CW00621377

**Praise**

## DANCE OF THE GOLDEN PEACOCK

'Set in Singapore and Burma during World War II, this tale follows a woman forced to flee military and personal conflict . . . Written with a colourful descriptive power, the book manages to bring emotion to the smaller scenes and minor people as well as the main characters'
— *Dorset Evening Echo*

## SUNLIGHT ACROSS THE PLAINS

'Absorbing novel of the romantic and glamorous allure of the Kenya of the 1930s'
- *Ellesmere Port Standard*

'A taste of intrigue, romance and social history'
- *Kensington and Chelsea Times*

'Kenya is the backdrop against which romance, family feuds, and passionate drama are set'
— *Doncaster Courier*

*Also by Catherine Dunbar
and available from Coronet*

Sunlight Across the Plains

About the Author:

Daughter of a coffee planter, Catherine Dunbar was born in India and grew up in Suffolk. She has since travelled and lived in all corners of the globe. She was a journalist for many years and wrote for the *Investor's Chronicle* and the *Financial Times*. She has written two previous novels, *The Nuthatch Tree*, which won the Mary Elgin award, and *Sunlight Across the Plains*. She lives with her husband and their two children in London and Sussex.

# DANCE OF THE GOLDEN PEACOCK

## CATHERINE DUNBAR

CORONET BOOKS
Hodder and Stoughton

First published in Great Britain in 1995 by Hodder and Stoughton
A division of Hodder Headline PLC

A Coronet Paperback

10 9 8 7 6 5 4 3 2 1

Dunbar, Catherine
Dance of the Golden Peacock
I.Title
823.914 [F]

ISBN 0 340 59444 6

Typeset by Phoenix Typesetting, Ilkley, West Yorkshire

Printed and bound in Great Britain by
Cox & Wyman Ltd, Reading, Berkshire

Hodder and Stoughton
A division of Hodder Headline PLC
338 Euston Road
London NW1 3BH

*To James
with Love*

## Acknowledgements

I would like to thank all those who gave so generously of their time to share with me their recollections of Burma and Singapore and in particular: Eric Battersby, Joan White, Pooh Johnson-Hill, Major Clixby Fitzwilliams and Sir Eric Yarrow.

The Golden Peacock shall be stricken
And the White Heron shall occupy its shady pool
But a sudden storm of lightning
Will drive the White Heron away

Ancient Burmese prophecy

# Prologue

*I*n the early days, when the kings of Burma preferred to build their palaces in Upper Burma, Rangoon was little more than a sleepy riverside hamlet.

True, the Mons had once established themselves along the Irrawaddy Delta; but although one or two of the Burman kings tried moving their capital south it was always northwards and inland that they eventually returned. Back to the central plains from which they felt they could control the warring Shans to the north and east and the Mons to the south.

The Irrawaddy Delta and that coastal strip held no particular interest for the insular Burman kings. In the end, it proved a costly mistake: for it was from this very area that their most tenacious invaders – the Europeans and their chartered companies – emerged.

Burma, wedged between India to the west and China to the east, could offer them enviable possibilities. They were drawn, not to the splendid palaces, nor the regal, exotic white elephants, but to the rice-rich paddy fields and the teak forests beyond. Their dreams were not of golden peacocks but of trading treaties and for the right to use Burma as a pathway to China.

Their arrival marked the beginning of Rangoon's growth. Gradually it started to thrust out beyond its rickety quay into the tall grass and lush jungle which surrounded it. And by the time King Thibaw had capitulated finally to the British and Upper Burma had joined Lower Burma under their control, the opening of the Suez

Canal in 1869 only succeeded in underlining Rangoon's importance.

This was the new face of Rangoon: a city uncompromisingly Victorian in its appearance, with its solid columned buildings, worthy of Leadenhall Street, set in wide straight streets. Gradually, among the employees of the Bombay Burmah Company or of Steel Brothers, came the first trickle of government officials and administrators and in their wake the Indians, the money-lenders and the coolies.

The pattern for the city was set then. The British had stamped the city with its own colonial imprint as unmistakable as the Peacock seal of the Royal Burmese Throne.

Over the next few decades Rangoon changed little. It stretched at the seams as it prospered, but remained resiliently Victorian, with that air of self-certainty. And why not? Though a war raged in Europe, Burma was too remote to be directly involved. Business was booming and the docks were busier than ever – though perhaps not quite as frantic as those of her precocious sister Singapore – as Burma strove to provide the raw materials for which England and America were so desperately clamouring.

So, here in Burma, in the early days of 1940, a sense of unshakeable confidence and security filled the air and people reminded one another of the music hall ditty which had echoed through the officers' messes between the two wars:

> *'Where was I when the war was on?'*
> *I can hear a faint voice murmur,*
> *'Where was I when the war was on?*
> *In the safest place, in Burma.'*

And for the moment, as the British in Burma determinedly set about their tasks, there seemed no reason to doubt these words.

No reason at all . . .

# 1

*I*t was the distant gong she heard first. The low, resonant boom drifted lazily across the mud-churned river, its echo breaking the stillness of the early morning.

Kate Lawrence, elbows planted firmly on the ship's worn wooden railings, turned at the sound, watching as a saffron-robed figure made his way along the palm-fringed riverbank. Ahead of him, through the dispersing mist, walked a small boy, announcing the monk's arrival to the villagers with steady beats on the gong.

To Kate it was this sight, even more than that of the bullocks being brought down to the river's edge to be washed, which made her realise that she was almost home. Not that Rangoon was home, of course – she still had to journey on to Singapore – but it was the feeling that she had finally left Europe behind, and India too, and at last was entering the achingly familiar world of the East.

She stretched out her arms behind her head and sighed. It was four years since she had been out here. Sometimes, during that time at school, she had wondered if she would ever return. But then war had been declared in Europe, and even though, in the late days of 1939, it was still branded a phoney one, her father had overridden her English grandmother's view that it would all be over in six months and had insisted Kate return to Singapore.

'Much safer for you to be out of England,' he'd written to her. 'Come home until it's all over.'

Kate had obliged willingly, but she had known it wasn't his only reason for asking her to return.

When he'd come home to England on leave eighteen months before she had realised instinctively that he was lonely. A widower could find life terribly tedious in Singapore without a consort and she knew her father hadn't recognised quite how much he'd come to depend on her until after she had left for England. She had always been her father's child, even when her mother had been alive.

So, now she was returning to Singapore. It would be a relief to be needed again. However kind her aunt and grandmother had been to her, she had always felt in the way.

Now all that would change. In a few short days she'd be back in the world she understood.

She leaned forward again, resting her small pointed chin against her cupped palms, eyes intent on the scenery slipping past her.

The light was changing now, the wreaths of mist lifting, drawn up into the valley by the warmth of the sun. Horizontal shafts of sunlight gilded the shaggy palm trees and paddy fields beyond. In the distance a small village appeared, and Kate, stretching up on tip-toe, was just able to distinguish the tight clusters of houses raised on stilts.

She brushed a strand of coppery-blonde hair back from her face and turned her head at the murmur of voices, the rumble of bullock carts. A small group of village boys was coming down to the river to collect water. There was a grace to their movements, a reflective lack of haste, which Kate found charming after the chaotic bustle of India.

Burma, in contrast, seemed secret and still.

The scents of frangipani and jasmine mingled with that of the river – evocative smells. She closed her eyes, feeling the river and the country absorb her into its green heart.

She sensed this might be her last chance of enjoying solitude but that didn't worry her. Vitality was her greatest charm. She let her head fall back with a sigh, her thick hair tumbling across her shoulders, exposing the soft whiteness of her neck – a slow, easy movement which disguised the restlessness she felt. There was a hunger inside her for something to happen. *Anything.*

A white and gold pagoda came into view, its straight-edged roof reflected in the sunlight. It was one of the many shrines they had passed that day, but for Kate, opening her eyes at that moment, its appearance seemed intertwined with her longing; its glistening brightness an omen. A promise that, if only she would wait awhile, she would not be disappointed by what fate held in store for her.

In her cabin a deck below, Kate's best friend Elizabeth Staveley bent her tousled head over the edge of the bunk, not in the least surprised to find it empty. In all their years at school together, she had rarely known Kate to indulge in the luxury of a lie-in.

She sank back against the pillows again, linking her hands behind her head. She was in no mood to hurry. It was not indolence, more the knowledge that the day must be taken slowly, because of its importance.

Elizabeth lay on her back, her eyes following the pattern of the cracks in the paintwork, trying to compose herself. Logically, it was sheer nonsense to feel so nervous, she told herself. After all, if she were sensible about it – and Elizabeth usually prided herself on being eminently sensible – it was most unlikely *he* would be there to meet her at the docks.

And yet, even to be in the same country as Martin again . . . She closed her eyes, hugging the memories with a smile.

Elizabeth had met Martin Downing three years earlier at her aunt's house in Chelsea. It had been an unpromising start. Martin had come to see her father, who was on six months' leave from Tavoy, to talk about joining the Burma

Civil Service. He had paid scant attention to the gawky fifteen-year-old in her too-tight dress, who had hovered hopefully in the background.

He had sat there, listening to Henry Staveley's argument that the ICS and India could offer greater opportunities, but though he'd accepted India could mean faster advancement, he'd been resolute that only Burma captured his imagination.

Elizabeth, watching the young man before her, with his mop of fair hair and expressive grey eyes, had recognised that he was someone who knew what he wanted, and that nothing her father could say would sway him from his intention. And she had fallen for him, and his quiet determination, then and there.

Over the next few months Martin had frequently called in at Tite Street. And each time she'd seen Martin leave with a volume tucked under his arm, she'd known he would have to return.

Then after he'd taken the Civil Service Exams at Burlington House, he'd gone back to Oxford as a BCS probationer, and Elizabeth had thought he had slipped from her life for ever. But, out of the blue, the following year, he'd written to her, asking if he might call by to borrow a book her father had mentioned. He even wondered if, remembering Henry Staveley telling him how well his daughter spoke the language, Elizabeth might be able to help with his Burmese.

The letter, written to her at Tite Street, had been forwarded to her at school and she and Kate had pored over its contents, Kate optimistically reading unintended innuendos into every line.

When she returned to Tite Street that summer, their friendship had gradually blossomed as Martin struggled with the appalling difficulties of what seemed a comparatively monosyllabic, tonal language. Martin would sit in the big armchair in the ornate drawing room at Tite Street, listening to her, his sensitive face aglow with interest as she spun out stories of Burma with the skill of Scheherazade. The tales of Thibaw and the medieval kingdom of Ava with all its ramshackle splendour, the intrigue, the treachery, the palace murders, took on a life of their own in the quiet of that elegant room.

Slowly the images of punts idly drifting on the cool waters of the Isis were replaced by those of sampans on the bustling blue-lilied Irrawaddy, and the noble spires of Oxford suddenly appeared dull and predictable beside the exotic picture of the sun glinting onto the golden-roofed temples of Mandalay.

It was only a matter of time, then. Elizabeth possessed a quality which Martin found more irresistible than either brains or beauty: something which drew him back time and again. A love of Burma.

Elizabeth could pinpoint the precise moment when their friendship had changed into something subtly different. Martin's twenty-first birthday at Chilgrove.

One moment they had been chatting with dozens of other people in the ballroom and the next they had been out on the windswept terrace and he had turned to her with a look on his face which she had never seen before.

He had leaned forward and taken her face in both his hands and kissed her on the lips. His long fingers had felt cool against the warm of her neck, their touch making her skin vibrantly alive.

Instinctively she closed her eyes now and shivered, remembering the questing sweetness of the first kiss . . .

'Come on, sleepy-head! You're not still mooning about in bed, are you?' Kate's teasing voice came from the doorway.

Elizabeth started. She had been so deep in reverie she hadn't even heard the cabin door opening.

She lifted her head indignantly. 'I'm not mooning,' she protested.

'You're missing the most perfect morning,' Kate said, coming to sit on the edge of the rumpled bed. 'And you can just see the tip of the Shwe Dagon glinting on the horizon. It's wonderful.'

'The Shwe Dagon! Already?' Elizabeth sat up. That meant they would be in Rangoon in only a few hours. She swung her legs over the side of her bed, catching sight of herself in the small mirror which hung over the wooden dressing-table. 'Oh, Lord, Kate. Just look at me!' She tried to ruffle some life into her dark locks. 'Honestly, it's this wretched heat . . .'

'I know,' Kate pulled a face. 'Mine's gone into cork-screws.' She pulled out a strand to show the effect.

Elizabeth glanced at her friend a little enviously. In truth, the springy tight curls did little to detract from Kate's looks. Somehow, even when caught in a rainstorm, Kate still exuded glowing vitality. Although not perhaps conventionally beautiful, she turned heads wherever she went.

Elizabeth glanced back at the mirror, pushing a despairing hand through her hair. 'Today of all days.'

Kate slipped off the bed and came to her side. 'I could do your hair the way I did it when we went to see your sister in Calcutta,' she suggested. 'Everyone commented on it.'

'Would you?' Elizabeth's face eased slightly. 'Of course, it'll probably all be for nothing. I shouldn't imagine he'll be there. He's right up-country, you know. Probably impossible for him to get time off.'

Kate, who had had this conversation with Elizabeth a score of times since leaving Marseilles, grinned. She started to move about the cabin, picking up the last of her belongings.

Elizabeth went over to the tiny wardrobe in the corner

of the cabin and pulled open the door. She had visualised to the final detail exactly what she was going to wear when they docked but suddenly the image wavered.

One dress after the other was unceremoniously dragged out and held briefly against her, before being discarded onto the bunk. None seemed right now.

'The blue one,' said Kate, gently, from behind her.

'Are you sure?'

'Absolutely. Besides, as I've told you, Martin won't care two hoots what you look like. He's been up in the jungle ever since he arrived out here, lonely and over-worked. He'll be so pleased to see you he probably won't even notice what you're wearing. Remember his last letter?'

Elizabeth blushed slightly. She had no secrets from Kate. Martin had somehow slipped into their friendship and been encompassed by it, rather than dividing them.

She sank down on the bed beside Kate. 'What if he's changed?'

'He won't have.'

'Oh, Kate, how can you be so sure of everything?'

'Because I'm a disgusting optimist, as you well know.'

Elizabeth smiled. Kate's remark neatly summed them up. Kate, the optimist, the daring one, she the realist. She glanced at Kate. She was aware for the first time that when they reached Burma there would be a parting of the ways. She longed to see Martin of course; but she'd forgotten it would mean losing Kate.

Kate stood up and glanced out of the porthole. 'Come on,' she said, stretching out her hand to pull Elizabeth to her feet. 'The Shwe Dagon is positively looming. Martin might be delighted to see you in your nightie, but your parents won't!'

Already the first pugmarks of industrialisation were visible on the horizon. Soon they would be crossing the mouth of the Pegu River and Rangoon would unfurl before them with the speed of an exotic flower blossoming.

Spurred into action, Elizabeth bundled the pile of clothes on her bed into her brown leather suitcase with shameless disregard. Then she washed quickly and changed into her cotton dress. No hesitation this time. A quick adjustment of the embroidered Peter Pan collar was all she would allow herself.

She turned then, holding out her hairbrush to Kate.

'And who's it to be this time?' Kate asked, brushing her friend's hair forward so that it fell across her face in long peek-a-boo tresses, covering one eye. 'Veronica Lake?'

'Certainly not!' Elizabeth protested, laughing as she pushed back her hair. She hoped Kate had remembered their conversation about Calcutta and was not about to experiment. Kate was prone to giving in to creative impulses, with varying degrees of success.

She watched as her friend moved this way and that, twisting the last section at the back into a soft chignon with deft swiftness. Dutifully, Elizabeth held out the pins to her with timed precision.

'Well?' Kate secured the last pin into place and stepped back to admire her handiwork.

'Perfect,' Elizabeth breathed with relief. Kate really had surpassed herself. The chignon seemed to ease the squareness of her jaw and make the whole outline more delicate. And by lifting her hair back from her forehead like that, Kate had contrived to show off Elizabeth's luminous brown eyes to their best advantage. The effect was one of quiet sophistication.

Elizabeth lifted her eyes to meet Kate's encouraging gaze and smiled, a new quiet assurance burning within her.

'London was in turmoil. Honestly Martin, you should

have seen Aunt Maude trying to put up her blackout curtains!'

Kate sat on the verandah of the Staveleys' house on University Avenue in Rangoon, half-listening to Elizabeth's excited chatter. Here in these peaceful surroundings on the lakes, with the soft breeze stirring the dry palms, it was impossible to think they had been part of that upheaval too. She recalled the cumbersome gasmasks, the tear-stained faces of the children being evacuated, the Anderson air-raid shelters hurriedly erected in back gardens, the waiting, nerves-a-tingle for something to happen. All that seemed an eternity away.

She leant back in her wicker chair, looking up at the darkening branches of the margosa tree which overhung the house, and breathed in the scents of the night, the honey-sweet fragrance of blossom almost sickly in its richness. The first faint white glow of the moon was starting to show as it slowly pushed its way into the purple-black sky.

Behind her she heard Elizabeth stir, coming to stand by the verandah steps, Martin by her side. They stood, arms draped over the wooden railings, hands touching, heads bent together. Their preoccupation with each other, their private smiles, their intimacy, formed a magic circle around them.

Kate turned her head away. She did not feel jealous exactly, just excluded.

'Less than a week and you'll be in Singapore.'

Kate swivelled round to find the stocky figure of Elizabeth's father, Henry Staveley, standing beside her.

She took a sip of lime juice, the glass ice-cold in her hand. 'I can't wait,' she admitted. 'It seems to have taken for ever even to have got this far.'

'I can imagine.' She saw him glance at Elizabeth and Martin and intuit her feeling of isolation. He caught up one of the verandah chairs and pulled it over to sit beside her. 'You were lucky to leave England when you did. Things very much look as if they'll hot up over there.'

'Do they? To be honest, everything seemed very quiet when we left. They kept talking about gas attacks and parachute landings, but nothing happened. Some of the evacuees were even returning to London.'

'Well, things are changing now. What with the Soviets pushing against the Finns and Mussolini beating his drum, Hitler is sure to feel justified in going for a full-out attack.' Henry Staveley compressed his thin lips. 'Glad you're both safely out of England, that's all I can say.' His dark eyes, so like Elizabeth's, met hers in a steady gaze. 'It won't be much fun over there when it starts in earnest.'

'And what about here?' One of the house servants offered Kate some more lime juice and she held her glass up to be refilled. 'Do you think the Burmese might take advantage of England's preoccupation and push for early independence?' It was what the Indians were doing. When they had stopped off at Calcutta, Elizabeth's sister, Charlotte, who had been posted out to India with her army officer husband, had been predicting a good deal of unrest there. The INA was having massive success recruiting new members.

'I hope it won't come to that here,' Henry Staveley said. 'U Pu has given his guarantee that the Burmese Government won't use England's present weakness for its own gain.' U Pu, the Burmese Premier, was solid, religious and pro-British. As long as he retained power all should remain calm in Burma.

Kate sat with her glass straight in front of her, cupped in both hands. 'And the Japanese?' She knew their reputation as aggressive opportunists. Like the rest of the world, she had been horrified by their infamous rape of Nanking.

'Still too involved with the Chinese to give much thought

elsewhere,' said Henry. He stretched inside the pocket of his white dinner jacket and drew out a cigarette case. 'At least, for the moment.'

'Which explains why I didn't see many signs of fortifications when I arrived at Rangoon,' said Kate. 'I wondered.'

Henry leant back in his chair, lighting up the short black cheroot he had extracted. 'There are a few trenches being dug, a few shelters, but that's about it,' he admitted. 'We've got a Volunteer Force, of course. Alex is rather involved with that.' Alex was Elizabeth's brother. He ran the family teak business down in Moulmein further along the coastline. 'I must say it's rather hard on the boys here. For the most part they've been told they're more use staying put than joining up. Very frustrating. Martin's just the same. Been told the ICS isn't releasing anyone at present . . .' Henry puffed at his cheroot, watching the smoke curl into the darkness. 'Good for Elizabeth, of course.' He turned his head slightly and gave Kate a conspiratorial smile.

'Yes.' Kate glanced over to where Martin and Elizabeth were standing. Elizabeth had her back to the railings and was holding on to the lapels of Martin's jacket, gently drawing him closer to her. Kate could feel Elizabeth's happiness even from here.

'I'm sorry you're not staying longer,' Henry said, taking another puff at his cheroot, then laying it aside in the silver ashtray. 'Rangoon doesn't give you much taste of Burma proper.'

'I should have liked to have seen Mandalay, if I'd have had the time,' confessed Kate.

'Alex would've been the one to have shown you that,' said Henry. 'Quite an authority on Burmese art and history. I'm sure he would have been delighted to have taken you up.'

'If you could have prised him away from his current string of girlfriends,' teased Elizabeth, coming over to perch on the arm of her father's chair. Kate laughed. Elizabeth's inability to keep track of her brother's bevy of admirers had been a standing joke at school. 'Mummy says he's being pursued by a very determined American girl at the moment. Her father's one of the bigwigs up at the oilfields. Anyway, Mummy says it will come to nothing. Apparently she didn't fare particularly well when Alex took her up to Pagan and beyond. Not at all interested in the pagodas, and even less in trailing through the jungle. Kept on talking about cool drinks at the Gymkhana Club!'

'Poor girl, I don't blame her,' said Henry, smiling. 'Alex really ought to stop putting these helpless creatures through these endurance tests.'

'They're not endurance tests to Alex. Just everyday living,' said Elizabeth. 'And to be honest, I think it makes sense to find out whether or not they're cut out for his lifestyle. No point marrying some girl who only wants to lead a pampered social life in Rangoon.'

The words were spoken lightly enough but Kate noticed Elizabeth glancing at Martin as she spoke, as if addressing him secretly as well. She saw them exchange a smile.

'So, Kate, have we quite put you off visiting Mandalay with Alex?' Henry asked with a chuckle. 'I assure you, he's not that bad! Elizabeth and Charlotte used to love heading off the beaten track with him. They'd always discover some hidden pagoda or shrine, some out of the way village.' He leaned back and picked up his cheroot again, remembering. In his youth he had been fond of heading up to the hills, too, of discovering the real Burma hidden away beyond the well-worn European paths. He glanced back at Kate, smiling encouragingly. 'So, my dear, you'll have to come back. See it for yourself.'

'Of course she's coming back,' said Elizabeth emphatically. 'She's got to. She hasn't even seen Anapuri yet!'

There was pride in her voice when she spoke of their rubber plantation. Kate had forgotten that this house by the lakes was merely a base for the Staveleys when they came to Rangoon. Anapuri was their main residence, carved out of the hills between Moulmein and Tavoy by Henry's grandfather. Elizabeth had always talked about Anapuri back at school. Kate glanced at her, wondering how Elizabeth would really re-adjust to that sort of isolated existence again.

The sound of the dinner gong rang out and Henry pushed back his chair. He could see his wife, elegant in a long low-backed dress, coming through onto the verandah to chivvy them on their way.

'We're coming, Joan,' he called out placatingly.

The moon was clear of the trees now, spilling its warm orange light across the lake and garden. Kate stood up and stretched. It seemed so peaceful, it was hard to remember that men were at war, not only in Europe, but just over Burma's border in China, too.

She knew little of China's internal struggles and even less of Japan's politics and ambitions. But the threads which loosely bound all their countries were tightening.

The soft, murmured warnings were there for all to hear, if only they would listen. But Kate and the Staveleys, walking through to dinner, heard only the sound of the wind whispering through the creamy white blossoms of the frangipani and the tinkling bells of a distant pagoda.

## 2

'You'll have to tell her, Mark. Straight away.'

Mark Lawrence rolled on to his side with a groan. Adorable though Sylvia was, she could be maddeningly persistent at times. He propped himself up on his elbow, looking at her across the long windowed room. She was sitting at the dressing table brushing her short honey-blonde hair with slow, determined strokes.

'Have a heart, darling,' he protested, ignoring the jut of her chin. 'Not the moment she arrives, surely?'

Sylvia recrossed her legs, a leisurely movement which parted the silken robe to expose them to full advantage. 'It's no good, Mark,' she said, putting down the silver brush. 'I'm not going to be hidden away like some leper. She'll have to know about us some time.'

'But not on her first day back!' Mark pushed an uneasy hand through his brown hair and sighed. He already knew how Kate would react to the news that he was intending to remarry. 'Give her a chance to settle in.'

Sylvia glanced into the triple-sided mirror. The cut-glass bottles and silver accessories on the table caught the sunlight and glittered back at her. She had been about to tell Mark that he pandered to the child but, seeing his anxious face, decided on a different tack.

'Rather you tell her than she hears it from someone else, surely? You know what Singapore's like.'

Mark did indeed know. Ever since he had met Sylvia Nicholson, four months earlier, there had been undertones of gossip. Their age difference – she was twenty-six, he nearly forty-two – his money, her room-stopping looks; the bored matrons of Singapore had had a field day.

Not that it worried him personally in the least. He knew what small communities could be like and was impervious to it all. But he had known the tittle-tattle speculation had hurt Sylvia at times, and had no intention of allowing Kate to be caught up in it as well.

'Well.' He hesitated. He had the image of Kate in his mind's eye, so eager to see him, so trusting. He felt like a Judas.

'Procrastination won't help, you know.' Sylvia stretched out her legs, sliding on her sheer silk stockings and clipping them into place.

Mark watched her as she stood up and crossed the carpeted room, moving in that smooth effortless way of hers. He could see the soft curve of her breasts as she leaned forward to pick up her yellow dress from the back of the chair. Really, she was stunningly good-looking, with those impossibly long legs and tiny waist. People might hint that he had been shanghaied by her, but he was happy to live with that. He had never felt more content, more alive.

She crossed over to the mirror again, stooping to fluff up her hair before turning back to him.

'So, we're agreed? You'll tell her tomorrow when she arrives?'

Mark pushed back the covers and stood up. He pulled on his black-printed Chinese dressing-gown, knotting it firmly in place. 'I had hoped you'd have a chance to get to know her a bit first,' he said.

'There'll be plenty of time for that.' Sylvia gave him her most charming smile. 'We'll end up being the best of friends, you'll see.'

There was a certain tight tone to her voice which he belatedly recognised as nervousness. For the first time he realised that she might be feeling more than a trace of anxiety about her forthcoming meeting with Kate.

He came across and put his arms around her. 'Of course you'll get on famously,' he said, looking down into her grey eyes with quiet understanding.

She stretched up to kiss him. She had not misjudged the man. She had come to Singapore to find someone to take care of her, to protect her from the more painful realities of life. Mark Lawrence would not let her down.

'Thank you,' she said softly, kissing him again.

He stretched out his hand, gently touching her cheek. He knew that Sylvia was far more vulnerable than people realised.

He had seen it, even that first time he'd met her at the Palm Court.

Newly arrived from Perth, she'd been surrounded by admirers, all pressing for her attention. Any girl's dream to have so many courting her, or so he would have thought. But, despite her smiles, her easy laughter, Mark had sensed she was wishing herself away from all this clamour. He'd waited, a little apart from the others, and suddenly she'd lifted her eyes above the heads encircling hers and had given him a look of something approaching despair. It had reminded him of a wild deer he'd cornered once as a boy with his father, the same fear, the same misjudged stillness.

He'd put down his stengah and elbowed his way through the crowd to her side, loudly declaring that it was time they left for their lunch appointment. Purposefully he'd reached out to her, and her slim elegant hand had immediately hooked into his – so tightly that he'd known he hadn't been mistaken.

'Thank you,' she'd said as he'd led her out of Raffles. 'I was afraid there'd be no White Knight to rescue me.'

Without a backward glance he had whisked her off for

lunch at the Tamagawa Gardens. No one had stopped them. His position as a much-liked and respected *tuan bezar* had been enough to quell any complaints as to the manner of his securing the lady. Besides, the old Singapore hands were an easy-natured bunch who knew Mark Lawrence was difficult to please.

Now all that had changed. Mark was well aware of the rumours of a broken engagement which surrounded Sylvia's arrival in Singapore but she'd been open about it. Besides, he knew he'd be a fool to suppose that, at her age and with her looks, Sylvia would have no skeletons in the cupboard.

That was the past. The present was here and now. He felt her young firm body shudder against the coolness of his silk dressing-gown and he tried not to think about Kate and what she would say about it all.

Singapore seemed reassuringly unchanged as Kate drove with her father towards their house in Tanglin Road. For all the fortifications and her father's tales of drilling the Volunteers and of practice air-raid warnings, it still retained its feeling of unassailable security.

'So – is it good to be back?' Her father stretched out his hand to cover hers, their fingers interlocking.

'You know it is,' Kate said, beaming. As she had come down the gangplank into the blast of hot air, the pungent, spicy smells had hit her with powerful familiarity. This was her home; the place that had filtered into her dreams through the cold damp fog of England. She glanced out of the window at the bustling crowd outside, the coolies and the Chinese and the Malays surging alongside their Bentley on bicycles and rickshaws and carts.

To Kate, the air seemed to crackle with opportunity. But then her father had often told her that Singapore was built on enterprise, on vision. From the moment that Thomas

Stamford Raffles had planted his flagpole on what was then a rat-infested, centipede-riddled, swampy island, it had been a magnet to all those who had adventure in their veins.

'There can't be another place like this in the world!' Kate exclaimed happily. 'I can't tell you how much I missed it all.'

She turned to her father, inspecting him closer. He appeared well enough – certainly the hollows under his eyes which had so worried her on his last visit to England had disappeared – but he seemed unusually preoccupied. She wondered if business were healthy or whether the war in Europe had taken its toll.

'How's everything at Lawrence & Marsden?' she asked.

'Fairly good. The boom in rubber and tin can only help us, but things in China are tricky now. The puppet government there is progressively freezing out all foreign trade and replacing it by Japanese monopolies.'

'Heavens! That will hit some of the agencies pretty hard.' Kate knew how many of the firms relied upon their trade with and through China.

'It has already.'

Mark Lawrence was aware that the world was changing. But then in the fifty or so years that Lawrence & Marsden had been operating in Singapore the company had had to adapt constantly. One had to find new markets as others closed. That was the nature of the beast.

Kate listened quietly as her father went on to outline the anti-Western restrictions which had been brought in, all of which were designed to cripple European and American interests in China. 'The Japanese are out to take what they can get, of course, and I'm afraid I can't see the British government doing much to stop them.'

A sudden hard spatter of rain sounded on the roof but Kate barely noticed. Singapore was given to periodic downpours.

'Thank heavens for rubber!' she exclaimed, glancing at her father. 'There've been no more strikes then?'

'A few.' Mark Lawrence shrugged. 'The trouble is, with the price booming, the workers want a share of the profit. They don't seem to remember that only a few years ago rubber was less than 8d a pound and the depression was so fierce that companies were close to bankruptcy and people were being laid off left, right and centre. All they can see is that the rubber companies are getting rich. The communist agitators are behind the strikes, so the managers say, and I'm inclined to agree.'

'Well, I just hope things don't get ugly,' said Kate with feeling. 'Though presumably it's still safe for people to travel around?'

'Heavens, yes!'

'Good.' Kate smiled. 'Then I hope you remember you promised me a holiday when I got over here. The Cameron Highlands, Penang.' She'd been looking forward to their trip together ever since he had mentioned it in his letter to her ten months ago. It would be like the old times. 'You promised you'd save up a good few weeks' furlough.'

'And I have,' he assured her. 'We'll all have a wonderful time!'

'All?' She peered up at him apprehensively.

His pale blue eyes flickered briefly across to her then fixed on some unseen object out of the window. 'Well . . .'

There was a moment of silence. Even the noise of Singapore street life seemed to still. She had the sense of walking on the rim of a volcano, aware of the warning rumblings at her feet.

She stretched out to touch his sleeve. 'Daddy?'

She saw him move uncomfortably on the leather seat. 'Listen, darling,' he said. 'There's something I've been meaning to talk to you about.'

\*      \*      \*

She would not cry. *She would not.* Kate folded her arms tightly across her chest, fighting back tears of self-pity and anger.

She stood, her back towards the sprawling lawns and white-columned house, watching the bright lights of the city below flood the sky as the last of the day faded. Even with darkness approaching it was still hot and sticky, and though she longed for the cool of the drawing room's whirring fans, Kate refused to go back inside. *She* would still be there.

She turned to glance resentfully back at the house. The moment she had met her, with those too-long legs and that full red mouth set into an exaggerated smile, she had known they could never be friends. There was something possessive about the way Sylvia had walked into the house, straight through to the drawing room without pausing, as if it were *her* home, not Kate's.

Kate had tried desperately to greet the other woman with some warmth, but it was hard to avoid feeling a certain rancour at the way Sylvia continually met her father's eyes in silent communications, drawing him away from Kate all the time; difficult not to let her heart harden a little as she watched the way her father looked at this intruder. How could he be in love with this vain woman, who was almost young enough to be his daughter?

That was what hurt, Kate knew. That love. All she had wanted was to feel needed again, loved. That was what she had missed so terribly in England.

The sour taste of jealousy was so strong it almost made her gag. It would have been difficult sharing her father with anyone, she knew; but with Sylvia it would be intolerable.

She headed down the steps towards the summerhouse, past the gardenias and the dark green Binjai trees. This had been her place of refuge as a child and she had sat here for hours, listening to the huge bamboos creaking in the wind, secure in her own little domain.

Ahead of her a chickak was slowly stalking along the side of the summerhouse, its pink belly showing under the transparent skin as it preyed on a brown beetle. Kate watched as it drew its body up like a cat preparing to spring, measured the distance and struck, hardly pausing to blink its small opal eyes.

Suddenly the lizard darted up the wall of the summerhouse into the shadows of the roof and a moment later Kate heard the sound of someone approaching.

'So this is where you got to.'

In the near-darkness, her father's white dinner jacket gave out an almost ghostly sheen. He looked taller than his six foot, more bulky.

'I thought you might come here.' He hesitated, a new but distinct distancing between them. 'All right, now?'

She shrugged, not trusting herself to speak just yet.

'I'm sorry it came as such a shock to you, darling. Truly I am. But once you get to know Sylvia you'll like her a lot. She's tremendous fun, you know.' He looked down at her a little awkwardly, hands plunged into his pockets. He hated confrontations. 'You will try with her, won't you? Please.'

'Of course.' Her voice shook slightly with the effort of saying those words.

'She so much wants the two of you to get along together. It's difficult for her, you know.'

'It's difficult for me, too, Daddy!'

'Don't you think I can't see that?'

There was a silence broken only by the clicking of the insects close by.

'Listen, Kate.' Her father cleared his throat and pushed

his hands deeper into his pockets. 'Darling, try and understand.'

The gentleness of his tone pierced through her fragile-thin defence. Suddenly she could stand it no longer. 'Daddy, don't marry her,' she begged. Her voice was little more than a whisper but it showed all her anguish. 'Please don't. She's not right for you. Can't you see?'

'Kate!'

Her father's face was suddenly forbidding; but she couldn't stop now. The need to express her true feelings was too great.

'I can see things you can't, Daddy. She isn't all sweetness and light, you know. Have you ever wondered why exactly she came up from Perth in the first place? I'll tell you. She came with the express purpose of finding herself a husband. A proper *tuan bezar*. I bet she even stage-managed your so-called chance meeting at Raffles!' She had a sudden vision of the chickak stalking its prey with ruthless precision, the brown beetle oblivious to its fate. Couldn't her father see that was what was happening to him? 'She's shallow and she's . . .'

'That's enough, Kate.'

'But Daddy . . .'

'I said, that's enough.'

Kate noticed the edge of weariness to his voice as if he realised that the battle he had hoped to avoid still threatened. He did not, she knew, want to have to choose sides; nor did Kate want to force him to do so. She was afraid, after seeing him with Sylvia and hearing his words now, what his choice might be.

'Dammit, Kate. I didn't plan to fall in love. It just happened. Can't you be happy for me? You, of all people, must have known how lonely I was.'

His words were like the turn of the surgeon's knife.

To give herself time to compose herself she looked over
her shoulder at the city behind her. The glow of lights
hung on the skyline like some glittering necklace against
the velvet gown of night.

Somewhere in the tall trees beyond the house a howler
monkey shrieked.

Her father cleared his throat again. 'About our holiday,'
he began, his voice tense and quiet. 'Do you still want to go?'

She lifted her head up, her eyes guarded. 'With Sylvia?'

'Just the two of us. Sylvia thought it might be a good
idea.'

'Ah.' It had not come from him, then, this crumb
of hope. She looked at him, seeing him quickly glance
over his shoulder towards where Sylvia was waiting on
the verandah. Following his glance she could make out
her diaphanous silver dress lifting and curling in the
light breeze. Her appearance made Kate painfully aware
that the holiday might be the last time she would have
alone with her father. 'I'd like to go with you,' she said,
braving a smile. 'Very much.'

Mark Lawrence's face lost its deep furrows. 'That's my
girl.' He held out his arms to her. 'And shall we try and
find that trail we went on in the Cameron Highlands last
time?' he asked, drawing her close. 'Remember that tiger
we saw?'

'Of course I do.' Memories flooded back to her. It had
been a perfect week.

She bent her head against his shoulder and as she did
so she became aware of the cloying scent of Sylvia's
perfume on his jacket. Kate wrinkled her nose distaste-
fully but, warm in his arms, she could not bring herself
to pull away from him just yet.

The lilting sound of 'Stormy Weather' drifted down
across the garden towards them. Sylvia, bored of waiting
on the terrace, had gone back into the house.

Kate felt her father draw back from her slightly. 'So, that's settled. We'll leave on Saturday, ' he said. She could see he was ready to return to Sylvia. 'Are you ready to come back up?'

'In a moment, yes.' She would have to face Sylvia then.

There was to be no escape.

## 3

'*I*sn't that the stunner we saw up at KL?'

'What?' Johnnie Matheson pushed back his fair hair from his face and glanced across the crowded dance floor.

'The girl we met at the Spotted Dog with her father. You remember?' Joe Langley nodded in the direction of a small group threading their way through the tables.

'So it is!' Johnnie put down his Tiger beer and smiled. He remembered that girl very well. He'd come into the Spotted Dog, after a hellish week up at the tin mines, only to see this apparition in a flame-coloured sheath dress, sitting aloof at one of the tables. She'd seemed blissfully unaware of the sensation she was causing and perhaps it was this youthful innocence which had held his attention.

He'd tried to engineer an introduction to her but had failed. Now, it seemed, luck had thrown him a second chance. She was with the Macphersons and he knew the old man quite well through business. Johnnie was not one to miss an opportunity.

He straightened his tie, smoothed back his hair once more, and stood up.

'Struth! You don't waste much time!' Joe grinned up at him. 'You haven't even finished your beer.'

'I'll be back in two ticks, more than likely!' Johnnie said, giving Joe a wink.

Joe knew he wouldn't. Johnnie knew just how to turn on the charm. He'd make a point of chatting up the old man and his wife first, before even acknowledging his angular daughter and then, finally, her friend.

Johnnie skirted the room once and then advanced on the small, unsuspecting group. Rob Macpherson, burly and high-complexioned with a small bristle of a moustache, saw him approaching their table and lumbered good-humouredly to his feet. He liked the no-nonsense young Australian and welcomed him with loud joviality. Singapore was all to do with whom you knew: with the right contacts it was easy to infiltrate the hierarchy. Without them, the doors remained firmly closed.

Introductions over, Johnnie carefully transferred his attention back to Rob Macpherson. He knew the girl was watching him. Though she made a great business of stirring her drink and talking to the skinny Macpherson girl he could see the occasional flicker of her eye in his direction, as if she were reluctantly drawn to him.

His place at the table afforded him a perfect view of her and he studied her unhurriedly under the guise of discussing the latest disruptions at the tin mines with Macpherson. Close to, he decided, she was even more attractive. Not beautiful, her features were too irregular for that, but there was something sensual and appealing in her face. Some hint of challenge.

He felt a frisson of excitement run through him and, glancing at the girl, wondered if she could feel it too.

Kate had noticed the tall Australian the moment she had walked into the room. He had been seated at one of the far tables with his small hawk-faced friend and as she followed the balding Robert Macpherson and his wife to their table she could feel his eyes on her. She hadn't glanced his way but she had known then with youthful certainty that he would try to come over to speak to her.

She glanced at him quickly now, unsettled. There were some men, she realised, who could give out the most powerful sense of adventure in the most mundane of surroundings. Alex Staveley, in Rangoon, had been one: here was another. Even deep in conversation with Macpherson, Johnnie Matheson managed to convey a sense of devil-may-care.

She heard an impatient stirring beside her.

'Well, do you want to make up a four for tennis or not, Kate?'

Kate started guiltily as Alice Macpherson's aggrieved tone cut across the whirring of the fans. 'What?' She hoped it wasn't too obvious that she hadn't been paying attention.

'At the Tanglin. Tonight at five. The Pearson twins have asked us to make up a four.' Alice spoke in slow pronounced tones as if dealing with someone with a severe disability. 'Then I thought we could all come home for a swim and supper . . .'

'Supper tonight?' Rob Macpherson broke off his conversation and swung round to face his daughter. 'Good idea.' He raised his hand, clicking his big fingers to summon the waiter, before turning back to Johnnie. 'I trust you'll join us, young man. I hear you're quite the Fred Perry! Do me a power of good to have a spot of serious tennis for a change . . .'

Alice opened her mouth to protest at the way her father had usurped her tennis party, then gave a resigned shrug. Her father always interfered. Besides, she'd seen the competitive look in his eyes and knew that he wouldn't be content until he had challenged Mr Matheson to a game of tennis and beaten him hollow.

She glanced at the young Australian, hoping he would have the good sense to lose to his host. Seeing his mischievous grin as he accepted her father's invitation, she had the disturbing feeling that Mr Matheson might not play by society's polite, unwritten rules.

It was a conclusion that Kate had come to, too. She smiled. After the Pearson twins, she decided, Johnnie Matheson was like a blaze of sunlight after a week of rain-filled days.

From where she sat on the shaded terrace, Kate could see the long spidery lines of the Malay fishing traps lacing the coastline and the low, shimmering green islands in the distance. It was blissful here and she was glad now that Johnnie had overridden her suggestion of Raffles and had brought her out to this spot instead.

'Another drink?' Beside her Johnnie stretched out his long arms and beckoned over one of the Chinese boys, who expertly balanced a tray of drinks aloft as he slid from table to table. 'Gimlet, this time?'

'I'll stick to orange juice, I think, thanks,' Kate said.

It was too sweltering for anything stronger. Even the wooden tables seemed hot to the touch today. Kate fanned herself vigorously with a small rattan fan, trying to remind herself that it was the heat she had missed most when she had lived in bone-chilling England.

Johnnie glanced across at her antics and smiled. He never seemed to be affected by the heat. 'We'll go down to the Tanglin after this if you like. You look as if you could do with a cooling swim. If you'd brought your bathers, you could have gone for a dip here and now.'

Kate put down her fan and laughed. It was just the sort of thing Johnnie would have done regardless of what other people would have thought.

The Chinese boy returned with their fresh drinks. Kate picked up the glass and pressed it against her forehead gratefully.

'You're supposed to drink it!' teased Johnnie, looking

across at her with amusement. Having spent his youth in the outback of Queensland, where it could reach 120 degrees in the shade, he found little discomfort in Singapore's heat. At least here there were clubs with swimming pools, punkah fans, obliging servants and every comfort known to man. No wonder everyone flocked here from up-country whenever they could.

'So,' Kate took a sip of her juice, 'how was your week up at the mines? Any more trouble?'

'Not really.' Johnnie gave a quick shrug. Ever since the winter of '35, when communist miners had taken possession of a coal mine at Batu Arang, there had been continued rumblings through the workforce in Malaya. It made no difference that the soviet had not lasted long; it had sparked off a series of disruptions whose reverberations were still being felt.

'Elizabeth says it's just the same in Rangoon,' Kate said.

In her last letter Elizabeth had written about the university students getting out of hand. It was nothing serious, but Kate knew Elizabeth was still pleased to be down at Anapuri, even though it meant being farther away from Martin. 'Her father says it's the *pongyis* who are stirring up the students . . .'

'I thought they were supposed to be peaceful blokes,' commented Johnnie. 'Above politics and all that.'

'They are,' agreed Kate. Though she remembered Alex Staveley telling her the monks had suffered greater losses under foreign rule than any other sector of the community. Hence, she supposed, the discontent. 'But I suppose it only takes one or two to fan up the sparks of discontent.'

'Too right it does! And now the workers have got hold of these cheap Jap bikes and can pedal from place to place stirring up all sorts. Makes our life infinitely more difficult, I can tell you!'

He gave her a wide grin and picked up his beer. It would be all he'd mention about what was happening up at the mines, Kate knew. Johnnie had the capacity to push any aggravations or difficulties behind him. He didn't allow the past to impinge on the present. She admired him for that and, encouraged by him, had made a great effort to banish the problem of Sylvia and her father from her thoughts, too.

'Stop fighting the inevitable,' Johnnie had advised her when she'd first told him about her father remarrying. 'You'll only earn his animosity if you make things difficult for him and the BT.'

The BT was Kate's unforgiving term for Sylvia. In a despairing moment while writing to Elizabeth, Kate had referred to her as the 'Brainless Tart' who'd cast a spell over her father. Elizabeth had promptly abbreviated that to 'the BT'. Kate approved. The act of reducing Sylvia to mere initials had somehow reduced her in importance, too. Objects were so much easier to discard emotionally.

Now she found the thought of Sylvia no longer choked her and felt she had Johnnie to thank for that.

She glanced at him, contemplating the deep-etched lines around his eyes, the fine sun-bleached hairs of his thick eyebrows, the slightly crooked nose, the wide mouth, all so familiar to her now. Their very sense of intimacy thrilled her. She wanted to stretch out and touch his face.

As if sensing her eyes upon him, he turned his head slightly to look at her. 'So,' he asked, putting his cool, smooth hand over hers. 'Where's it to be tonight? Raffles? Or should we join Joe and his party at the Great World?'

'What about the Tanglin?'

'With Alice?'

Kate nodded. Ever since she'd met Johnnie they had joined forces with Alice Macpherson and one of her friends at the weekend. It had meant that Kate could avoid telling her father precisely where she was going and with whom, Alice acting as convenient cover. For the time being anyway she wished to keep Johnnie separate from her life at home, for him to be part of her new, independent world. Besides, perversely, she felt that her father had forfeited any right to share in anything remotely personal between them.

Johnnie put down his beer. 'Do you think, just this once, we might dispense with Alice?' he asked. He began to trace the line of her hand with his finger.

'But I'm staying there, remember?' Kate reminded him. 'While Daddy's on honeymoon . . .'

She closed her mind to the thought of her father and the BT cavorting together for five weeks while they toured Australia and the islands.

The only consolation was that the wedding was over now. No more Sylvia twittering on about what colours to choose for the marquee, and whether the tables should be decked with camellias, frangipanis or orchids, or which hymns to choose for the service at St Andrew's cathedral, or whether or not the ice-sculptured swan would be large enough to hold sufficient caviar for all the guests.

Now it was over and Kate was staying with the Macphersons for the next few weeks. She had thought it had been a wise choice, but now, Alice, once her key to freedom, suddenly seemed her potential jailer.

'Well?' asked Johnnie, looking across at her pointedly. 'Can we escape the Fearsome Foursome, or not?'

'Leave Alice to the charms of singles with Eric Pearson, you mean?'

'Something like that. She might even relish the chance of not being massacred by us on court for once.' His face crinkled into an easy smile. 'There's a terrific cabaret on at the New World, so Joe tells me. And the Filipino saxophonists there are the best in Singapore . . .'

'Well . . .' The thought of being able to dance cheek-to-cheek with Johnnie without Alice watching her every move like an over-zealous Cerebus was exceedingly tempting.

'Live a little.' There was a slow huskiness to his voice which made her pulse race.

'Why not?' Blue eyes met grey. She smiled. Johnnie made bending the rules seem so simple she thought as she felt the light, approving pressure of his hand on hers.

Elizabeth Staveley blotted the final page of her letter to Kate, put down her pen and stretched languidly.

Outside the dusk was drawing in, the last of the light filtering through the meticulously neat rows of rubber trees which marched into the distance as far as the eye could see. Elizabeth smiled at their perfect symmetry. She knew others might find their rigid conformity oppressing, but to her they seemed merely reassuring.

She was glad to be back at Anapuri. Kate's fears that she would be lonely after her sociable life in London had proved unfounded. The tranquillity of her days here suited her for the moment. She didn't see much of Martin, of course, but she had a feeling that even if she'd remained in Rangoon, he would not have been able to get down there with any more regularity. Besides, in his latest letter he had said he'd a very good chance of being posted down to Moulmein or Mergui after he'd taken his final exams and those were only a few months away.

From the sitting room next door she heard the sound of the gramophone being cranked up and a few moments later Billie Holiday's voice, rich with the echo of nightclub blues, filled the air.

She stood up, went to the door and pulled it open sharply. 'Alex!' she called out with exasperation. 'Honestly, must we have the same record three times in a row!'

Alex raised his dark head and regarded her benignly over the top of a crumpled newspaper with appraising green eyes. 'Driving you mad, is it, Sis?' he asked with brotherly provocation.

Elizabeth picked up the nearest cushion and threw it at him. 'Frankly, yes,' she said, for good measure pitching another pillow his way.

Alex dodged the offending missile, putting out a hand to catch it deftly. 'All right, I give in,' he told her, smiling affably. 'Next time you choose!'

'I have every intention of doing so. Really, Alex, you have no taste whatsoever!'

He grinned at her, unmoved. Theirs was an easy relationship. 'I thought you were supposed to be writing letters.'

'I was.' Elizabeth came over to flop down in the deep-seated chair beside him. She swung her long bare legs so that they dangled over one chintz upholstered arm. 'I wrote to Martin earlier. And I've just finished one to Kate . . .'

'Have you indeed?' Alex's voice was faintly teasing. 'And how is the lovely Kate?' he asked.

'All right, I suppose.' Elizabeth made a faint moue and lifted her shoulders. 'Still upset about her father remarrying, I think. But surviving.' She adjusted her position slightly so that she could see her brother more clearly. 'Anyway, she's settled back into Singapore pretty easily. She's even talking about getting herself some sort of Volunteer job.'

Alex, listening to Elizabeth as she went on to describe her friend's antics, could well imagine Kate needing some sense of her own usefulness to keep boredom at bay. He could see her in his mind's eye, just as she had been when he'd met her in Rangoon that day, her face full of spirit, her every move wonderfully vibrant and alive.

'So, what happened with you and Father down at the village today?' asked Elizabeth. 'Did you manage to sort out the difficulties with Hla and Pe?' Hla and Pe were the sons of the local headman and had recently come back home from Rangoon.

'For the moment.'

Elizabeth laced her fingers under her thick, dark hair, pushing it up from her warm neck. Even with the punkah fan going it was incredibly warm in this room.

'Isn't it odd how those boys have suddenly become so awkward?' she said. 'It's ever since they went up to Rangoon University and became involved with that political hard core. Hla is particularly troublesome, so Daddy says. Even his own father doesn't know how to deal with him. He had hopes of Ko Hla taking up the law but Hla has given all that up now to become more active with this nationalist party. And his brother just follows in his footsteps. It all seems such nonsense to me . . .'

'I don't suppose they see it in that way,' Alex remarked matter of factly. He had to admit, though, that Ko Hla was proving difficult to deal with at present. He'd always been slightly mutinous, even as a child, albeit that as children they had been friends. Not any more. Not since Hla's interest in politics.

Elizabeth lifted her shoulders in a light, eloquent movement. 'But why all the fuss? I thought the British government had already agreed to discuss giving the Burmese Independence.'

'To be considered in due course, yes. But the likes of Aung San and his nationalist party and the students at Rangoon don't want to have to wait. They want the power now. I have to admit I can't say I entirely blame them.'

'Alex!'

He laughed at her indignation. 'Well, I don't. But I would rather it was achieved by peaceful means than by agitation and sedition. And it goes against the grain to have the likes of Hla and Pe secretly stirring up trouble around Anapuri.'

Elizabeth stood up and went over to the gramophone. The record had ended, though it still revolved on the turntable with a faint hissing sound. 'But you and Daddy have managed to put a stop to all that now, haven't you?' she remarked, carefully removing the record from the gramophone and bending down to replace it in its cover.

'Pretty much.'

Alex turned his head slightly away from her. He was lying, of course. This sort of thing did not just die away. It was impossible to stop once it had started. Aung San might have disappeared from the limelight and the young communist student leader, Thein Pe, along with him, but the ripples left by the stones he had thrown into the nationalist pond continued to lap against the water's edge.

Alex watched Elizabeth as she put her chosen record onto the felt-covered turntable, slowly cranking up the gramophone again, then he stood up restlessly and went over to the window.

He wouldn't tell Elizabeth as much, but if his investigations were correct, it seemed likely that the nationalists had chosen Tavoy as a base for their activities.

He had no actual proof, of course.

But he had a feeling that the trouble with Hla and his associates was only just beginning.

It had been an exhilarating evening. Kate, threading her way through the noisy crowd, stepped nimbly aside as a trio of acrobats somersaulted past her, skimming past the plump Malay soto soup seller and coming to a halt one after the other, only inches away from the burning charcoals of the satay food-seller a few stalls away.

All around her the New World pulsated with life. Men

and women of every shape and nationality edged their way slowly round the vast concourse, passing along the line of brightly lit, flimsy stalls, the cabarets and side-shows. Strollers mingled with diners and revellers, the soft melancholy wail of saxophones vied with the metallic crooning of a Chinese girl; sounds, sights, smells, assaulted her every sense.

Johnnie reached across and took her hand, tucking her arm through his. 'Enjoying yourself?'

'Tremendously.' Kate beamed. She had grown used to the bland uniformity of England. This vast, multi-national melting pot oozed interest and excitement. 'Oh, do look!' she said, pointing to where a makeshift stage had been erected.

A Chinese play seemed to be in progress. Sumptuously dressed actors, highly rouged and powdered, scurried backwards and forwards in the curtained wings, while on stage an imperious Chinese character, complete with huge forked beard and fiercely arched black eyebrows, was acting out the dastardly tale of the wrath of the Gods. Kate loved the fierce drama of these Chinese plays, the powerful, unforgiving stories. As a child her father had often taken her to watch these tales, and she had sat mesmerised as he had explained each action to her, the symbolic structure of each piece.

'Heaven knows how we'll be able to find Joe again,' Kate commented, laughing. She looked out across the dance floor, past the Chinese girls, slim in their high-collared, straight-cut Shanghai gowns, sitting at the tables which edged the floor. There had to be at least a couple of thousand people packing the cabaret from wall to wall.

'A death defying mission if you ask me! So . . .' He turned to look down at her. 'Shall we cut our losses and run? It's too late for Raffles I know, but what about a visit to Bugis Street? Or perhaps a spin up the coast before I deliver you home? It's a perfect night for it . . .'

'A drive would be wonderful.'

'Come on, then.' Johnnie took her hand, his fingers closing tightly around hers. 'Joe's quite old enough to find his own way back!'

Soon they were out on the coast road, Kate's hair tossing in the wind as they sped on, Johnnie driving at breakneck speed, past the brown huts of the Malay kampongs, the road white as dead coral in the car lights.

At last Johnnie stopped the car. Here, just a few miles out of Singapore city it was another world; peaceful, serene, unspoilt. No noisy crowds, no throbbing bands, only the call of the fishermen floating on the night air and the dull echo of sampan oars.

It was only when Kate got out of the car that she realised that she had often come here before as a child. She stood for a moment, watching the gleaming form of a square-sailed junk as it drifted past, its curved hull reflected across the moonlit water.

'You all right?' Johnnie asked. 'You've gone awfully quiet.'

'Miles away. Sorry.'

'Penny for them.'

'My father used to bring me up here, that's all.'

'You and your father used to do a lot together, didn't you?' Johnnie said, pushing his hands into his pockets and staring out across the sea.

'Used to, yes.'

'Ah, yes. The dreaded BT.' Johnnie grinned across at her, his voice light and teasing. Kate was forced to smile. It was impossible to brood with Johnnie around.

They walked down to the beach in silence, the crabs scattering at their approach. Somewhere a little further back along the coast a shore-level searchlight threw out its blue light like a probing finger across the sea. Kate sat down on the trunk of a fallen tree, tilting her head back. Away from the bright lights of Singapore city, the sky seemed even more lustrous.

Johnnie lowered himself onto the sand beside her, following her gaze. 'The outback's the place,' he said. 'Jesus, you should see the skies there, so clear . . .' He leant back against the smooth bark of the tree, his hands behind his head. 'I remember when we were kids, my father used to take us camping. All four of us. Way into the outback . . .'

He talked then. He told her about his childhood in Queensland. His father had been an engineer and they'd had a comfortable, easy life until his father had been killed in a mining accident. His death had put an end to Johnnie's dreams of university and following in his father's footsteps as an engineer. Instead, he'd been forced to leave school and get a job cutting sugar cane, a task which he might still have been doing, had not some cousins of his mother's written offering him a job on their farm outside Perth.

'So you left Brisbane for good?'

'Yes.' Johnnie fished inside his jacket pocket and drew out his cigarette case. 'Seemed too good an opportunity to turn down. They'd got no sons of their own and, although it wasn't promised as such, it was pretty much understood that they'd see me right in the future . . .'

Listening, Kate realised how little she'd known about Johnnie until now. Normally he was not inclined to talk about himself and skitted lightly over the past.

'Then why did you leave?'

The question hung in the darkness between them. She heard the click of his lighter and his sharp intake of breath on the cigarette.

'I met Vee . . .'

'Vee?' Her voice tightened a little. She knew instinctively

this must be the girl who Joe, in garrulous mood, had told her Johnnie had been crazy about once.

'Yes. She lived on a station in Toodyay close to my cousins.'

He'd fallen for her as completely as Anthony for Cleopatra. He could still recall the first time he'd seen her standing in one of the paddocks, leaning up against the weather-beaten railings, with her waist-length blonde hair pouring across her shoulders like molten gold. 'God! But she was pretty! Tall, long-legged like a gazelle . . .'

There was a tenderness in his voice which made Kate look down at him sharply. She tried to keep the small sliver of envy from stirring within her. She had never heard Johnnie speak like this before.

'So what happened?' she asked quietly.

He gave a light shrug and drew on his cigarette again. 'We had a monumental row. She wanted to live in the city, I was happy in the outback. It seemed to be my mother and father all over again. She'd only been happy in Brisbane and he out in the bush. Anyway, Vee stormed off to Perth to her aunt's in Peppermint Grove and I was too bloody-minded to go after her. By the time I'd swallowed my pride and gone down to Perth she'd already got some rich fellow in tow. Yachts, fast cars, smart restaurants . . . I couldn't compete.' He gave a hard, sharp laugh. 'I don't think she loved him, but she loved what he could offer her. I thought she'd see sense and come back to Toodyay, but she didn't.'

'Oh, Johnnie, I'm sorry.' She touched his shoulder lightly with her fingertips, sensing that he somehow blamed himself for losing Vee, regretted his own inaction. 'So,' she probed gently, 'then you came up to Malaya?'

He nodded into the darkness. 'A friend of my father's who'd been with him in the mining business offered me the job. The farm had lost its appeal by then. Besides, my younger brother was coming of an age when he could take over from me . . .' There was a silence, broken only by the soft lapping of the water against the shore. Johnnie adjusted his position, sending a crab scuttling for shelter. 'At any rate,' he continued flatly, 'Vee was engaged by then. There was nothing to keep me in Perth.' He took a long, last drag on his cigarette and then stabbed it out in the sand. He turned to look at her full-square for the first time since he had started speaking, giving her that untidy grin of his. 'God knows why I'm telling you all this . . .' He laughed a little awkwardly.

'I'm glad you have,' she said softly.

He took her hand in his, turning it over slowly and kissing the palm. 'Anyway, that's all in the past now. All over and done with . . .' He leant forward and took Kate's face between his strong hands, looking deep into her eyes. 'All that matters is here and now. Don't you agree, Kate?' His hands were cool against her skin as he drew her face towards him. 'My beautiful, beautiful, Kate.'

He began to kiss her then, softly at first, then purpose-fully. The surge of excitement that engulfed her took her by surprise. She felt the hungry force of his kisses, her heart thudding almost painfully in her throat beneath his insistent mouth.

She felt his hands on the thin cotton of her dress, his fingers slowly undoing the small pearl buttons. The sudden heat and delight of desiring, and of being desired in return, seemed to fill every part of her.

She reached up and tightened her arms around his neck, greedily returning his kisses. And he, looking down at her, seeing her beauty, thought not for the first time how easy it would be to fall in love with her.

He bent down to kiss her again and behind them the soft call of the fisherman, as he drifted slowly past in the darkness, went unheard.

## 4

*T*he Sea View Hotel was crowded. It always was on a Sunday, when half of Singapore seemed to congregate there for lunchtime drinks.

Kate glanced round the pillared terrace, nodding in the direction of a dozen or so of their friends who called out to them. She would have preferred somewhere quieter, but Johnnie had insisted on driving out on the East Coast road to this spot. Stuck up-country all week, he missed the bustle, and liked to be surrounded by people when he came down to Singapore.

'Come on, there's Joe and Eileen,' said Johnnie, taking her arm. 'Lucky for us they got here early!'

They eased their way past the tightly packed tables towards Joe, stopping briefly to chat with Eric Pearson, who was sitting with Alice Macpherson at one of the wooden tables nearby. Usually quieter than his twin brother, George, today Eric seemed to be still running on a high from the excess of alcohol he'd consumed the night before.

He was busy enthusing about the cabaret show they'd seen at the Great World. 'How on earth did that simply enormous woman squeeze herself into the cannon in the first place, that's what I'd like to know!'

'With difficulty,' Johnnie pronounced solemnly.

'Next week there's some splendid show or other coming over from America,' Eric went on, unabashed. He nodded briefly at the Chinese boy who had come to the table and placed a packet of cigarettes and some matches at his elbow. 'A trio, I think. Terribly well known, though, what their names are, for the life of me I can't remember.'

Listening to Eric, Kate observed that the war in Europe seemed to have little effect in curtailing the entertainers arriving in Singapore. If anything, the flow of artists from America appeared to be on the increase.

She turned her head as the orchestra on stage finished a catchy Ivor Novello number with a flourish. It was the sign for everyone to take their seats.

A hushed expectancy hung over the terrace. Everyone knew what was about to take place next.

They had just reached their table when the orchestra struck up a loud resounding chord. There was a general clearing of throats and the last drinks were finished and put down. The Sunday ritual at the Sea View Hotel had begun.

When first they'd come here and the Sunday lunch-time drinkers had burst into song, she and Johnnie had been hard-pushed not to show their amusement. Johnnie, dangerously close to laughing out loud, had pronounced it a load of silly nonsense to be sitting here listening to all the Poms singing such a soppy song.

But when the second chorus of 'There'll always be an England' had begun, they both started singing as lustily as the next person, and Kate had been appalled to find a lump in her throat by the final rousing chord.

It didn't seem to matter that the war was so distant. Sitting there, singing along with the unmelodic throng, there had been a sense of camaraderie between them. The war might be ten thousand miles away, but the newsreels and the papers had shown graphic details of what was happening in Europe. And now with the Dutch army capitulating, and the French and the British being pushed back by the advancing German forces in Belgium, there was an even greater sense of patriotism than ever.

Each and every one of them all through that May had seen the long line of weary, retreating soldiers flickering across the screen on the Pathé News at the local cinema. It had been a sobering sight.

Beside her, Johnnie was singing with relish. His voice was deep and clear, though more inclined to volume than sweetness. She watched him now as he ebulliently bellowed out the last part of the chorus.

He smiled at her and winked. Years of singing in isolated outback pubs had left him totally unconcerned that his rendering would hardly be considered mellifluous.

Kate loved his complete lack of embarrassment. It was part of his unaffected, easy-going charm. The more she got to know Johnnie, the more she admired him. No airs. No pretence.

She felt his hand brush against her leg. A tiny movement, but just the touch of his fingers against her thigh made her body hum and buzz with a current all of its own. Beneath the cover of the table she felt his hand gliding up the smooth silky expanse of her stockings, his thumb stretching past the ribbed band at the top to knead the soft bare flesh above it.

'Johnnie!' she whispered, only too aware, even here in this crowd, of the blissful swimming sensation that was washing over her.

'What?' His clear grey eyes looked straight into hers with mock innocence and he grinned across at her like a mischievous schoolboy.

She reached out to put her hand firmly over his, stopping the light, compelling pressure. She felt she would simply dissolve beneath his touch if he continued. 'Behave!'

'I am.'

'You most certainly are not.' But she was laughing with him all the same. The expression in his eyes was so lively and his confidence so tangible it was impossible not to.

Now she could fully understand Elizabeth's preoccupation with Martin only too well. On the stage behind them the orchestra started to play a slow-moving melody. It was a piece that Johnnie and she had danced to together at Raffles the night before and Kate remembered the feeling of being in his arms as they had danced, the warmth of his mouth against her hair.

Beneath the table she felt Johnnie's hand tighten on hers. He did not look at her, but she knew he was remembering too, and the pressure told her all she wanted to know.

Elizabeth stood by the shuttered window watching her father and Martin walking back to the house, heads bent together in deep conversation. Even from here she could see Martin's expression and that look of intense concentration, so typical of him, made her smile to herself.

'Darling, leave the two of them to it!'

Her mother's gently teasing voice came from behind her. Elizabeth turned, half smiling.

'But they're taking such ages!' she complained, tapping her fingers with rhythmic impatience against the windowsill. 'Honestly, what can they have to discuss? It isn't as if any of this has come as a surprise!'

'Maybe not,' admitted Joan Staveley, easing her arms around her daughter's shoulders. 'But it's an important step, you know. It mustn't be rushed . . .'

She looked down at Elizabeth whom she still thought of as the baby of the family. Somehow it was a shock to think that Elizabeth was going to be married.

'So, my darling,' she pushed her hand through her daughter's long dark hair, looking down at her tenderly. 'We get you back, only to lose you again!'

Elizabeth made a face. 'I know it seems like that, but it's not really *lose*, Mother! We're going to be in Rangoon for the first few months . . .' Martin had been lucky enough to get a posting there, though it was unlikely to be for more than a year at the most. 'You'll be able to come and see me every few weeks if you want . . .'

Her mother laughed. 'I hardly think Martin will relish the thought of his mother-in-law descending too often, darling,' she said emphatically. 'I should think you'd end up in the divorce courts if I were to inflict that on you both!'

'Nonsense,' Elizabeth bent to kiss her mother's smooth white cheek. 'You know Martin's very fond of you. I think he misses his family more than he'll admit.' Though Martin had never complained, she knew he had found the first year or so in Burma quite lonely. Yet she also knew he didn't regret coming. Burma, its beauty and its people, had more than lived up to his expectations.

'He's coped admirably,' Joan Staveley said with feeling. She knew how lonely it could be, miles from anybody. As a young bride she had felt desperately homesick at first in Anapuri. It was one of the reasons they had kept the house in Rangoon.

'And now he's got me,' pronounced Elizabeth happily.

'It's lucky for him that you love Burma so much,' her mother said. 'It'll make all the difference.'

'That's why he fell for me in the first place!' Elizabeth declared roundly. 'I knew I had him the moment I told him those little snippets about King Thibaw's court!'

'I see. The poor boy had no chance then?' teased her mother.

'None.'

Outside in the garden where the native trees and bushes clashed in a riot of colour, the *mali*, watering can in hand, was moving through the jungle of flowers with

infinite care. Joan Staveley observed him, knowing that
for all his tending, when the monsoons came the English
flowers, having valiantly survived the murderous sun,
would be decimated in a moment.

She turned back to her daughter, more pressing matters
on her mind. 'I suppose we ought to be sensible and
talk about the wedding. There'll be masses to do. Presumably you'll want to have the reception at University
Avenue?'

'I hadn't really thought about it.' Elizabeth's voice was
deceptively casual but she sensed her mother was right.
For one thing, she must write to Kate straight away. If
Kate hadn't yet found herself a job, she might be able
to persuade her to stay a few months rather than a few
short weeks – providing she could be enticed to leave
her divine sounding Australian, that was. It was worth
a try.

Elizabeth had missed Kate enormously. As close as she
was to Alex and her mother, she still held certain things in
reserve. With Kate she had no secrets at all and she missed
their late-night chats, their intimacy.

The sound of footsteps on the gravel pathway made
Elizabeth look up and her father's rumbling voice carried
across the hallway as the verandah door was pushed
open.

'Well, dear boy, that's that. Part of the family now.'

She smiled. Her father's relief at having finished with
the whole business was obvious. He was not one for
formalities.

They came into the sitting room, trailing one after the
other, both looking faintly flushed, like schoolboys who
had been conspiring how to escape having to take tea with
an aged aunt.

'I think drinks are called for,' said Henry, coming
over to take his wife's outstretched hand. He stood for

a moment looking down at her. Small and petite, her blonde hair still unflecked with grey, she seemed little changed from the day they had married.

He knew that she hadn't always found their marriage easy, but her loyalty had never wavered even through their most difficult moments. And there was nothing more that a man could ask of a woman.

He cleared his throat a little self-consciously, aware of creeping sentimentality taking hold. 'Damned good show this,' he said loudly, smiling approvingly at Martin. 'Can't tell you how pleased I am, dear boy. And to think we believed we'd never get rid of her!' he teased.

'Daddy!'

'Not true, of course, darling! Not true at all,' he said, leaning over to kiss Elizabeth's forehead fondly. 'Now, what about that drink? The verandah, I think.'

Elizabeth took Martin's arm, leaning her head against his shoulder. She let out a sigh of sheer happiness.

From the moment she had arrived with Kate in Rangoon and had seen Martin standing there on the wharf, her dreams had begun to shape themselves into realities.

And now, safe here in Martin's arms, her hopes seemed finally to have grown and blossomed into certainties.

Kate sat stiffly under the pencil palms at Raffles, holding her drink in front of her with cold, tight fingers.

Something was wrong. Desperately so.

She glanced over at Johnnie as he stared distractedly at the bulb of light in the centre of the table among the flowers, watching as he turned and tapped his small gold lighter on the table top. She had never known him so withdrawn. He hardly seemed to be aware of her presence.

'Johnnie, are you all right?'

'Of course.' He forced a smile but his reply was mechanical.

'Father didn't say anything to you, did he?' They had just come from Tanglin Road.

'What about?'

'Us.'

'Should he have done?'

The laughter she half-expected to see in his eyes was not there. 'No. I just thought . . .'

What had gone wrong? The evening had started with such promise. She'd even been blessed with Sylvia's absence – she had caught some bug on the last few days of her honeymoon and was still indisposed – and as far as Kate could remember there had been not even the slightest hint of tension between her father and Johnnie.

But something must have happened, something to make Johnnie's usual ebullience shrink into this remote passivity.

'Johnnie?'

He stopped running his fingers around the rim of his glass and looked up.

'Won't you tell me what's the matter?'

He gave a half-smile. 'It's nothing. Really. Just tired, that's all.' He tried to force some life into his voice but it still sounded flat. 'Had a hell of a week and it's catching up with me.'

From the ballroom behind them they could hear the band jitterbugging into a lively piece. Several couples left their tables and crossed the lawn on their way to the dance floor. They watched them go in silence. Johnnie took out his cigarette case and extracted a cigarette. 'Not giving you much of an evening, am I? Sorry.'

She watched him flick open his lighter and take a long draw at his cigarette. 'Is it something I've done?' she asked quietly. 'Is that it?'

'You?' The surprise in his voice was genuine. 'Heavens, no. You mustn't think that.' He stroked her cheek with the back of his large, roughened hand. 'I've just got one or two things to sort out, that's all. Something unexpected has cropped up.'

She waited, but he said nothing more.

After a while, he stubbed out his cigarette and took her hand. 'Come on. Shall we dance?' he said. 'The band's playing its heart out tonight. Must be pay day!'

Kate took his arm and they made their way across the lawn, past the pillared overhead galleries to the ballroom. Johnnie slipped his arms around her and drew her close, moving slowly in time with the music.

For all that he held her near, she could still feel the distance between them. Used to his infectious enthusiasm for life, Kate did not know how to deal with this new, introspective Johnnie. She felt awkward with him, unsure. And it came as no surprise when he told her that he was too tired to go on to Bugis Street that night, and suggested instead that he take her home.

'Daddy? What happened between you and Johnnie when I went out to fetch my cape?'

Mark Lawrence lifted his head from his papers to see Kate standing before him, arms folded across her emerald green satin dress. She seemed a far cry from the relaxed, confident girl of earlier that evening. 'Nothing happened between us. Why?'

Kate looked away, not quite ready to meet his searching gaze. She traced the line of the chintz-covered sofa with the tip of her finger. 'He was just terribly quiet tonight, that's all. Not at all like his usual self.'

'Tired, most probably,' laughed her father. 'You girls always think us fellows have got boundless energy. That we can work all week and then dance all through the weekend. The old bones just can't take it all the time, you know!'

'Hardly old bones! Johnnie's only twenty-six,' Kate returned. Her father was probably speaking from personal experience on these matters; Sylvia, no doubt, had run him ragged in the past.

Her father saw the tension in her stance and pushed his papers aside. 'Several of the managers up at the mines have been released from duty because their call-up papers have finally come through, haven't they?' he asked. 'That must mean that Johnnie is doing all their work, as well as his own, until the replacements come up from Australia. Probably dead on his feet!'

Kate hesitated momentarily. She remembered Johnnie mentioning that Joe Langley had left but she still didn't think that was the cause.

'No, it was something else.' She came and perched on the arm of his chair, draping her thin arms across his shoulder. 'Are you sure you didn't say anything?'

'Positive.' Her father gave a sharp nod of his head as if to emphasise the point. 'You were only gone a few minutes, my dear. We spent most of the time discussing what's happening in France and Belgium at the moment – I must say, it's a rotten business our troops being cornered at Dunkirk – but that's about all we talked about. No sweet words about you, I'm afraid. Though he did show a passing interest in the photographs of you . . .'

She twisted towards him at that. 'Which photographs?' She hoped to heaven her father hadn't had the albums out. He was quite capable of that.

Her father caught her apprehensive look and, guessing her train of thought, smiled.

'Only the ones on the piano,' he said reassuringly, giving her a playful grin. 'Duly admired, they were. He thought the one of you on your seventh birthday with your new

pony was the most telling. Said your chin still tilted like
that.'

'Did he?' Kate had to smile now.

'He did.' Her father adjusted his position slightly.
'Though I must say, my dear, I don't know what
you've been saying about Sylvia.'

'Sylvia?' A twinge of guilt began to stir within her. She
hoped Johnnie hadn't been indiscreet.

'Yes, Sylvia. Your Johnnie couldn't believe it when he
saw her photograph. He was obviously expecting her to
be like one of Macbeth's witches. Quite shocked he was.
You know, Kate, it's about time you declared a truce on
this one. Sylvia is part of this family now, whether you
like it or not. She's my wife.'

'I know, Daddy.' Kate felt suitably contrite. Tonight,
sitting here with him in the sitting room, she had felt
almost as relaxed as in the old days. Perhaps Sylvia
wouldn't change things between them too much after
all, perhaps everything would settle down a bit now. 'All
right, Daddy, a truce. I promise I'll make an effort.'

'Good girl.' He seemed visibly relieved. 'Now, don't you
worry about that young man of yours. By next weekend
he'll be as right as rain and raring to go!'

'Perhaps you're right.'

'I'm sure I am.'

She felt the encouraging pressure of his hand on her
shoulder. She wanted so badly to believe him.

She leaned forward and gave her father a kiss goodnight
on his prominent forehead, momentarily reassured by his
words.

Johnnie drained the last of his black coffee and pushed
himself back from the table. Outside he could hear the
low rumbling of the machinery working in the tin mines
on the honeycombed hillside opposite.

It was ten o'clock and he knew he should start his rounds but today he had other things on his mind. Kate, for one.

He picked up his hat and paused, running the rim slowly through his large, capable fingers. Dammit! Why did life take one's dreams and turn them upside down to make a mockery of them? Over the past few months he had found himself falling in love with Kate, had felt easy in her company as he had done with no other woman since Vee. And now this.

He jammed his broad-rimmed hat onto his head and stepped outside. As he started down the path the heat wrapped itself around him like a cloak, even at this hour making his white shirt cling to his lean body, like a half-sloughed skin of a snake.

He walked on past the honeycombed hills, trying to think back over the past few days, trying to clear his mind so that he could view the events with calm objectivity. But past and present mingled together into one blur, so that his emotions, usually held at arms' length, came crowding in on him, swamping him.

He knew one thing, though. He could not leave everything unsaid. For all his easy-going manner, he prided himself on honesty and knew he could not live with that deceit. If he tried to bury it, it would undoubtedly rise to the surface at some future date and poison their relationship in the end. He was sure of that.

So, this Sunday, when he saw Kate for lunch at the Rex, he would have to face her. Tell her the truth.

Whatever the consequences.

Kate glanced at her watch. They were having drinks at the Macphersons' and she had to meet Johnnie in an hour. She tried to concentrate on what Eric Pearson was saying, but his long drawn-out tale about a business deal he'd pulled off against some Chinese rivals seemed interminably boring and it took all her willpower to pretend interest.

She wished Johnnie were here. She'd been thinking of him more than ever this past week. So much so, that she'd even imagined seeing his grey Chevrolet skimming down Tanglin Road yesterday on her way back from the Swimming Club. That was the trouble about being in love. It seemed to dominate everything in one's life.

She glanced up, suddenly aware that Eric was looking down at her expectantly.

'Oh, I'm sorry, Eric. What were you saying?'

He gave a sharp cough of embarrassment. 'I was asking if you'd care to come to the Alhambra Cinema with me on Thursday? There's a frightfully good new film on. American.'

'Oh.' She saw her mistake now. Eric, used to more forceful rebuttals, had seen hers as vaguely encouraging. 'Thursday? I'm not sure . . .'

Eric pushed his floppy straight hair back from his face. 'You've got to come. Really you must. It's the one where they do that amazing dance routine. You know . . .'

He started to demonstrate, shoulders swinging, feet tapping, then, flinging out his arms, he tried to twirl around. He was no Fred Astaire. Halfway through the slow routine he tripped clumsily over his own two feet, staggering slightly forward so that the drink grasped tightly in his hand splashed all over Kate.

Blushing violently, he delved into his pocket and drew out a pristine white handkerchief and began to dab vigorously at the mark on Kate's dress.

'Eric, leave it!' Kate implored, seeing that he was only making matters worse.

'I haven't ruined your dress, have I?' Eric asked remorsefully, wishing now he'd been drinking the champagne rather than the orange-based punch.

'I'm sure you haven't.' Nevertheless she'd have to go home and change. She couldn't possibly go to lunch with Johnnie like this.

She left Eric still stammering his apologies and made her way up to the house to find her father.

'Fine. Absolutely,' Mark Lawrence said, only half-listening to her request for the *syce* to take her home so that she could change, and then carry on to the Rex before returning for him at the Macphersons'. 'And call in on Sylvia, could you?' he added as she turned to go. Sylvia was still under the weather and had missed the Macphersons that morning.

It only took Kate a few minutes to arrive back at their house in Tanglin Road. As the car purred its way into the tree-lined driveway she saw the familiar outline of Johnnie's Chevrolet drawn up outside. He'd said he'd try to get down earlier if he could, but she hadn't expected him to succeed.

She ran excitedly into the house, flinging down her bag onto the round mahogany table in the hallway with such haste that it only narrowly missed the huge bowl of orchids displayed in its centre.

'Johnnie?'

Kate crossed over to the sitting room and glanced in. The sun-filled room was empty.

She turned, about to call out his name again, then stopped. She had suddenly become aware of the very stillness of the house. It was filled with an odd silence, almost suffocating in its intensity, which seemed to wrap itself around the rooms.

She came back into the hallway, her feet light upon the highly polished floor. She moved slowly, almost hesitantly. She became conscious for the first time of the sound of soft murmured voices from upstairs, the whispered words amplified beyond their natural value.

For no apparent reason she suddenly felt cold and she wrapped her arms tightly around herself. Then she very slowly began to climb the stairs.

She should have announced her presence, she knew that in retrospect. But without thinking she walked straight to the door of her father's and Sylvia's room and, with only the merest breath of a knock, pushed it open.

There was a flurry of movement as the two figures sitting entwined on the bed pulled apart.

A rush of sensations burst inside her head as she saw a startled Sylvia turn towards her and hastily pull her silk wrap across her shoulders.

Kate stared at the other figure on the bed. 'Johnnie!' She had been expecting something, but foolishly not this. Never this.

She felt as if all the breath had been knocked out of her body by a violent blow across the chest. She took two steps backwards and groped for the door handle with shaking fingers.

'Kate! It isn't what you think!' Johnnie was on his feet in a second, heading off her exit. 'Kate, listen to me!'

He put his hand out to touch her but she pulled away from him angrily. 'No! Don't you dare!'

'Kate, listen, I want to explain.'

'Explain?' Her voice was venomous. 'How can you explain this, for God's sake?'

'Listen, you've got to understand. Vee and I . . .'

'Vee?' She flung the name back at him. 'What the hell's she got to do with *this*?'

As she saw his gaze flicker over her shoulder towards Sylvia she became aware of some hidden force drawing them together.

There was a silence. Johnnie was still looking at Sylvia.

'Tell her, Johnnie,' Sylvia said quietly.

There was something in her voice which made Kate look at her then. She saw the expression on her face as she stared at Johnnie, saw the deep-rooted tenderness in her eyes and sensed the powerful intimacy of old.

'Oh, God.'

The truth struck her with the force of a rocket-borne missile. She put out a shaking hand to the wall to steady herself.

'We didn't know.' Johnnie held up his head and looked Kate straight in the eyes. 'I swear to you we didn't. How was I to know that the wretched BT was Vee all the time? My Vee? You never told me the name of the woman your father was marrying. We never met. It wasn't until last weekend that I had any inkling of what had happened. I saw the photograph of her then. On the piano.'

'Oh.' So that was what had happened.

'I wanted to tell you,' Johnnie said. 'That evening at Raffles I wanted to tell you. But I didn't know how. It all seemed so preposterous, somehow. So tangled.' He covered his face for a moment, taking a deep, steadying breath. 'And then I knew I had to come and see Vee first.'

'Oh did you?' The gentleness of his tone when he spoke of Sylvia lacerated her already aching heart. Her voice was whip-thin and stinging with scorn and hurt. 'You thought you'd just come and seduce her for one last time, I suppose. For old times' sake.'

He didn't even flinch. 'It wasn't like that, Kate.'

'Oh no?' She flung the words back at him. 'I know what I saw, Johnnie.'

'Nothing happened between us, Kate.' Sylvia's insistent voice came from behind them. 'I swear to you, nothing happened.'

'Because I conveniently arrived when I did,' said Kate, all her bitterness coming together in a rush. 'And if I hadn't, what then? Would you really have stopped at a few mere kisses?'

Her mark hit home. She saw that Sylvia had the good grace at least to drop her gaze to the floor.

'So,' Kate's thin arms fell limply to her side. 'What are you going to do now?' she asked Sylvia quietly. 'Are you going to leave my father?'

'No!'

'Why not?'

'We're married, for heaven's sake.'

'But you love Johnnie.' Kate saw them glance at each other and knew it to be true. 'You love Johnnie much more.'

Sylvia didn't deny it. All she said was: 'I can't leave your father. I couldn't do that to him. Not now.'

'What do you mean "not now"?'

There was a silence. Sylvia stared down at the floor.

'What do you mean?' Kate persisted.

At last Sylvia lifted her head to meet Kate's gaze.

'I'm having his child, that's why I won't leave him,' she said slowly. She couldn't bring herself to look at Johnnie.

'Jesus!'

Kate heard Johnnie's whispered breath of surprise. He hadn't known, then. She closed her eyes, covering her face with weary hands.

What a mess it all was. What a hopeless, tangled mess. And each one of them losers in their own way.

She looked at Johnnie, forcing herself to face the fact that this was the last time she'd see him. No point pretending. It was over. They could never even be friends with this between them.

'I think you'd better go now,' she said, trying, but failing, to hide the anguish in her words.

'Kate, I didn't want it to be like this,' he said softly. He stretched out to take her hand but she pulled away from him. Just to feel his touch again would be too painful for her.

'Please go, Johnnie.'

She saw him glance at Sylvia, saw her slow, sad nod.

At that moment she realised she hadn't stood a chance. It would always have been Vee for Johnnie. She would only have been second best, a shadow of that other. Johnnie had been merely fooling himself to think otherwise. She saw that now.

She went down to the sitting room. She couldn't actually bring herself to watch him leave. She was conscious only of the sound of his car drawing away, the crunch of his wheels on the gravel driveway. Then silence.

She stood by the french windows fighting back the tears that pricked at her eyes, a terrible hammer-blow of emotion beating within her.

She knew she couldn't stay here in this house with Sylvia. It just wasn't possible to sustain the pretence. She needed to get away, to escape the mockery of the past few days.

And even as she struggled to come to terms with this decision she saw the solution unravel itself before her like Ariadne's ball of thread. She knew what she would do.

She would go to Rangoon and Elizabeth.

## 5

*C*hurchill's gruff voice cut across the silence of the Staveleys' large, airy sitting room, drowned a few moments later by a deafening buzz and high-pitched whine from the wireless set. The hills around Anapuri played havoc with reception, making it almost impossible to hear any of the news, but Henry Staveley tuned in to the BBC World Service every morning and evening, regardless of the appalling quality of sound.

Kate sat on the sofa, one leg drawn up under her, leaning forward slightly so that she could catch the faint, oscillating tones which were coming from the wireless set again.

For the first time in the few months since she had left Singapore, the news from England sounded a little more positive. By all accounts the young RAF lads had acquitted themselves superbly, defying all the odds to inflict heavy losses against the Luftwaffe and putting pay to the threat of an immediate German invasion. They had bought the British a respite, and at the same time given them back some of their old sense of pride. After the horrors of Dunkirk and the fast-following fall of France, they needed that.

'Damn!' Henry Staveley's exasperation at the newscaster's voice petering out again was all too obvious. 'What was that last bit about the Americans?'

'Britain's agreed to lease them some suitable sites,' said Kate, frowning as she tried to remember the exact words, 'for their greater security against the unexpected dangers of the future . . . at least, I *think* that's what he said.'

'That means against Japan, no doubt,' said Henry. 'Good. The more committed Roosevelt feels towards the British, the better for all of us.'

Kate glanced across at him as he lit up his cheroot, aware of his concern about Japan. It had already put pressure on the French authorities in Indo-China to block the transit of supplies to the Chinese Nationalists, and had compelled the British to do the same by closing the Burma Road.

It was a show of power they could all have done without.

At least this latest report from England about the leasing of bases, albeit overshadowed by the daring exploits of the pilots in the Battle of Britain, was a significant sign that Roosevelt was preparing his people for America's more active role in supporting the Allies; a sign that Japan's move to make the belligerent General Tojo Minister of War had not gone unnoticed.

Kate sat hunched close to the wireless, listening to the last of the news.

'Anything else of interest?' Elizabeth asked, glancing up briefly from her magazine as the newscaster gave his final summary.

'Not really.'

Kate straightened slightly, pushing her thick hair back from her face, her thin wrists with their prominent knobs of bone protruding from beneath the sleeves of her blue cotton top. The truth was, though she wouldn't dream of admitting it to Elizabeth, there had only been one small item which had really interested her. A few short sentences about the movement of Australian troops. Stupid, she knew, but she couldn't help it. Despite everything, she still thought of Johnnie. Although she could never forgive him, she couldn't pretend that she didn't still think of him, recall the fun they had together, remember his smile, his touch, his kisses. And, remembering, didn't wonder where he was or what he might be doing.

The trouble was she could ask no one where he had gone. Alice knew nothing save that Johnnie was no longer coming down to Singapore at weekends, and Kate didn't like to ask her father. Although she had never confessed to him what had taken place that day at the house, telling him only that her relationship with Johnnie was over and that she needed to get away for a while, she suspected that he knew more than he would admit to. Certainly, during that last week before she had left for Burma, she had felt the stirring of tension at Tanglin Road, felt a new coolness between her father and Sylvia.

But however much she disliked Sylvia, however much she blamed her for what had happened that day, Kate was still glad she had not spelt out Sylvia's perfidy to her father. With new-found maturity she knew it would have injured her father far more than Sylvia.

She lifted her head slightly at the sound of the door opening as Elizabeth's mother came into the sitting room.

'So, have you girls decided when you are going up to Rangoon?' Joan Staveley asked as she crossed the room, coming to sit on the sofa opposite Kate. 'I must say, I think it'll be simply hideous there in this weather, but Elizabeth seems quite determined.'

Kate grinned. 'She is.' Elizabeth had already started to plan how she would furnish her own home, even though she and Martin were to start their married life at the house in University Avenue. The trip to Rangoon was to sort out the wedding list at Rowe & Co.

'Well, for heaven's sake, don't let her drag you round town all day. She's quite capable of it, especially once she gets into the bazaars,' warned Joan. 'I can tell you,

I might be coming up to Rangoon with you both but I have no intention of trailing round after Elizabeth. I learnt my lesson long ago.'

'And don't let her loose in Hok Eong's, either!' Henry Staveley piped up from his corner.

'Daddy!' Elizabeth lifted her head from her magazine with a muted cry of protest.

'Pots and pans, that's what you're looking for this time,' her father reminded her, a smile breaking across his square-jawed face. 'Not baubles and bracelets. Strict instructions.'

'Strict instructions indeed,' Elizabeth rallied. 'Says who?'

'Martin.'

'What nonsense! Martin's far too generous-minded to say such a thing.'

'That's what worries me,' Henry chuckled, leaning forward to stub out his cheroot. 'Far too bountiful a chap. I shall have to take him aside and warn him of your extravagant tendencies.'

'Daddy, you can hardly call me extravagant,' Elizabeth protested.

'Except where one thing is concerned . . .'

Kate and Elizabeth's mother caught each other's gaze across the room, knowing the answer only too well. 'Jade,' they said together and laughed.

Elizabeth grinned unselfconsciously. 'All right, jade, I admit it. My one weakness,' she acknowledged. 'But you can blame Alex for that. If he hadn't come back with all those pieces from Mogaung.' Her dark eyes were suddenly alive with the recollection of his prized assortment. 'And what a time he'd had! Do you remember his tale about encountering those Chinese ruffians with their pony caravans and chow dog? He swore they were opium smugglers.'

'Probably were,' said Henry matter-of-factly. It was well known that Chinese bands regularly came across the Shan Hills with more in their packs than mere legal commodities. 'Still, they sold him some pretty fine pieces of jade, I remember. There was one piece of that wonderful dark green quality.'

Elizabeth saw the glint in her father's brown eyes. 'And you criticise *me* for having a weakness for jade, Daddy. Really!'

Kate smiled. Elizabeth and her father always bantered like this. She turned her head to glance out of the shuttered window.

Outside the sun was taking advantage of the break in the rain to filter across the tops of the thick leaved rubber trees. Across the valley endless acres of systematically planted dark green heaveas spread out before Kate's gaze, row upon meticulous row, like a sea of even treetops. Personally, Kate found the landscape forlorn and dismal, though she would never have admitted as much to Elizabeth, who she knew shared her father's unwavering love of Anapuri.

'Now then,' Henry Staveley pushed back his chair and glanced at his watch as if suddenly aware of how late it had become. Usually he was out on the estate before six o'clock. 'Any takers to join me while I do my rounds?'

'Yes, I'll come.' Elizabeth put down her magazine and stretched. 'What about you, Kate?'

'Love to.' Early morning, before the sun had had a chance to penetrate the thick canopy of trees, was one of her favourite times on the estate.

The first workers were already moving soundlessly among the trees by the time Kate and the Staveleys came down the verandah steps. Kate watched as they shifted swiftly from tree to tree, making a quick, skilled incision in each trunk with their curved knives before passing on to the next, leaving the bleeding latex to seep slowly into the porcelain cup suspended below. Trees were tapped early in the morning before it became too warm, to prevent the latex drying too quickly and decreasing production.

They began to walk down a passage of trees, pruned of all limbs below the 15-foot line and looking, Kate always thought, like a column of neglected telegraph poles.

After a few minutes Henry stopped to chat to one of the tapping assistants whose job it was to check the coolies' work. He examined one of the trees close by, taking out a sharp little knife and prodding its thin blade into the tapping incision to check its depth. If the labourers cut too deeply they would make a tiny wound in the thin membrane that surrounded the trunk. Each such cut would grow into a knob which would make the tree difficult to tap properly. On the other hand, if they didn't cut deep enough the latex flowed too slowly and rubber production decreased.

They waited while Henry examined two more trees, then they continued on their way. A thin layer of leaves crackled softly beneath their feet.

Somewhere in the forest beyond a deer belled to its mate, its call carrying across the still of the morning. Kate turned her head. She loved that sound. Once, when she had been in the Cameron Hills with her father, they had managed stealthily to approach a magnificently antlered stag as he called across the misty hillside to his mate. He'd been so heart-struck that he'd been oblivious of their proximity and she had almost been able to stretch out her hand to touch his sun-dappled coat. She could remember that moment so clearly.

She felt Elizabeth slip her arm through hers. 'It isn't allowed, you know.'

'What isn't?'

'This mooning for your Australian.'

'Ah.' Kate smiled. 'Actually I was thinking about my father.' Though Kate knew in truth that Johnnie was

always in the shadows of her thoughts. 'I was thinking about one of our last trips to the Cameron Hills
together.'

Elizabeth gave her arm an understanding squeeze.
'There'll be more.'

Kate shrugged. 'Maybe.'

'You know,' Elizabeth suggested, by way of diverting
her, 'once the rainy season is over, why don't we take
a trip up to Pagan and Mandalay? We could even get
Daddy and Alex to come with us.' A green mottled
lizard made its way between the line of rubber trees just
ahead of them, the leaves rustling loudly as it scuttled
by. 'You were only saying the other day how much you
wanted to see Upper Burma.'

'And I do.' Kate concentrated on the disappearing tail
of the lizard, not quite able to meet Elizabeth's penetrat-
ing gaze. 'But it's just a question of timing. I shouldn't
stay too long after the wedding.'

'There's no need to hurry back to Singapore, is there?'
Elizabeth asked, surprised. From all that Kate had told
her she imagined the last thing Kate wanted was to go
back.

'Not really. But . . .' Kate hesitated. Singapore was still
her home, whatever had happened there, and she knew
that she would have to go back sometime soon. She was
not one to run away from difficulties. She said as much to
Elizabeth, trying to dispel the nauseating picture of Sylvia
and the expected baby from her mind.

Elizabeth's hand tightened on Kate's arm briefly, as if
she understood the tangle of her friend's emotions. 'Well
then, if you have to go back, we'll have to go north
before the wedding, that's all there is to it,' she said
firmly. 'Heavens, I don't know why I didn't think of it
earlier. It's a perfect excuse to escape all the pre-wedding
tensions. Daddy will join us like a shot!'

Kate laughed. Even though it was two months to go until the wedding, Henry Staveley already wore the expression of a shell-shocked soldier whenever his wife tried to discuss the finer details of the reception with him. She could see, for reasons of everyone's sanity, that Henry's removal might prove propitious.

They walked on between the scarred rubber trees until they reached the brow of the hill. Below in the distance lay the low tin-roofed sheds where the cans of fresh latex would be brought to be weighed and registered at the end of the morning. Kate had only been down there twice and then had been fastidiously careful not to touch the milky fluid, for the overpowering eggy smell was appalling. She had stood well back from the latex being poured into the huge cement troughs, wondering how these workers, and those who later loaded the pressed spongy white cushions of latex, could ever quite rid themselves of the foul-smelling odour which must permeate their skin. The rumour that they had difficulty in finding themselves girlfriends did not surprise her in the least!

Beside them, Henry gave the tapping assistant the last of his morning instructions and then turned round to face them.

'Well, you two, are you going to join me down in the factory?' he asked, taking off his wide-brimmed hat and wiping his brow with a quick mop of his handkerchief.

'Not this morning, Daddy,' Elizabeth said firmly. She slipped her arm through his, to ease his disappointment. 'Sorry, but it's not exactly Chanel No. 5 down there, is it?'

'It might not be,' Henry conceded ruefully. 'But it's an important part of the rubber business, however unpleasant it may be. There's no escaping that.'

'I know, Daddy. And one can't simply look at the good side of everything.'

Kate knew that this was a frequent theme of Henry's. Hard work and sacrifice had made Anapuri the profitable estate it now was, and Henry wanted his children to realise that.

'Anyway,' Elizabeth pressed on, 'I suppose Kate and I ought to be getting back. We've got a few things to organise for our trip to Rangoon.'

'Ah yes, Rangoon.' Henry replaced his hat with a resigned shrug.

In truth he hadn't really expected Kate and Elizabeth to come down to the sheds with him, though he would have appreciated their company. He was used to these solitary treks. Joan was not in the least bit concerned with the manufacturing side of the estate and had long since ceased to do the rounds with him.

He quickly scanned the sky through the arch of trees.

'Probably wiser to get back anyway. Looks as if there'll be a terrific downpour in a moment.'

Glancing up, Kate saw that the previously blue sky had become leaden. She hoped the deluge would be short. She found the days when the sun hardly penetrated the monsoon steams oppressive. Somehow here, away from the coast, the damp green trees and the muggy thick air seemed to cling about her like a depressed relation.

Without warning she felt a sudden acute longing for Singapore and the sparkling expanse of blue seas which surrounded it. There, each wide avenue seemed to end in a turquoise splash of ocean. There, one could stand at the highest point and see right across the Straits, the horizon seeming to stretch for ever. There . . .

She stopped. It would never do. She pushed the familiar images from her mind determinedly.

Ahead of her Elizabeth was saying: 'I'm hoping Martin will be able to come down to Rangoon while we're there. If he can arrange a dentist's appointment, that is.'

'Another one?' Kate caught up with Elizabeth and gave her an impish smile. 'That makes at least four in the last few months. Don't you think his boss might be getting just the tiniest bit suspicious that the rapid decay of Martin's teeth seems to have coincided with your arrival?'

'Nonsense! Everyone's teeth deteriorate out here,' returned Elizabeth matter of factly. 'He'll just think Martin's have disintegrated sooner than most.'

The first drops of rain started to fall, drumming against the scruffy foliage of grey-green. They quickened their pace.

'Anyway,' Elizabeth continued as they dodged the fast forming puddles. 'He hasn't said whether or not he'll be able to come yet. He might be too busy.'

Kate heard the merest hint of longing in her voice. Kate knew Elizabeth's moments with Martin had been disappointingly hurried, snatched like hasty sips of water on a dusty trail.

'But *if* he comes down, will you . . . you know . . .' Elizabeth went on hesitantly, her cheeks flushing slightly.

'Distract your mother for a few short hours?' put in Kate with a grin. 'Of *course*.'

She was becoming quite a dab hand at diversion. On their last visit to Rangoon Kate had persuaded Joan Staveley, a keen equestrian, to join her on the weekly Sunday paper chase which took place early in the morning before church.

It had been a hair-raising episode, far more dangerous than any hunt Kate had ever attended, with various borrowed mounts, not entirely under control, setting off at a furious pace. They had returned as hot and exhausted as their ponies, to find Martin and Elizabeth seated discreetly at opposite ends of the cool sitting room, looking demure and unimaginably correct, though Kate suspected that a few minutes earlier they had been locked in a passionate embrace.

Beside her now, Elizabeth slowed her pace slightly despite the driving rain. 'I'm sorry I've dragged you into this dreadful chicanery,' Elizabeth said. 'Do you mind terribly?'

Kate laughed. Elizabeth could be unbelievably proper sometimes. 'Of course I don't, silly. Anyway, I don't see it as lying. It's more the gentle bending of the truth.'

The trouble was, Elizabeth thought as they walked on towards the house through the deepening puddles, as much as she hated this deception, and as a dutiful daughter she did most terribly, she could not help herself. The need to be with Martin negated all else.

And Kate, walking beside her, saw the look on her friend's face and understood.

She knew the power of love only too well. Knew the price one paid, and the heartache, too. And as they ran up the verandah steps she determined to be more judicious next time and never again to allow herself to fall so completely into its grasp.

Below them, driving his battered truck down the slippery mud-churned track leading to the sheds, Henry Staveley was thinking about the power of obsession too. Of a different sort, though no less demanding.

Anapuri.

Even the sound of its name on his tongue made a small dart of pleasure shoot through him, just as it had his father before him. Yet, strangely, when Henry's father had first come out to Burma, rubber was the last thing on his mind.

The Staveley brothers, Edward and George, had arrived in Rangoon in 1882 as eager young men in their twenties. They had come, like so many of their kind, to join the trading companies mushrooming in Lower Burma, dealing mostly in rice and teak. Opportunities seemed limitless and, although King Thibaw and Queen Supayalat were still holding court in Mandalay, Lower Burma seemed to echo the new free economic climate of Hong Kong and Singapore.

In the years that followed George and his brother flourished. They took on forestry leases, purchased a teak mill at Moulmein, and built warehouses along the wharves of the Rangoon River. By 1890, both men had married well and Edward had returned home to England to run the London side of the business.

In time, George was all set to follow too, but then Fate stepped in. One of the companies which Staveley Brothers dealt with over-committed itself speculating in rice and, unable to meet its debt, offered George Anapuri and two other rubber plantations in part-payment.

George had no interest in rubber, but knew it was a commercial prospect. On his way to look over Anapuri, as the little boat had slipped along the coastline past Moulmein, on past where the jungle closed in over the land, tumbling down the low cliff-sides, shining pagodas clinging to the most inaccessible spurs, he had watched the majestic white cranes soaring across the tree-tops and felt his spirits lift.

It had only taken one brief tour of the house there for George to make up his mind. Built on grand scale, with wide verandahs and vast airy rooms and views which stretched across apparently endless mountains, it seemed to George a fitting and majestic residence, every bit as elegant as Edward's new house in leafy Surrey. He determined to agree a settlement.

George never regretted his decision, though it cost him his wife. Grace had taken one look at the mountainous jungle spot George had chosen for their home and had promptly packed up her bags for England. His only pre-condition for her leaving was her agreement that once his son became of age he would be allowed to come out to Burma.

Grace had acquiesced, sure that Henry would take one look at the steamy paddy fields and impenetrable jungle and, hating them as much as she had done, would return with the speed of winged Mercury to the soft English countryside.

George had insisted, sensing his son would not.

It had taken Henry less than a week at Anapuri to become as captivated as his father. It was a lonely life, though. That was this Eden's serpent. And after his father's death, only three years after Henry's arrival in Burma, it became even more so.

Those were dark months, hard years, when solitude became isolation, and had it not been for the company of a soft-skinned Burmese village girl, Henry might have left Anapuri, for all its beauty. Ma Kyin had seen him through the darkest moments, comforting him through the longest nights.

She had known it could not be for ever. Finally he had told her that he had decided to return to England to find himself a wife, and reluctantly he sent her back to her village to start a life, and marriage, of her own.

He had never told Joan of this past secret love. And though Henry sometimes thought she suspected the truth, it remained unspoken between them.

It had ceased raining. Henry stopped the car and got out, slamming the door behind him.

'All our sins remembered . . .' The line, unbidden, came to him. Henry frowned. Now why should he suddenly think of *Hamlet*, of all things? The frailty of human nature . . .

A milky sun was beginning to burn fiercely through the canopy of trees, creating a pearly vapour of steam. In the hazy half-light Anapuri took on an almost mystical quality, like some enchanted forest rising out of the mist.

The imagery pleased Henry. It was moments like this which made all the hardships and sacrifices fall into perspective.

Henry took one last look behind him then, whistling softly, started off down the narrow muddy track towards the sheds.

Later, much later, he would remember that line from Hamlet.

## 6

*G*radually Kate's eyes became accustomed to the sudden darkness of the enclosed stairway. She thought the steps would go on for ever but then *thanaka*, jasmine and sandalwood filled the air and she knew that they must be nearing the entrance to the Shwe Dagon at last.

'Shouldn't we buy something as an offering?' she asked Elizabeth as they made their way towards the head of the stairs, past the little stalls selling flowers and good luck charms.

'I suppose we should.'

Elizabeth's voice showed no enthusiasm, though. Having promised he would try and make it down to Rangoon – if only for a day – Martin had sent a note this morning to let her know that he couldn't get leave after all.

Elizabeth had tried to hide her disappointment but not even the unexpected arrival of Alex, on his way up-country, nor his surprisingly prompt agreement to join them in Mandalay at the end of the month, had dispelled her gloom.

The trouble was, Kate thought, Elizabeth's despondency threatened to affect them all, and Kate had suggested this visit to the Shwe Dagon to raise her friend's spirits. Ever since that first morning when she had seen the sparkling golden spire of the Shwe Dagon pagoda, shining like a motionless flame in the distance as they had sailed up the Rangoon River, she had felt drawn to its magical aura.

'Well, what do you think? Was it worth the climb?'

Elizabeth asked, smiling. The sheer beauty of the place was working its charm on her already.

'How can you ask? It's quite, quite wonderful!' Kate replied, her eyes very bright.

Yet, it wasn't just the beauty of the place, Kate thought. True, the bell-shaped pagoda plated with slabs of pure gold and the thousands of diamonds and gems encrusting its tip were dazzling, but it was more than that. There was an air of calm serenity, which seemed to draw one in.

'It's almost like a small religious community up here, isn't it?' said Kate, looking at the little groups gathered about chatting together.

Kate, who had found churches in England somewhat austere, immediately felt a sense of warmth and life here. There seemed no air of stilted reverence to mar the simplicity of devotion.

'Did you know the Shwe Dagon is the most sacred of all the Buddhist temples in Burma?' Elizabeth said as they stopped at one of the eight cardinal points which marked the planetary posts round the base of the pagoda. 'They say that in their time each of the four Buddhas left a relic to be enshrined here. Heaven knows whether it's true or not, but the Burmese seem convinced enough.'

'And why not?' Kate said. 'We Christians are supposed to believe in some equally incredible deeds too, but because it's our own religion we think that's quite acceptable.'

'Arrogant, aren't we?' Elizabeth laughed.

'Utterly,' Kate agreed fiercely. 'And that's one thing Burman Buddhists are not. I have more than a sneaking regard for both them and their faith.'

'A secret convert, eh?' Elizabeth teased. 'You're as bad as Alex.'

Kate could well imagine his sympathies would lie with the Burmans and Buddhism. She smiled. 'Of course, the trouble is, there's no point my changing religion,' she said. 'No point at all. I'm told that in order to reach Nirvana one has to extinguish all passions and desires completely.'

'No hope for you then.'

Kate laughed. 'None whatsoever.'

They walked on for a moment in silence, the marble terrace warm to their feet after a day's fierce sun. Above her Kate could hear the bells gently stirring in the light evening breeze. Dusk was one of the most perfect times at the Great Pagoda. The glow of the setting sun caught the golden spire, so that it shimmered in its own intensified light.

They started back down the stairway. Below them, coming from the foot of the steps, they could hear a raised indignant voice. It was quite out of keeping with the stillness of the place, and as they drew closer Kate saw that the strident tones belonged to a heavily built Englishman. He was protesting forcefully against the request that he and his companion take off their shoes before being allowed into the temple, incensed at the refusal of the attendant to give in to his demands.

'For heaven's sake, man, in the past it's been permitted,' he was shouting, looming aggressively over the small frame of the Burman. 'Why not now?'

What he said was true, of course. Kate knew that in the past the Burmese had tolerated the British keeping their shoes on when visiting even the most holiest of places, despite the sheer lack of reverence such an act showed. But not any more. The rise in nationalist feeling had changed such kow-towing to the wishes of the British.

Embarrassed by the fuss he was making, Kate and Elizabeth walked quickly past the Englishman who was still angrily decrying the absurdity of the law.

And glancing at the string of curious bystanders pausing on their way up to the pagoda, Kate saw that they were looking at the Englishman with a new expression. Not alienation exactly, more a stiffening of resolve.

Alex Staveley bent warily over the huge grey bulk of the patient stretched out on the ground before him. Lying there, looking so peaceful, it was hard to believe that Shwe Sein could be anything other than docile, but Alex was not fooled.

Years of experience had taught him to treat all elephants with the utmost respect, and Shwe Sein, who could be unpredictable at the best of times, was likely to be even more so now she was so obviously ailing.

He edged gingerly forward, syringe in hand, aware of Shwe Sein's bright eyes watching his every move. It didn't help to have the *mahout* at his elbow urging him vocally to take care.

'The very devil, Shwe Sein, *thakin* . . .' he insisted. Having put up with her temper for years, he had his own scars to prove it and happily rolled up his sleeve to show Alex one of Shwe Sein's more impressive deliverances.

'Thank you, Ba Maw, just what I need to cheer me up,' Alex said with feeling.

'The very devil,' Ba Maw repeated with a cheerful smile. 'But better than the buffalo, eh, *thakin*?'

'Infinitely so.' Alex laughed. Injecting a buffalo was a notoriously difficult task. Apart from its mean temper, its skin was so thick and tough it was almost impossible to pierce with a needle. At least an elephant's hide, though certainly not thin, was soft and supple.

Encouraged, Alex stretched forward and picked up a handful of Shwe Sein's skin just on the barrel of her ribs, praying that she wouldn't bulge out her ribs and make it impossible to hold on, measured the thickness of two layers and quickly pushed in the needle.

He held his breath, waiting for the expected explosion. To his surprise the elephant showed no reaction whatsoever.

Alex let out his breath slowly.

'Good God, is she dead?' he exclaimed in amazement, glancing quickly down at the huge bulk before him. But the little beady black eyes merely blinked at him demurely.

Alex had to laugh. He could see it was a game to her. Next time, no doubt she would try and kick him, or stamp on him, or worse. Just to keep him on his toes.

For the moment, though, Shwe Sein was content to play the perfect patient.

He left her in the safekeeping of her *mahout* and started back across the camp. It was still early in the morning, but the other *mahouts* had already left with their elephants and Alex, whistling up his dog, set off down a series of barely distinguishable dank forest trails towards their distant, faint shouts.

Alex loved his visits to the forest camps. In many ways it was the most enjoyable part of his job. Though he had to admit that to come out here for two or three weeks, and then to return to Moulmein or Rangoon, meant he had the best of both worlds.

When it had first been decided that Alex would take over the family teak company rather than the rubber plantation in Anapuri, Henry had declared that it was essential for him to be *au fait* with the whole business of teak. Accordingly, it was agreed that Alex should spend the best part of a year working alongside one of their forestry managers to learn the grass roots of the business.

It was a decision that had stood him in good stead.

Alex had known little about the teak business when he had first arrived back in Rangoon, but after a few months of observing the trees being selected and girdled – a process, he learnt, which stopped the circulation of the sap so that the trees would dry out and be easier for the elephants to handle, and light enough to float when they were felled three years or so on – he felt confident enough to supervise his own team of around thirty workers and elephants.

He quickly mastered the art of finding the most economic route to bring the felled trees down through impenetrable forest to the rivers and of picking the precise spot in a dried-up creek which, when the rains came, would fill up sufficiently to carry the logs down to the main rivers. He learnt about the training of the elephants, the workings of the *mahouts*, he studied and watched until even his dreams were peppered with images of dancing teak trunks.

For a whole year his only interest was how to get an ample number of good trees girdled, and the required number of logs measured and dragged down to the river banks, for the first stage of their journey to Moulmein or Rangoon.

He learnt how to cope with mud and more mud, with leeches and scorpions and snakes, with Dacoits and government officials, to become immune to the vociferous growth of green mould which daily appeared on his every possession, even his precious books, and he worked harder, physically, than he had ever worked in his life.

When he had returned to Burma after finishing his schooling in England and spending three pleasure-packed years at Cambridge, Alex had impressed his father with his capacity for hard work. But he'd shown no interest in running Anapuri. The rubber business was too orderly for him, too controlled. Alex thrived on challenge and diversity and the Burma jungle proved much more suited to his temperament.

As he had steamed up the muddy, brown Irrawaddy

River on the first stage of his journey to Kunchoung he had had the sense of finally coming home. As a child he had often travelled up-country with his father, but those images had been lost amid the cold playing fields of an English boarding school. Now they tapped gently on the door of his memories.

Alex found himself growing increasingly interested in Burmese ways, in the country's complex history. In his spare time he sketched the little villages they passed through and its people – and since Staveley Brothers' forest leases were spread around assorted parts of Burma, he had a chance to observe not only the Karens, but the Shans and Kachins, too.

'*Thakin!*'

The shout brought Alex sharply out of his reveries. He quickened his pace towards the curve in the river ahead, where the elephants were trying to disperse a huge log jam.

He immediately pinpointed the problem. One of the middle-aged female elephants had been straightening up the key log of the jam when her young calf must have slipped on the wet rock beside her and fallen into the rock pool below.

He was unhurt as far as Alex could tell, but too frightened to try and scramble out and his mother, having received no response to her first small encouraging noises, was beginning to panic.

Lifting her trunk she began to trumpet with all her might. The sound was deafening. Worse, Alex knew that the other elephants soon would be affected by her frantic calls of alarm. He could already hear the working elephants upstream beginning to rap the ground with their trunks, the low anxious rumblings starting along the line.

Alex tightened his grip on his rifle, listening to a cacophony of trumpeting echoing round the hills. It was a dangerous moment and he had to be prepared to act fast. Even the most mild and good-tempered animals could run amok when they sensed panic.

Then, just as Alex was beginning to think that it must all end in utter chaos, the calf decided it was not such an impossible task to scramble out of the shallow pool, and in two quick splashes mother and son were triumphantly reunited.

As soon as the other elephants heard the short reunion pipings they gradually quietened down and soon afterwards order was restored to the team once more.

Drama over, Alex replaced the safety catch on his rifle, letting out a palpable sigh of relief. He had not relished the thought of a stampede.

He went down to check on the youngster. 'He won't make that mistake again,' he commented to the *mahout*, with a little nod at the glistening wet calf, who was now clinging to his mother's side as tightly as a limpet.

'No, *thakin*. And tonight his mother will lecture him long about foolhardiness of rock climbing.'

He turned at the thudding of footsteps. Roy Palmer, Staveley Brothers' Forest Manager for the area, was racing down the track towards him. He'd obviously been alerted by the rumpus.

'No need for alarm. All's well,' Alex called out to him reassuringly. 'Just some calf trying out his water wings, that's all.'

'Not very successfully, if that noise was anything to go by,' Roy declared with a grin. 'Is he all right?'

'Perfectly.'

Roy took off his bush-hat and wiped away the sweat which was pouring off his moon-shaped face. A small, stocky man he was permanently affected by the heat.

Alex walked up the track to meet him. He liked Roy. It was Roy who had been his first mentor. He was one of the old types of forestrymen whose attitude towards those for whom he was responsible was laid down in an unwritten primary law of the jungle. 'In an emergency your men and "Boys" come first; your dogs second; and you last.'

'So, are you coming back to base camp with me tomorrow?' Roy asked Alex. He pushed his greying hair back from his face and replaced his hat.

'No, I'm back to Moulmein.'

'Back to civilisation, eh?' Roy laughed. The truth was he hated the towns and avoided them at all costs. 'And didn't I hear you say you were off to Mandalay for a few days after that? No peace for the wicked, eh?'

Alex caught his speculative smile. 'Not what you think at all,' he insisted. 'As it happens, I'm meeting my sister there.'

'Are you indeed?'

'Yes,' said Alex ignoring Roy's sceptical tone. He did not mention Kate. He wasn't sure why exactly.

'I see.' Roy continued to eye him suspiciously but said nothing more. He looked faintly disappointed. As a confirmed bachelor, he found Alex's amorous entanglements a source of great entertainment.

They started back up the path together. 'Any more plans for the mill?' Roy asked after a while.

'Not for the moment,' Alex told him. 'After last year's modernisation, Father's a bit keen to hold fire.' The introduction of the band saws had at least given them the chance to keep up with their competitors. 'We've bought another warehouse over at Rangoon, though.'

Alex paused, ostensibly to whistle up his dog, but in truth to give Roy a chance to get his breath back. Even though the slope wasn't steep it was an effort in this heat.

They moved on slowly. Alex was aware, listening to Roy's laboured breaths, that his mentor was getting old.

It happened quickly out here in the jungle. Less than a year ago Roy would have more or less sprinted up this incline.

He felt a sudden futile spasm of anger that the jungle would eventually sap every ounce of energy from this old man, who loved it so.

They walked on in silence. Alex, feeling the dripping green mass of the forest press down upon him, thought suddenly of Mandalay and its mirror-still moats and its rose-brick palace walls, and knew that it would be a relief, for once, to leave this place.

## 7

'Can't you feel it? Close your eyes tighter, much tighter than that, and be still.'

Kate, standing by the Western Gate of the Palace at Mandalay, three weeks later, shivered involuntarily. There was something about this place, beautiful though it was, which made the hairs on the back of her neck stand on end.

Even before Alex had started recounting the massacres which had taken place here, Kate had felt the echoes of the past. She hadn't needed him to tell her of the dreadful murders, of Queen Supayalat's plot to rid herself of rivals, and how under the cover of a *pwe* she had ordered eighty or so members of the royal family to be bludgeoned to death.

Kate glanced across the lily-clad moat, so serene now. It was past this very spot, so Alex was saying, that in King Thibaw's time the cartloads of murdered princes, with their mothers and sisters, all covered in red velvet sacks, had been carried before being thrown into the Irrawaddy.

'Even the noise of the *pwe*, with the musicians being ordered to play louder and louder, was not sufficient to block out the sound of their screams,' Alex grimly went on. 'It continued for three days, so they say . . .'

'Alex, please!' Elizabeth protested sharply.

Kate, though, was fascinated, despite the graphic details. Alex was full of these little gems of Burmese history and she'd been caught up by his enthusiasm. She'd discovered he had the capacity of being able to bring a scene to life, with only a few short words. A rare quality, which seemed to emphasise his great love of the country.

'But did no one try and stop Supayalat?' she asked him. In truth she supposed everyone would have been too terrified to oppose the Queen's orders. 'What about Thibaw himself?'

'No, certainly not Thibaw,' replied Alex. He turned slightly, looking beyond the line of the crenellated pink walls of the city to the blue Shan hills in the distance. 'He was weak and foolish, completely under Supayalat's thumb. It was rumoured that he was not even the son of King Mindoon, but that of a *pongyi*. At any rate, he was the least of the king's sons, so by rights he should not have come to the throne at all.'

'Then how did he?'

'By the plotting of Supayalat's mother. She tricked Mindoon on his death-bed. He'd wanted his favourite son, the Nyaungyan Prince, to be king. By all accounts, he was very learned and very pious.'

Kate looked up at him. 'So if Thibaw hadn't come to the throne, there might even have been a Burmese king still?'

'Perhaps there might, yes,' Alex agreed, a slightly wistful note to his voice. 'Though it would have been a tricky time for whomever came to power. You have to remember the British and the French and the Italians were all scheming against each other, trying to win favours in court. Perhaps even the Nyaungyan Prince couldn't have triumphed over their combined machinations.' He gave a light shrug. 'Who knows? Certainly he was far more intelligent than Thibaw, and had none of his liking for copious quantities of French wine . . .'

'And he wouldn't have had the dreadful Supayalat by his side,' put in Elizabeth. As far as she was concerned, the queen was the more evil of the two and she said as much.

Kate, looking past the massive white gateway, tried to imagine what the City of Gems must have been like when the Kingdom of Ava was in power at Mandalay. Then it would not have been full of beefy red-faced soldiers in their drab dusty khakis, but slender Burmese dressed in rough gleaming silks with flowers and jewels in their hair.

'Come on,' Henry Staveley stirred impatiently by the car. He had none of Alex's sentimentality about the Burmese crown. To him it was quite obvious that if a king were polygamous and produced countless offspring, problems and intrigue would abound. 'Let's get a move on, shall we? Cartwright's expecting us at five,' he said, his mind turning now to the drink waiting for him inside the fort. 'And it's too damned hot just standing here . . .' As if to emphasise the point, he took off his hat and wiped his brow. The wet brim had scarred his forehead and he rubbed the skin briskly with one hand as if to erase its mark.

They drove on beyond the salmon-pink walls and the wide moat choked with lilies and pink lotus. Inside, Ford Dufferin – the British had promptly renamed the City of Gems – even with its regimental lines, and polo ground and hospital, seemed strangely lifeless and empty. During Thibaw's reign it would have been packed tight with bazaars, barracks for the royal bodyguard, houses for the court officials, audience chambers.

There would have been music too, strange native music, heavy with drums and gongs and cymbals, pierced by the thin sweet note of flutes and silken-stringed harps. Always the music. It was said that for all the years Thibaw existed in the palace, he had music played for him day and night. Silence woke him into a dreadful awareness.

There was no music today as Kate and the Staveleys drove round the compound. Yet, for all its air of present day imperial decorum, Kate was not disappointed.

Alex caught the look in Kate's eyes. 'Wait until you see the palace itself,' he said. 'It's only a pale shade of what it used to be, of course, but the proportions are still pure elegance.'

'Alex, we're having a drink first, for heaven's sake!' said Elizabeth pointedly. She knew only too well that Alex was quite capable of blocking out everything, once he became absorbed. She could see he'd already forgotten about Cartwright. 'Honestly, Kate, if you're not careful he'll run you ragged. He'll have you walking up Mandalay Hill in no time.'

'Mandalay Hill? Now there's an idea.' Alex turned to beam at them across the car.

'No! Absolutely not,' Elizabeth was adamant. She'd forgotten the extent of Alex's energy. 'Have you any idea how many steps it is to the top?'

'A few.'

'A lot. Over seventeen hundred to be precise.'

'But well worth every one of them. Really, Kate, don't let my sister's lack of stamina put you off. The view from the top is really quite splendid.'

'I'm sure it is,' countered Kate. 'And I can assure you, I'm not so easily put off. Tomorrow I have every intention of climbing to the top.'

'Oh, Lord! We've got two of them now, Daddy,' Elizabeth said, turning to her father with a groan. 'I'd forgotten how maddeningly energetic Kate could be, too. We'll have to stick together you and I to try and bring some sanity into this trip, that's all there is to it.'

'Quite so,' said Henry with a quick nod of agreement. 'And the first step to sanity is to find Cartwright and have that drink.'

They turned down one shady road, then another, skirting the north side of the maidan until Henry finally pulled up outside a two-storeyed house with wide verandahs surrounding it on each level.

Almost immediately, a short cherubically bald man came down the steps to greet them.

'Peter!' Henry climbed out of the car and went to greet his old friend with a hearty handshake. 'Good of you to offer to put us all up.'

'Delighted, old chap. Don't see enough of you.' Peter gave Henry a friendly slap on the back and then turned to greet each one of them in turn. 'Now, come on in, do. No point standing around in this heat.'

Inside it was wonderfully cool. The drawing room had no windows, but there were five slatted double doors which all stood open to let in the air, with green curtains hanging across the doorways to keep out the direct rays of the sun.

'So, what's been happening here since I was last up?' Henry asked Peter, as he helped himself to an ice-laden drink from a silver tray which an Indian servant was holding in front of him. He felt more relaxed now, having had a quick wash and a change of clothes.

'Not a lot,' Peter returned with a shrug of his heavily-set shoulders. 'There's talk of raising a few more Burma battalions. Darley Tucker – you remember him, course you do – he's to be given command of one of them. And we had General Macleod, GOC Burma, up for a short visit the other day, trying to get things stirred up a bit. What with the Japanese occupying air-bases in French Indo-China, there's a feeling we should be a bit on the alert.'

'Quite.' The signing of an alliance between Japan and Germany and Italy didn't help matters either.

'Not anything to worry about, of course,' Peter went on quickly. 'After all, it isn't as if Japan has occupied Indo-China fully as yet, it's only air-bases. And as we all know, Burma is of little military or strategic use to them.

The Tenasserim airfields, perhaps. Maybe even Rangoon
to stop the flow of military aid to China, but beyond that
nothing.' He kept his voice light enough. He did not add
that Macleod had made a point of taking aside a selected
number of military officers and telling them, in the strictest
confidence, that if the Japanese were to invade Burma, that
the Burma forces would be vastly outnumbered and that
there could be no possible hope of reinforcements.

Henry pulled out a cigarette case and drew out a
cheroot. Across the room he caught Alex's watchful gaze.
Alex had consistently told him that if the Japanese were
to invade they would come across from Siam, despite
the fact that Joshua Tait, the British high commissioner
there, repeatedly insisted that Siam would not allow the
Japanese into their country without a good hard fight.
Henry wondered if, after all, Alex might have a point.

'So,' Peter picked up his stengah from the polished teak
table beside him, 'how's Joanie? Didn't want to come up
with you?'

Henry took a puff on his cheroot. 'Too busy in Rangoon.
The wedding's in less than two months . . .' He knew,
though, that Joan wouldn't have come anyway, wedding
or not. She wasn't interested in up-country expeditions,
preferring to stay in town whenever she could. At
the back of his mind was the niggling thought that
Anapuri seemed to hold little joy for her these days.
When Elizabeth married, what would happen then? He
pushed the question away, turning to Peter and saying
instead: 'You're coming, of course?'

'To the wedding? Wild horses wouldn't keep me away.'

'Glad to hear it. Old Beeky's coming, you know.'

'Not old Beeky? Good Lord! Haven't seen him in an
age. Last time must have been three or four years ago.
Riot of a time, we had. Well, you know old Beeky. Did
I tell you about it?'

Outside on the verandah, Kate smiled, listening to the deep guffaws as Peter described his last hair-raising encounter with Beeky.

'Really they're nothing short of a couple of school-boys,' exclaimed Elizabeth as another peel of laughter rang out from the drawing room.

'Nothing wrong with that,' Alex said, appearing out on the verandah to join them. 'Good to see the old man enjoying himself and relaxing for a change.'

He came to stand beside Kate, leaning his long tanned arms against the teak balustrade. 'Feeling more refreshed now?' he asked.

Kate nodded. She had lain in the tin tub pouring can after can of cold water over her shoulders and back until every inch of her body had felt cool and reju-venated. It had been blissful.

From Alex's other side she heard Elizabeth saying: 'Now Kate, don't fall for Alex's seemingly innocent enquiry, for heaven's sake. If you admit for a moment to having even an ounce of energy left, he'll suggest some ghastly hike somewhere.'

Alex laughed. Kate noticed he didn't deny such a motive. She looked up and found him surveying her reflectively.

'Well?' he asked.

'Told you so,' Elizabeth said victoriously. 'Honestly, Alex, you've got all of tomorrow to see the Golden Palace.'

'But it's such a perfect evening, why waste it? So won-derfully cool. Besides, tomorrow we're climbing Mandalay Hill, remember?'

'Alex!'

Kate's face lit up. Filled with pent-up energy herself she could understand Alex's desire to explore only too well.

Alex straightened, pushing himself away from the balus-trade. 'Well, I'm for the Golden Palace. Kate, what about you?' There was just the suggestion of triumph in Alex's smile when she agreed.

Ten minutes later they were mounting the white stone steps to the entrance of the palace, Alex leading the way through.

'Do you see how high the Lion Throne is raised up, so anyone who entered had to look up in order to behold the king?' said Alex.

They walked slowly on towards the throne. The whole place was eerily empty. No longer were there any Aubusson carpets; no lacquered and gilded Burmese chests, no elegant couches. No *chowkidar* was there to guard treasures and possessions long since removed.

They met no one, saw no one as they walked on through the rooms. And no sounds penetrated the deep, deep silence save those of their own footsteps. There was something unbearably sad about it all. This, then, was all that was left of the glorious Kingdom of Ava.

She felt a slight comforting pressure on her shoulder. The touch was light but Kate was aware of the sense of safety and reassurance it conveyed.

'You're supposed to be marvelling at the beauty of the place, at its symmetry, not being besieged by the ghosts . . .' Alex teased softly.

'Oh, Alex, I *know*. And it's not even as if they were a particularly pleasant bunch but to come to this nothingness, it's frightening almost. It makes one aware . . .' she hesitated slightly, unable to shape the words.

'Of one's own mortality?'

She gave a small nod. 'And perhaps even more than that. Of the world's . . .'

'Oh, not the world's, surely. Just power's impermanence. The king is dead, long live the King, that sort of thing. It's healthy, in a way.'

'Do you believe that?'

'Yes, I do as a matter of fact. I don't believe the world can go forward without change. However painful that may be. The kings of Ava made the mistake of not changing with the times.' He didn't add that the British might also suffer the same fate if they were not careful.

It was getting dark inside the room. This side of the palace faced eastwards and no rays of sunshine penetrated the audience hall. 'Now, come on,' said Alex, taking one last glance about him, 'let's go and look at those spires again. You were in too much of a rush to appreciate them properly last time.'

Outside, the sky was turning an impossibly deep pink. The pyathats with their curling roofs and the seven-tiered spire, the white and gold pagodas, and the teak buildings, carved, fretted and painted, stood out in brilliance against the huge dark Shan hills to the east and the deepening sky to the west.

'Alex, it's perfect,' said Kate, her mood lightening immediately. 'I only wish Elizabeth had come with us. The palace will have none of this magic in the morning.'

' 'Course it won't. And Elizabeth knows it, too. But then my guess is she had her own reasons for staying behind . . .'

'Like what?'

'Writing to Martin for one. She hardly misses a day. Abélard and Héloïse have nothing on this pair, I can tell you.'

'You shouldn't mock.'

'I wasn't, I assure you.'

There was something in his voice which made her look at him more closely. Standing there, with the soft warmth of the sun on their backs watching the light fade from the sky at Mandalay, Kate sensed that beneath that wry humour there was a certain gravity to him that she had missed before.

He was more complex than she had imagined at first. Now she glimpsed something more formidable, more enigmatic beneath that boyish charm. She could see why he always had a string of girlfriends pursuing him. He was a man of strength, yes, but of unexpected gentleness, too. It was a rare combination.

They were silent for a moment, watching the sun's last rays caressing the gilded spires of the palace, each of them lost in their own thoughts.

After a while, she heard Alex say quietly: 'We should go back and rescue poor Elizabeth, I suppose. There's a limit to how long she can pretend to be still writing that letter to Martin. She'll have had her fill of the major's reminiscences long ago.'

'More than likely.' Kate smiled.

'The worst thing is they're always the same stories, too! Elizabeth and I have heard that tale about the major and Beeky a dozen times at least.'

As they began to retrace their tracks back along the tree-lined road towards Cartwright's house, they heard the persistent *tonk, tonk, tonk* of a coppersmith bird calling from a mango tree close by. Then, rising above it, from down in the lines, came the brisk tones of the bugler on duty sounding 'Retreat', the distant cadence curling about them for a moment before drifting out across the red and gold spires into the still, warm night.

Martin Downing, seated in his airless room overlooking the dusty compound, felt in dire need of one of Elizabeth's bolstering letters at that precise moment in time. The day had not gone well and he felt more than usually exhausted.

It had started close to midnight last night with the pariah dogs baying at the moon. Ever since Martin had arrived in this village, for some peculiar reason one dog had taken up a position outside his bungalow. This week, others had arrived, settling down about thirty yards away from the compound gate, and letting out sharp, loud yelps relentlessly all night. After several attempts to shoo them away – first with words and then with stones – Martin had finally resorted to letting off a couple of barrels over their heads.

This last act had failed to deter the dogs for more than fifteen minutes but had earned him both the wrath of the deputy commissioner and a painful shoulder, bruised by a heavy kick from the rifle. Furthermore it was the finals of the tennis match at the club after work that evening. He and Blake, representing Ferguson's department, were to play two Bombay Burmah forestry chaps. Ferguson had made it clear how important it was that they win.

God! What an evening it had been, he thought, cringing now at the memory of it. Six-Two, Six-Love. He and Tony Blake had been massacred and Ferguson had barely spoken to them afterwards at the club.

There was nothing he could have done to save the match either, he thought now, dispassionately watching a *tucktoo* clinging to the wall by the bookcase, flat and motionless like a heraldic dragon. His demon serve, usually aided by his height and his powerful shoulders, had turned into something resembling a donkey drop, a gift to anyone.

He put his hand down, stroking the soft head of JoJo, his black and white spaniel. If only Elizabeth had been here, she would have laughed about it all, told him it didn't matter in the slightest.

That was the one disadvantage of being so far up-country, of being out on a limb. The rules were made by the men themselves. Martin's previous boss had been an easy-going sort, and his amicable disposition had rubbed off on all he dealt with. It had been a pleasure working for McGuire, but Ferguson's pettiness was quite another matter. It had made the English community waspish and narrow-minded, encouraged them to scandalmonger over cocktails. Thank God he was being posted down to Rangoon for a while.

And yet, except for Ferguson, he had loved this part of Burma. He had loved the people themselves and the villages. He loved the freedom of being able to travel into the countryside for a day's shooting, and going on fairly lengthy tours of inspection, snatching a few hours to try for jungle fowl, partridge, snipe or duck for the pot.

He loved the tours, too, riding in leisurely fashion across the country with his bench clerk, looking at crops and stopping at the villages to confer with the headman to check registers and, as sub-divisional officer, to sort out any problems that had arisen since his last visit.

Outside there was a stirring high up in the peepul tree. A flock of green pigeons were up there, eating the berries, the tree shimmering with their activity.

Martin stood up, and Jojo immediately stood up too, wagging her tail, eager for a walk. 'Not yet,' he told her, trying to ignore the appealing look in her eyes, then relented. 'All right. But only a *short* one . . .'

He got back to his bungalow about half an hour later to find Tony Blake waiting for him on the verandah, sitting quite happily, drink in hand.

'Thought I'd come and find you,' said Tony pleasantly as Martin came up the path. 'How's the shoulder?'

'It'll be fine tomorrow.' Martin flung himself into the wicker chair opposite. 'Sorry about the game, by the way.'

'Doesn't matter,' said Tony, giving an airy wave of the hand. 'But I thought I'd better warn you. There may be repercussions.'

'What sort of repercussions?'

'Well apparently, there's a move afoot to release the more junior members of the department for officer training at Maymyo. Those considered dispensable.'

'And?'

'Well, officially, of course, you shouldn't fall into that category . . .'

'But?' Martin sensed he knew from the way the conversation was going.

'Ferguson was muttering after the game that he thought someone who took pot-shots at dogs in the middle of the night wasn't quite the calibre of man he wanted to keep on his team overly much. He thought he might be able to persuade the powers-that-be that you could be considered dispensable. Vindictive bugger that he is.'

'Good God!' Martin roared with laughter. 'Doesn't he realise that that's what I've been pushing for all along?'

'Have you?' Tony looked surprised. He had imagined himself to be the bearer of ill tidings.

'Absolutely.' Ever since Alex had somehow wangled to go on the training course earlier in the year, Martin had been biting at the bit to go up to Maymyo, too.

'Good heavens, you'd better not let Ferguson know that. He views it as some sort of punishment. He's so wrapped up in the Service he can't imagine anyone would want to spend time out of it, for whatever reason.'

'Then I'll look suitably aggrieved when he tells me.'

'Good man.'

Martin stretched out his hand and topped up Blake's glass from the whisky bottle Myin Ka had placed on the glass-topped table, then carefully poured himself a measure.

'Maymyo, there's a thing. And to think I was ready to kill those dogs last night,' he mused, grinning at Blake.

Later that night when the pariah dogs started systemically baying at the moon outside his gate again, instead of reaching below his bed for the tin case with his rifle in it, Martin merely pulled the pillow over his head with a resigned chuckle. It was impossible to wish them harm after the immense service they had done him.

## 8

'*I* don't know why Martin's so pleased about the possibility of being sent up to Maymyo,' murmured Elizabeth, turning slightly so that the dressmaker could make the last tiny alterations to her shot silk wedding dress. 'He knows how much I'd set my heart on being in Rangoon. It's so wretched.'

Kate raised her head, hearing the grievance in Elizabeth's voice. 'But he's been positively *aching* to go on this officer training course, you yourself said as much,' she pointed out.

She sat on the smooth covers of the bed, watching the dressmaker readjusting the tiny covered buttons at Elizabeth's waist. In the past few weeks Elizabeth had lost weight, Kate noticed, and the dressmaker was softly tut-tutting as she deftly pinned a sleeker, more svelte line. 'Remember how cross he was when Alex managed to get himself on that course, and how envious when he got those letters from his friends from Oxford recounting their exploits in France and Africa?' Kate went on. 'How frustrated he was to be so out of it all? This is his first real chance to feel involved, it's natural he should feel pleased. Besides, you'll be coming back down to Rangoon after the training is finished, won't you?'

'I shouldn't imagine so. It's much more likely we'll get sent to some faraway up-country posting. These plum jobs in Rangoon don't exactly wait around.'

Elizabeth, Kate saw, was not about to be mollified. It didn't matter that the hill station of Maymyo was a perfectly pleasant place to start one's married life, that it had green rolling country and carefully cut rides through the woods, that the climate was cool enough to merit a blanket at night, that there was a decent club and a swimming pool. Elizabeth had set her heart on Rangoon and University Avenue and was bitterly disappointed to be thwarted.

'Anyway,' Kate said. 'It's pure rumour at the moment. You may find it comes to nothing.' Kate thought this more than likely, despite Martin's optimism.

She stood up and went to the window. Outside they were erecting a marquee in the garden. Elizabeth had wanted the reception to be held here at University Avenue, and although her mother had indicated that the Pegu Club would have been much simpler, Elizabeth had held firm.

'It's looking wonderful out there,' she said encouragingly.

'Is it?' Elizabeth's shoulders lost a little of their stiffness. 'Do let me see.' She took a step towards the window but was promptly admonished by the dressmaker who mumbled, through a mouthful of half a dozen pins, something piquant about the impossibility of fastening a moving target.

Kate grinned at her. 'See, one thing at a time.'

'That's fine coming from you,' Elizabeth retorted without malice. 'You're as bad as Alex, juggling a dozen things at once.'

Kate ignored the jibe and said, with as much dignity as she could muster: 'Blake said energy is eternal delight.'

'Did he indeed? Then he'd obviously not been to Burma and had to put up with this steamy climate.'

Downstairs they heard Joan Staveley issuing orders, rallying the servants to clearing the dining room. With only twenty-four hours to go before the wedding there was still a lot to be done and Joan's voice reflected her mounting tension.

'I suppose Daddy's shut himself in his study?' Elizabeth remarked matter of factly.

'At the first battle cry this morning, yes.'

'He's better out of the way, actually.' Elizabeth began to slip out of her dress, the dressmaker hovering about her like an expectant father about to be handed his precious first-born. 'He annoys Mother by being so ineffectual.'

There was a loud crash from the dining room followed by several shrill commands from Elizabeth's mother, then more crashes.

Kate hesitated, unsure as to whether she should go down and see if she could help or not. In a strained moment, such an offer might be regarded as mere interference.

Then, amid more sharp directives, another voice, quite calm and unruffled, rose above the general furore: 'My, my, Mother, aren't we getting things a teeny, weeny bit out of perspective here?'

Both girls laughed and looked at each other with relief. 'Alex!'

'And not before time,' came Joan Staveley's voice from downstairs.

A few minutes later, Kate saw Alex striding purposefully across the lawn to supervise the men erecting the marquee. There was something very soothing about his presence. In a few short moments he had dealt with a number of problems, alternating between charm, diplomacy and cajoling where necessary, and a perceptively lighter mood filtered through the rooms. Even Henry dared to emerge briefly from his study.

By the time the dressmaker had left and Kate and Elizabeth had come downstairs Mrs Staveley had regained her composure and peace reigned once more. Alex, employing a swift and decisive rearguard action, had soothed and wheedled the house back into order.

'So, ready for the big day?' he asked Elizabeth brightly, looking up as she came into the drawing room.

Elizabeth braved a smile. 'As ready as I'll ever be, I suppose . . .'

'Marquee's looking super. Clever choice of yours.'

'Thank you.' Elizabeth's voice, though steady, seemed small and diminished.

She sat down and accepted the drink Alex held out to her gratefully. How silly it was, she thought, that despite the fact she *desperately* wanted to marry Martin she was already feeling a jangle of nerves about tomorrow.

She took a sip of her gimlet and then turned to her brother, another thought coming to mind. 'Alex, you will take extra care of Martin tonight, won't you?' she said earnestly. 'Nothing too wild, promise?'

Alex leant back in his chair. 'Now, Lizzie, would I ever . . . ?' he began, grinning mischievously.

'Yes, you most certainly would! I seem to remember that Charlotte was terribly cross with you after Richard's stag party,' Elizabeth reminded him.

'That was hardly my fault, was it?' Alex protested truthfully. He pushed his ungovernable dark hair back from his face, contriving to look as hurt as possible. 'It was Richard's army friends who were culpable that night, not me. They were quite determined to make his last night as a bachelor wholly unforgettable.' They had succeeded, too, he seemed to remember. God! the places they'd gone to. He found himself smiling at the recollection.

'So what we need tonight is a bit of decorum,' Elizabeth was saying, her words bringing him back to the present.

'Quite.'

Kate heard the solemnity of his voice and smiled. She had a feeling that the evening that Alex and Martin's friends had planned would be anything but refined.

'And you will have him at the church on time, won't you? I'd hate to have to keep on circling in the car, waiting, like Mary Garnett. The organist had practically run out of pieces to play by the time Dick finally arrived. Do you remember how ghastly it all was?'

'Terrible.' Actually Alex couldn't remember, but he knew now was not the time to admit as much. Elizabeth, he could tell, was perilously close to high emotion and needed to be handled with kid gloves. 'Lizzie, trust me. I'll make sure Martin's at the Garrison by four,' he assured her.

Kate noticed that there was no laughter in his green eyes now, no suspicion of teasing, as if he sensed how wafer-thin his sister's composure was at this moment.

'You won't be late?'

He smiled. 'Not even by a minute.'

'Promise?'

'Scout's honour.'

Kate was sure Alex had never been a scout in his life, but Elizabeth looked so impossibly relieved at his promise that it seemed inappropriate to point out this minor fact.

'I told you it would all go off perfectly.'

'You did, Alex.'

They were standing on the verandah, looking down towards the lakes. Kate had never known a more sublime evening.

'Bridegroom was in place at ten to four. Did you see?'

'I was most impressed.'

'Of course, it was a miracle of modern science to get him there at all. Let alone on time. There was a stage earlier on in the afternoon when he was having so much difficulty trying to string two words together that we thought we might have to employ a ventriloquist to do his part.'

Kate laughed. 'As bad as that, was it?'

'Worse.' Alex grinned.

'And I thought you were supposed to be looking after him.'

'I was. I *did*. I can't tell what state he would have been in if I hadn't been there. Those BCS fellows are *lethal*.'

Across the lawn Kate could see the guests, champagne glasses in hand, making their way down to the marquee for dinner. In their elegant long dresses and dinner suits they made a beguiling picture set against the lakes, gold-streaked with the last of the sun.

Alex turned slightly towards her. 'I suppose we ought to go down. They'll be serving dinner in a moment.' He pushed himself away from the railings, but made no further move. 'Shall I escort you through?'

'Shouldn't you be looking after some elderly relation or other instead?' asked Kate, mindful of his obligations.

'Would you rather I did?'

She hesitated only a moment. 'No.'

'Then I shan't.'

They continued to stand on the verandah watching the last of the light fading from the lakes, neither of them in a hurry to join the throng. After a while, Alex stretched inside his jacket pocket and drew out a slim cigarette case.

'So, what are your plans then, Kate?' he asked. Kate heard the snap of his lighter and the sharp intake of breath as he lit his cheroot. 'Are you planning to stay on in Rangoon a while yet?'

She lifted her shoulders slightly. 'I shouldn't think so. It's back to Singapore, I suppose.' She was aware, when she spoke, of the lack of enthusiasm in her voice.

She wrapped her arms around her slim, bare shoulders as if protecting herself from the future and what lay ahead. When she looked up she found Alex's green eyes regarding her reflectively.

'You do know, Kate, that you can always stay on in Rangoon, don't you?' His voice was gentle.

She sensed he knew what had happened in Singapore, that Elizabeth must have told him about Johnnie and Sylvia. And yet she felt no embarrassment. She was comfortable in Alex's company, because he was so like Elizabeth in a multitude of ways; not only in looks and mannerisms, but also in a deeper sense.

'I don't think it would be a sensible idea to put off going back,' she said, turning her head away from him, looking across the garden.

'Don't you?' He seemed genuinely surprised.

'No.' She gave a slight but definite shake of her head, pushing back a lock of hair which had fallen across her face. 'I think there comes a point when procrastination does more harm than good, Alex. The time has come to go back. I should see my father, at least.'

'And lay a few ghosts to rest?'

'That too.' That would be the most painful part. For all the months that had intervened, she couldn't help wondering how she would react if she saw Johnnie again. She was conscious of a tiny moving speck of anxiety.

The lanterns around the garden had now been lit and they cast pools of yellow light across the lawn. Alex leaned his shoulder up against the verandah post, taking a leisurely draw on his cheroot.

'You know, Kate, you don't have to stay there, *per se*. You could go and see your father and then return to Rangoon. There's plenty you could do here . . .'

'Perhaps.' The goal of going back to Singapore had so dominated her vision that she'd not seen beyond that. Now, she supposed she should consider other choices. 'Though I'm not sure where I'd stay if I came back. Elizabeth seems to think it unlikely that they will be coming back to Rangoon after Maymyo . . .'

'That's just Elizabeth talking. They may not even be sent to Maymyo and even if they are, I'm sure they'll come back here. Elizabeth looks for the downside because she likes to think she's being a realist, but it means she errs on the side of caution most of the time.'

'Perhaps there's some merit in that,' returned Kate with feeling.

Their eyes met. They both knew she was thinking about Johnnie.

'That's not your nature, Kate,' said Alex. 'You need excitement and challenge. I suspect you'd be bored to death being careful after a while.'

'Perhaps I wouldn't,' she said. 'Perhaps it would be an enormous relief. Elizabeth seems to have handled her life so much better than me so far.'

'Just differently.'

Kate leant forward against the teak railings again, the light from the lantern on the verandah shimmering across her backless apricot silk dress, like a dancing, flickering flame.

'It's all seemed so simple for Elizabeth,' she declared.

'Only because she fell in love for love's sake,' maintained Alex. 'That helps.'

'Of course it helps,' Kate said. For some reason she felt mildly irritated, as if he had set some puzzle which she couldn't quite understand. 'Why else does one fall in love?'

'Oh, Kate, surely you know,' he said. She was aware he was watching her intently. 'For the *adventure* of loving. Why else?'

His inference was clear. Kate felt herself stiffen. How dare he belittle her feelings for Johnnie. To put it down to adventure.

Her chin jerked up towards him. 'As it happens, Alex, it wasn't like that, if you must know.' She flung the words at him, the rawness of her emotions apparent. She was furious at the sheer gall of the man. 'I *loved* Johnnie, don't you understand that? It wasn't some sort of game, for God's sake.'

'I wasn't trying to say it was, Kate.'

'And I certainly don't need a lecture from you of all people about love.'

'Dammit, Kate, you misunderstand. I was only trying...'

The rest of his words were lost in the loud jovial greeting which came from the bottom of the verandah steps.

'Kate, there you are!' Tall and bespectacled, Paul Morrison, Martin's best man, was advancing cheerfully up the steps towards them. 'I've been looking for you everywhere. Best man's privilege to escort the chief bridesmaid through to dinner, don't you know? I thought you'd forgotten.'

'Oh.' She had. She looked at Alex.

He made a slight conceding bow of the head towards Paul. 'But, of course, you must take her through, Paul,' he said. His voice was mildly encouraging, as if he were handing on a cumbersome package.

Kate swished her pleated skirt to one side and started down the steps towards Paul's outstretched hand.

'I'll leave you to the elderly aunts, then,' she called over her shoulder to Alex, her voice poisonously sweet.

'Yes, do that.'

She stalked on, her hand resting lightly on Paul's arm, determinedly refusing to even glance behind her. All the same, when they were finally seated at their table for dinner, she couldn't help noticing that when Alex arrived he was escorting not some decrepit octogenarian but a pretty dark-haired friend of Elizabeth's, who seemed to be hanging on his every word.

Conversation at dinner, Alex found, fluctuated from the frivolous to the serious, from the hot favourite for the forthcoming Rangoon Races and the Governor's Cup, to discussing what might be the effect of the ambitious U Saw succeeding U Pu as Premier of Burma.

'Actually I don't trust him an inch,' admitted Alex, when asked his opinion of the new premier by Tony Blake. 'Without scruples entirely. He knows that to keep himself in power he must achieve an early independence for Burma, and he'll sell his own grandmother to get it.'

U Saw was a very different kettle of fish to the quiet, old-fashioned U Pu. He controlled a leading newspaper and had a body of youthful adherents known as the Galon Army, which he used to overawe his political opponents.

'They're somewhat like the Blackshirts in England, I suppose,' said Alex, when pressed further by Blake's wife about U Saw's army. But then, Alex reflected, U Saw wasn't the only politician to have his own private army: Dr Ba Maw – who had recently been arrested for making a seditious speech – had his Dahma Army, and U Maung Maung had his Green Army. It was as if they sensed that the real struggle for power would come after the British had left, and were already putting their chess pieces in place.

Alex leant back in his chair, his gaze flickering around the marquee. He spotted a splash of apricot twirling its way spectacularly around the dance floor. Kate was dancing with Paul Morrison. They moved well together, carried on the tide of melody.

Alex picked up his brandy glass. Watching Kate as she spun effortlessly round in Paul's arms, he suddenly realised he did not want to leave for Moulmein without making his peace with her. The argument, which he now acknowledged he had unwittingly provoked, had been ridiculous, but it had taught him how tender her wounds still were, and that she wasn't ready for honesty yet.

He waited until she had returned to her table, pink-faced and glowing after a foxtrot.

'Kate?'

The pale flecks of her blue eyes were so icy as she turned her head towards him that he didn't have to ask if she were still angry with him.

'Kate, this is silly. Can't we call a truce?'

'A truce?' Her voice held no warmth. 'No white flag?'

'All right. I apologise. Is that what you want? I'm sorry.'

'For being a pompous prig, you mean?'

He was determined, despite her deliberate goading, not to lose his temper. 'Yes.'

His reply took the wind out of her sails. She had expected a denial. 'Well . . .' There was a pause in which she turned more fully to face him. 'And you were wrong, you know.'

He hesitated the barest moment. 'I see I might have misjudged the situation.'

'You did, yes.'

He fought down the urge to tell her what he knew to be true. Evasion was preferable to honesty at this moment.

Behind him the band had started playing again. He stretched out his hand to Kate. 'Am I forgiven enough to be granted one dance?'

'Possibly.' She was giving little ground but he noticed her eyes had lost their chill.

He led her onto the dance floor and slid his arm around her, his hand spanning her back, where the white skin was left bare by the deep backless curve of her silk dress.

He held her lightly against him, aware of the scent of her hair.

'Kate . . .'

She glanced up at him, stiffening slightly. 'Not another lecture, Alex.'

'It wasn't going to be.'

'Good. Because I couldn't take another one. Especially about love. And especially from you.'

He saw then that she was still spoiling for a fight, that her anger was just below the surface, ready to burst through like an underground spring.

It had been a mistake to dance with her. He could see now that instead of rebuilding the bridges it would only end in more acrimonious accusations.

'You've always had it so easy, Alex, haven't you? Girls falling at your feet . . .' She was determined to push him as far as she dared, blustering to hide her hurt. 'You talk about love for adventure's sake, that's something *you'd* know about, of course.'

The music around him seemed to intensify, to wrap itself around him, enclosing him so tightly that it was almost impossible to breathe.

'Kate, this is ridiculous,' he said. Or at least tried to say.

Suddenly he became aware that his head hurt like hell. That there seemed to be a thousand tiny feet stamping around in his skull. Worse still, that despite the heat he was shivering with cold.

He lost the rhythm and stumbled and looking down he saw Kate staring up at him, concern in her eyes.

'Alex, are you all right?' There was no hostility in her voice now.

'As a matter of fact,' he said, managing an apologetic smile, 'no.' It had been coming on all evening but he'd tried to ignore it; now there was no chance of escaping it. He could feel the beads of sweat gathering on his face.

He stumbled again, reaching out to Kate for support.

'Alex!' He felt Kate take his arm. 'I'll get somebody.'

'Kate, no! Don't cause a fuss. Just help me back to the house, will you? I'll be fine once I'm there.'

'Alex . . .'

'Please. I know what I'm doing. Just get me up to the house.'

'Are you quite, quite sure?'

He nodded. He didn't have the energy to speak any more. He'd seen other men come down as quickly as this, but when he'd succumbed to malaria in the past, it had come upon him slowly, not with the speed of an express train hurtling through a tunnel.

They started back, taking slow and deliberate steps. He hardly remembered getting up to the house. He was aware of one of the servants helping him upstairs to his bedroom, and of Kate disappearing to find the blankets he had instructed her to fetch.

'Alex, are you sure you want all these blankets?' He forced open his eyes to find Kate standing at the foot of his bed. 'You'll boil alive.'

'That's the idea.' He was lying in bed with two thick sweaters over his pyjamas, but despite the bulk he was still freezing. 'Just pile them on top.'

'All four of them?'

'Yes.'

'And the hot water bottles?'

He nodded, mustering a smile at the incredulous look on her face. He knew what he was doing, though. It may not have been orthodox hospital treatment, but it always worked well enough in the jungle.

He lifted his head slightly as Kancha came in with the aspirin. He took three. His head ached, as did every bone in his body, he alternated between feeling frozen and boiling, and he was racked with limb-breaking spasms. But soon, in an hour or so, if he were lucky, the ague would pass. The trick was to sweat, lie still for about half an hour or so, then to start with the quinine, a good twenty grain dose. As long as his temperature didn't rise much above one hundred and four he shouldn't have any problems. For the moment, though, he felt wretched.

He glanced over the mound of blankets at Kate.

'Go back to the party. I'll be right as rain.'

'Are you sure there's nothing I can do?'

'Positive.' He heard the rustle of her apricot silk dress as she moved towards the door. 'And Kate . . .'

She looked across at him. His eyes were half-shut, showing slits of exhaustion. 'Yes?'

'Thank you.'

Her face suddenly relaxed, a warm smile dispelling the earlier tension between them.

Later that night, much later, as Alex turned fitfully amongst the mound of blankets, he thought he saw a glimpse of apricot standing over his bed, dreamlike, watching over him.

But he couldn't be sure.


Kate stood in the doorway watching as Alex gingerly eased his way out of bed.

'Are you certain you're fit enough to be doing that?' she asked pointedly, watching as he bent forward to put on his morocco slippers and then struggled to stand up.

'Absolutely.' As if to prove his point he began to grimly walk up and down the room, trying to force some strength back into limbs which seemed incredibly weak after a mere four days in bed.

'Shall I come back later?' asked Kate, somewhat amused by his antics. She had a book in her hand, *The Seven Pillars of Wisdom*. She had intended to read to him.

'Don't go.'

'I've got better things to do than stand round here watching you stride up and down this room.'

'I'm well aware of that.' All his charm was in his smile. 'But don't go. Only ten more to do.'

'Honestly, Alex!' But she came and sat in the small high-backed chair by the window all the same.

Down among the bamboos by the lake a coppersmith bird tapped with its metallic voice, on and on, like the beat of a little hammer in the hush of the late afternoon. Kate started turning the pages of the book to find her place.

'Mother back yet?' Alex asked, as he wheeled round to do another lap.

'She came back about four. She wasn't long at the Gymkhana Club.' The bridge tiffin party hadn't been as prolonged as usual.

'And I suppose Father left for Anapuri this morning?'

'Very early, as a matter of fact.'

Kate saw that Alex had stopped his pacing. She knew what he was thinking. That Henry liked being in Rangoon less and less and his mother more and more. Over the last year the difference between them had become even more pronounced. And it would get worse. Joan had no intention of retiring to Anapuri.

'Damn and blast it!' Alex came over and sat on the edge of the rumpled bed. 'She still thinks she'll manage to persuade him to go home to England. She'll never succeed, you know. After his last home leave four years ago, he was adamant. Nothing will make him budge from Anapuri.'

'No, I think you're right.'

'Both are so unbelievably stubborn.'

She smiled at him. 'Family trait.'

'Nonsense.' He leant back against the superfluity of plump, white pillows.

Lying there, his dark hair flopping across his face, Kate thought he looked like a naughty schoolboy. She was terribly glad that he hadn't left for Moulmein the evening of Elizabeth's wedding before they'd had a chance to patch things up. It would have been such a waste. Such a sorry end.

'So . . .' He put his hands behind his head, looking across at her. 'Did I tell you that Eric Barnaby came in to see me yesterday while you were out swimming?'

'The BCS chap?'

Alex nodded. 'That's him. Now, it may not be of any interest, but he was saying that they could always do with extra assistance there. Typing, that sort of thing. I thought I'd mention it, you know, if you were thinking of coming back.'

Alex had been full of similar ideas these past few days. Kate put down her book with a small smile. 'But Alex, you know I can't type . . .' Surely, she thought, he couldn't have forgotten how long it had taken her yesterday to do that letter to the mill in Moulmein for him.

'Heavens, don't let that stop you.' Alex adjusted his position on the bed slightly so that he could see her more clearly. 'Anyway, you *can* type.'

'Alex, I can't.'

'Yes, you can. It's just that you happen to do it very, very slowly.' He gave her a beaming smile. 'Besides,' he went on encouragingly, 'Eric seemed to think it wouldn't matter all that much . . .'

'Oh.'

'Very keen he was, in fact. Wanted to know when you could start . . .'

Kate hesitated only a fraction of a second. 'And what did you say?' She stood up and went over to the window.

'That I didn't even know if you were coming back after Singapore.' He looked up at her with intense concentration. 'Are you, Kate?'

Kate turned slightly, tracing her fingertip along the line of the windowpane. It was icy cold to her touch. She was aware of crosscurrents in her life which hadn't

been there four days ago, unable to ignore any longer
the subtle change which had taken place in the relationship between herself and Alex since he had become ill.
Somehow, she sensed, they were poised to pass beyond
the realms of mere friendship.

'Are you?' she heard him ask again.

She let her hands fall back to her side. There was a
heartbeat's pause in the now silent room.

'Yes, Alex,' she said, turning round to face him. 'I rather
think I shall be . . .'

And the certainty came to her as she spoke.

## 9

Mark Lawrence bent over the deep, white laced cradle and swept up his baby daughter into his arms. He never ceased to be amazed by her perfection. At three months old she showed all the hallmarks of grace and beauty; she was tiny, peach-skinned, blue-eyed with a mass of wispy impossibly blonde hair and a small rose-bud mouth.

Behind him came the soft tread of someone coming up along the passage and he turned, giving a quick, guilty glance over his shoulder. Sylvia did not approve of him disturbing Louisa on a spontaneous whim.

'It's me! Don't panic!' It was Kate.

'Only taking a quick peek.'

Kate unleashed a conspiratorial smile. 'Won't tell. Promise.' She came into the room and crossed over to her father's side, touching Louisa's cheek gently with her forefinger. 'And how's my little poppet today? Beautiful as ever.'

Mark Lawrence glanced across at Kate and smiled. Her easy and ready acceptance of Louisa was more than he had dared hope for. He felt chastened that he had expected some tiny measure of jealousy from her when she had returned to Tanglin Road. From the very first moment Kate had seen Louisa, the baby's placid sweet charm had worked its spell.

Of course he was aware that Kate's calm acceptance of his new daughter might reflect the fact that she now felt a mere observer at Tanglin Road. Sylvia had stripped out

the rooms, changed the decor, and altered the gardens –
all with the utmost imagination and skill Mark had to
admit – but, nonetheless, he had seen his daughter's
face as she had climbed out of the car that first day
back, and had understood her thoughts. Mark knew the
house had lost its magic for Kate, that the warm childhood memories had evaporated.

Yet he sensed that their disappearance, though painful, had released her, as if severing the umbilical cord.
He could feel her independent strength now, her air of
freedom.

He stretched forward and put Louisa back in her cot.
She made no cry of protest, instead she lay back gazing up
at them kicking her legs, wide-eyed and perfectly content.
Kate had not been such an easy baby, Mark reflected.
Even at a tender age she had found the confines of the
cot far too restricting and had protested vocally at its
boundaries.

He watched her as she bent over the cradle, fastidiously tucking in the Viyella sheet which lightly covered
Louisa. For all the traumas in her life, she seemed happier,
more content, than he had ever known her. She had
even coped with coming back to Singapore, where the
spectre of Johnnie still hung over them, perhaps always
would.

It could not have been easy for her, but his daughter
had never been one to avoid unpleasant tasks. When
she had arrived back from Burma, Johnnie's whereabouts
was the first subject she had brought up as soon as she
got into the car for the drive back from the docks.

'Might as well clear the air and get the question over
and done with, Daddy, then we can all relax,' she'd said
with her usual forthrightness.

'Absolutely,' Mark had agreed. But he hadn't really
been able to answer Kate. He had not seen Johnnie since

the day of the Macphersons' party. And neither had
Sylvia. He had disappeared from their lives as completely
as a stone dropping into still, deep water.

'So you don't even know if he was called up or not?'
Kate had asked.

'No. But I'd be surprised if he hadn't been.' Most of
the Australians had. 'Couldn't really say, though.'

The truth was, when Johnnie had walked out of their
lives that day, Mark had been careful to slam the door
tightly after him. His marriage to Sylvia had staggered
through the crisis and had reached a sort of comfortable
equilibrium. What was past was past and best forgotten,
and he would do nothing to disturb that peace. For
Louisa's sake, if for no one else's.

'So . . .' He turned back to Kate, pushing away those
thoughts. 'I'm going down to the office in about fifteen
minutes. Would you like a lift to the Tanglin Club for a
swim?'

'That would be perfect. I'm meeting Alice Macpherson
there later on this afternoon after she clocks off from the
Alexandra.'

Mark had forgotten the Macpherson girl was doing
voluntary work at the hospital. He glanced at Kate,
remembering something he'd heard that morning.

'I know what I meant to tell you. Did you know
she's about to become engaged?'

'Good heavens, no. To whom? Eric Pearson, I presume.'
Kate knew they had been seeing a bit of each other
since she had left Singapore.

'Right. Old man Macpherson told me this morning.
Pleased as punch he was. It'll bring their two family
companies together and make them quite a formidable
force in the Far East.'

He saw Kate glance quickly at him. 'The dutiful daughter, eh?' she said. 'I've rather failed you on that front,

haven't I? It would have given Lawrence & Marsden a shot in the arm to have merged with Pearsons.'

'Actually, I enjoy being small and independent, if you must know,' Mark told her truthfully. 'But if you feel that badly, darling,' he teased, 'there's always George, isn't there?' He gave her a wicked smile, knowing full well her opinion of Eric's twin brother.

'Suddenly I think small and independent's the way we want to stay,' returned Kate with feeling. 'Anyway, we're busy enough as it is, aren't we?'

'Absolutely.' All the firms in Singapore were feverishly trying to match output to demand, and for once patriotism and profit lay in the same direction. Kate had even come in several times to help in the office. Mark had been impressed at how quickly she had picked up the running of the company.

If she had been staying in Singapore he would have suggested her involvement on a more permanent basis. With most of the civilians devoting much of their spare time to civil defence duties, staff were quite thin on the ground. On the other hand if she *were* to stay on longer in Singapore he knew that she would probably join the Volunteers anyway, working as an auxiliary at the Alexandra Hospital like Alice, or doing secretarial work at Fort Canning or some such.

Overrated nonsense, it all was, in his opinion. There were thousands of under-utilised military men in Singapore as it was. They could be put to very good use, instead of being bored to death waiting for something to happen.

Of course the civilians in Singapore wanted to help the war effort in some minor way – and he'd been one of the first to offer his services – but Whitehall had made it clear that the local government must give priority to rubber and tin production, over the training of military volunteers or the construction of defence works. Who was he to argue? Especially when he'd seen the old-fashioned, essentially World War I equipment that they were to train with.

No, leave it to the military proper. And as long as General Bond and Brooke-Popham and Air-Marshall Babington could stop squabbling over how Malaya should be defended and by whom, all would be well.

After all, Singapore was practically a fortress. Hadn't sixty million pounds gone into strengthening the defences over the past few years? Heavens, the Japanese wouldn't stand a chance.

Besides, the majority of well-informed people believed that the Japanese were too tied up in their present difficulties with China to branch out on fresh ventures, and in any case were fearful of a Russian rear attack.

He expounded on this theme as he walked down to the hallway with Kate.

It was only when he reached the car that he stopped to consider that the steady influx of troops arriving in Singapore, far from making the civilian community more alert and battle-ready, had only served to make them more complacent.

It was an impossibly clear night and a full moon lit up the silver line of river which lay just beyond the tennis courts and rugby nets.

From the room behind her Kate could hear the sound of a piano tinkling away and, rising above it, muffled laughter and chatter. She liked the informal atmosphere of these up-country Malayan clubhouses. They were so much more relaxed than the formal atmosphere of Singapore high society.

She leaned forward against the verandah railings, looking out across the padang. It was her father's suggestion that they come out here for a few days. Just

the two of them. She knew that, with only a few weeks
to go before she left for Rangoon, he was orchestrating
his farewell to her. It was his final offering. Tomorrow
they were to return to Singapore.

Kate had been grateful for these few days alone with
her father. However hard she and Sylvia had tried to
bury their differences, it had been an uneasy truce, and
she had leapt at her father's suggestion that they tour the
Cameron Highlands together for a few days before coming
on to stay with some old friends of his, the Rawlinsons,
who lived just outside Kuala Lumpur.

These past few days had been like the old times and she
had to admit that, whatever else, Sylvia seemed to have
succeeded in making her father happy. .

How much of it was mere papering over the cracks,
Kate did not know. Nor did she wish to find out. It was
enough to see that her father's face was no longer gaunt
and pinched, nor his eyes shadowed with dark hollows.
Love was a fragile thing and one took one's happiness
where one could.

'So, are you ready to leave?' Her father had come out
onto the verandah. Down below, in the compound, the
cicadas hesitated briefly and then continued their loud
chorus.

'Have Jack and Mary finished their game of bridge?'
Kate looked across at her father as he leant forward, both
arms resting on the railings. He'd grown a moustache while
she'd been in Rangoon. It suited him, making him seem
younger, somehow, more dashing and debonair.

'Jack's on his last rubber, if his cards are anything to go
by. He's bid a grand slam and Mary's furious with him.
He should only be in two spades.'

Kate laughed. 'And they were doing so well when I
looked in earlier.' Jack Rawlinson always insisted on
playing bridge at the slightest opportunity, though after

a few drinks he invariably over-bid so wildly that he and his partner always went down spectacularly. 'Oh dear, that means we'll have to endure a blow by blow dissection of the game on the way home.'

'*If* they're talking to each other,' her father put in.

'As bad as that?'

'Worse. If looks could kill then Jack would be in the mortuary by now. We'll need bracing up, I can tell you.'

'Then yes,' she said to his unasked question, 'I will have a nightcap before we go.'

'Wise girl.' He went over to the doorway and banged his hand against the old-fashioned circular bell to summon the boy. 'Do you want drinks out here or inside?'

'Out here, I think,' Kate replied. The overhead fans in the clubhouse were notoriously temperamental.

They settled down at one of the glass-topped tables looking out across the river and the line of areka trees, whose tall white trunks gleamed silver in the moonlight. The cicadas increased their volume, for a moment almost succeeding in drowning the noise from the clubhouse.

After a while her father said: 'So, are you looking forward to going back to Burma?'

'I am, yes. I shall miss Singapore, of course. But Rangoon does have its compensations.'

'Alex Staveley for instance?'

His question caught her completely by surprise. 'Good heavens, Father, whatever makes you mention him?'

'You talk about him an awful lot, you know.'

'Nonsense.' She couldn't bring herself to look at him. She knew he was smiling at her. 'Listen, Daddy, there's nothing between us.'

'Nothing?'

'Nothing. And I'm not even sure there will be. I don't want to rush into anything, not after . . .' She hesitated the merest second, 'Not after Johnnie.' She glanced at him quickly to check his reaction. 'I charged into that without thinking and look what happened. No, this time I'm going to take things very, very slowly.'

'You do care for him though?' Her father's voice was gentle. She saw he had no wish to pry but needed to reassure himself.

'Yes.' A variety of expressions chased across her face. 'Yes, I think I do.'

Her father reached out and covered her hand with his. 'I'm glad. You have such a capacity for loving, Kate. Don't shut it away.'

'I shan't.' She swirled the contents of her glass in a sharp circle so that the ice clinked against the edge. 'I just want to be absolutely sure before jumping in with both feet this time.'

Mark, who had been on the point of telling her that no one could be absolutely sure of anything as far as love was concerned, held back. Instead he said: 'I understand, Kate. Really I do. And in many ways I feel I'm to blame for your débâcle with young Matheson.'

'You?' She put down her glass with a clatter. 'Don't be silly, Daddy. It had nothing to do with you.'

'But I was so involved with Sylvia, wasn't I? Not much help to you when you needed me.'

She felt his hand squeeze hers. 'I'm a selfish bugger when it boils down to it, Kate.'

'Daddy, it doesn't *matter*.'

'Oh, but it does. And I want you to know, Kate, you're well cared for. Financially, that is.'

'Daddy, you don't need . . .'

'Oh, but I do,' he broke in. 'I want you to know that I've set up a trust fund for you and Louisa, and should anything happen to me you're to get controlling interest of the company.'

'That's far too generous. Really, I couldn't accept such an offer.'

' 'Course you could. This last month or so you've shown me you've got quite a flair for business. Make the old man happy, eh?'

She only hesitated for a second. She could see that giving this final parting gift meant as much to him as receiving it did to her. 'Thank you, then,' she said quietly.

'Didn't want you to leave without knowing that your future's secure. Always a place for you back in Singapore, you know.'

She understood what he was saying. That if things between herself and Alex did not work out then she had a certain future here with Lawrence & Marsden. He was offering her the security he thought he had failed to give her last time.

'Now then, that's all said and done with.' Her father slapped his thighs, relieved to have the business finished. He pushed a hand through his short-cropped hair. 'Time to go, don't you think?'

Inside they could hear Mary and Jack noisily discussing the play of the last hand. 'Definitely time,' returned Kate, catching his look and grinning.

'What we need to take their minds off the wretched game,' said Mark, 'is something to otherwise engage their energies. Some sort of diversion . . .'

'Absolutely,' agreed Kate. 'Something jolly.'

As it happened a distraction was awaiting them on the journey home. But it was of a far more dangerous kind.

## 10

*K*ate glanced out of the car window. The pale shafts of light from the headlamps flickered across the unlit roadway as they jolted their way along the jungle-lined track towards the Rawlinsons' rubber plantation.

Outside it seemed perilously dark. The full moon, which had cast out such a clear light less than an hour ago at the clubhouse, had now retreated behind a bank of clouds. In the darkness everything seemed to have grown motionless and rigid.

Ahead of her Kate could see the tense stiffness in Jack's long back as he concentrated on driving in the murky half-light. A dull thwack sounded against the rattling windscreen, signalling the end of a large moth, but apart from that, beyond the soporific purr of the engine, there was only a sharp-edge silence.

'Jesus! What's that?'

Suddenly Kate was almost catapulted out of her seat as Jack jammed on the brakes.

'Someone's come off the road ahead,' Kate's father peered out through the dust-smeared windscreen to where he could just make out the awkwardly-angled tip of a silver bumper gleaming dimly in the headlights.

Jack secured the brake. 'Better take a snifter,' he murmured, pushing open the car door. 'Won't be long.'

'I'll come with you,' said Kate's father, climbing out before Jack could refuse. 'Any sign of anyone?'

'Doesn't seem like it.'

'Shall I come, too?' asked Kate. She started to move

forward, but her father placed a restraining hand on her arm.

'No, stay put with Mary, will you?' Until he knew exactly what was out there he didn't want Kate with him. 'Easier just the two of us.'

Kate watched the two tall figures disappear beyond the pool of yellow light cast by the headlamps. She could hear the low murmur of their voices from the shadows, the sound of a car door being pulled open and then closed sharply again, then silence.

'Are you all right?' she called out.

'All's well,' came her father's reply. 'No need to worry.'

They appeared a few minutes later and climbed back into the car.

'No one seems to have been hurt, thank goodness,' Jack said over his shoulder as he started up the car again. 'But goodness knows where Mitchell has gone.' Most estate cars were known to the planters in the district and Jack had recognised at first glance that the battered black Ford had been Gordon Mitchell's. 'Probably gone on to our place for help, knowing him. It's only half a mile down the road and his own estate is a good four miles in the opposite direction.'

Kate saw Mary's round face tighten into a grimace. 'You don't look too pleased at the thought,' she commented, faintly amused.

Mary was not one to camouflage her feelings. 'Mitchell's not one of my favourite men, if you want to know the truth,' she admitted. 'Too opinionated. Too tough on his men, too.'

'Oh, he's all right,' said Jack, easing the car into first gear. 'Bit of a bully, perhaps, especially when he's had a drink or two. But he's an amusing enough chap.'

'Ghastly,' said Mary under her breath to Kate. 'Loud

mouthed and intolerant.' She dropped her voice still further and proceeded to tell Kate what a furore Mitchell had caused at the club's last New Year's Eve bash when he'd struck one of the boys for bringing him a beer which wasn't quite chilled enough.

Apart from when Jack played a particularly appalling hand at bridge, Mary was the most amenable of creatures and Kate could well imagine how much she disliked having a neighbour such as Mitchell.

In the front of the car Jack was silent. He either hadn't heard Mary's criticisms or was simply refraining from commenting. Kate had learnt that planters tended to stick together, whatever. Neighbours were few and far between and it didn't pay to fall out with them.

They continued to drive slowly down the red laterite road towards the Rawlinsons' house, all the while peering out into the darkness in case they should happen to see Mitchell wandering down the roadside. There was no sign of him.

It was as they arrived at the entrance of the estate that they sensed something was wrong. Ahead of them the bungalow was ablaze with lights and on the verandah steps two of the boys stood stiffly to attention, decidedly ill at ease.

'What the hell?' Jack quickly glanced over his shoulder at Mary and then put his foot down for the last hundred yards of the track. He was out of the car almost before it had screeched to a halt outside the bungalow.

'Mitchell's brought trouble, if I'm not mistaken,' said Mary grimly, wrenching open the car door. She sped up the verandah steps with surprising speed for her ample form, Kate following close in her wake.

Inside they found the short, wiry figure of Mitchell lounging, whisky in hand, in one of the deep armchairs in the sitting room. One of the 'boys' stood uneasily in

the doorway. Mary and Kate walked quickly through
into the brightly lit room.

'And they attacked without provocation?' Kate heard
Jack asking as they came in.

'Completely.' Sitting there in his khaki shorts and long
stockings and open-necked shirt, Mitchell looked relaxed
enough under Jack's questioning. Kate noticed, though,
that his skin seemed pale under his deep tan, and his
steel-grey eyes moved restlessly from Jack to Kate's father
and back again, as if checking that they believed his story.
'It's the damn commie bastards stirring things up again,'
he said, his nasally voice harsh.

'They usually only picket the workforce,' commented
Jack. He glanced uncomfortably at Mark.

'And nothing out of the ordinary happened today?' Kate
noticed her father was studiously careful to keep any note
of accusation out of his voice.

'Not really, no.' Mitchell stood up and went to the
window, drawing back the curtain with a quick sweep of
his hand. He turned back to them. 'Not until this evening,
that is. Then a whole bunch of the blighters surrounded
the house . . .'

'But why?' Jack leaned forward, frowning deeply. It
made no sense.

Mitchell shrugged his sinewy shoulders. 'Wanted me out.'

Jack and Mary exchanged looks. So far the communists
had only tried to intimidate the workers and had left the
white community pretty much alone. 'But you must have
done something,' Jack insisted.

Mitchell tossed back his whisky. 'Well, if you must
know, I had a set-to with one of the troublemakers
this morning. Bloody man deserved it. Been stirring up
my workforce all week.' He put down his empty whisky
glass on the mahogany table by the window and looked
across at them defiantly. 'You've got to teach the beggars

a lesson, that's what I say. Show them who's boss.'

'You've certainly done that, Gordon,' remarked Mary
tartly. 'Haven't you?'

'Listen, Mary, if you don't show them you mean
business, you'll get nothing but trouble,' said Mitchell,
unabashed.

Listening to him Kate thought how incredible it was
that Mitchell seemed incapable of realising his mistake.

It was a view obviously shared by Mary. 'And what
have you got now if it's not trouble, Gordon?' she asked
him quietly. 'Fair and firm, Gordon, that's the way. Not
out and out brutal.'

'Gordon only did what he thought was best,' Jack
broke in quickly. 'Don't let's argue now. What's done
is done.' He turned back to Mitchell who was still standing by the window, peering out across the verandah.
'And you say when you left there were fifty or so of
the fellows outside your house?'

'More than that, probably. They were stoning the house
and baying for revenge. So I hopped out the back way,
jumped into the Ford and made a run for it. Seemed the
smart thing to do.'

'Smart!' Kate heard Mary snort derisively under her
breath.

Jack stood up and pushed a hand through his greying
hair. 'Well, I only hope they don't try and follow you
here.'

'I don't think there's any chance of that,' Mitchell said
quickly.

Too quickly, thought Kate, suddenly aware of how
many times he had glanced nervously out of the window
since their arrival.

God! He *did* think they were coming. That was why
he was so uneasy. She glanced across the room at the
others.

There was a tense silence as each one of them realised the truth.

'Damn!' said Jack. He looked down at his whisky glass for a moment, then said: 'I suppose you've at least had the sense to call the police and warn them there might be trouble?'

'I rang them as soon as I got here. They know about the mean-tempered mob at my estate, yes.'

'And here? Did you tell them that it was quite likely to boil over onto this estate, too?'

Mitchell looked faintly subdued.

'Gordon, did you only mention your own estate? For crying out loud!'

'They know I'm here. They're bright enough to work out what that means,' said Mitchell, his voice showing a tinge of aggression. When cornered, Kate could tell he was the sort of man to come out with both hands fighting. She was disliking him more and more.

Jack stood up. 'Right then, I suppose I should phone police headquarters and put them in the picture,' he said. He carefully avoided Mitchell's truculent glare. 'Then I think we should get ourselves organised. Just in case. Mary . . .'

'I know.' Mary was on her feet instantly. Her voice was crisp but calm. 'The twelve-bores are in the study. I'll bring them through.'

'Just a precaution,' Jack stressed. He turned to Mitchell. 'And I don't want you blasting off with both barrels willy-nilly, do you understand?'

'A couple of shots and they'd run like hell,' said Mitchell. 'You don't want to allow them too close to the house, you know, Jack.'

'Gordon! We'll have no shooting unless it's absolutely necessary, do you understand?' said Jack fiercely. His pale blue eyes behind his steel-rimmed spectacles were bright with anger.

'But . . .'

'This is my property, I'll have you remember, and I'll handle the situation *my* way, not yours. Don't you think you've stirred up enough trouble as it is?'

He didn't wait for Mitchell's answer, but turned on his heel and went out into the hallway to make his phonecall.

There was a silence. Kate was afraid that Mitchell would prove a liability. He was like a loose cannon running, uncontrolled, through their ordered lives.

'No good treating them with kid-gloves,' said Mitchell, to no one in particular. 'We have no *authority* over the natives now. Not like in the good old days.'

He stood by the window, facing them with his arms firmly folded, defying them to disagree with him. His angular face wore an arrogant smile and Kate guessed he knew their opinion of him and couldn't care less.

There were a few hard-core men like him in Malaya – too many if the truth be known – and Kate believed they did the British cause irreparable harm.

'Well, that's done,' said Jack coming back into the room. Kate thought how tired he looked, his shoulders stooping slightly. 'And I've told the boys to close the shutters and turn off the lights throughout the house. No need to broadcast the fact that we're here.'

'I don't believe they'll come,' said Mitchell. He flicked at the curtain moodily with one sun-blotched hand.

Jack said nothing, but from his face Kate guessed he knew more than he was willing to pass on for the moment.

They heard the first faint sound of murmurings as the boy was carrying round the second tray of whiskies. Kate stiffened. There was no mistaking that sound. It was a deep, murmurous, dangerous hum, like the buzzing of an angry swarm of bees.

'Get away from the window, Gordon!' called out Jack. 'If they see you it will only infuriate them further.'

There was a heavy thump on the roof. Everyone started and looked up. The mob had started stoning the house. A fusillade of rocks and pebbles started to rattle against the walls and roof like a furious burst of hail.

'Bolt that bloody door, someone!' cried out Mitchell. He was no longer smiling quite so cockily.

'No! No!' Jack stopped the boy mid-action. 'It's fatal not to face them.'

'I agree,' said Kate's father. Up until this moment he had left most of the organising to Jack for fear of seeming to interfere, but now he felt he must say his piece. 'It's imperative that at least one of us goes outside and confronts them openly. We should at least acknowledge their grievances.'

'Poppycock!' declared Mitchell. 'Talking to them won't make the least bit of difference. You'll only get rid of them with a show of force.' As if to emphasise his point, he made a move to the front door, gun in hand.

'Jesus, Gordon, do you never learn?' asked Jack savagely, pushing him behind him back into the room. 'I've told you before, this is my estate, and I'll do things my way. And I'll have you staying out of sight for the time being, if you please.'

'You're making a mistake.'

'Shut up, Gordon, will you?' said Mary fiercely. Her small round face was etched with anger and for a moment Kate thought she might even strike Mitchell. But at the last moment she seemed to catch Jack's warning glance and seize hold of herself.

Jack turned to Mitchell. 'Listen, Gordon, if things get really nasty, *then* we'll do it your way, but not until then, do you understand?'

'On your head be it.'

'Fine.' Jack glanced across at Kate's father. 'Are you ready?'

'You lead the way. I'm right behind you.'

The boy pulled open the door for them and they slipped quickly out onto the verandah. The noise out there was deafening. Kate could hear menacing jeers and catcalls and shouts and for a moment wondered if perhaps Mitchell had not been right after all. She hoped to heaven that they all would be safe. There was no telling what an angry mob might do.

There were more thunderous yells and lumps of laterite came hurtling against the bungalow with a crashing thud. Kate could make out numerous angry voices shouting out Mitchell's name, drowning Jack's attempt to speak.

Then, as if at a signal, the noise seemed to subside. Kate felt herself relaxing the merest degree. It meant that the mob was not completely disorganised. Somewhere in that violent horde they had a leader or spokesman. At least that gave Jack and her father a chance. If they could start a dialogue then the need for violence might diminish.

She heard Jack's voice pleading with them for calm. Then above that, another rose up from the crowd in the compound.

'Our quarrel is not with you. We have come for Mitchell. The man he struck this morning is in hospital and may die.'

'You can't settle your grievances in this way, surely you know that?' Jack called across to him.

The man shifted in the darkness. 'If you send Mitchell out the rest of you will not be harmed,' he said. Beside him, the crowd murmured softly in agreement.

'You know we can't do that.'

'Our quarrel is not with you. Send out Mitchell to us,' the man repeated, 'and you will not be hurt.'

From inside, Mitchell peered over Kate's shoulder at

the crowd gathered beyond the verandah lights. 'Just remember that fellow's face,' he said vehemently. 'When this is all over I'll make dead sure he gets hauled up in the courts for this! I'll have that man deported if it's the last thing I do.'

The crowd outside were murmuring again, their voices gathering as one. 'Mitchell! Mitchell!' they began to shout simultaneously.

'The buggers!' Mitchell's rage was such it nearly choked him. 'Jack should never have let them near the house.'

Kate was aware he was making for the doorway. 'Gordon, stay out of sight,' she shouted, knowing what his presence might do to the crowd. She put out her hand to try and stop him pushing his way past her, but Mitchell thrust her aside with an oath and propelled himself through the doorway.

The change in the crowd was immediate. One minute they had seemed almost subdued, ready at least to listen to Jack. Now there was a thunderous bloodcurdling roar from the compound and a sudden shower of stones hit the bungalow, snapping against the shutters and the walls like a battle roll.

All chance of reconciliation was lost then.

'Jack! Get back in,' urged Mary from the doorway. She could see the glimmer of several curved *dahs* among the crowd. 'For God's sake, if Mitchell wants to play his silly games let him, but don't you go risking yourself on his behalf. And you, too, Mark.'

Kate felt her throat constrict with sudden fear. The mood out there was ugly. If the crowd were to attack they would stand no chance. The din seemed to swell to such a volume that it drowned all Jack's pleas for order.

The mob seemed about to surge forward, but then for the briefest of moments, they appeared to hesitate as if aware of something Kate couldn't see or hear. Seconds later, the sound of a number of trucks rumbling down the long driveway cut across the silence.

'Thank God,' said Mary under her breath. 'The police!' Kate knew she'd been convinced that it would all end in bloodshed.

Kate saw the core of the crowd halt in their charge, looking back over their shoulders towards the approaching reinforcements. Several of them began to move hurriedly away from the compound, backing off into the darkness. They knew the penalty if caught. Deportation was the one punishment most dreaded by the Indians and Chinese in Malaya, for it cut off a financial lifeline to their families.

The shuddering sound of vehicles approaching grew louder, and then Kate heard a resonant sharp shout as the sergeant in charge ordered his sepoys to step down from the trucks and line up. She could see a small nucleus of rioters standing their ground, but their numbers were vastly depleted already. The sight of the sepoys, bayonet rifles in hand, had frightened off all but the most contentious.

'Prepare to fire : . .'

Kate felt her stomach tighten at the sound of the command. Were they really going to open fire on that dwindling crowd?

Beside her Mary clutched at her arm. Make them fire over their heads then, Kate uttered in silent prayer.

'Fire!'

There was a roar, a rolling echo, across the compound. The foremost section of the rioters fell to the ground like a swathe of hay, but just as Kate was about to cry out in protest she realised that they had only flung themselves down in panic, for some were already scrambling to their feet.

The unbroken line of sepoys raised their rifles a second time and fired again. Now even the most dedicated of the rioters could see they would never get their man. Worse, surrounded by the police, they realised that their own cause was hopeless. Those who had not been wily enough to fade like shadows into the night now found themselves surrounded. They were dragged off unceremoniously to the waiting trucks.

Kate knew it would not be a happy fate that awaited them. The courts did not treat those who threatened a white man kindly.

'God! What a night.'

Kate turned away from the open doorway, suddenly exhausted. She sank down into the soft depths of the nearest armchair and, leaning forward, put her head into her hands. She was shaking. She felt as if her body was suddenly about to give way to all the fears she had fought to control.

'I thought we'd had it at one point,' admitted Mary, coming to sit beside her. 'When Mitchell went out onto the verandah.'

'It was almost as if he *wanted* a riot.'

'Wasn't it?' Mary agreed. That thought had crossed her mind too. Almost as if Mitchell were testing his power. She gave a small, involuntary shudder.

A few minutes later, Kate's father came back into the sitting room, accompanied by Jack and Sergeant Callow.

'We're back to headquarters now, if you chaps think you can manage from here on. But for the sake of prudence we'll leave a man on guard here for tonight,' Sergeant Callow addressed them with calm confidence. A man with a job well done.

'And Mitchell?' Jack asked.

'We'll escort him back to his estate. I don't think he'll have any more trouble with the rioters, but we'll leave a double guard there for a day or two. Just in case.'

'Good idea.' Jack held out his hand to the sergeant.

'And thank you. Without your men I think we'd have been in a pretty pickle.'

'Surprising how nasty a crowd can get when they've had a bit of toddy,' agreed Sergeant Callow, diplomatically putting the riot down to an excess of drink. He brushed at a small speck of dust which marked his otherwise immaculate khaki uniform. 'And of course we've got to contend with these agitators as well. They don't help. But it'll all be quiet and forgotten tomorrow, I guarantee. Always is.'

He turned his head as Mitchell came in, rifle still in hand. He was wearing that same supercilious smile which had so annoyed Kate just before the mob had appeared. He seemed either totally unaware of or, worse, unperturbed by the fact that his actions had put them all in such danger. Instead he appeared almost exhilarated by the night's events.

'Damn good show getting those ringleaders like that, Callow,' he said, slapping the sergeant on the back. 'Teach the beggars a lesson, eh? Can't have them stirring up trouble for the whites, can we?'

Callow shifted uncomfortably. It was true that for discipline's sake he could not have handled the matter differently, but sometimes he wondered why he was always risking his neck for people like Mitchell.

'Let's get you home, shall we?' he said. 'Leave these good people in peace.'

Mitchell seemed not to notice the lack of warmth in Callow's voice. 'Fine. And perhaps your men can give me a tow on the way back. Had a slight mishap in the car on my way here. No real damage but I'm off the road. On second thoughts, I've a good mind to get the beggars from my estate to push it home for me tomorrow. Got to show them who's boss, eh, Callow?'

Mary made an inarticulate sound at this comment,

jerked out of her by seething anger, but it was drowned by Mitchell's deafening laugh.

Watching him leave Kate felt her outrage almost boil over, too. Mitchell was jaded and smug, living a life full of comfort and luxury which had been gained neither by merit nor worth. Kate was aware that this was British colonial rule at its worst. It frightened her a little to see it so close at hand and to observe the havoc it wreaked.

In Mandalay, Alex had spoken of the Kingdom of Ava failing to see that the winds of change were blowing. And for the first time she saw that the British were just like the Golden Peacocks, just as vulnerable to outside forces and, possibly, just as much in danger of losing their throne.

And with men like Mitchell on their side, undermining the trust and goodwill which it had taken years to build up, who needed enemies to hasten the demise?

## 11

*P* assing the turbaned *jagger* standing at the entrance of the Raffles Hotel, Kate, now back in Singapore, went through to the cool marble-flagged hall beyond. The day had been stifling, and she wished she had arranged to meet Alice at the Tanglin Club rather than here. A refreshing swim after a hard day's work would have been blissfully invigorating.

Opposite the Long Bar the band was playing a leisurely foxtrot and a couple were slowly easing their way round the dancefloor. Kate sat down at one of the tables and glanced around the room. Alice was nowhere in sight but she was invariably late these days. Between the Alexandra Hospital and Eric, the time she had for herself was decidedly limited.

Kate ordered a drink and sat back to wait for her. She was almost at the end of her stay in Singapore now. On Thursday she was due to leave for Rangoon again.

It had been a visit of mixed fortunes. On the one hand, she had rediscovered her old relationship with her father, partly thanks to her involvement with Lawrence & Marsden; on the other, she now felt that she no longer had a home. Tanglin Road was Sylvia's, she had branded it with her mark so completely that it would be impossible for Kate to ever feel comfortable there.

Singapore might be full of childhood dreams and experiences and it would always be part of her, but for the first time Kate felt she had grown beyond its limits, reaching out to new worlds.

'Kate! My word, I thought it was you.'

A harsh twangy voice cut into her thoughts. Kate put down her iced lime and looked up to see a small, wiry figure, trim in khaki uniform, crossing the room towards her. She recognised him at once.

'Joe Langley! What a surprise.' He hadn't changed one bit. Still as sunny as ever. 'It's been a long time.'

'Hasn't it just?' He stood over her, beaming down with obvious delight. 'Can I join you?'

'Of course, please do. I'm just waiting for Alice Macpherson. You remember her, don't you?'

'My word, yes.' Joe pulled out one of the chairs and sat down beside Kate. He took out a tin of Players from his inside top pocket and extracted a cigarette. 'You look terrific, Kate, you really do. Life must be treating you well,' he said, eyeing her appreciatively. 'How long has it been?'

'Almost a year, I suppose.'

'Must be. Last time was at the Sea View Hotel, wasn't it?'

'You were there with Eileen.' How easily it all came back to her. Johnnie singing 'There'll always be an England' in his raucous voice. 'How is she, by the way? Do you still see her?'

'Eileen?' Joe gave her a beaming smile. 'I should say so. We got hitched about four months ago.'

'Oh, Joe. I *am* pleased.' She had liked the uncomplicated and lively Eileen.

'Good news, eh? Eileen's supposed to be back in Melbourne, but it seemed silly for her not to stay put in Singapore so we could see each other. Unofficial of course, but Eileen's father is an important *tuan bezar* here so the authorities just turn a blind eye. Of course, if things hot up she'll go back to stay with my parents, but it doesn't seem likely for the moment, does it? Bored stiff we all are. Half our lot are in North Africa and they're seeing some real action. Not like here.'

Kate nodded sympathetically. Again and again she had heard the British troops complaining that they had nothing to do in Singapore.

'But I suppose if the rumours about the Russians signing a Neutrality Agreement with Japan are verified, then it changes the whole complexion of things, doesn't it?'

'Too right it does.' If the Agreement was signed, then Japan would be free to push all her forces southwards to Indo-China. It made the whole of the Far East very vulnerable. 'I was saying just that to Johnnie only the other week.'

'Johnnie?' The mention of his name caught her by surprise. Her hand trembled slightly as she reached for her glass. 'You've seen him, then?' She tried desperately to keep her voice calm, her face passive.

'Only briefly. He's not my unit,' said Joe lightly. His small button-bright eyes darted across Kate's face. 'He hasn't been in touch, then?'

'No.' Kate twisted her glass round so that the chunks of ice rattled against the sides.

'Now that I find surprising,' said Joe. He leant forward and stubbed out his cigarette. 'When I saw Johnnie that night he told me he had decided to brave it and call in at Tanglin Road. Said he'd realised what a mistake he'd made last year.'

'Did he?'

Kate felt myriad emotions stir within her. Though she had often thought about Johnnie since returning to Singapore, she found herself strangely unprepared for what Joe had to say.

'Bitterly regretted it, so he said,' Joe went on.

'Oh.'

Kate studied the ice in her glass. In many ways she was glad that Johnnie had changed his mind at the last minute about visiting. He'd left it far too long to try and gather the threads together again, and Kate wasn't sure how she'd feel if she were to see him again.

Their relationship had been too short-lived to have any real lasting shape to it, that was the trouble. There had been no real substance. Slowly she had come to realise that in Burma. Whether it was due to the brevity of the relationship, or merely the combination of their two characters, Kate could not be sure.

All she knew was she had changed during the past year. And that to some measure Alex was the cause.

She looked up to see Joe observing her over the top of his ice-cold Tiger beer. 'So, he didn't call?'

She shook her head. 'And tomorrow I leave for Burma.'

His thin suntanned face tightened slightly. 'That's that, then, isn't it? Well, if I see him again I'll tell him what an opportunity he missed!' He paused for a moment, wondering if he could have misunderstood what Johnnie had said to him. The trouble was he couldn't remember the conversation exactly, several pints having blurred his concentration by the time he'd met Johnnie that evening. He was certain, though, that Johnnie had said he was going to visit Tanglin Road. Something about handling it all rather badly, he was sure of that much.

A second couple were now on the dancefloor. Kate watched them circle unhurriedly round. It was too hot to do more than a slow shuffle.

'When you next see Johnnie, say I asked after him, won't you?' she said to Joe. She couldn't quite trust herself to send her love. It seemed to be opening up too many possibilities.

'Too right I will!' Joe returned enthusiastically. 'I'm sorry you're off to Burma so soon, though. I'd have liked to have invited you up to "Fairfield" for dinner. Eileen will be most upset to have missed seeing you again.'

'Yes, I'm sorry about that.'

'Can't be helped though. Next time, perhaps.'

It did not seem the right moment to question whether or not there would be such a thing.

'And talking of time,' Joe said, glancing swiftly at his watch, 'I think I ought to rush. I only meant to pop in for a quick one on my way back from Fort Canning, but when I saw you I couldn't resist coming over to say hello.'

'I'm *so* glad you did,' said Kate. She meant it too. His presence had tied together a few loose threads, stretching back into the past and bringing them neatly into the present. It had been less painful than she'd imagined it might be.

The band burst into a catchy Ivor Novello piece as Joe stood up and stretched across the table to shake her hand. 'Me, too. Wouldn't have missed it for the world.'

'Goodbye, Joe. Give my love to Eileen.'

'Will do.' He picked up his khaki hat from the table and put it under his arm. He hesitated the barest moment. What Johnnie had said to him that night was coming back to him now. Something about Sylvia. He was about to say as much to Kate but stopped. Glancing at Kate's composed face he knew that certain things were best left unsaid. She was going back to Burma. Best to leave it like that.

'Goodbye, Kate. Safe trip.' He lifted his hand in a quick farewell salute and then passed unobtrusively through the crowd and was gone.

Kate sat quietly for a moment looking down at her ice-frosted glass. Curious how life twisted and turned, weaving extraordinary patterns. She had finally come to terms with the fact that Johnnie had slipped from her life for ever. And now this. The strange perversity of life's unpredictability seemed to rise up to taunt her.

Oddly enough, it no longer seemed to matter. Having seen Joe, having spoken about Johnnie again at last, however briefly, the air had somehow been cleared and the keen edge of her pain finally dulled.

She knew she was ready to go back to Rangoon and Alex and to risk her chances there.

Whatever they might be.

## 12

*A*lex Staveley walked through the clearing of bamboo to where the ground rose, free of scrub, above the bullock track. Behind him the camp hurricane lamps glowed orange, like a pumpkin-covered candle at Hallowe'en.

It was very dark. The star-studded sky above had a pure intensity that seemed to draw him upwards into its midst.

Alex loved these sorts of nights, their vivid brilliance. A faint breeze was fingering its way through the tall expanse of trees, across the brittle fronds. After the heat of the day, it brought relief like an ice-cold hand on a fevered brow.

'Alex!' Turning, Alex saw Roy Palmer coming up the path towards him. 'Chow's ready,' Roy called out, eagerly beckoning him to return to camp.

Alex waved in return but made no immediate move. A week into their tour together and the tedium of camp cuisine was already beginning to have its effect. Roy, on the other hand, possessed of either an iron stomach or an indifferent palate, never seemed to lose his penchant for campfire stews.

From somewhere across the valley came the hiccough of a tiger followed by the loud howl of a pariah dog barking in response. Then all was quiet again.

Alex stood for a moment listening to the breeze rustling through the wide domes of the gold mohur trees. Then hearing Roy call out his name again he whistled up his black mongrel dog and started back to camp.

Roy was already tucking in happily by the time Alex arrived.

'You took your time,' he said with a grin, gesturing towards the pot hanging over the fire. 'U Tun was a bit worried I'd scoff the lot. Still plenty left though . . .'

'Good.' Alex was careful to sound enthusiastic, for U Tun, the cook, was hovering close at hand. Alex knew he did his best with the most basic of equipment and supplies and he had no wish to offend him.

' 'Fraid it's jungle fowl again though,' said Roy, with an apologetic wave of his veined, weatherbeaten hand. 'That's all I seem to be able to shoot these days. Must be losing my touch.'

Alex grinned. In truth Roy had never been able to hit anything much other than jungle fowl. He wasn't overly bothered. The tour would be coming to an end in the next few days or so. He and Roy had only one more forestry lease to visit together then Roy would be heading back down to base camp.

Alex had other plans. He'd only told Roy that he was going to continue further up the Shan Hills to Lashio, ostensibly to look for some jade pieces to enhance his collection. The reality was far more complex.

Alex's journey northwards stemmed from a meeting almost a year before, when he had gone up to Maymyo for the officers' training course. Almost as soon as he had entered the cadet school he had been approached by one of the senior officers and asked whether he would be willing to do a 'spot of reconnaissance work', gathering general information about local conditions and sentiment when he returned to Moulmein.

Alex's contacts among both the Karens and the Shans where Staveley Brothers held their forest leases were deemed to be of the utmost importance, since it was thought that if the Japanese decided to attack Burma they would come overland through the north-eastern section.

Alex had readily agreed. However, there were a few drawbacks – as he was subsequently to discover.

The first and foremost was the lamentable state of existing intelligence in Burma. Whereas the Japanese had infiltrated most sections of the Burmese community – they even had agents in most of the post offices throughout the country – the British had a very flimsy network. Coupled with this, Alex found that his hard-won information, when passed on to headquarters – and thence presumably to New Delhi and London – was invariably disregarded. As far as he could see the Chinese contacts he had were deemed to be unreliable, and the reports he'd gathered about the Japanese extending airfields in Siam, strengthening bridges, improving roads to take heavier traffic, were thus more or less ignored.

But, for Alex, the most disconcerting thing of all was the supposed need for secrecy. 'The trouble is if you tell one person, you might as well tell the whole damn world,' the officer had said that first day. 'So, it has to be no one, not a soul, do you understand?'

'Of course,' Alex had agreed. It hadn't seemed to matter then. But now, suddenly, it did.

Because of Kate.

He wanted to explain to her why he frequently had to disappear without any real warning. He hated deceiving her, hated his forced absences from her, hated the whole show. Now that the Russians had signed their treaty with Germany, now that the Japanese, with the approval of the Vichy government, had taken bases in southern Indo-China, it seemed increasingly likely that their real objective would be either Malaya, the East Indies or the Philippines, and Alex knew that Burma was as vulnerable as the rest.

So, he kept his secret from Kate and his parents. Kept

his secret from everyone. But it wasn't easy. He was too open a character for deception.

'So, it's up to Lashio at the end of the week, is it?' Roy asked, putting down his tin plate with a clatter. The two dogs raised their heads expectantly, sensing their turn would come soon.

'Just for a few days, yes.'

'And then back to Moulmein?' Roy shifted slightly away from the smoking fire and drew out a huge white cheroot, the sort that would have made a Burman proud.

'Probably.' Actually Alex was certain he'd go there. The army had moved their 4 BURIF infantry brigade down to the Tenasserim area to protect the airfields in that part of Burma, and he often liaised with Micky Merton, the intelligence officer, on the ground. 'But only for a short while. I'm hoping to go up to Rangoon at the end of the month.'

Roy cast Alex a speculative glance. 'You do seem to be spending a lot of your time there . . .' he commented with a wide grin.

'Nonsense,' said Alex firmly, eluding Roy's look of conjecture. The truth was he didn't spend nearly as much time there as he wanted. Although he called at University Avenue to see Kate as often as he could, it still seemed they only saw each other for the briefest of moments. He was not surprised that she seemed to want to take things slowly between them. He'd hardly shown himself a candidate for reliability over the past month or so. Not his fault, of course, but he could not tell Kate that.

Beside them the dogs stirred as U Tun collected the plates and took the blackened pot off the fire. Caspar, Alex's black labrador cross, turned to look at his master, waiting for the command, tail thumping slowly against the dusty ground with anticipation.

Alex stretched out to stroke his head and the dog pushed

his wet nose into the palm of his owner's hand, his dark velvet eyes alert with expectation. Now seven years old, Alex had had him since puppyhood and Caspar guarded him most jealously.

It was one of the things that had impressed him about Kate on their first meeting – the fact that Caspar had taken to her at once. He could be a choosy, sulky old fellow when the mood took him and he certainly hadn't regarded Alex's American girlfriend with the same congeniality.

Alex leant back in his canvas chair, his thoughts turning to Kate. She crept into his mind rather often these days, and when the likes of Merton stopped sending him off on those time-consuming jaunts, when things settled down a bit, he would be able to find the time for them to be together at last.

When . . .

For the first time he was aware of a vague sense of alarm, but he brushed it away. He couldn't allow himself to think that things might deteriorate rather than improve. As a means of self-protection he must look to the future with sublime, unfettered confidence. It was the only way.

The trouble was, the more information he gathered about what the Japanese were surreptitiously doing, the more concerned he became.

Even now, there were few, if any, air-raid shelters in Rangoon, and yet it was generally accepted that the Japanese, if they attacked, would be likely to mount a concentrated air strike against the city.

And what about the eastern frontier, which the so-called military pundits had declared 'impenetrable jungle' because of its range of steep hills? He knew that area well, and though it would prove difficult for motor transport, he wasn't so sure it would prove an obstacle to the Japanese if they were really determined to push in that way. Especially if they had help from the Burmese nationalists.

'My, you're miles away tonight,' declared Roy, looking across at Alex with a toothy grin. 'Rangoon I presume, with the lovely Miss Lawrence?'

'Wrong, actually,' Alex took childish pleasure in contradicting him. Ever since Roy had somehow prised Kate's name out of him, the old fellow had delighted in teasing Alex about Kate's existence.

'Goodness, that does surprise me!' Roy picked up his glass of whisky, giving Alex a speculative look. 'Don't tell me the lovely Miss Lawrence has fallen from favour?'

'You know, Roy, you're becoming more and more nosy as the years go on,' Alex declared roundly. 'Can't a fellow have a bit of privacy and peace, for once?'

'Absolutely not,' Roy pronounced, gleefully pleased to have provoked a reaction. 'First law of the jungle. Everything is shared between friends.'

'Well, I don't hear anything about your after-hours activities,' Alex pointed out. 'Do I?'

'That's because there *are* none, old boy,' Roy admitted quite happily, grinning still further. 'I rely entirely on you to bring a little interest into my own small, grey world.'

'Nonsense,' said Alex. But he suspected it was true. Roy was a confirmed bachelor, totally addicted to jungle life, on whose shoulders the so-called sophistications of the city did not fall easily.

'Besides,' said Roy, stubbing out his cheroot with the heel of his boot, 'I have a confession. For reasons unknown, I have taken a shine to your Miss Lawrence.'

'But you've never even met her!' protested Alex.

'Makes no difference,' said Roy, carefully picking out a flying insect which was trying to commit suicide in his glass of whisky. 'I feel I know exactly what she's like. I can even picture her precisely, in my mind's eye. Perfection.'

Alex suspected that Roy had transformed Kate into a rather voluptuous Clara Bow lookalike. He wondered if he should disillusion him and decided against it. What was there in life if not dreams?

He leant back in his chair. Talking about Kate had brought her very forcefully back to mind. Sitting here, under the vast canopy of stars, she was suddenly real to him. He could almost smell the sweet freshness of her springy soft hair, feel the suppleness of her body against his as they danced. Recall each expression, every inflection of her velvet-rich voice.

And, remembering, he found he was missing her more than he cared to admit. Even to himself.

He bent down to stroke Caspar's ears, concentrating on the black, well-formed head, careful to avoid the shrewd, knowing look in Roy's eyes.

'I do believe he's going to let us down.'

'Alex? Never. He'll be here, just you wait and see. He might cut it a bit fine, but if he said he'll be here for the do at Government House, then he will.'

Kate didn't know whether to be pleased or annoyed by Elizabeth's touching faith in her brother. As far as she was concerned, during the past month or so, Alex had walked an increasingly fine line.

She watched, faintly exasperated, as Elizabeth stood in front of the long mirror repinning the diamond star brooch onto her blue and gold silk dress.

Elizabeth looked radiant. She had the glow of early pregnancy upon her and carried herself with new confidence. Her eyes were bright, her brown hair thick and lustrous, and her skin had a healthy, glowing peachiness to it. Impending motherhood quite obviously suited her, although Elizabeth was at present complaining bitterly about her thickening waist.

'At least Martin doesn't seem to mind, that's the important thing,' Elizabeth said, turning sideways to survey her rounded form critically in the mirror.

'I should jolly well hope not, too!' Kate declared, faintly surprised by Elizabeth's easy acceptance that Martin might have a right to mind. 'After all, he's partially responsible for the expansion, isn't he?'

Elizabeth laughed indulgently. 'Oh, but I don't think men see it in that way.'

'No, I'm sure they don't.'

'You shouldn't care so much, Kate.' Elizabeth adjusted her brooch minutely, then glanced up. 'I don't.'

Kate turned away and walked across to the window. She pulled back the frilled curtain and glanced down to the lake, rosy pink in the setting sun.

'I suppose it's that wretched brother of mine that's making you so out of sorts?' Elizabeth said after a moment. 'I'm sorry about that.'

As soon as Elizabeth said it, Kate knew that was the core of her discontent. She gave a little shrug. 'It's part of it, I suppose.' She wouldn't admit to more.

'Really, he is impossible.' Elizabeth came to stand beside Kate at the window. 'But if it helps at all, I can tell he's keen, whatever you may think.'

'Can you?' Kate's face was controlled. 'How?'

Elizabeth gave a small shrug. 'Oh, little things.'

'Then why does he keep disappearing all the time?' Kate asked, for the first time voicing the crux of the matter. 'It's almost as if he's got some other girlfriend hidden away in Moulmein or somewhere or other.'

'Oh, not that. Alex is a faithful soul when it comes down to it. I expect he's just terribly busy at work . . .' Her voice trailed off slightly.

The trouble was, Elizabeth had to admit she was as perplexed as Kate. She had been so pleased when Alex and Kate had obviously taken a liking to each other. Her two most favourite people, destined, in her eyes, to be a perfect match. And yet, one look at Kate's face told her the path of true love had not been smooth. She almost felt she should take Alex aside and warn him to pull his socks up, but she knew Kate, fiercely independent, would hate such interference. Perhaps she had hoped for too much too soon.

Kate, for her part, would have liked to have opened up her heart a bit more to Elizabeth. The thing was when she was with Alex everything seemed so right. Then just as she was sure that at last they were going somewhere in their relationship he would disappear from her life again. It was all so bewildering. She cared for him deeply but because of his inconsistency she was afraid to give full rein to her emotions.

She was about to put this to Elizabeth when they heard a loud commotion downstairs in the hallway.

'Alex!' Elizabeth looked at her triumphantly. 'I told you he wouldn't let you down.'

'Yes, you did.' Kate spoke in a carefully neutral voice. She had no intention of letting anyone know how ridiculously pleased she was that Alex had come.

'Shall we go then?'

'Might as well.' Kate traced a line on the window with the tip of her finger. She hoped Elizabeth couldn't hear the hollow thumping of her heart.

'I need my cape. Do you want to go on ahead?'

'No. I'll wait here for you,' said Kate, glad of the few extra moments to calm herself.

By the time they came downstairs everyone was waiting for them in the hall, ready to leave.

'Come on, you girls,' said Henry Staveley impatiently. He and Joan had come up for this reception at Government House and Henry was fussing in case they were going to be late.

From behind them, Alex stepped forward. Seeing him,

heart-stoppingly handsome in his dinner jacket and black tie, made Kate falter in her resolve to be cool with him.

'I'm sorry I'm late. I was held up,' he said. He seemed genuinely apologetic. No mere threadbare conventionality, this. 'With the rains we've been having lately the roads are hellish. Had you quite given up on me?'

'Almost,' she admitted.

Close to she noticed how tired he looked, the skin beneath his eyes was soft and darkened, and for the first time she acknowledged the unspoken effort he'd made to be with her. Her expression softened slightly. She had missed him terribly over the past few weeks.

'Come on, then,' said Henry, ushering them all forward with an expansive wave of his hands. 'Time and Wavell waits for no man. Alex, there's not enough room for us all in the one car, so will you take someone in yours?'

'Of course. Kate?'

Alex held out his hand to her and Kate took it, feeling his strong broad-tipped fingers encase hers. She was aware of the slight pressure of his hand against hers, and just his touch made her draw in the breath at the back of her throat. He always managed to have that disconcerting effect on her.

He was watching her with that expression in his eyes which made her both exhilarated and perturbed. And very alive. Useless to fight it or pretend. She wished that they were not going to Government House to some formal reception. Their time together was so short, she was loath to share it with others.

He must have read her thoughts for as they drew up in front of the wide stone building he turned to her and said: 'After this, would you like to go on to the Silver Grill?'

'That would be lovely, yes.' She would have happily gone anywhere with him.

'Good.' He beamed at her. 'We'll see if we can escape

early, then. Even though everyone expects Wavell to be at the reception, I doubt we'll have much chance to meet him anyway. The bigwigs will have cornered him already.'

'Poor man. He's been on the hop ever since he got here. And I thought India was supposed to be his easy posting after the rigours of the Middle East!'

'It is.' Alex climbed out of the car and led Kate up the steps.

Inside it was a fearful crush and as far as she could see Wavell was nowhere in sight. As Alex had said, if he were there at all, he'd probably have been snared already. Wavell, having just succeeded Auchinleck as C-in-C India, had come to Burma to assess the military situation for himself, and everyone was eager to know his opinions.

Kate, working with Eric Barnaby in Government House, had already seen him briefly from afar. Small, stocky, not very approachable, Wavell nonetheless had the ability to inspire confidence. Word had gone round Government House that he had been shocked by the extent of unpreparedness in Burma's defences, and was stressing the fact that Burma was India's bastion rather than Singapore's rear. What would actually be done about the situation, if anything, was a different matter entirely.

By the end of the evening Kate had heard a thousand theories. The trouble was most centred around the belief that reinforcements should be sent into Burma. As Alex had already pointed out to her, he doubted whether Wavell had more troops to send.

'Heavens, am I pleased to get out of that!' Kate exclaimed as Alex led her back to the car after the reception. 'I've had my fill of strategists tonight. It seemed all of Rangoon had an opinion to voice.'

'Oh, it does the civilians good to think a bit,' said Alex, starting up the engine. 'They're far too complacent in the main. It's probably the first time they've actually had to

consider whether an all-weather road should be built from
Assam to Burma, or what they can all do personally to
help should the military need arise . . .'

'Well, you're a fine one to talk,' commented Kate,
pulling her black silk-lined cape across her shoulders
more tightly as the car sped forward past a rickshaw toiling
along the road. 'You haven't exactly rushed forward to be
counted yourself, have you? Even my father in Singapore
has joined the ARP, you know.'

'Has he? Sensible fellow.' Alex fought back the com-
pulsion to tell Kate the truth about his involvement.
He'd found tonight particularly hard, for there had been
a definite division between the military and the civilian
groups present. Each one barely tolerant of the other, and
the convivial Dorman-Smith trying his best to straddle the
two camps.

'I'd have thought you of all people wouldn't have
enjoyed just sitting around,' Kate went on. It had always
struck her as odd that Alex, so usually in the thick of
things, had seemed to hold back on this.

Alex thought of giving her a lecture on the need for
resources to be shipped to England, but he knew the
excuse would sound lame on his lips and held back.
How much simpler it would have been to have been
honest. Instead he said: 'You're probably right. I shall
have to give it serious thought, I suppose.'

'Even your father is going on the Auxiliary Force reserve to do a musketry course, you know,' Kate went on.
Though she knew Henry had complained like mad about
the antiquity of the arms they were supposed to use.

'Well, if Wavell manages to reorganise things as he
hopes then I'll offer my services like a shot,' Alex said.
'Be one of the first.' He gave her a sideways glance, hating
his duplicity. It was like a silent, false note between them.
'Now, since I've had Tarlington *et al* pushing their views

of Hutton and Wavell down my throat all evening, do you think we might give military matters a rest for the remainder of tonight?'

'Of course.' In truth Kate felt as if she'd overdosed on possible government tactics too.

'So where to now?' Alex asked, anxious to steer the conversation onto less stormy waters. 'The Silver Grill, or is there somewhere else you'd rather go?'

'The Silver Grill's fine. Elizabeth told me they've got a really good blues singer there at the moment,' said Kate.

'Have they?' Alex perked up at the news. 'Now did I ever tell you that Billie Holiday is one of my favourite singers of all times?'

'No. But I seem to remember Elizabeth mentioning something along those lines,' laughed Kate. 'Didn't she break the record because you insisted on playing it so often?'

'Threatened to, at least,' Alex grinned. 'No soul, that's Elizabeth's trouble. Now did I complain when she played Ivor Novello day in, day out? Absolutely not. Though I can't pretend I'm not delighted that Martin's inherited those now, along with the rest of her motley record collection.'

'I bet you're secretly addicted to her collection. Probably even hum a selection from *Snow White* when you and Roy are wandering down your little forest tracks,' teased Kate.

'Couldn't,' protested Alex, his liquid-green eyes returning her laughter. 'The elephants wouldn't stand for it. Sensitive creatures, you know.'

Kate giggled. She knew that Alex was only stirring and that, judging from his own collection, he actually had rather catholic tastes in music.

They drew up outside the club and went in. The smoke-filled room was crowded with drinkers and diners and they were shown to a table in one of the far corners from where they could see the small band on the raised platform opposite. The much vaunted singer, presumably having a break, was nowhere in sight.

Alex ordered their drinks. A handful of their friends, who had evidently also come on from the reception, waved to them from another table, signalling for Alex and Kate to join them.

'Do you want to?' asked Alex, indicating the beckoning gestures with a nod of his head.

'Join them? Not particularly, unless you do.'

'No, I don't.' Alex seemed very sure about that.

Kate smiled at his certainty. It was what she had hoped he would say. After a few moments she felt him touch the back of her hand with his forefinger. 'I would like to dance with you. If you'd care to?'

'Yes, I would,' said Kate. 'Very much.'

'Good.' His finger moved lightly up the line of her arm. She felt her bare skin tingle in response to his touch, and the tiny space between them seemed to vibrate with a current of its own.

From across the room the band started up a slow foxtrot. Alex took Kate's hand in his and led her onto the dancefloor. He held her lightly, hardly touching her soft white skin. He danced exceptionally well, and they fell in effortlessly together, Kate being swept round in his arms as if it were the most natural thing in the world.

It was too noisy to try and speak. As the music changed beat they moved closer, an infinitely small distance.

Before long other couples had joined them, jostling for space on the dancefloor, and soon it was almost too crowded to do much more than sway a little.

Not that Kate minded. Just to be here in Alex's arms was enough. There was a certain simple pleasure in dancing with him, in holding him so close.

She felt his mouth brush against her hair and instinctively pressed her body closer to his. She could feel the firm contours of his body, his lean strength. He dipped his head to touch the ivory silkiness of her shoulders with his mouth, the coolness of his lips against the heat of her skin making her breath quicken.

She wondered if he knew the effect he was having on her.

'Hallo,' said someone as they slid past on the dancefloor. 'Wasn't the reception fun?'

'Yes,' she and Alex said in unison and laughed. It was obvious neither of them had the remotest idea whom they were addressing through the smoke haze.

In a little while the music ended, the dancers returned to their tables and the floorshow began. The singer had a rapturously deep, gravelly voice, the sort Kate normally loved, but tonight she found she couldn't concentrate on the dark-haired breathy-voiced vocalist. She was too aware of Alex beside her.

For the first time, she was conscious that without him her life felt slow and dull, without colour or meaning. She only wished she knew what his feelings for her truly were.

Later that evening, on the drive back to University Avenue, they stopped by the lakes, the moonlight dancing across the still dark waters like pale, flickering candlelight.

In the darkness she sensed him move towards her. He leant over and, slipping his hands inside her cape, drew her to him, kissing her with urgent tenderness.

'God! I've been dying to do that all evening,' he confessed and with an odd shaky laugh buried his face in her hair. 'Too many damn people in the club tonight, that was the trouble. And I thought I'd have you all to myself . . .'

She tilted her head, stretching out to touch his face, running a finger gently across his cheek. He caught her hand with his, pressing it hard against his face for a moment, then twisted his mouth round to kiss the soft hollow palm.

The world settled around them, velvety dark. She closed her eyes, shutting her mind to everything but the sheer physical pleasure of feeling him against her, the touch of his mouth, searching, probing.

His hands moved beneath the folds of her cloak, sliding across her bare shoulders, pushing aside the thin straps of her evening dress.

Kate felt her breath catch in her throat, her heart beating so fast she thought it would burst. She wanted him so intensely that her body ached with desire, but at the same time she was afraid.

'Alex,' she whispered. She knew if they didn't stop now, they never would. Her body stiffened minutely.

He stopped at once, feeling the slight change in her. 'It's all right,' he said gently. He raised his head, kissing the curve of her neck. 'I'm sorry. Couldn't help myself. Did I . . .'

'No.' She spoke quickly to reassure him, bending her head slightly so that her cheek brushed against his hand. 'It's just I want to take things slowly, Alex. It's just . . .' Her voice, little more than a whisper, faltered. She couldn't bring herself to mention Johnnie's name.

He drew away from her, just far enough to focus on her with avid green eyes. 'I do understand, Kate,' he said softly. 'Really, I do.' But he wondered if she could even half guess how fiercely he longed for her.

'I just need a little more time . . .'

'I know.' He kissed each bare shoulder, slipping the thin strap of her satin dress back into place. His mouth was warm and she could feel the curve of a smile in it. 'There's no need to hurry, Kate. I can wait. We've got all the time in the world.'

But there Alex was wrong.

In Japan the Prime Minister, Prince Konoye, had been forced to resign and his place had been taken by the Minister of War, General Tojo.

Had Alex but known it, the last piece in the chess set had finally been put into place.

## 13

*M*artin Downing stepped aside to let a bullock cart pass him on the narrow pitted track. The bullock, its wooden yoke dangling against its dusty shoulders, plodded by, drawing behind it a low flat cart containing a family of Burmese in their brightly coloured cotton.

The air smelt of heat and dust and dung. It was late afternoon and the sun was still fierce, despite the beginning of a breeze blowing up from the sea. Martin could feel the sweat running down his forehead and wiped it away with a vigorous sweep of his handkerchief. This was his last task of the day and already he was looking forward to getting back to the house and sitting under the punkah fan with a beer in his hand.

Still, he had few complaints. This posting to Mergui suited him well enough. The Tenasserim coast was lush and attractive and the sea was strewn with islands veiled in tropical foliage, every one of them a veritable beach-comber's paradise. In the olden days, Mergui was a port of Siam, and it was here that Samuel White had tried to set up his independent empire, had become too greedy, and had eventually been massacred by the Siamese. Martin had heard the story time and again, but had scant sympathy for White, whom he considered little more than a pirate, deserving of his ignominious end.

There was one thing that Martin actively disliked about Mergui, though. Its distance from Rangoon. In the normal course of things he wouldn't have minded, but Elizabeth, six months pregnant now, was experiencing some minor problems and it was deemed more sensible for her to remain with Kate in Rangoon for the time being.

He missed her passionately. That was the trouble with having shared one's life with someone, however briefly. Their absence made a great abyss in one's days.

It was the evenings that he found the most difficult. However kind and friendly the other BCS people were down here, and they were certainly that, it was still an empty and silent house that he came back to. He had taken to reading at night, slightly ashamed now that he no longer leapt upon the likes of Gibbons, but took comfort in good light thrillers like Edgar Wallace or Agatha Christie.

Overhead he heard the great whoosh of a hornbill flying past and then, further away, the sound of a gibbon calling. He put his handkerchief back in his pocket and continued walking.

From behind him, came the sound of a car approaching and Martin automatically hugged the side of the track, waiting for it to pass. Instead, it drew alongside him and slowed to a crawl.

'Alex, good heavens, what are you doing here?' Martin asked with delight, recognising the driver. Suddenly, anxiety flooded his face: 'I say, nothing's wrong is it? I mean, nothing's happened to Elizabeth?'

'Heavens, no. She's as fit as a fiddle,' Alex returned quickly. He hadn't intended to frighten Martin. 'It's just that I was down this way, seeing a business contact. I was hoping to commandeer a bed off you for the night. Think you can put me up?'

Martin grinned. 'Be delighted to.' The thought of his evening stretching beyond the pages of *Ten Little Niggers* filled him with sudden pleasure. Alex was always good company. 'Just got one last call to make . . .'

'I'll drive you,' said Alex, pushing open the door.

'Wouldn't say no.' Martin climbed in thankfully. 'My

wretched banger's on the blink.' He hoped to God it would be fixed by the following day. It was too damned hot to walk. 'So,' he said, giving Alex a sideways glance, 'Elizabeth was well when you saw her?'

'Terribly. The doctors want to keep her there for a little while, but she's hoping that if her blood pressure settles down a bit she'll be able to join you here by Christmas. She's bored stiff in Rangoon without you, I can tell you.'

Martin felt secretly pleased that Elizabeth was feeling the separation as much as he. Somehow he'd imagined her, surrounded by her friends and family, managing quite well without him. It had accentuated his sense of loneliness.

He was aware that Alex was saying something about Dr Cotte. 'You mean the old girl at Thandaung?' he asked, pushing the thought of Elizabeth temporarily from his mind.

Alex sounded his horn at a bullock cart which was blocking the road. 'Yes, have you seen her lately?'

'Not recently, no.' Dr Cotte was an aged American lady, who had devoted her life to the welfare of the Karens. The hill-people would travel for many miles across precipitous jungle country to be treated by her. Martin had first met her with Henry Staveley, when he had just come out to Burma, but had not ventured up to that part of the Karenni hills of late. He was surprised by Alex's interest, and said as much, but his questioning was met with adroit evasion.

Martin appraised Alex with a quick sidelong glance. This subtle hedging seemed to be becoming more and more of a pattern. He wasn't sure of Alex's reasons but he was beginning to suspect. And now these questions about Dr Cotte and the Karens . . .

He wondered where it was all leading. All he knew was that Alex was far more involved in military matters than he admitted, and although Martin was pretty much convinced that Burma would escape any involvement in the war, he saw Alex's dealings as a safeguard. He would make certain that Alex promised to get Elizabeth out of Rangoon, to Maymyo or wherever out of harm's way, at the first hint of trouble.

He was being over-cautious, he recognised, but knowing that Elizabeth would be safe and secure, whatever happened, would make his stay at Mergui that little bit more bearable. He would make sure he obtained his assurance from Alex tonight. Just in case.

In another city, other promises were also being extracted that evening. Johnnie Matheson, lying naked in the dishevelled bed, was aware that some of them, granted in the heat of the moment, might not be met. He stretched out and flung aside the bedsheet.

'You're not leaving?' The muffled voice beside him sounded piqued.

'I must. I'm late as it is.' Gently, he tried to disentangle himself from Sylvia's supple arms and legs, which were wrapped tightly around him. 'If I stay any longer I'm likely to be court-martialled.'

'We're both taking risks, you know.' Her legs coiled more insistently against his. 'It isn't just you.'

Johnnie glanced at the voluptuous body lying before him. 'I'm well aware of that,' he returned bluntly. In many ways he felt that Sylvia was gambling for even higher stakes than he was. He didn't know what would happen if Mark were to find out.

Sylvia's mouth pressed against his ear. 'Just five minutes more . . .'

'Vee, honestly, I can't. I've got to go.'

'All right. Go, then.' She fell away from him with a pout, giving him a little peevish push with her foot.

Johnnie, used to her sulks when he had to leave, was careful to say nothing. The trouble was, neither of them was really cut out for this kind of duplicity. It pushed and frayed at their nerves. But what other choice was there at present?

He turned his back on her, climbed out of bed and started to retrieve his clothes. He knew she was watching him, cat-like, from the rumpled bed. Knew, too, that if he turned or hesitated once he would be lost.

That was how it was between them. Their passion for each other was all-consuming, and he knew now that neither would ever be able to escape the other. It had been foolish of him to ever suppose otherwise.

He'd tried. God knows, he'd tried to stay away from her. But he hadn't been able to. An obsession, that was what it was. Fatal and blinding. He'd tried to explain that to Joe Langley when he'd seen him a few months ago, but Joe hadn't understood. He'd even thought Johnnie was talking about Kate, not Sylvia. Johnnie hadn't bothered to try and put things straight. It was too complicated to explain.

He started to fasten the buttons on his khaki shirt, carefully one by one, concentrating on each one with furious determination. When he was dressed he would look at her, not before.

'Johnnie?' Her muffled voice came to him from the folds of the sheets. 'There's something I've got to talk to you about.'

He could sense by her tone this was no kittenish distraction. He turned away from the mirror and saw that her face was anxious and stiff. 'Vee, what's wrong?' he asked. He crossed the room and came to perch beside her on the bed. 'What is it? Mark?'

She shook her head. 'But I'm frightened, Johnnie,' she said, her voice little more than a tight whisper. 'I've got this terrible feeling that he's going to find out about us. You know I said I saw Edna Carlington outside the flats when I arrived here.'

'Yes. What of it?'

'Well, what I didn't tell you was that it wasn't the first time she's spotted me coming in here.'

'Damn.' Edna Carlington was the veritable town crier.

'I don't think she's put two and two together yet, but it won't take many more chance encounters before she does. We've got to find somewhere else to meet, Johnnie. It's just getting too risky for me to come here.'

Johnnie pushed his hand through his ruffled fair hair with a sigh. If Sylvia knew just how many problems he'd had getting the use of this flat she wouldn't relinquish her hold on it quite so freely.

And yet, he knew they could not risk their affair becoming public knowledge.

'Johnnie?' Sylvia was sitting up now, knees drawn to her chin, the crisp white sheet wrapped around her. 'You're not cross with me?'

'Of course not. It can't be helped.' He saw that she was holding out her hand to him for reassurance and he took it tightly in his. 'I'll ask around, there's sure to be somewhere else.'

'If only it didn't have to be like this all the time.' There was more than a trace of bitterness in Sylvia's voice. Her eyes were suddenly wide and dark and uncertain. 'God! How I hate it.'

It was Johnnie's sentiment precisely, but he took care not to show it. 'When this wretched conflict is all over, it'll be different,' he insisted. He hated to see how hunched her slim white shoulders had become. 'We'll both be free to do what we want then. You can leave Mark and we can go back to Perth together. Start a new life.'

'Yes.' It was a game they played all the time. Neither of

them had worked out the repercussions and practicalities of such a move.

'You've got to be brave, my darling. It won't be for ever, I promise.'

'Won't it?' Sylvia lifted her head, pushing a strand of blonde hair despairingly back from her face. 'Sometimes I feel all this will just go on and on. I almost wish the Japs *would* attack,' she said, a catch in her voice. 'Then the British could give them a good hiding and we could be finished with all the talk and speculation. Then at least we could start to live normal lives again.'

He put his arms around her and tilted her face up to his.

'But it isn't that simple, is it? There's still Europe. Even if we put the Japs in their place here, there's North Africa and the Germans to contend with.' It was a gentle reminder that he'd still be a soldier and would have to go wherever his battalion was sent. 'Besides, you've forgotten one tweeny weeny thing, Vee.'

'What's that?'

'That if your wish came true and the Japs attacked, then I'd be right smack in the middle of it.'

He spoke lightly, laughing as he kissed her.

But when he looked down at her, he saw the stricken look on her face and wished that he'd held his tongue.

Afternoons with Sylvia were not meant for brutal truths.

He bent to kiss her, to reassure her, and she stretched up and began to undo his tie.

And this time, he made no move to stop her.


Kate followed Alex across the perfectly manicured green lawns of the Turf Club, watching as he tore up yet another betting slip in disgust. It was the first Saturday in December, the day of the Governor's Cup, and the bookmakers were making a killing with the ever-eager public who packed the enclosures.

'That last one must have had only three legs, I swear it,' said Alex, tucking her arm through his with a grin. 'I should have taken your advice and gone for the chestnut.'

'Yes, you should,' Kate told him. 'It came third.' She grinned, pleased with her success. Normally she was not so lucky at the races. 'So much for your insider's tip!'

'That'll teach me to listen to trainers' gossip.'

'Well, at least that was the last race and you won't be able to throw away any more of your money.'

Alex laughed. 'And if I start saving now I might even have enough for the next Governor's Cup.'

'Possibly.'

They walked back across the lawns, arm in arm, past the covered stands. Kate could see a small party of Chinese and Burmese lined up to collect their winnings, chattering excitedly amongst themselves. It always amused her to see how seriously the Chinese, in particular, took their gambling. They bet on practically anything. It was almost a creed to them.

Kate could remember being a young child in Singapore and driving through the Chinese quarter, seeing little groups huddled at the side of the road, betting what her father had insisted was probably their entire week's wages, on the turn of a single dice.

She'd been terribly upset when she'd seen one of them obviously lose everything, but her father had told her that the Chinese had a completely different view of these things, much more philosophical and accepting, not like an Englishman who'd be ready to fetch the loaded shotgun at such a setback.

Kate wasn't sure she would ever understand the workings of the oriental mind completely, but then, she suspected, nor would most of the British who'd endeavoured to make their homes out here.

Later that evening, watching the cabaret at the Strand

Hotel, she was quite sure that the Chinese probably understood the British just as little. Here they were packed into a crowded fuggy room – a practice blackout was in progress so every window had had to be tightly shut – with a rather stout lady singing a comic song, and concluding it by throwing up her skirt to show them the seat of her panties emblazoned with the Union Jack.

They all roared their approval, applauding like fury, and even the Dorman-Smiths seemed amused by the antics though Kate was sure that had the Chinese seen them now they would have thought them more than a little mad.

The mood of gaiety continued well into the night and the next morning it was a very sleepy crowd who attended the service at the Garrison Church. Even Alex, whom Kate had never known to be other than bursting with energy, seemed a little subdued, readily agreeing to a quiet day.

Kate was glad. Over the past few months Alex had rushed from place to place, and it was wonderful to have him all to herself. Today they had swum together at the club, picnicked, and were now sitting leisurely on the verandah at University Avenue, drinking gimlets and watching the moon cast its fluttering pale light across the lake.

'Are you back to Moulmein tomorrow?' Kate asked above the unmistakable sound of Glen Miller and his band coming from the gramophone in the sitting room behind them.

'Yes. Then I want to go down to Tavoy,' said Alex. 'I ought to check up on Father. It's the first Governor's Cup he's ever missed, you know. He's always come up for it in the past.'

'So your mother was saying.' Kate glanced at Alex, knowing that he was worried about his father, who now had become a virtual recluse at Anapuri. 'I'm glad she came up, though. The break's doing her good, I think.'

'And Elizabeth. I think my sister's rather enjoying being mummycoddled by Mother. Takes her mind off Martin.'

'She's still very cross about the doctors refusing to let her go down to Mergui for Christmas, though,' Kate told him. 'She swears blind that she's feeling perfectly all right, you know, but they won't believe her. I've got a horrid feeling that one day she'll just up and go regardless of what they say.'

'Martin won't let her. He's got more regard for doctors' opinions than she has. If they say Elizabeth must stay put, then he'll make sure she does, regardless of what he feels personally about it.'

Kate knew Alex was right. 'Poor Martin, torn between duty and desire. He must miss her terribly.'

'He does.' Alex remembered his visit to Mergui and how Martin had done nothing else but talk about Elizabeth all evening. He tried not to think of the rash promise he'd made that night, pushing it determinedly to the back of his mind.

The record had long since ended. Alex got to his feet and went inside, riffling through his collection. There didn't seem to be a tremendous choice.

After a moment's silence Kate heard the gramophone being cranked up and the soft lilting lyrics of 'They Can't Take That Away From Me' drifted out onto the verandah.

She was aware that Alex was standing in the doorway behind her, leaning against the frame, watching her. 'Aren't you coming to sit down?'

'Come and dance with me,' he said softly.

She stood up and went to stand before him, aware of a sudden sense of stillness between them. Wordlessly he folded his arms around her and they began to move together, to the soft lilting music.

She felt his lips brush her hair and tilted up her face to

his, putting her arms around his neck. He bent his head down to hers and she began to kiss him, gently at first and then hungrily as her body began to hum with purposeful excitement.

She had the feeling of ecstatic anticipation, piercingly aware of her own readiness. She knew Alex was aware of the change in her, the receptiveness of her body to his touch.

It was she who was asking for him, she who slowly undid the buttons of his cotton shirt to slip her hands beneath its crisp whiteness to touch his skin, the flesh smooth and muscled beneath her fingers. It was she pressing her supple body closer against his, insistent, demanding.

'Kate . . . ?' He hesitated, holding back, as if wary of his own longing. 'I think we should . . .'

'Don't stop, Alex.' She went on kissing him. 'Please don't.'

'You know what you're saying?' He looked down at her, his expression still guarded. 'Are you sure?'

'Utterly.' She knew her instinct was right. She had waited long enough. So had Alex.

He kissed her long and deeply, and then without another word he took her hand and led her upstairs. They went to her room, tucked away by itself at the end of the passageway. He closed the door softly behind them and locked it. Then he came over to her, standing facing her, very close but not touching.

'It's all right,' she said again. Purposefully she kicked off her shoes, and began to unfasten the catch on her dress.

The last vestiges of his self-control crumbled then and his hands were strong and urgent as they struggled with the tiny buttons of her dress. It fell to the floor with a soft whispering sigh and he pulled her down gently onto the narrow bed beside him. She felt his strong fingers cup her small breasts, and then his head came down, his tongue darting across her nipples, fluttering over them until they hardened.

He moved over her, breathing in the scent of her, then his mouth travelled down along the silky softness of her skin, exploring and teasing.

With the piercingly sweet careful passion of an expert lover he lifted and carried her along, then released her, only to sweep her tantalisingly up again, leading so skilfully that she followed, too exhilarated to feel awkward or exposed.

Only for a second did she falter, then she moved with him, for him, caught up by the waves of overwhelming pleasure which rippled through her quivering body.

She had no regrets. As she lay there in his arms in the damp and luxuriant languor of after-love, she could only think of how much she loved him. How right it had been. She pressed her body against his, and he drew her into the circle of his arms, kissing her soft hair.

She fell asleep curled against him, but when she awoke as the first light of morning stole across the sky, she found that he had gone and she was alone.

She lay in bed, not willing to move yet, afraid that if she did she would erase some of the dream-like serenity which hung about her like folds of cloth, filling her every sense.

Gradually she became aware of stirrings downstairs. The muffled sounds of a household awakening, of breakfast being served on the verandah.

Then there was the sound of footsteps, Alex's, she knew. There was a tap at the door.

'Kate?' His voice was soft, urgent.

'Yes?'

The door opened. She glanced up, eagerly awaiting him.

As soon as she saw him standing there, white-faced and rigid, she knew something cataclysmic had occurred.

'Alex, what is it?'

He didn't speak for a moment. When he did his voice was hollow with a sort of desperate exhaustion.

'We've just heard it on the news,' he said.

A cold finger of fear ran down her spine. Gone was her sublime feeling of happiness. 'Heard what?'

He crossed the room towards her. 'It's the Japs,' he said, sinking down on the bed beside her. 'They attacked Pearl Harbor at dawn. There was no ultimatum, no declaration of war. Nothing . . .'

'Oh God.' As far as Kate had been aware, the Japanese were supposed to be involved in peace negotiations with the Americans. She now saw it had all been a pretence, a front.

'They've more or less wiped out the American fleet.' There was a brief pause. He took her hand in his. 'There's more, too, I'm afraid.'

'What?' Her mouth was suddenly terribly dry.

'The Japs bombed Singapore last night and they're reported to have landed in the north of Malaya. The latest news is that they've been repelled at Kota Bharu, but they also are said to have landed at Singora and Patani.'

Kate's tongue seemed to have cleaved to the roof of her mouth. It seemed impossible that the Japanese had taken on two of the mightiest powers head-on. Such unbelievable arrogance. They couldn't possibly stand a chance, despite their surprise initiative. It would only be a matter of time before they were beaten back.

Yet she was aware of a peculiar sense of unease, of foreboding.

She let out a long, drawn out sigh and buried her head against Alex's shoulder, hoping to find comfort there.

A few hours ago her life had seemed so perfect, bright with anticipated happiness.

All that had changed now.

## 14

*H*ow could anyone have foreseen how quickly one disaster after another would strike Malaya? Mark Lawrence, making his way back to Tanglin Road past the shelled Raffles Place, still couldn't believe what had happened.

In a matter of days the Japanese had managed to bomb Singapore, seize the strategic Kota Bharu airfield, move in on Penang, and now this: the news that the battleships *The Prince of Wales* and *The Repulse* had both been sunk.

Somehow Mark felt that this loss was almost more grievous than the destruction of the American fleet at Pearl Harbor, because he and Sylvia had actually met and entertained some of those British officers who had been killed. God! he could hardly believe it was only last weekend that they had all been laughing and joking together.

It had had a devastating effect on the morale of the people of Singapore.

Mark couldn't pretend that he wasn't concerned, for all the government's flag-waving propaganda. From the very beginning the British had lost the initiative. Prevarications by Whitehall – and Brooke-Popham, he suspected – had made it impossible to launch the proposed 'Matador' plan to enter southern Siam and pre-empt any Japanese attack before it reached Malaya.

Now, in the first few days of the campaign, air control had been lost and the naval base was nearly empty. It would be the army which would bear the brunt of the campaign, and though Mark knew the soldiers had been chaffing at the bit to get out there and fight, he wasn't sure how well-trained or equipped they really were. Time would tell, of course. Perhaps that was what he was worried about.

And he was worried. All the reassurances they'd had about the Japanese not being able to penetrate the jungle were proving totally misguided, though he had personally been surprised that the Japs had managed to bring heavy equipment through such difficult terrain. It was another sign that the British had underestimated Japanese determination.

As the car eased to a halt outside the house he tried to push aside his misgivings. It wouldn't do to show concern; bad for morale. Besides, when the Japanese had first bombed the city, Mark had tentatively sounded out Sylvia about returning to Perth with Louisa. Sylvia had been adamant about staying put.

It had surprised Mark a little. He'd known how frightened Sylvia had been of the bombing and he had thought that she might leap at the chance to leave. She'd shown she was made of sterner stuff and he'd been secretly rather proud of her resolve.

Of course, they had agreed that if the bombing became really extensive, or the Japanese threat intensified, then they would review the situation, for Louisa's sake. What Mark did not know, of course, was that it was neither he, nor duty, which was keeping Sylvia in Singapore at all.

As the night advanced and the rain stopped, Johnnie became aware of the strange restless stirrings of the jungle about him. Used to these movements and sounds, he was unconcerned, but he knew there were a few of his men whose skins crawled at the unfamiliar noises. There was very little he could do to reassure them, though. He found it increasingly difficult enough to keep up morale as, day after day, they heard muffled rumours that the Allied troops had been ordered to pull back further towards Singapore.

What a mess it had all been. It was bad enough for his bunch on this side of Malaya, but by all accounts it had been even more of a débâcle on the west coast. Missed opportunities all along the way.

And the powers-that-be had told them how easy it would be to hold back the Japs!

He lay back, cigarette in hand, watching the moon climb over the black wall of jungle. It didn't do to have brooding moments like this, he knew. Inevitably, all that happened was that he thought of Sylvia.

He watched a wisp of smoke curl up to the thick canopy of trees overhead, wondering when he'd next get a chance to see her. As a liaison officer he'd been more fortunate than most, legitimately being able to get down to the island with comforting regularity. Now he supposed it might be a little trickier. Still, he'd always been a lucky devil. Somehow he'd wangle a way of getting back to the island. He had to. The thought of seeing Sylvia was the only thing that kept him going in this miserable place.

Singapore was always such a tonic by contrast, too. It seemed so blissfully unbothered by the war, even now, so confident. Of course, the place was a safe fortress. Everyone knew that. But he sometimes wondered if the civilians there had any idea of what was actually going on in Malaya. What the 'strategic withdrawals' really meant.

What would actually happen, Johnnie didn't know. Reinforcements were rumoured daily to be on their way, and he supposed once they arrived the Allies would be able to shore up their defences and push the Japanese back up the peninsula. It was just a matter of time, that was all.

He stirred and stubbed out his cigarette. At least here they'd had time to dig in their defences well. He smiled, remembering their first war-time assignment when they'd proudly taken up their position to guard the aerodrome at Kluang, only to discover that all the planes on the airfield were dummies: mock-up models made out of cardboard and timber slats. Even the planes concealed in the surrounding rubber plantation had been dummy mock-ups. The boys couldn't believe it. It had obviously fooled the Japs, though, because barely had the boys set up the guns before a flight of Jap planes swept over and bombed and strafed all the dummies to bits.

They were ready to get on with some real fighting. And though all seemed quiet for the moment, he had a feeling that their wish would be granted all too soon.

'Do you think they'll come back, Alex?'

'Yes, I do, I'm afraid.'

Alex and Kate were standing in the newly dug slit-trench at University Avenue in Rangoon, heads just visible, elbows resting on the warm, damp grass.

The skies were clear now, but only moments before there had been seventy or so Japanese bombers overhead, heading for Mingaladon airfield. Over in that direction smoke was now rising in great clouds as the last dull thumps of bursting bombs echoed through the air.

At least the warning system, by telegraph from observers in Tenasserim, had proved adequate. They'd had about forty minutes' notice, time enough for the RAF Buffaloes and the American Volunteer Group to get themselves airborne, and to be on the ready for the Japanese.

In the distance the anti-aircraft gun renewed its barking as the enemy bombers headed back to the city in arrow-head formation. Bombs crumped in rapid succession, the sound rising above the throbbing of the aeroplanes.

Alex saw clouds of dense smoke billowing up to the sky from what looked like the heart of Rangoon itself. 'That'll be the waterfront, I presume,' he said soberly. 'Jesus, I hope the workers down there had the sense to get to the slit trenches.'

They'd had practices, of course, but Alex knew that the sheer fascination of watching the dog-fights might have momentarily distracted the workforce from taking cover.

He hoped to heaven it hadn't. It only took a few minutes for disaster to strike.

High above them a British fighter sped past on the tail of one of the bombers, and a few seconds later a trail of smoke burst from the Jap plane.

'God! He's got the blighter!' Alex was full of admiration. The Allied planes were hideously outnumbered but they were putting up a tremendous fight.

He watched, faintly envious, as the glittering form of the fighter skimmed past. The war had heightened his passionate longing for adventure and, despite his intelligence gathering escapades, he fervently wanted to do more.

Overhead they heard the splutter of an engine as a crippled plane circled, looking for somewhere safe to land.

'Is it one of ours?' Alex felt Kate grasp his arm anxiously. He could almost hear her holding her breath.

He shielded his eyes, staring up into the sky. 'No,' he said, taking in the glittering, sleek form, 'definitely a Jap Zero fighter. And definitely on its last legs.'

Even as he spoke, from nowhere, an American 'Flying Tiger' came tearing up from behind with an earth-shattering burst of gunfire. The Japanese fighter flared like a spent rocket and dropped.

Alex let out a small explosive shout of approval. 'God! Those Americans know how to fly, don't they?' he said, beaming at Kate as they watched the Tomahawk wheel off into the distance.

They certainly had a lot to thank the Americans for. After Pearl Harbor the American Volunteer Group had moved down from Magwe to Mingaladon. Without them Rangoon would have only had one RAF squadron of Buffaloes to protect it. They would have stood little chance all alone against the might of the Japanese. It'd been tough enough as it was.

The skies were clear now. Alex clambered out of the slit-trench, giving his hand to Kate to help her scramble out. From the verandah they saw Elizabeth waving to them. 'So, you survived the terrors of the slit-trench then, I see,' she teased.

When the cold shriek of the air-raid signal had sounded Elizabeth had flatly refused to join Alex and Kate in the slit-trenches which Alex had insisted on having dug at University Avenue.

'Honestly,' she'd wailed at her brother, 'I'm six months pregnant, there is absolutely no way I'm going to leap down into that thing! Even if I *could* get down, there's not even the slightest chance of my being able to get out again, believe you me.'

Alex had let her stay – muttering something about not setting a very good example to the servants – on the proviso that she shelter under the kitchen table, an instruction which he secretly suspected Elizabeth would have totally ignored, had not Joan Staveley insisted on keeping her daughter company to ensure her safety.

Alex had looked at them both, unimpressed. 'A bloody fiasco, this!' he had complained, with more than a little truth. 'What on earth's the point of having a trench you won't use it?'

The trouble was he could understand their feeling of lack of urgency. The air-raid warning system was so long drawn out it had taken ages for the Japanese bombers to actually appear. Alex had had a devil of a time trying to make the servants stay put, and he'd had to fight hard to curb his own sense of restlessness, stifling the temptation to climb out again after only a few minutes.

'Next time remind me to bring some supplies,' he joked to Kate as they made their way up the steps to the house after the All-Clear. 'If we're going to be stuck in the damned thing for hours on end we might as well make it as enjoyable as possible, don't you agree?'

'Oh, Lord,' laughed Kate, grimacing at him. 'You don't mean you're seriously going to make us climb into the beastly thing every time there's a scare on, do you? I think the table gets my vote.'

'And mine,' said Elizabeth and her mother in unison from the drawing room.

'Rebellion, eh?' Alex laughed easily with them. He had to agree it seemed an awful performance for very little gain.

But later that evening, after he'd been down to Rangoon where he'd gone to volunteer his help after the raid, he was in an entirely different mood. He still felt in shock. The scenes he'd witnessed at the docks had been horrific. There'd been a fleet of lorries clearing corpses from the streets, and the hospitals had been so full they had had to leave the wounded simply lying in the corridors.

'It's slit-trenches for you all, inconvenient or not,' he insisted, brushing aside Elizabeth's complaints. This time he was not going to give in to his sister. 'If you'd seen what I did today, you wouldn't argue.' He took a stiff swig of whisky, trying to forget the harrowing sight. It had been nothing short of carnage. 'There were over two thousand dead down by the docks.'

He saw Kate put down her drink, her head jerking up at his words. '*Two thousand?*' He knew she couldn't believe the extent of the casualties. Sixty-one people had been killed in the first air-raid on Singapore, so the papers had said, and that had seemed high enough. She turned terribly pale. 'But how, I mean . . .'

'The bastards just rained down stick upon stick of anti-personnel bombs on them,' Alex told her savagely. He rubbed his hand over his eyes wearily. 'I've never seen such butchery. And there's probably another two thousand or so wounded.'

It had been a day of nightmare proportions. The pavements had been strewn with the dead and the dying and there had been total panic. The whole of the Botataung quarter east of the main docks had been gutted, and if the fire brigade hadn't held fast the city, mostly wooden houses, could easily have burnt to the ground. Alex hoped to God he didn't have to face anything like that again.

He sank forward on the sofa, elbows on knees, head resting in his hands, utterly exhausted.

'Alex?' Beside him, Kate gently stretched out her hand to his. 'You should try and get some sleep.'

'Probably should.' The trouble was Alex knew that the moment he closed his eyes the gruesome images of the wounded and dead would rise up to fill his mind again. It wasn't a sight he cared to remember.

He straightened slightly and reached out to pick up his whisky glass, wondering vaguely how long it would take to get the city back to normal again. The fires were now under control, the dead and wounded had been seen to, but when he had left the city late that night there had been a steady mass exodus of Indian coolies and their families in progress. The Prome Road was full of frightened inhabitants, bundles on their heads, naked children by their side, all heading for India.

Somehow, Alex supposed, something would have to be done to entice them back, for without the Indians the port would be paralysed and no military supplies or reinforcements could be unloaded. It was just another headache for the already reeling government.

At least it wasn't his problem. He'd got enough of his own for the moment.

He leant back, hugging the whisky glass to his chest, thinking about the news he'd heard in Rangoon today. The Japs, having taken over Victoria Point in the southernmost tip of Burma, were now reported to be on the move again. Where they would strike was still not certain, but Alex's guess was that it would be down towards Tavoy, since that was where the Thakins, who supported the Japanese, were the strongest. Alex had already heard rumours that villages were being visited by a party of Thakins, all wearing a kind of khaki uniform. They had been led by a young Burman who'd told the villagers that the Japanese would be coming as liberators, not conquerors. The young Karen *havildar* who had brought Alex this information also told him that the young Burman – whose description fitted Aung San, the leader of the Burmese National Army – had urged the villagers to cooperate with the Japanese when they came, and to hinder the British in every way possible.

This, coupled with the report he'd heard today that the Japanese were massing in great strength across the border at Rahreng, filled Alex with growing alarm.

He realised he would have to go to Tavoy to check things out for himself.

*          *          *

When Henry Staveley saw Alex's car coming up the dusty track his first reaction was one of surprise. He was due to come up to Moulmein and to take the train to Rangoon himself that day for the Christmas festivities and had expected that Alex would already be there.

'Come to chase me up, have you?' he asked wryly, watching Alex step out of his car. 'Joan think I'd duck out at the last minute?'

'Not a bit of it.' Alex laughed and pushed back his thick, dark hair from his face. 'We knew you'd come. You've never been able to resist roast turkey and all the trimmings.'

'So, it's all still on, is it?' Henry had wondered what state Rangoon would be in after the news of the bombings.

'Of course, it's still on,' returned Alex, accompanying his father up the steps and into the house. 'The Japanese might be able to do a lot of things, but cancelling Christmas is not one of them!'

Henry laughed and sank down onto the sofa under the cool of the fan. 'So, what brings you down this way, then?' he asked. Alex was not one to make needless journeys.

'Actually,' said Alex, deciding on candour, 'I wanted to know exactly what was happening down here. Thought you could put me in the picture.' He helped himself to a glass of lime which the boy had brought in. 'Like how much trouble you've been having with the Thakins recently.' He waited until the servant had left the room before continuing: 'And whether Aung San has been travelling around this part, spreading his gospel about how the Japanese are going to treat them as equals.'

'I've heard that he's been visiting the villages round here,' admitted Henry. 'And some of our boys have been murmuring about the Japanese being comrades of the

Thakins. The naïvety of it all. The Japanese are just using the students for their own ends.'

'*We* know that. But the Thakins are so anxious to get independence that they don't care what they risk to obtain it.'

Henry shifted his position slightly. 'Not much we can do about it, is there?' he said resignedly. 'Counter-propaganda won't work. Too late for that.'

'Far too late,' agreed Alex. Despite the fact that the Burmese Government and the Premier, Sir Paw Tun, still supported the British, Aung San and his faithful were nevertheless gaining strength.

'You know, Father,' Alex spoke carefully, knowing the effect his words would probably have, 'I'm wondering if it might not be sensible for you to stay a while in Rangoon after Christmas . . .'

'I'm certainly not going to be frightened off by a few wet-behind-the-ears students, you know!' said Henry bristling at the very thought.

'They're hardly that, Father. And they've probably got the might of the Japanese army coming in their footsteps, don't forget.'

'I don't forget anything.' Henry stood up. He was too disturbed to sit still any more. He stamped over to the window, staring out across the line of rubber trees. 'You can't seriously expect me to just abandon Anapuri.'

'I don't. But it is starting to seem increasingly likely that the Japanese *will* come, Father,' said Alex quietly.

'And when they do they'll have to deal with our boys. And if by any mischance they still happen to get through then I'll be ready for them,' said Henry defiantly. 'By God, before they take Anapuri I'll make damn sure that I burn every last scrap of rubber, break up the machinery and destroy everything. They'll not find one thing on this estate that they'll be able to make use of, that I promise.'

Henry's voice was shaking with emotion. It seemed almost sacrilege to speak of Anapuri and the Japanese in one breath.

'Anyway, I think you're being a shade pessimistic, Alex, if you ask me,' he said, turning back from the window. 'You talk as if they'll just walk in over the borders.'

'They've got our boys to contend with, certainly,' agreed Alex. And more reinforcements were said to be on the way from India, too. 'But if the Japs join forces with the Thakins . . .'

'If you're so damned concerned with discovering what the Thakins are up to, then you should find out where the Ma Kyin's boys are,' Henry broke in.

His voice was faintly irritated. Alex had touched a raw nerve by suggesting that Anapuri could possibly be in any sort of danger. Henry simply wouldn't allow himself to contemplate the thought.

Alex watched his father quietly for a moment, then he took a small cheroot out of his cigarette case, lit it and inhaled deeply. 'Both Hla and Pe joined the movement in their Rangoon university days, didn't they?' he asked, after a slight pause.

'Yes, so I believe.' Henry was staring out across the grey-green meticulous lines.

'Strange, that, in a way.' Alex watched a wreath of smoke curl up to the ceiling fan. 'They were so terribly pro-British when they were younger.'

'Yes.'

'The change in them came almost overnight, I seem to remember.'

Henry did not reply, but his back stiffened almost imperceptibly.

'Always wondered what exactly it was that prompted so thorough a conversion. Especially since you were always so good to their family.'

'No more than to the others,' said Henry. His heart thumped painfully against his ribs. It was a lie, of course. He knew it and so did Alex.

He could not bring himself to look at his son.

He supposed that at some point he should tell him the truth. But now now. Not for the moment. He held back instinctively.

Henry felt a sudden black mood claiming him, the tiny speck of doubt which Alex had planted in his mind growing to engulf him. Surely his son must be mistaken about the Japanese. Old Pelly, the DC, had once told him that even a leaf couldn't fall in the Tenessarim without him hearing about it, and Pelly had given him no indication that anything was amiss. Alex *must* be wrong.

But if it *were* so, if the Thakins were leading the Japanese into Burma and towards Tavoy, then Henry knew that Anapuri would be in their path. Anapuri would be destroyed.

Hla and Pe would see to that.

For all things past.

He folded his arms across his chest, casting his son a sideways glance.

'I rather think,' he said, turning back from the window, 'I ought to go down and check the factory. Do you want to join me?' His voice showed none of his inner apprehension.

'Actually, I should go.'

Henry nodded. It was what he had expected.

'I'll see you in Rangoon tomorrow then.'

'Yes.' Alex stubbed out his cheroot. He looked up, his eyes searching his father's face and for a moment Henry thought he was going to say something more. Instead, he stood up without further comment.

Henry followed him outside and watched him drive away down the dusty track until the low rumbling of the car faded. Then he turned and started to make his way out through the avenue of tall trees, stopping to examine one of the tapper's work. But even as he dug his knife into the small slit on the scarred grey trunk, he shivered, despite the heat.

For already, it seemed to him, he could hear the soft echo of alien feet trampling their way through his beloved Anapuri.

'I shan't go, Kate, that's all there is to it.'

'But it makes so much sense, Elizabeth, surely you can see that?' Kate was aware that she was fighting a losing battle in trying to persuade Elizabeth to join her mother on the boat leaving Rangoon for India that Wednesday.

The trouble was, sitting out here on the verandah at University Avenue, it seemed so calm. Apart from Christmas Day, when the Japanese planes had come streaming over the city again, Rangoon had been virtually left alone these past few weeks. She could see why Elizabeth felt it safe to remain here.

'You know what Martin said,' began Kate, trying a different tack.

'Martin's an old fuss-pot,' Elizabeth returned with a mixture of affection and exasperation. 'I know he'll be secretly pleased I'm still here. It hasn't been much fun for him these past few months without me, you know.'

Kate did know. Alex had told her what a miserable state Martin had been in down at Mergui.

'He'll worry about you,' Kate pointed out. She fished out an insect which was practising its backstroke in her glass of lime juice. 'That's almost worse than missing you.'

'*I'm* the one who's worrying,' said Elizabeth. 'If those reports are true . . .' She couldn't bring herself to finish, as if by so doing it would give some credence to the rumours which were spreading through the city.

Kate was silent. She'd not heard from Alex for the past few weeks either. She knew he was down near Moulmein somewhere, but hoped to heaven he hadn't gone to Tavoy. The latest, suitably guarded, reports seemed to indicate that the Japanese had started to make pretty strong advances there.

She closed her eyes and turned her face up to the last rays of the sun, blocking out all negative thoughts. She had to have faith in the future. After all, a brigade of the 17th had now arrived and had been posted down near Moulmein. They would be able to stop any Japanese advance surely?

All the same, when Joan Staveley joined them on the verandah a few minutes later, Kate grew more and more silent listening to her argue with Elizabeth about leaving Burma. She knew Joan was counting on her to help persuade Elizabeth to go, but somehow she couldn't bring herself to do so.

For, as they sat there with the sun dipping down behind the lakes, her thoughts swung to Alex and all her theories about the importance of leaving were turned on their head. After all, how could she force Elizabeth to do something which she herself had no intention of doing?

And suddenly, listening to Joan talking about India and safety, she understood Elizabeth's obduracy. To leave would be to cast off that last thin thread which bound them to those whom they loved.

And she knew then that she could never leave Burma without Alex.

## 15

*S*ylvia put down her silver-backed hairbrush and pushed back a strand of hair from her face with an impatient gesture.

'The answer is no, Mark,' she said irritably.

'But for heaven's sake, Sylvia, they're our friends . . .'

'*Your* friends, Mark, not *ours*,' she corrected, glaring peevishly at him in the mirror. 'And I have no intention of turning our home into a boarding house. You're too soft, Mark. We can't have just anybody descending on us here.'

Mark gave one of his low, controlled sighs which she found so annoying.

'Jack and Mary aren't just anybody, Sylvia,' he said purposefully. 'I've known them for years.'

'But they're hardly a bundle of fun.'

Sylvia made a great play of making a Joan Crawford mouth for her lipstick.

Out of the corner of her eye she saw Mark move over to the window, and stare stonily out across the garden. Normally he would avoid an argument at all costs, but this time she sensed that he would not give up. He was terribly fond of Jack and Mary, and had been appalled when they had arrived in Singapore with their pitifully few possessions, along with hundreds of other refugees from Malaya. She'd been shocked too, in truth, but not to the extent of being moved to play Lady Bountiful. Homeless or not, she most certainly didn't want them moving into Tanglin Road.

Mark, though, had other ideas.

'Good God, Sylvia, they've lost their home, their livelihood, everything,' he began again, turning round to face her. 'It's the least I can do for them. When Kate and I were up there a year ago and there was the riot at the plantation . . .'

'Not that again, *please*,' Sylvia said witheringly. It still rankled that Mark had managed to find the time to go off on holiday with Kate, whereas he hadn't suggested so much as a day trip to Johore to her, declaring himself far too busy.

She stretched out her legs and adjusted her silk stockings. The fact was it just wasn't convenient to have Jack and Mary to stay. It would make her brief clandestine meetings with Johnnie even more tricky.

'Have a heart, darling. It's only until they get themselves sorted out with a passage to England. Just a week or so.'

It wouldn't just be a week, she knew that, but she refrained from saying as much. She sensed that if she were cunning she could turn all this to her advantage.

She dabbed on her perfume, deciding on a change of tack. After all Mark, if he so chose, could quite simply insist that Jack and Mary stay with them, regardless of her own sentiments. It would be far more sensible to capitulate gracefully now and make him feel indebted to her.

'Well . . .' She allowed herself the sigh of a generous-hearted woman tried beyond her strength by the insensitiveness of others. 'A week or so, then. As you say, we can't let friends be homeless, can we?'

She turned alluringly towards him, leaning back in her chair a little so that the soft folds of her wrap parted slightly. She knew the impact her beauty still had on him.

He came over to the dressing table and she allowed him

to kiss her. 'It will only be for a short while, darling, I promise.'

She saw he was gratifyingly grateful for her acquiescence. She smiled.

Later she would mention to Mark the dear little emerald and diamond necklace she'd seen in da Silva's . . .

'Tavoy's gone. We've got our orders to evacuate.'

The news, dire though it was, did not come as any surprise to Martin. Ever since the Japanese bombardment of the airfield at Mergui, he had been aware of this possibility.

He glanced at Yarnold, the District Commissioner, knowing how hateful he found the situation. Yarnold was the sort of man who would have preferred to have remained behind, and have risked capture and internment by the Japanese, rather than leave the people whose welfare had been entrusted to him. Martin was inclined to agree with him. How could they ever expect to be looked up to and trusted again after this withdrawal? It made a mockery of all their time out here.

Nevertheless, orders were orders, and Martin knew that the situation was such that there was no time for melancholy or regret. Regardless of his own personal opinion, there was the welfare of other civilians at stake: the tin miners and rubber planters and their wives and children who must be removed to safety.

So Martin busied himself with the evacuation. The first batch of civilians, together with most of the troops, left by the first ship for Rangoon. Martin, who had volunteered to complete the demolitions with a handful of other civilians, was to stay on.

It was to be a fraught two days.

All the while Martin was aware of the Japanese closing in on them. Everything that could be of military use to the enemy – petrol, rubber, boats, tin or money – had to be destroyed. There seemed so much that there were moments when Martin was sure that they wouldn't finish their task in time.

But finally they were done.

That night, under cover of darkness, Martin and the 'last ditchers' made for Tenasserim Island, fifty miles out to sea on the western edge of the archipelago.

They were in sombre mood. Most felt caught on the horns of a dilemma – Martin, in particular, who felt it was disgraceful to go, lunacy to stay. It was only the strengthening thought of Elizabeth which kept him going.

Gradually as he thought about her, his anger about having to withdraw began to fade. He might not approve of the orders, but he had no wish to be like the officials at Victoria Point, who had not received their orders to withdraw in time and had been taken by the Japanese.

He closed his eyes. He could picture Elizabeth very clearly at this moment and suddenly he realised how much he needed to hold her in his arms again. What he would give to be able to lay his head against her soft comforting breasts, to be able to bury his face in her silky dark hair, to hear her soothing voice whispering to him in the darkness.

He cheered himself with the knowledge that it was only a short time to go. Only a few more days.

He found himself clinging to the thought with the grim tenacity of a limpet to a slippery wet rock.

As it happened, a day later Martin found himself not in Rangoon as he had expected, but Moulmein.

Martin was under the impression when he'd left Mergui that he was to join Yarnold in Rangoon. Instead he somehow found himself in the Moulmein area with Pelly who assured him that with the British forces in strong concentration around Moulmein, the situation was pretty much under control.

The only thing that concerned Martin was that there was no news of Henry. From what he gathered from the military, the Japanese troops advancing upon Tavoy should have missed Anapuri and he was certain that Henry would have stayed on at the estate rather than pulling out down to Tavoy. Certainly, he had not come to Moulmein.

'We sent some chaps up there last week,' said one of Pelly's assistants. 'Told him it was time to clear out.'

'And?'

The assistant shrugged in an exasperated gesture. 'And nothing. Stubborn old fool wouldn't listen. Told us he'd come in his own time.'

Martin wasn't surprised. No one had ever been able to make Henry do something he didn't wish to do.

'And is it still safe to get up there?' Martin asked him.

'Safe? Who can say? No one knows where the Japanese are, exactly.'

'Possible, then?'

'Possible, yes. I say, Downing old chap, you can't go risking your neck for an old fool like that. What's possible one minute isn't the next, with these damned elusive Japs.'

'It shouldn't take me more than a few hours there and back,' Martin pointed out. 'I know the way like the back of my hand.'

Now that the thought was in motion it wasn't possible to push it aside. Martin was a man of duty. He'd fulfilled his obligation seeing the civilians out of Mergui, and now he saw it as his responsibility to persuade Henry to come down to Moulmein. He owed it to Elizabeth. She'd expect it of him.

It was this thought, the knowledge that he wouldn't be able to face Elizabeth unless he at least tried, that spurred him on. Pelly was talking of evacuating the last of the civilians from Moulmein within the next few days and Martin was determined that Henry would be amongst those leaving for Rangoon.

Somehow he'd get him to leave Anapuri.

It was close to sundown by the time Martin finally came through the trees to the familiar winding path which led to Anapuri.

It had taken him much longer than expected. Already the darkening shadows seemed to be pressing down around him. But, despite having to take cover from Jap overhead planes from time to time, Martin wasn't discouraged. The villagers on the way had been friendly and supportive, and he was sure that once he'd managed to persuade Henry of the foolhardiness of remaining at Anapuri, the journey back would take far less time.

It was as he came over the last hill that he felt the first inkling that something might be wrong. A curl of smoke, just visible in the failing light, was rising in the distance.

He drove on cautiously. Although he was still certain that, as yet, there were no Japanese troops in the area, he knew a fire at Anapuri indicated that Henry had already begun his 'scorched earth' policy, a sure sign that the enemy were closer than he had at first thought.

He came to the last bend, expecting to see the friendly glow of lights from Anapuri bathing the line of rubber trees, but ahead were only deepening grey shadows. There was no one here, no one at all. Not even a tapper in sight. A fearful premonition made Martin's heart begin to pound.

Turning the battered truck in front of the house he drove down the uneven track towards the factory. There was no need to go all the way down. One quick glance and he knew all he needed to know. The smoke rising from the skeletal building was not the first hesitant strugglings of a fire, as he had imagined, but its last dying gasps. This blaze wasn't new. It had begun several days earlier, by the look of it.

He turned the truck once more and edged his way back to the house. He was aware, for the first time, that his hands were shaking, and sat still for a moment, clutching the wheel tightly in an effort to calm himself.

He would have to get out and investigate. A sharp stab of fear was running through him like a cold knife.

He picked up the antiquated revolver from the front seat beside him, and then pushed open the truck door, starting purposefully up the path towards the house.

At the verandah steps he halted, aware that the door to the house was slightly ajar. Had it been that way when he'd arrived? He couldn't remember.

He stood stock still, swallowing hard, then steeling himself he began to edge his way forward, one slow step at a time.

'Henry?' he whispered into the darkness. His voice seemed to stick in his throat.

Silence.

'Henry, are you there?'

Still no reply.

Martin stood on the verandah, his face wet with sweat. There was nothing for it. With infinite care, he nudged open the door.

Inside, so dense were the shadows that he almost stumbled in the hallway. It took him a moment or two to focus. When he did, he felt his stomach coil and tighten like a spring at the sight of the rooms before him. The house was in chaos. Tables and chairs had been knocked over, drawers opened and the contents strewn on the floor. The quiet, serene orderliness of the house had been torn apart. He had no doubt now. The Japanese had been here.

One question went hammering through his mind then: had Henry managed to get out before the Japanese arrived? Certainly there was no sign of him, but as Martin moved slowly from room to room, he dreaded what he might find.

He had no doubt that if the Japanese had found his father-in-law then he would have stood little chance. But gradually, as Martin moved from room to room, he consoled himself that as far as he could tell, upstairs and down, the house was empty.

It was as he was coming down the stairs from Henry's bedroom that he heard the faint tread of footsteps in the drawing room below. The hairs on the back of his neck bristled at the sound, his mouth suddenly bone-dry.

He hesitated a brief second then, putting one hand out to the banister to steady himself, began his stealthy descent, walking with infinite care, toe to heel, soundlessly, tightening his grip on his revolver.

He could hear the dull scrape of drawers being opened.

Jesus, make it Henry, please, he thought. Martin froze, still as an animal which senses danger, listening as the footsteps seemed to draw closer. A shadow fell across the doorway and with shaking hands he slipped the safety catch off the revolver in readiness. It was a woman who stood there not a Jap soldier. A Burmese.

'What the hell do you think you're doing?' he asked, coming down the last of the steps, revolver held out in front of him.

As he drew closer he saw the gleam of silver in her hand. A common or garden looter then, presumably after the pitifully few objects which the Japanese had overlooked.

He felt his indignation boil over, incensed at the sight of such a base act, and waved the gun at her angrily.

'Give me that!' he cried out furiously, stretching out his

other hand to her to retrieve what he saw now was a silver photograph frame.

He took another step forward, gesticulating wildly, then stopped in his tracks, recognising the intruder for the first time.

'Good God, it's you, Ma Kyin.'

Ma Kyin was the headman's wife, mother of Hla and Pe. No looter this, at all. 'What on earth are you doing up here?' His voice was steadier now.

Outside it had begun to rain. Martin could hear the sudden drumbeat against the roof. He peered through the half-light, suddenly seeing how tight and pale was Ma Kyin's face. 'Where's everybody gone, Ma Kyin? Where's Mr Staveley?'

'They took the *thakin* . . .'

Ma Kyin's voice trailed away, lost in a small sob.

Martin bent over her small frame taking hold of both her slender hands in his. 'But where, Ma Kyin? Where did they take the *thakin*?'

Ma Kyin bent her willowy neck. He thought he saw the glisten of tears on her cheeks and put out a comforting hand and touched her thin shoulders. 'Ma Kyin,' he urged. 'Tell me. Where is Mr Staveley?'

She stiffened then, taking a deep shuddering breath. 'Come . . .' She lifted her head. 'I will take you to him.'

Martin hesitated, dreading the next question he knew he must ask. 'Is he . . . is he all right?' He couldn't bring himself to voice his worst fears.

Now it was Ma Kyin who couldn't speak. She put her slim brown hands up to her face for a long moment, then wiped away the tears with one slow movement of her hand, one side at a time.

'What happened, Ma Kyin?' Martin urged again gently.

'The *thakin* was trying to destroy the factory,' she whispered.

'I saw that,' Martin said. 'But they came too quickly, I presume. He had no chance to leave.'

The merest hint of a smile, infinitely sad, crossed Ma Kyin's face. 'He never *was* going to leave,' she said quietly. 'He would never willingly abandon Anapuri, Japanese or not.'

He realised that Ma Kyin was speaking again.

'When they came, he didn't try and run and hide. He'd told the workers to go at the first hint of the enemy, but he himself . . . No . . . He stayed to face them. He was not afraid, you know.'

'No, I can imagine that,' said Martin quietly.

'Even when they tied him to the tree and he knew he was going to die.'

'Oh, God!' Martin felt tears begin to prick his eyelids.

'He died with dignity. The *thakin* . . .'

Her voice caught in a half sob. She couldn't go on. Couldn't tell him how the Japanese had strung Henry up to one of his precious rubber trees and then used him for bayonet practice. Couldn't tell him how they hadn't even had the decency to finish him off properly, but had left him there, laughing at him, abandoning him to die in drawn-out agony.

Martin stood there, hands together prayer-like, unable to speak for a moment. It was impossible to think of Henry, so vital, so energetic, being dead. He glanced at Ma Kyin, aware that she had taken Henry's death almost as badly as he had. For some reason she was blaming herself for his death, but nobody could have done more than she had done. He told her as much. It seemed to comfort her.

He saw her take a deep, shuddering breath.

'Come,' she said softly, beckoning Martin out of the house.

He followed her as she led the way out beyond the

compound through the canopy of trees. Only a short distance it was, but with each step Martin felt his heart become more leaden. He knew instinctively what he would find. He moved reluctantly forward, then stopped at Ma Kyin's side.

Before him, the shallow, freshly dug mound of earth seemed poignantly small and humble. No cross, no in- dication of who lay beneath the newly turned soil. He watched as Ma Kyin stepped forward and placed the small silver frame on top of the rain-soaked grave. A picture of Henry himself, he saw now, and felt a surge of remorse that he had ever thought that Ma Kyin was taking the tiny frame for her own purposes.

So, he thought, Henry would never have to leave Anapuri now. The blessed shade of the rubber trees would cover him for ever.

He turned, hearing Ma Kyin saying something about Alex helping to dig the grave.

'He was here, then?' he asked, his surprise plain.

'Two days ago, yes,' said Ma Kyin.

'But he was supposed to be in Rangoon.' This was partly why Martin had come up to Anapuri himself, taking on the responsibility of bringing Henry back to Moulmein.

He felt faintly despondent, let down by his double sense of failure.

A wasted trip then. All this. Poor Elizabeth. He won- dered how she would take the news about her father.

'You must leave, *thakin*.' He was aware of Ma Kyin's thin small hand on his arm. 'The Japanese are on the move even now . . .'

'Yes.' The rain was still falling heavily. Martin took off his hat, spilling a pool of water from the brim. 'I suppose I should head back to Moulmein.'

'I must warn you,' cautioned Ma Kyin, 'there is talk that

the Japanese are about to advance towards Moulmein.'
The bush network was invariably correct, too.

'But there's still time for me to get back, surely?'
Martin's voice was suddenly tight. Such a rapid advance
was something he hadn't foreseen.

Ma Kyin gave a noncommittal shrug. 'Perhaps. But
Rangoon is where *Thakin* Alex went. Moulmein is no
longer safe, and even the Salween and Sittang Rivers
might not be so easily crossed in time.'

Martin nodded. He rapidly made his plans. Rangoon it
was then. It was where he should have been with Yarnold
anyway. He would skirt north of Moulmein. Then, if the
worst came to the worst, if the Japs looked as if they
might prove a problem, he could always head up to the
security of the Karenni Hills.

There at least he knew he would be safe.

The decision made, he turned and gave one last farewell
salute to Ma Kyin and started back towards the truck.

She was still standing there by the grave when he
reached the truck and as he drove off down the track
he thought that, despite the driving rain, he could see
her shadowy shape bent over the rain-soaked mound.

It was raining heavily in Rangoon that night, too. Kate
sat in her bedroom watching the steady downpour beating
against her window, the rivulets running down the glistening windowpanes.

Downstairs she could hear the low murmur of voices as
Alex and Elizabeth spoke on into the night, brother and
sister united in grief. She shivered, tightening her arms
across her body. It barely seemed possible that Henry
was dead. Why hadn't he left Anapuri when he'd had a
chance to do so? He must have known he wouldn't stand
a chance against the Japanese force, must have known he'd
be killed if he stayed to face them.

Perhaps, quite simply, it was what he had secretly wanted. To die at Anapuri. Alex believed that. Certainly he'd told Elizabeth as much.

When Alex had arrived late that evening, Kate had hardly recognised the damp, dirty, unshaven bulk standing in the hallway. One glance and she'd known something hideous had occurred, but even so, she'd been unprepared for the awfulness of his news. He'd told them about Henry, about Ma Kyin, and how she, alone, had been brave enough to cut Henry down. Because of her, Henry had died, not strung up like a chicken to one of the rubber trees, but with a smidgen at least of dignity.

They owed Ma Kyin a great deal, Kate knew, though even now she wasn't quite sure why the headman's wife had risked so much for Henry's sake, and Alex had been decidedly evasive when she and Elizabeth had tried to dig further.

No one mentioned Martin, as if by taciturn agreement that they would not tempt the gods by so doing. Yet, they now knew that Mergui had been evacuated and that Yarnold had arrived in Rangoon already. Elizabeth had been told that Martin was following with the so-called last ditchers, and should be arriving in Rangoon shortly. She was not allowing herself to consider other possibilities, Kate knew.

So, for the moment they would stay in Rangoon, waiting.

For how long, though, Kate couldn't say. Alex had already spoken to them about leaving the city, if only to pull back to Maymyo and it was rumoured that the government – at least the non-essential workers – would up-sticks and head for Maymyo before too long. Kate supposed she would have to be among them.

Elizabeth, she knew, would be reluctant to leave, but Rangoon would be no place for a pregnant woman alone with the Japanese less than a few hundred miles away.

'Kate?'

She propped herself up on her elbow, turning at the sound of Alex's voice.

'How's Elizabeth?' she asked, as he pushed open the door and came in.

'Taken it all rather badly, actually.'

He stood in the doorway for a moment, leaning warily against the frame, then crossed the room and perched himself on the edge of her bed.

'It's the shock, I suppose,' Kate said, moving her legs slightly to one side to make more room for him. 'She'll miss him terribly.'

'We *all* will.' There was a sudden sharp intensity to his voice which betrayed the fragility of his own emotions.

Kate put her arm around his shoulders, pulling him round so that her cheek rested against his neck. 'I know. I'm so sorry, Alex. So terribly sorry.'

'He didn't deserve such an end.'

'No.'

Kate tightened her arms around him.

For a long moment they lay there in silence then he cleared his throat slightly and lifted his head to look down at her.

'Listen, Kate,' he said, taking her hand in his. 'I think you and Elizabeth should leave for Maymyo.'

'When?'

'As soon as possible.'

'But we've been through this, Alex. Apart from the fact that I can't simply throw in my job and disappear up to Maymyo just like that, you know as well as I do Elizabeth's set on staying here. At least until Martin comes.'

'He may not come in the next few days as she thinks he will,' said Alex purposefully.

Kate glanced at him, wondering if he knew something she did not, or was merely being over-cautious.

'And if he doesn't, I don't want her waiting here *ad infinitum*,' Alex continued, his fingers closing convulsively on hers. 'I promised Martin I'd see she was safe.'

'But she won't go without him,' Kate protested. 'She's superstitious about leaving without him, that's the point. She's frightened for him.'

'Well she can be frightened for him in Maymyo,' said Alex with uncharacteristic curtness.

He let go of her hand and, standing up, went across to the window, yanking back the curtain to reveal a still tempestuous night. 'She's got the baby to think about as well.'

'Oh, Alex, it isn't that simple . . .' Kate began.

'Nothing is, Kate,' Alex said, spinning round to face her. 'And I can tell you it's going to get a bloody sight more complicated before all this ends.'

There was an edge to his voice which made her glance across at him. 'God! What do you know that we don't, Alex?'

'What I know is common knowledge,' returned Alex with a weary shrug. 'That we're up to our necks in generals all pulling in different directions, that our men are ill-equipped, some barely trained. Hutton and Smyth don't care for each other overly much and every day the Japanese are pushing that little bit closer.'

'But the army *will* stop them, won't they?' Kate asked. Like all the civilians, she had a touching faith in the army's ability to defeat the enemy.

She saw Alex hesitate just a fraction. 'The Japs won't give up without a fight, Kate. They're tenacious so-and-sos. Even if we do push them back from Moulmein, it won't be their last attempt . . .'

'So you think it'll be a long drawn-out affair, then?'

'Yes.' The other possibility was unthinkable. 'That's

why you must make sure Elizabeth sees sense and goes up to Maymyo.'

'All right,' she said slowly, suddenly realising how desperately important it was to him. 'I'll try. If Martin hasn't arrived in Rangoon by the time Government House starts to move out, *if* that's what they decide to do, then I'll make sure Elizabeth comes with me to Maymyo.'

'You won't let her be silly and remain in Rangoon waiting for Martin?'

'No. Not even if I have to bodily drag her up the Mandalay Road shouting and screaming all the way. There, does that satisfy you?'

'Perfectly,' he said, grinning at her. 'How could I have ever doubted your gentle, persuasive powers?'

'How indeed?'

It seemed the first light-hearted moment of the evening and Kate, looking across at him, had a glimpse of the teasing Alex of old. He'd seemed so detached, so withdrawn, all evening, she'd found it difficult to stretch beyond the barriers.

The trouble was they'd had so little time together since Pearl Harbor, fleeting moments here and there when Alex had arrived and gone almost in the same breath. There'd been no time to show their love for one another.

Now again, she sensed, he was about to leave.

'Alex?'

He turned back from the window, pushing his hands wearily across his face. She saw how gaunt he looked, how dark the shadows were beneath his eyes and she longed to reach out to him, to beg him not to go.

But instinct told her he had enough to worry about without such demands. Now was not the time to show her doubts and fears, to ask for promises or reassurances. It would only make her love a burden to him, and she was too much of a free spirit herself to want that.

Yet, for all that, she was a little afraid. With the world in such turmoil she could see that their burgeoning love might never have the chance to blossom and grow.

The war was sweeping them along in different directions, even now. And she was aware, suddenly, how fragile happiness was, and how easily it could all slip away from her.

## 16

*A* lex was not the only person thinking about the problems of evacuation. In Singapore Mark Lawrence was debating the same issue.

During the last few weeks the bombing attacks on Singapore had increased, and even though the Press – censored admittedly – said the Allies were holding the Japanese successfully in check, the increasing numbers of refugees flooding into Singapore told a different story. To Mark it appeared that the fighting was taking place further and further south, and despite the government talking about 'new British lines' and the Allies 'successfully employing leapfrog action to slow the Japanese down', as far as he could see Malaya was systematically being abandoned and the Japanese were still coming down the mainland.

Like everyone else, he'd supposed that the Japs would get the surprise of their lives when they met the well-dug-in Australians and other hardened troops at the Muar line, and that there they would finally be brought to a halt. But it just didn't seem to be happening. Apart from when the Australians had managed to ambush the Japanese at the Gemencheh River Bridge, the Allies had had little success and the latest news from Yong Peng did not seem any better. One or two of Mark's colleagues had already arranged for their wives to leave for Australia as a precautionary measure, since increased Japanese bombing of the city was more than likely.

It was time, Mark felt, for Sylvia and Louisa to leave.

He jabbed at the slice of chilled papaya and lemon juice on the plate in front of him. Sylvia, for reasons of her own, still seemed reluctant to go, pointing out that many of the refugees who had turned up in Singapore from the mainland – Jack and Mary included – had refused passages to Australia, preferring to wait for a ship bound for England, and arguing that if things were really all that bad then surely they would have had more sense of urgency.

It was a reasoning Mark found hard to fault, but with the news that Kuala Lumpur had fallen he'd made some enquiries about ships leaving Singapore, and now that the latest batch of bombing had put the drains out of action, there seemed to be more reason than ever to get Sylvia and Louisa out of the city. Typhoid was always a possibility and Mark wouldn't risk anything happening to his baby daughter.

He swivelled in his chair to watch her through the verandah railings as she tottered about the garden, the *amah* close at her heels, arms outstretched in readiness lest she topple. At fifteen months old, Louisa already seemed to sense the legacy of grace and beauty which was hers.

Looking at her now, her soft blonde curls gleaming in the sunlight, he felt a lurch of protective love. No, for Louisa's sake, he must arrange a passage for them to Perth. He wouldn't allow Sylvia to argue this time.

He put down his fork and, pushing back his chair, stood up determinedly, glancing quickly at his gold watch. Sylvia would still be upstairs, having her breakfast in bed at this moment. She hated what she considered to be such early starts to the day.

He went up the stairs and, pushing open the door, looked in. Sylvia was sitting up in bed, silk wrapper across her pale shoulders, cup of lemon tea in one hand, a letter in the other.

'I thought you'd left for the office,' she said, glancing

up at his entrance and putting down the page she was reading.

'Not quite. I wanted to talk to you first.'

'Oh?' Sylvia bent her willowy neck, concentrating on her lemon tea. 'What about?'

'About leaving Singapore.'

'I thought we'd settled all that. I thought we'd agreed I'd stay.'

Mark was aware of the eddies of tension and hostility in her voice and manner, conscious of the unspoken challenge. Of late, life with Sylvia had become one long simmering row which never seemed to have anything approaching a real issue, but which seemed to bubble with quibbles and dissatisfactions.

'Things have changed. I don't believe it's safe for you to stay in Singapore any longer.'

Sylvia barely lifted her head. 'But we're due for reinforcements any day now. That'll change things, surely?' she persisted. 'Besides, I thought after the Indian troops' success at Niyor things were looking up. And the Australians seem to be holding their own against the Japs.'

'Not any more I'm afraid,' he told her bluntly, disinclined to shelter her from the truth now. 'The latest reports are that they're withdrawing . . .'

He had her attention at last. He saw her head jerk up.

'The Australians? Are you sure?'

'Apparently it's been a shambles.'

Her face lost most of its colour. He'd frightened her, he could see that. He wasn't sorry. If it made her see sense then he'd achieved his objective.

'Well?' he asked, pushing home his advantage. 'Do you now understand why I want you to leave?' He watched as her slim fingers fidgeted with the edge of her letter. 'You will go, won't you?'

Sylvia didn't answer for a moment. Beside her, on the

crisp white sheet, lay Johnnie's latest missive. It had been written only three days before, and though it mentioned the possibility of some small skirmish there'd been only confidence at the outcome. Now . . .

She closed her eyes, not allowing herself to think about the consequences. She was sure Johnnie would be all right. Johnnie had the luck of the devil. But what about the rest of them?

If the reinforcements didn't arrive soon then they'd all be in a terribly tight corner. She'd been so obsessed with staying so that she could see Johnnie that she'd not really thought about much else.

'Well?'

She opened her eyes to see Mark staring down at her. For the first time she was frightened, aware that the enemy might indeed be on their doorstep, aware that the rumours she'd heard yesterday that the Chinese were no longer accepting 'chits' and would only take cash, an unheard-of occurrence in Singapore where goods had been bought on the chit-signing system since Raffles' time, could actually have some credence.

In that moment her sense of self-preservation came to the fore.

She might love Johnnie, but, realist that she was, she knew it was a love based primarily on passion. To stay in Singapore against Mark's wishes would be to risk too much. Though she had blithely said she would leave Mark for Johnnie, the truth was she had no wish to lose the security, comfort and wealth that her husband offered her. She had come to rely on it. If she insisted on staying this time Mark might become suspicious, start to ask awkward questions.

Besides, Mark's remarks about the Australians being pushed back had alarmed her. For the first time she acknowledged the unthinkable: that the Japanese could take Singapore. And, by all accounts, the Japanese were not merciful victors.

She knew then, for her own sake, she must leave Johnnie to his own devices. She could not jeopardise her own safety any longer. Not even for him.

She took a deep breath, her fingers unconsciously tightening about Johnnie's letter. 'You're quite right, Mark,' she said, her voice sweetly indulgent, giving no hint of her inner turmoil, 'it makes sense to leave.'

Mark was careful to show neither relief nor triumph at her decision. 'Then I'll book a passage for you and Louisa as soon as possible,' he said quietly. 'You may have to leave at short notice, I'm afraid.'

Sylvia nodded, ostensibly studying her carefully manicured nails. She wouldn't allow herself to think of the full consequences of her decision. She must think about herself, her own survival.

But silently, despite her resolution, she found herself praying that Johnnie would keep himself safe and, having done so, would forgive her for her desertion.

Up ahead the Gordon Highlanders had at last knocked out the Jap machine gun post which had been causing such havoc to the withdrawing troops, but Johnnie, looking around him at the weary remnants of his battalion, thought it had done little to boost morale.

The trouble was the boys were too bloody exhausted.

It wasn't just the fighting, it was the incessant rain, the falling back to one ill-prepared position after another, and the knowledge that, try as they might, they still hadn't been able to give the Japanese the hiding they had so confidently expected they would. That was what had really worn them down.

It didn't help to be told now that they'd been up against 12,000 guards from the crack Japanese troop, the Imperial

Army Japanese Guards. Six foot two some of them had been, highly trained in jungle warfare, well equipped, and hardly a pair of spectacles among them. So much for all the propaganda about little short-sighted puny men who were afraid to fight at night! Jesus! And to think Intelligence had even tried to convince them that the Jap bullets were so small that they wouldn't hurt much . . . Tell that to the convoys of wounded being ferried back to Singapore, Johnnie thought bitterly.

The truth was they hadn't ever stood a chance. Johnnie knew that now. Once the Japanese had established complete command of air and sea, it had been just a matter of time. However bravely the troops fought, it was impossible to win a peninsula war with neither navy nor airforce backup. It was like trying to win a boxing match with both hands firmly tied behind one's back.

It was almost risible. The Jap Zeros could pinpoint their position with unnerving accuracy, picking them off in their own time from the skies, and every time the Allies had managed to get some sort of hold on the Japanese infantry, they had somehow managed to slip behind the Allied lines, often by dropping fresh troops off along the coastline, and had taken them from the rear. How could anyone compete against those advantages?

From behind him came the sound of a plane. Instinctively the troops along the track scrambled for cover.

'Bloody hell,' said the man beside Johnnie as they dived into a shallow ditch, 'where did he spring from?'

'God knows.' Johnnie watched grimly as the Zero circled then dived straight down the road in front of them, machine gunning the luckless few who were too slow to find refuge. The plane was skimming so low over the trees that Johnnie could see the face of the pilot in the cockpit.

'How the hell did the bugger know where we were?' asked Johnnie's companion. 'Beats me.'

The answer to this question was apparent almost immediately as a scuffle broke out further up the line. It transpired an Indian Sikh, with a white turban and long flowing shirt, had been caught signalling a few minutes before the raid. Obviously a 'Fifth Columnist', he was one of the many local natives aiding and abetting the Japanese by signalling the position of Allied guns and other strategic targets, an additional hazard they could well do without.

At least this time the casualties had been reasonably light.

Johnnie had been present, a few days earlier, when the Japs had blown to bits a small well-camouflaged native hut which the Indian Army was using as its headquarters.

He'd heard a sudden 'whoof' and the hut and the men had completely disintegrated, the blast jolting his truck more than a hundred yards away. Later he'd heard that a Malay farmer had ploughed a ditch pointing to the concealed hut being used by the Indian Brigade, and had then filled it in with water to highlight its location for the enemy. It was typical of the Fifth Column activities they were up against in Malaya.

Johnnie looked about him now at the pockets of men crouched by the side of the track. The number of able bodied men who could fight had dwindled dramatically over the past few days and looking at the dispirited, ragged bunch he had an uneasy feeling that there was no possible way this war could be turned around.

There was, of course, talk of reinforcements arriving at last in Singapore, but quite frankly he couldn't see what difference that would make now. It was more aeroplanes that were needed, and without them he was desperately afraid that the patriotic young reinforcements would be mere lambs to the slaughter, sacrificed for no good purpose.

He hoped he was mistaken.

He stirred and stubbed out his cigarette. Somewhere in the distance he heard the scream of the shells as a Jap mortar attack began. At least it wasn't his boys who were getting it this time. He rubbed his face wearily, trying to ignore the gnawing hunger pains clawing at his stomach. They hadn't had a decent meal in days.

There was an order from the front to move on, but no sooner had it been passed down the line and they had all started to clamber out of their various hiding places than they heard the sound of the plane returning. Johnnie dived hastily back for cover into what was now becoming an increasingly familiar drainage ditch, his erstwhile companion tumbling down on top of him a few seconds later.

'Sorry about that, mate,' he said apologetically, disentangling himself from Johnnie with a sheepish grin. 'But you can't hang around when those Nip bastards come overhead . . .'

Johnnie's reply was lost in the din of the enemy plane strafing the track, skimming low over the trees, his guns riddling the area so forcibly with bullets that mud and debris came raining down on top of Johnnie and his compatriot like an eruption from Vesuvius.

'Jesus, that was close.' They lifted their heads the barest inch to inspect the damage.

Less than twenty yards away one of the lads, Nornton by the looks of it, had caught it in the chest, and another had had his leg smashed to pieces. Somehow, Johnnie supposed, they'd have to put together makeshift stretchers and get the blighters moved out to the recovery position and then out to CCS.

The trouble was that the Japs opened fire on any vehicle, whether marked with the Red Cross or not, and it was touch and go whether or not the ambulances would ever get through to Singapore. But they had to try. They certainly weren't going to risk leaving any wounded behind.

Rumour had it that the badly injured boys from the 19th, whom Colonel Anderson had left behind at Parit Sulong Bridge, under the protection of the Red Cross flag, had all been summarily massacred by the Imperial Guard. It was even said that the Jap bastards had tied the wounded men's hands together behind their backs, poured petrol over the lot of them and then set them alight. They'd finished them off by driving their tanks over them. Whether it was true or not, it was clear that the Geneva Convention was not bedtime reading for the Japanese command.

The ear-splitting sound of enemy fire had died away. Tentatively Johnnie edged his way out of the ditch and then zig-zagged his way up through the trees towards Nornton, dropping down into the hollow beside the wounded man.

'Take it easy, Nornton,' he said, bending down over the whimpering boy. He quickly tried to assess the damage but it was difficult to judge the extent of the injury. Blood was everywhere. Someone, he noted dispassionately, had pushed a rolled jungle hat between the lad's teeth to stop him moaning out loud. As if the Japs didn't know precisely where they were anyway. 'We'll have you out of here in no time,' he continued gravely, putting one hand on the boy's bloodstained, exposed shoulder. 'The fellas are just getting a couple of stretchers together and then we'll try and get you taken up along the line to Casualty Clearing.'

Whether it was his words or his tone Johnnie didn't know, but Nornton suddenly quietened. He didn't seem to need to ask for any guarantees. Perhaps he knew that at this stage in the game none of them could.

A short time later two of the men came along with a makeshift stretcher and, grunting with the effort, slid Nornton's heavy, unresisting body into place. Sweating and clumsy with tension they set off up the line, crouching, legs bent like apes, while those remaining watched them anxiously, unconsciously waiting for the high-pitched whine of mortars or the peppering of rifle shots.

Mercifully none came. Johnnie saw the men visibly relax. It was small triumphs like these that kept them going.

The light was starting to fade. They had orders to regroup and start to pull out. There were the inevitable muffled groans from the men, most of whom had collapsed in exhausted groups and huddles on the ground, but in truth Johnnie thought they were all secretly relieved to be on the move again. There was no pretence this time. They all knew they were pulling back towards Singapore.

Johnnie bent down to pick up his kit bag and rifle. The thought of Singapore cheered him. No, to be precise, it was the thought of Sylvia. If they withdrew onto the island itself he was sure he would be able to find a way of sneaking off to see her. He'd missed her, more than he could say, these past few weeks.

They marched on cautiously, each man trying to see beyond the blackness of the jungle to what lay beyond.

Perhaps tonight, thought Johnnie, a smidgen of hope rising within him, they might be lucky enough to gain a respite. No Japanese rearguard action for once.

But a few miles to the north of their position dark shapes were already moving along the moonlit road and soon the sound of spattered gunfire rose above the soft murmurings of the jungle.

Johnnie gave a resigned sigh and called his men to the ready.

There was to be no letting up, it seemed. It was going to be another busy night.

A wave of intense heat buffeted Mark Lawrence's face, forcing him backwards as he battled against the fierce flames coiling around the riverside godowns.

He lowered his helmeted head against the blistering blizzard of sparks, unable now even to distinguish one building from another in the general blaze which raged for acres along the waterfront. This night had been the worst so far, he thought, wincing as a piece of jagged glass embedded in the hosepipe tore into his skin. He glanced absently down at the palms of his hands. They were raw and bleeding: just one of the many hazards of the job.

Over to his right he heard a shout for more hose and a moment later another of the volunteers sped forward with a new length. Not that it would make much difference. The dock buildings seemed permanently ablaze these days, and as far as Mark could see these particular godowns had been packed with highly flammable material – possibly engine oil or palm oil or even latex stored as liquid.

He felt a tug on his arm and, turning, found that one of the Cantonese volunteers had come to relieve him so that he could have a break and a cup of well-earned tea from the Central Fire Station van.

It wasn't until he was sitting down on the kerb, another soot-smeared fireman sprawled beside him, that he realised how exhausted he was. Weariness was a disease of epidemic proportions in Singapore these past days. No one had slept in weeks.

He leant back, tea in hand, enjoying the momentary respite. Hard to believe how fast things had deteriorated in Singapore since Louisa and Sylvia had left. They had barely got out in time. Since their departure the Japanese had forced the Allied soldiers to a man to retreat back onto Singapore island, and now the enemy were encamped outside Johore Bahru, just on the other side of the causeway.

Singapore was under siege and though certain *tuans* had insisted when the causeway had first been blown up that the island had been made secure and all was still well, even they had had to change their tune during the past few days. The Japanese were expected to make a landing on the island at any moment.

Now it was virtually impossible to obtain a place on the packed ships leaving the harbour. The horror stories of weeping, frantic families trying to get tickets on those last boats, with people actually fighting each other on the docks for a place, stampeding over women and children to get up the gangway, had been bad enough. But what had appalled Mark most of all was that some of those responsible had been people he had *known*. He could never have believed they could behave like that. Panic, it seemed, was capable of changing even the mildest of people overnight.

He, himself, had elected to stay on. Singapore was his home, after all. He couldn't just walk away.

Besides, he thought, tossing out the last dregs of his tea onto the rubble-strewn road, if the unthinkable happened, if Singapore couldn't hold out against the Japanese and all hope was lost, then there was always the last-ditch plan of the motor launch at the Telok Ayer Basin which old Hutchinson had said was standing by to take the 'faithful few' to Sumatra. They should be quite safe on that.

The Dutchman beside him stretched and stood up. It was time to get back to work. Overhead searchlights swept the sky, crisscrossing each other, and then in the north Mark saw a faint flash of red followed by blue. Distress rockets of some sort, he supposed, giving the matter little thought.

He might not have been so complacent had he known the truth.

For what he had seen, in fact, were the rockets sent up by the Japanese to announce that the first assault wave of the 18th Chrysanthemum Division had been successful in landing on the north-west coast of Singapore.

*       *       *

On a whispered order the infantry moved forward. Another fiasco, thought Johnnie angrily. Why the hell hadn't the command been given for the searchlights to be turned on the moment the enemy had been spotted bobbing across the black water towards the island?

And what of the counter barrage which had been planned for the moment of attack? The British guns, so ideally placed, had remained mute. Why? Some cock-up from HQ he imagined, which had effectively let the Japanese land virtually unopposed.

Now, of course, a few of the guns were opening fire, but it was a question of too little, too late. The Japanese were already ashore along the entire front and, as far as Johnnie could make out, swarming through the maze of jungle, trying for an attack from the rear, as usual.

Johnnie stumbled in the darkness. God! it was impossible to see a thing, or even to know in which bloody direction he was facing now he'd lost sight of the Strait. It was a catastrophe of the first order.

Suddenly there was a flash and a violent explosion just ahead of him. He stopped, confused, aware that the huddle of men behind him were just as dazed, unsure even whether it was their own troops or the Japanese who were firing on them.

Either way, one thing was blatantly clear to Johnnie. By sheer bad luck the Japanese advance had opened a gap between the Australians and the Indians, and somehow the Japanese troops had managed to sneak past them already.

Worse still, if Johnnie's little pocket of men were anything to go by, the Australian fighting force was now split up into disorientated groups, all out of touch with their brigade and all trying desperately to find their way back.

It was the beginning of the end.

He felt a small shudder run through him, despite the heat. Thank God Sylvia had managed to get out of the place in time.

He hadn't thought that when first he'd come down to the city after that gruelling retreat. He'd so wanted to see her. He'd used all his skills to commandeer a motorbike and in desperation had gone round secretly to Tanglin Road, only to discover she had left without warning. A few short lines, that was all she had written – a note stuffed under the door of their hideaway flat – a few short lines saying Mark had insisted that she should leave. Mark! As if the wishes of her bloody husband were suddenly so important.

He'd almost wept in rage at her inconstancy and had promptly disappeared off to a whorehouse in Macpherson Road, where he'd spent most of the night and all of his money.

But now, little more than a week later, he could see how mistaken he'd been. If she had stayed, as he'd asked her to do, what mess would she be in now? Johnnie was not one to dwell on the consequences of his own actions but for the first time he acknowledged, a little ashamedly, how unutterably selfish he'd been in trying to persuade her to stay on in Singapore. And, despite himself, he felt a grudging respect for Mark, who by all accounts had made sure Sylvia had got to safety but who had stayed behind himself when, presumably, he could easily have wangled it to leave the city as well.

There was a volley of small arms fire up ahead, which was quickly returned. Johnnie called his troop to a halt, aware that in the distance each side was firing blind at each other. He hesitated, unsure of which way to turn. All he knew was, somehow, he must try and find a way through to the safety of Bukit Timah. At this moment it was all he could hope for.

*            *            *

The force of the blast lifted Mark clean off his feet, sweeping him up and sideways like a swimmer in a stormy sea. He'd abandoned the car and dived for cover as soon as he'd heard that ominous faint whistle, but this time he hadn't been quite quick enough. The succession of high-explosive bombs had fallen with a roaring thud, cracking the street wide open.

Choking dust filled his mouth and he was aware of crashing masonry, of dirt and dust and fragments, and of other bodies flying through the air. Then it was pitch dark.

He lay there, aware that he was pinned beneath an immense weight of material, unable to move and, more frighteningly, unable to breathe properly. Half the street seemed to be covering him, rubble pressing into every part of his body.

Dully, he began to distinguish between the different weights crushing against him. It was not all stone and rubble. Somewhere pressed against his face and head, the weight, though just as heavy, was less rigid. He knew instinctively it was another person, possibly two. He tried to call out some words of encouragement but it was impossible even to whisper. He felt himself drifting in and out of consciousness, not sure what was real and what was not.

An age seemed to pass. About him there seemed an eerie, uneasy silence. Lying there in the darkness, the feeling of claustrophobia growing with every second, Mark felt a wave of panic rising up within him. No one seemed to be coming to his rescue. What if they didn't realise he was here?

Of course they did, he frantically tried to tell himself. The street he'd been driving down when the planes had screamed overhead had been packed and he'd noticed a dozen or so Australian soldiers milling around by the corner shop. Surely they would remember seeing him too, and wonder?

Then dimly, as if from miles away, he was aware of the faint sound of scrabbling, of voices. A thin shred of hope stirred within him, but he was too tired to feel more than that. He was floating, floating, almost as if he were no longer part of his own body. Determinedly, he forced himself to focus on his pain, to feel the rubble, to concentrate, too, on the body on top of him, on that life-giving pocket of air which it had so mercifully provided.

The Australian voices became louder. Gradually, minute by painful minute, Mark felt the crushing weight diminishing, and the light getting steadily brighter.

The last of the rubble was painstakingly cleared away and the bodies on top of him carefully lifted up. Despite their removal, Mark still couldn't move his limbs. It was as if all the pressure was still there.

Confused, he let himself be hoisted up and carried to the waiting ambulance. As he passed by, one of the soldiers put a torn and tattered jacket across Mark's chest, and it was only then that Mark looked down at his bloodstained body and saw that his clothes hadn't survived the blast. The force of the bomb had literally torn them off him.

'You'll be all right, mate. Just wait and see,' the Australian said encouragingly as Mark was loaded in beside two young Australian soldiers who'd been caught in the blast. 'You three fellas are out of it now, lucky blighters.' He grinned. 'The delights of St Patrick's for you. Not like us poor saps . . .'

Mark didn't have the energy to tell him that he was neither army, nor Australian. It hardly seemed important anyway. Everything in Singapore was in such chaos.

As the ambulance rattled its way northwards, Mark drifted in and out of consciousness, comforting himself with the knowledge that whatever happened to him at least those whom he loved were out of harm's way. Sylvia and Louisa would nearly be in Perth by now, and Kate, if her last letter was anything to go by, would be well clear of Rangoon and the approaching Japanese.

As it happened, Kate had not even left Rangoon. At the precise moment her father was being ferried across Singapore to St Patrick's Hospital she was, in fact, in the garden at University Avenue trying valiantly to lug an extremely large and heavy teak chest across the now ragged and unkempt lawn.

Her progress was painfully slow and her sense of humour not in the least improved by Elizabeth, hugely pregnant, who was sitting on the verandah steps calling out advice.

'You know, you've gone awfully red in the face,' Elizabeth announced unhelpfully, watching Kate struggle forward another inch or so. 'I don't think you ought to be doing that at all. You'll probably rupture something . . .'

'Think I already have,' said Kate with feeling, giving the trunk another push.

'Perhaps if you pull it, rather than push . . .'

'I tried that, remember?' retorted Kate frostily.

'Oh, yes, so you did. Wasn't terribly successful, was it?'

'No.'

There was a merciful halt in the conversation, as Elizabeth took a sip of her drink. Kate edged the trunk forward a few more inches.

'What you really need,' said Elizabeth, putting down her glass and observing the sweating form of her friend collapsed on top of the chest, 'is some rollers underneath it.'

'Probably.'

'Or some wheels.'

'Actually, Elizabeth, what I could really do with is two

good strong men to put this bloody thing in the slit-trench
for me,' said Kate, exasperation suddenly getting the
better of her. 'Forget the wheels.'

'It was your idea to do this,' said Elizabeth, unruffled
by Kate's outburst. 'Remember?'

'I do, yes,' admitted Kate.

It had been an impulse which she had come to regret
several times over in the past half an hour.

She straightened up, wincing slightly with the effort.
Pointless to mention to Elizabeth that it was, in fact,
her family treasures that Kate was trying to save by
burying them in the teak chest before the looters arrived. Elizabeth refused point-blank to accept that such
a thing might happen to University Avenue, despite the
increasing evidence of such occurrences in other districts
where occupants had long since left.

Elizabeth put down her drink and stood up, coming to
lean over the verandah railings. 'I don't suppose there's
anything I can do . . .'

'Not really.'

'Didn't think there was. Look, why don't we just leave
the other trunk. It all seems so pointless, this.'

'You won't think that when we come back to Rangoon.'

'*If* we come back.'

Kate grinned. 'Don't be such a pessimist. *When.*'

'All right, when,' said Elizabeth grudgingly. 'But the
point is, even if you do manage to haul the wretched trunks
down into the slit-trenches, will we ever find them again?
Look how long the grass has grown and the *mali* has only
been gone a few weeks. It's practically a jungle already.'

'Long John Silver managed to find his treasure and he
was gone for years,' insisted Kate, not willing to admit
that she had the same misgivings, too.

'Long John had a map,' pointed out Elizabeth.

'Well, there you are,' said Kate blithely. 'That's your

entertainment worked out for the afternoon then. Twelve paces to the left, six to the right and start digging by the magnolia tree.'

'Very funny.'

'Actually,' said Kate seriously, 'a map is a splendid thought. They always say that when you return to a place it never looks the same. Your mother wouldn't exactly thank us if we have to dig up the entire lawn just to find the chests, would she?'

'Nor would the *mali*, since undoubtedly the task would fall to him.'

'Quite.'

The doorbell rang in the distance. Elizabeth straightened up and made a move towards the verandah door. Since half the servants had left with her mother and she and Kate had given the others permission to leave over the past few days, it was very much a question of doing everything oneself.

'Wait, for heaven's sake,' Kate insisted, abandoning the chest and running up the verandah steps to Elizabeth's side. 'You never know who it might be.'

'Looters would hardly ring the doorbell,' Elizabeth pointed out, smiling because she knew full well Kate would never be so overly cautious about answering the door herself.

'Polite ones might.'

'Nonsense,' Elizabeth said, obediently following Kate through the drawing room into the hallway.

Kate hesitated the barest second and then pulled open the heavy front door. Before her stood a tall, moustached army officer in khaki uniform. He was standing, arms folded, looking somewhat ill at ease.

'Mrs Downing?'

Kate saw he had an envelope in his hand. Her heart stopped still. 'No. Mrs Downing is . . .'

She felt Elizabeth push past her.

'I'm Mrs Downing. What . . . ?' Elizabeth's voice died in her throat as she took in the envelope and the uniformed officer standing in the doorway. 'Oh, God!' Her voice was barely audible. 'It's Martin, isn't it?'

'Listen, Elizabeth, it might not be about him . . .' Kate began, but even to her own ears her voice sounded false.

'It is. I know it is. You open it, Kate.'

Kate hesitated, then stretched out her hand to take the yellow envelope from the self-conscious young officer. It was a job he obviously did not enjoy.

She glanced at Elizabeth. 'Are you sure?' she asked gently.

Elizabeth nodded slowly.

After a long moment's stillness, Kate began to tear open the envelope. Her fingers felt tense and stiff, and she fumbled awkwardly, her heart pounding with fear.

She pulled out the sheet of paper, trying to hold it steady in front of her, but her hands were shaking too much.

She faltered. 'Do you want to read it, Lizzie?'

Elizabeth was staring numbly ahead. 'No, I couldn't,' she said, shaking her head with sudden violence. 'You read it, Kate. Please.'

Kate swallowed hard carefully smoothing out the page. The typed letters jumbled and blurred in front of her, then miraculously formed themselves into words.

Kate cleared her throat, lifting her head at last. She was aware of Elizabeth watching her with fearful intensity. She felt tears pricking at her lids.

'He's dead, isn't he?' said Elizabeth seeing Kate's face.

'No, Lizzie,' said Kate very, very quietly. 'No, he's not.' She took a deep shuddering breath. 'He's very much alive. They've written to say that they've had word he's reached the Karens.'

'Alive, but . . .'

'Here.' Kate thrust the note at Elizabeth, fighting back the tears of relief and happiness. So all their badgering of the authorities to try and find out what had happened to Martin had finally paid off. 'You'd better read the letter yourself. Seems your old man did rather well for a desk wallah.'

Elizabeth hugged her. Kate could feel her shaking in her arms.

'I *knew* he wasn't dead,' Elizabeth said, giving a squeal of delight. 'I told you, didn't I?'

Kate beamed. 'Many times.'

'You *see*.'

Kate left her, feverishly reading and re-reading the note, and stepped outside into the sunshine. How quickly one good piece of news could dispel the bad. It was too, too wonderful.

She turned to see the young army officer clambering onto the front seat of his jeep beside his driver.

'I'm glad it was good news,' he called out. He'd obviously expected the worst. 'HQ didn't brief me or I'd have saved you all that agony. I was a bit worried there for a moment, seeing that Mrs Downing . . . well, you know. That's why I hung around a bit,' he added, almost apologetically. 'Thought we might end up having to make a quick dash to the hospital.'

'So did I,' admitted Kate wryly.

She stood for a moment, regarding the two men in the vehicle, and as she did so a sudden thought came to her.

It was too good an opportunity to miss.

She came up to the jeep, leaning casually against the door. 'I wonder,' she said, giving them her most bewitching smile. 'I don't suppose you could help, could you? You see, I was having a small spot of bother with something just before you arrived.'

She watched appreciatively as the two strapping lads stepped obligingly down from the jeep.

Two good strong men. Really it was like manna from heaven. The teak chests would be in the slit-trench in no time.

## 17

'*I*t's my fault,' said Elizabeth. 'I should have told you when they first started. It's just that I was always under the impression that first babies took ages to come.'

'Not this one.' Kate took her hand. The contractions were now coming hard and fast. 'Managing all right?' she asked, as Elizabeth's hand tightened on hers.

'I wish I could walk around.'

'You can move as soon as the air-raid finishes,' Kate told her. 'It can't be much longer.'

'Much longer and it'll be too late,' commented Elizabeth, managing a weak smile. 'Honestly, what a time for it to choose!'

Kate adjusted her position on the floor beside Elizabeth. 'At least it waited for us to get to Maymyo,' she said.

There had been a moment on the Mandalay Road on the way up last week when Kate, after driving over a particularly nasty series of potholes, had thought they might have to do an emergency stop by the roadside.

'Hospital would have been better.'

'Nonsense. Much more cosy here.' Kate's voice sounded confident enough, but she still secretly hoped that the all-clear would sound shortly and that they'd have time to make a quick dash to the hospital. Either that, or Mrs Ferris who lived next door and was a VAD would return from her shift at the Military Hospital.

Beside her, Elizabeth tensed suddenly as another contraction gripped her.

'I wish Martin was here,' she said very softly, her voice catching between gasps. 'I always thought, well hoped, he would be here when the baby was born . . .'

'At least you know he's safe,' comforted Kate, pushing Elizabeth's damp hair back from her forehead.

'But I do worry about him.'

'Of course.'

'Poor Martin. He'll hate being in hiding. I know him. He likes security and stability in his life. He isn't like Alex who'd thrive on the adventure of it all.'

'He's shown he's tougher than you thought, getting through to the Karens like that,' Kate said. She picked up one of the towels she had bundled under the table with them when the air-raid siren had first sounded. 'At least they're loyal to the British and will look after him even if the Japs overrun their area.' She began to dab at the beads of sweat on Elizabeth's clammy face.

Elizabeth closed her eyes. She was like a butterfly pausing on a flower, fluttering, gathering strength.

After a moment, she said: 'The note said he might have to stay put for a while. It sounds like they've been cut off by the Japs already.'

'Perhaps he'll find a way through,' Kate tried to console her.

Secretly she doubted it. There were terrible rumours of the British pulling back across the Sittang River in such a rush that they'd blown up the bridge with half their troops still on the other side. If it was true, then it was a disaster of the first order and it meant that Rangoon would almost certainly fall.

She couldn't allow herself to think that in all probability Alex was in the midst of all that mess. She hadn't heard from him since January and every day there seemed to be news of further British retreats, the only advantage of which, as far as she was concerned, was that it must be bringing him closer to her. She desperately longed to hear from him, to know he was safe.

She glanced down as Elizabeth eased her position on the assorted pillows arranged under the table.

'Actually, I hope Martin doesn't try to get through,' Elizabeth was saying, her voice showing the edge of her weariness. 'I'd hate to think of him being hunted by the Japs each day. He's not cut out to live on his wits. Not like my brother . . .'

She stopped speaking suddenly, clutching Kate's hand in a vice-like grasp, as the strength of the last contraction caught her by surprise. 'Kate . . .'

'I'm here.'

'I don't think I'm going to be very brave.'

'You're doing wonderfully.' Kate began to breathe loudly and deeply trying to instil some sort of cadence back into Elizabeth's own breathing.

Elizabeth followed Kate's lead, trying to breathe through her pain, puffing and sweating with the effort. She could feel the rhythm of her body changing, feel the insistent bulkiness of the baby's head pushing against her.

'Oh my.'

Her cry was drowned by another, more persistent, wail. At that precise moment the All-Clear siren, with perfectly maddening timing, echoed across Maymyo.

'Lot of jolly use, now,' observed Kate wryly. 'Honestly, if I . . .'

'Kate!'

The urgency of Elizabeth's voice stopped Kate mid-sentence.

'One last push,' she encouraged.

'I can't,' Elizabeth began to whimper. She felt as if there was a searing pain thrusting its way right through her, tearing her apart.

'Yes, you can. You're nearly there,' Kate urged. 'You

can't give up on me now. I can see its head. One last push. That's all it'll take.'

'Just one?' Elizabeth's voice was tinged with suspicion.

'Absolutely.'

Actually, Kate's estimation was on the low side, but when Elizabeth's daughter, tiny and purple-faced, slipped squalling into Kate's waiting hands, she forgot all her resentment at Kate's bullying and bold-faced lies.

'She's so beautiful,' she murmured, taking the perfectly formed infant into her arms.

'Isn't she, just? You clever thing,' whispered Kate.

She sat, legs drawn up, watching mother and daughter. Elizabeth was looking down at her child with rapt attention, her face bright with elation, her hand touching the small, damp head with the utmost tenderness.

And watching them caught up in their small private magic circle, so wonderfully complete, so loving, Kate felt a tiny unexpected stab of envy.

Maymyo, thought Kate, could be compared to a swan at the moment. On the surface it might appear peaceful and serene but beneath the water it was paddling hard.

Already she was aware of subtle changes. The Shan farmers no longer brought their supplies into town from the countryside and although the 'S and T boys' went on foraging expeditions, so there were no shortages exactly, the sense of plenty had gone. Petrol was in short supply and, worst of all, the sole bank in Maymyo, the Bank of Upper Burma, now had closed its door. By sheer good fortune Kate and Elizabeth had a reserve of cash in hand, but it wouldn't last for ever.

Every morning as Kate bicycled off to work she saw the Karen nanny packing a basketful of baby commodities for Henrietta Anne, ready to be taken down to the slit-trench in case of air-raids.

Kate knew it couldn't continue like this for very much longer. The club seemed to be increasingly full of tired and wounded officers of the KOYLI who, though undaunted, no longer spoke confidently of victory.

A few weeks after the baby was born Kate came back to the house one March afternoon to find Elizabeth sobbing quietly in her bedroom.

'Elizabeth, what is it?' she asked gently, coming into the room. Instinctively she glanced over at the cot, but Henrietta was perfectly well, sleeping peacefully. Another thought rushed at her and for a moment she hesitated, half-afraid, then: 'Is it Martin?'

Mercifully she saw Elizabeth shake her head. She came across the room to sit on the edge of the bed beside her. 'Then what?' she asked gently, putting her arm around her.

Elizabeth swallowed, fighting back another sob. 'I saw Ann today . . .' she said, taking out a small linen handkerchief from her skirt pocket and blowing her nose. 'You know, the girl with the baby slightly older than Henrietta. The one whose husband is with the BURIFs . . .'

'Yes, I remember.'

'Well, she came to see me today to say goodbye. Seems she's been told she's being flown out to Calcutta some time in the next few days.'

'Oh, Elizabeth, I *am* sorry,' Kate sympathised. 'You'll miss her terribly.'

Elizabeth looked faintly irritated and Kate realised she had misunderstood her.

'Kate, no, you've missed my point completely,' she said stiffly. 'That's not it at all. Don't you see, if all the army wives are being moved out as Ann says, then it's my guess it won't be long before there'll be a general evacuation.' She blew her nose again. 'And I don't want to go. It was bad enough leaving Rangoon, but to leave Burma altogether . . .'

Kate was aware that Elizabeth was looking at her, waiting for her advice.

Usually so forthright, Kate knew she should tell her that she was being silly and that of course she should go, but then she saw the anguished expression on her face. She knew, too, how she herself would feel about losing Alex. Not a day went by without her thinking of him. She closed her eyes now, briefly, trying to remember every line and angle and hollow of his face, every tone and inflexion of his voice, making them sharp and distinct in her mind. She would not allow herself to think of him as anything but safe.

'No one can make you go, Elizabeth, not if you don't want to,' she said quietly after a pause. 'But don't you think if you were to get an offer of a flight out, it would be wise to take it?'

Elizabeth shifted her position slightly. 'That's what Ann said,' she admitted, scrunching her handkerchief up into a tight little ball and stuffing it back into her pocket. 'She said I've got Henrietta to think of now.'

'Which you have.'

'I know. But . . . oh, Kate, can't you see, it's like wilfully cutting the last tie with Martin?'

'He'd want you to leave, Elizabeth,' insisted Kate gently. In truth he probably thought she'd gone already.

'But what if he's trying to get through the lines to me?'

'It's unlikely. You said yourself that he was not much inclined to heroics.'

'But I don't want to leave,' Elizabeth said with conviction. 'Not until I *really* have to.' She lifted her head and regarded Kate hopefully. 'You haven't been told anything yet, have you?'

'About pulling out?'

Elizabeth nodded.

'No.' There'd been a few rumours but she supposed they'd stay put in Maymyo until Dorman-Smith decreed otherwise.

'Then if it's safe for you to stay, it's safe for me, surely?' There was a thread of hope in Elizabeth's voice. 'I could stay as long as you, couldn't I?'

'If you were certain of a flight out,' Kate pointed out.

'I'm sure I'd be all right.' Elizabeth felt a sudden surge of confidence. 'Besides, Ann did say that Meisha MacKay was staying on. She's a VAD at the Military Hospital and she and a few others have said they'll remain while there's work to be done there.'

Kate could see that Elizabeth's mind was made up. She wasn't too happy with her decision though. What had occurred in Singapore could easily take place in Burma. She still didn't know the details of what had happened to her father.

Over in her cot, Henrietta stirred but did not wake. It was as if she knew that, around her in that darkened room, decisions were being made that would affect her future.

Kate pushed her bicycle up the garden path, abandoning it against the side of the house with relief. It had been a long day and she was looking forward to having a hot bath – using the precious, last piece of their imported soap – and an early night.

Inside the house, Elizabeth had just finished feeding Henrietta. It amazed Kate how quickly the baby was growing. Not only in size but in character too. A smile here, a determined kick of a well-muscled leg there, all signs that she was no longer merely that little heartbeat of life that she had once been.

Kate sat down at the table and poured herself a cup of tea from the freshly brewed pot.

'What a day,' she said, stretching.

'Tired?'

'Absolutely bushed. What about you?' She glanced at Elizabeth who had put Henrietta across her shoulder and was patting the baby's back.

Elizabeth smiled. 'Actually I managed a nap this afternoon for once.'

'Well done.'

'Could still do with some more, though.'

'Not surprised,' said Kate. Henrietta had been particularly restless last night.

They turned at a tap at the front door.

Kate stood up. 'I'll go,' she said, walking through to the small hallway.

She pulled open the front door, letting in the waft of warm, scented frangipani. The garden was in darkness, but beyond the weak beam thrown out by the hallway light she could just discern a tall figure standing with his back to her.

He swung round at the sound of the door opening and as he stepped forward into the pool of light, she felt the breath leave her body.

'Alex!'

Her voice was little more than a whisper.

'When did you get here? How . . .' She couldn't believe it. He was here. Safe.

He stilled her questions with a kiss, drawing her into his arms and kissing her hungrily.

'God! I've missed you,' he said, tightening his hold on her.

She pressed her face into the fabric of his shirt, drawing in the breath of him. It still didn't seem possible that he was here, suddenly, after so long a silence.

After a moment, he released his tight hold on her and she stepped back a little. He was still as handsome as ever, but his face was older somehow, thinner. She sensed he had been through a lot since she'd last seen him in Rangoon. Later she would ask him about it, but not now. She didn't want to spoil the moment.

She moved her hand to catch hold of his. 'We ought to go in, I suppose. Elizabeth will be furious if I try and keep you all to myself. Besides . . .' She stopped, about to tell him about Henrietta, then decided it really ought to be Elizabeth's surprise.

'Besides what?' He tilted his head slightly, smiling curiously.

'Just wait and see,' she told him firmly, laughing as she led him in.

Elizabeth was already on her feet by the time they reached the drawing room, Henrietta bunched against one shoulder as she held out the other arm in greeting.

'Alex! This is *wonderful!*' she said, hugging him tightly. 'And this,' she went on, releasing him so that she could bring her baby proudly into full view, 'is Henrietta Anne Downing.'

Alex peered down at the baby, untucking the shawl slightly so that he could get a better look, examining her face closely.

'She's very like you,' he said gently after a while, smiling up at his sister. 'Going to break a few hearts when she's older.'

'She *is* beautiful, isn't she?'

'Very.'

'Do you want to hold her for a moment?'

'Please.' He took her carefully but by no means gingerly.

As if sensing the change of arms Henrietta stirred, opening her eyes for a moment and staring up at the stranger who now held her. He stroked her cheek with the back of his finger, talking to her softly, and Henrietta, having obviously summed Alex up to her satisfaction, nestled into the crook of his arm and smiled up at him contentedly.

'Your youngest conquest yet,' Elizabeth pronounced laughing. 'You haven't lost your touch, I see.'

'Girls are best at this age,' Alex told her with a grin. 'They don't argue.'

'Alex!' protested Kate. 'Any more of that and we won't ask you to stay for dinner.'

'Sadly, I can't anyway,' he said. Then, seeing their look of dismay: 'I have to meet someone for a drink later on.'

'Oh.' Kate tried to swallow her disappointment.

'Can't get out of it, I'm afraid. It's a chap called Calvert. Was up at Cambridge with me,' Alex explained, passing Henrietta back to Elizabeth. 'He used to run the Bush Warfare School up here, training British guerrillas for use in China. Now he's got other ideas about how to use his men. Wants me to meet another chap with the same notion.'

'If it was Mike Calvert I remember him well,' said Elizabeth, putting Henrietta back in her Moses basket and firmly tucking her in. 'Mad as a hatter. Are you sure you ought to be getting mixed up in some hare-brained scheme of his?'

'Using guerrillas is not hare-brained, Lizzie. And it's a damned shame the authorities don't recognise the fact,' said Alex forcefully. 'And because of their lack of interest it's been left to individuals, like Stevenson and Dickinson and Seagrim, who had to practically beg to stay behind, to try and form some sort of resistance behind the Japanese lines. God knows if they'll get proper support. God knows if they'll get equipment.'

Such was his passion that neither Kate nor Elizabeth spoke for a moment.

Alex had told Kate, once the war had broken out, that he'd been involved in some type of 'intelligence work' before the Japanese invasion, but she had thought that, since he seemed to be loosely attached to the army proper, when they retreated so would he.

Now she had her doubts and it frightened her.

'For goodness sake, Alex,' she said. 'You're not seriously thinking of staying on if the British army pull out, are you?'

'If I'm asked to, of course I will,' he returned calmly. 'That's why I'm meeting Calvert and this chap, Wingate, later. To see if I can be of any use to them.'

Kate looked helplessly at Elizabeth for support. 'But Alex, you've hardly any military training. It would be sheer madness to disappear behind the lines like that.'

'I've spent years with the Volunteers and Mike seemed to think that was sufficient,' he said tight-lipped. Actually Calvert had said that the only thing of importance was guts, endurance and determination and Alex knew he had plenty of those.

Kate watched him across the table. She felt him withdraw slightly from her, felt him let down a thin barrier. She couldn't pretend. She didn't want him to go with Wingate. In truth, she wanted him with her, safe, even perhaps coming out with them to India.

Now it seemed he was going to leave them in the lurch and disappear off on some scheme verging on insanity.

There was a tense silence. Elizabeth bent over the baby and made a great business of tucking her in again.

'Goodness Alex,' she said, straightening up, the tension leaving from her face. 'I quite forgot to tell you the good news. We heard from Martin.'

'Did you?' Alex stopped stirring his tea and glanced up at his sister, grateful for the change of conversation. 'That's wonderful. Did he manage to scrape through to Rangoon then?'

'Not Rangoon, no. The Karen Hills.'

'Even better.' Since Rangoon had fallen the Karen Hills

were safer by far. 'I expect quite a few of the stragglers will end up there now that the Japs have Lower Burma.'

Elizabeth fiddled with her teaspoon. 'I don't suppose many of them will manage to get as far as here then?' she asked Alex.

Kate knew where this was leading. She wanted to know what the chances were of Martin rejoining them in Maymyo.

Alex, it seemed, had the same thought. 'He's safer to stay put, Lizzie darling,' he said gently. 'And *you'd* be wiser by half to leave Maymyo while there's still time. The whole place is turning into a shambles.' Toungoo, Prome, Taungwingyi, all in chaos as far as the British were concerned.

'But . . .'

'Not buts, Lizzie. Honestly, you have little Henrietta to think of now. Martin can look after himself. She can't.'

Though his voice was muted there was a steeliness to it which made Kate realise that the situation was far worse than even she had imagined.

'You don't understand, Alex . . .' Elizabeth began.

'I do, Lizzie. But you've got to wake up to what's happening. Listen, Lizzie . . .'

In a low voice, almost as if he were speaking to a child, Alex began to explain the military position. He told her about the disastrous battle at Sittang Bridge, how the British hadn't been able to hold their position there, nor at Rangoon, nor at Prome. There was no doubt, he said, that slowly and relentlessly the Japanese were pushing their way up Burma and that nothing could stop them and nowhere would be safe.

'Not even Myitkyina?' Kate asked quietly. That was where she'd heard that the government would pull back to shortly. It was rumoured that the army would pull back there too, so that presumably the government and the refugees would be protected and could leave under the care of the troops if necessary.

'Myitkyina's far enough north to hold out for a while,' agreed Alex, 'but you've seen what the Jap Zero planes can do, Kate. My advice is, if you get an offer of a flight out, take it. And if you can't do that, then get your hands on as much petrol as possible so that you can leave pronto if the need arrives.'

Kate didn't dare tell Alex that Elizabeth had already been offered a flight from Shwebo a few weeks before, which she had determinedly turned down and as a result would hardly be offered another one.

She saw Alex glance at his watch.

'God, is that the time?' he said, standing up rapidly. 'I ought to be on my way to see this chap Wingate . . .'

'Already?' Elizabeth asked. 'We've hardly seen you.'

'I know, I'm sorry. But I can't keep Mike waiting. Apparently Wingate is due to fly out tomorrow and Mike seemed to think it pretty important that I should meet him. Quite a character, they say. Was in charge of taking Haile Selassie back to Ethiopian territory through the Italian lines. God! what a journey that must have been.'

Kate looked up at him. Once again she was conscious of that thin thread of excitement in his voice. She could feel the exuberant energy which lay just below the surface, the tide of purposeful vigour which was bubbling away simply waiting to break through.

He came over to kiss her, hesitating slightly, aware of the slight distance between them.

'I'm sorry, Kate,' he said, spreading his hands out in a helpless gesture. 'Look, if I can, I'll try to get back later on.'

'It's all right, I understand,' she said, desperately forcing a smile.

'I mean it, Kate,' he insisted again. 'I will try.'

He put his arms around her and she closed her eyes, trying to concentrate on the feeling of their enclosed warmth.

Even now she was aware that he was drifting away from her and that this new preoccupation had taken him into a world in which she had no part.

It was eleven o'clock and Alex had still not arrived.

Kate was conscious of the silence. Elizabeth had already gone to bed and Henrietta lay asleep in her Moses basket, her breathing slow and steady.

She stood up and went over to the window, pulling back the black-out curtain a whisker. She felt restless tonight, unsure of her ground. She had wanted to see Alex so badly all these months, but now his unexpected arrival had only served to spark off unforeseen tensions within her. She felt she was struggling in quicksand, desperate for firmer ground.

Outside a bat dipped in front of the window, turning and skimming off across the garden. Kate let the curtain fall back into place and returned to the sofa. She flung herself down and picked up a book.

A few minutes later she heard the sound of footsteps on the path and then a faint tap at the door.

'Alex?'

She pulled open the door hurriedly at his acknowledgement.

'Thank heavens, I was just beginning to worry about you . . .' she said.

'Sorry. It all took longer than I expected. Fascinating though.' He stepped into the lighted hallway. He looked bright-eyed with exhilaration, so strong it was almost tangible.

'Wingate was worth meeting then?' Kate asked.

'Absolutely.' Alex paused. It was difficult to describe

the man he'd just met. Though it was obvious he was not in great form physically, it didn't seem to matter. After only a few minutes Alex had been aware of Wingate's tremendous, driving spirit. With those intent staring eyes, that thin face and straggly beard, he had exuded the aura of a man of destiny. Alex was not in the least surprised that Mike Calvert had been so taken with him. He was so obviously an unconventional man and an unconventional soldier. A man, in short, whom anyone with half an ounce of adventure in his bones would long to follow.

Alex thought about telling Kate this, but instinct held him back. It would be difficult for her to understand that there was a dangerous undercurrent to the war that stimulated rather than made one afraid.

Kate, for her part, went over to the sofa and sat down, drawing her legs up underneath her.

'So does this mean you'll be joining Calvert then?' she asked slowly.

'Yes.' Again she felt him drawing back from her. 'It's more or less agreed.'

'I see.' Kate wished she could show more enthusiasm but a great weight seemed to be pressing down upon her. 'Do you know when?'

Alex shook his head. 'Not exactly, no. There are a few things to be sorted out yet.' He came to sit beside her, sliding his arm around her shoulders. 'Kate, I have to do this. Try and understand.'

'I am. It's just . . .'

She hesitated. How could she explain, when she barely understood her emotions herself?

Alex took her face between his hands and began to kiss her, gently at first, then more urgently, his fingers teasing open the buttons of her dress.

'Kate . . .' He breathed out her name on a sigh.

Unresisting, she allowed him to slowly undress her. He

bent over her, his mouth moving along the line of her thin white body. At his touch every nerve in her body fluttered in response. All these months she had longed for him, longed to feel him deep inside her, possessing her. Now, as his face hovered over hers, every part of her responded, pliant and willing under his touch.

Afterwards, though, lying in his arms, a succession of conflicting emotions tumbled through her. She had wanted him to make love to her, but she had wanted reassurance too. To feel the sense of emotional closeness as well as the physical. Somehow, tonight, that had eluded her.

'Alex?'

He turned towards her drowsily. His dark hair fell across his forehead and he pushed it back with an unhurried gesture.

'Have you any idea how long you'll be in Maymyo?'

He propped himself up on his elbow. 'No, not yet. Calvert seemed to be quite keen on getting my papers through as fast as possible. Seems there's a chance of getting a unit into action quite soon.'

'I see.' Kate felt apprehension slide into her stomach and settle. 'Alex, you will be careful, won't you?'

'Of course.' He took her hand. 'Listen, Calvert is far more careful than Lizzie gives him credit for. I can tell you, having been with the army proper when they were in retreat over the Sittang, I would sooner put in my lot with Mike than with a bunch of indecisive old generals any day. He knows his stuff and he's competent as hell. When I went with him on a couple of incursions earlier on this week he was tremendous.'

Kate looked across at him. 'What do you mean earlier this week?' she asked, a sudden cold premonition sweeping through her. 'I thought you'd only arrived here today.'

'No, Tuesday. As soon as I got here I met up with Mike,' he said, his eyes flicking over her, his voice matter of fact.

Kate felt herself stiffen slightly. She had craved Alex's presence so deeply these past few months that she would have moved mountains in order to see him. She had naïvely assumed he'd shared that longing.

Now she saw that she and Alex approached this affair from entirely different positions.

'Kate?'

She glanced up to see him looking across at her, a frown furrowing his brow.

'What is it?' he asked.

She gave a helpless shrug. 'I had no idea you were here in Maymyo,' she said, unable to keep the disillusionment from her voice. 'No idea you were even *safe*.' A niggling worm of discontent threaded its way through her emotions.

'Look, I'm sorry,' he said. 'But be fair. There's a war on, you know.'

There was a silence. In the next door room Kate could hear Henrietta's muffled sighs.

Alex spread his hands out in a helpless gesture. 'I don't understand what you expect from me.'

'I can see that,' Kate said bitingly. 'And what exactly do you expect of me, Alex? That you can just turn up and I'll take you into my bed whenever you feel like it.'

'For heaven's sake, Kate.'

'Well, isn't it that way, Alex? You go off on your little adventures and leave me behind to pick up the pieces.'

'You're being bloody unreasonable,' he threw back at her, furiously. 'They're hardly little adventures, as you so call them, Kate. For God's sake, don't you know what's happening out there?'

She pushed back her hair, tight-lipped. 'Of course I do.'

'Well then.'

She knew now what this was all about, this sudden anger

of hers. Commitment. Or rather lack of it. That though she was sleeping with Alex he had never once made any mention of a shared future. Nor was he likely to. She had thought it was the war that had come between them. Now she wasn't so sure that was the true cause.

Beside her Alex sat up, aware of the abyss deepening between them.

'You're such a child, Kate. Love isn't all hearts and flowers,' he said. 'And you can't always keep trying to put it into neat little boxes.'

'I don't ever do that,' she said, rebelling against his words. 'That's not fair.'

'Oh, but you do,' he contradicted. 'Your idea of love is to keep a kind of balance sheet. If I love you then I must be loved equally in return,' Alex smiled wearily. 'Love isn't like that. It's about taking risks. It's about *trust*. Somehow you don't seem to see that.'

'Because, so far, taking risks hasn't exactly had the best results,' she threw back, bristling at his gall. 'First there was Johnnie, and then . . .'

'Sod Johnnie!' Alex said fiercely. He swung his legs over the edge of the bed. 'That was then, this is now, Kate. Let it go, before it suffocates you.' He glared at her, his green eyes flint-edged. 'Stop weighing the pros and cons all the time. Take a few chances.'

'That's easy for you to say,' she said, leaning forward to hug her drawn-up knees. 'You haven't so much to lose.'

Alex stood up and started to dress. 'So what exactly are you saying?' he asked fiercely, buttoning up his shirt. 'Do you want to end all this? Is this what we've been leading up to?'

For a moment Kate didn't speak. She couldn't believe that Alex had so misunderstood her. She desperately wanted more from him, not less. Perhaps it was just a symptom of their deteriorating relationship that he could have so failed to have grasped the truth.

Alex leant against the doorway, arms folded. 'Well, Kate? I need to know where I stand, too,' he said, fighting to keep his wrath in check. 'What exactly do you want? For me to make promises I'm not sure I can keep?'

She struggled to keep her composure. 'You don't even begin to understand, do you?' she said bitterly.

'Obviously not.' He thrust his hands deep into his pockets. 'And I'm beginning to think that whatever it is you want, I can't give you.'

Kate couldn't look at him. 'I'm beginning to think so, too.'

He let out an exasperated sigh. 'I thought I knew you, Kate. I see I was wrong.' His dark face was tight with anger. 'I was under the impression we had something worth trying for.'

There was a moment's silence.

'God!' he said savagely. 'You're a bloody fool, Kate.'

His words were like a lighted match thrown into a box of fireworks.

Kate swung round to face him, eyes blazing. 'How *dare* you speak to me like that?' she shouted, a great tidal wave of emotion sweeping across her. 'Just go, why don't you, Alex? Go on, get out of here.'

'Kate . . .' He took a step towards her.

She put up a shaking hand to stop him. 'Just go, Alex. For God's sake, leave.'

'Is that what you really want, Kate?'

'That's what I want, yes.'

'Then it's over?'

She didn't speak for a moment and when she did, it was barely above a whisper. 'Yes, Alex. It's over.'

He stood for a second looking down at her, then without another word he turned abruptly on his heels and left.

She heard the sound of his footsteps receding across the drawing room to the hall, the sharp click of the door being opened and shut, then nothing. He had gone.

Silence filled the house.

She desperately wanted to run after him, to call him back, but she knew it would be pointless. Alex wouldn't change. Nothing would. It would only prolong the agony.

It was over.

She sunk her head against her knees, the tears which had threatened all evening starting to fall. She sat there, rocking backwards and forwards, sobbing quietly.

'Kate? What's wrong? What is it?'

She bit back her tears and lifted her head to see Elizabeth standing barefoot beside the bed, her white cotton nightgown glimmering in the darkness like moonlight on water.

'Where's Alex?' Elizabeth asked, coming to sit on the edge of the bed. 'I thought I heard him . . .'

'He's gone.'

Something in Kate's voice made Elizabeth aware of the seriousness of this statement. She waited.

'It's finished between us, Elizabeth.'

'Kate, why?' Elizabeth's anguish was genuine.

'I just knew it wasn't going to work between us, that's all.'

'Oh, Kate.' Elizabeth knew there was no point in recriminations. Kate had always been one to see everything purely in terms of black and white. And yet . . . 'Oh, Kate, what have you done?'

'Done? I've extracted myself from a relationship that was leading me nowhere, that's what I've done,' said Kate in a voice which defied criticism.

'And now?'

Kate gave a short, over-bright laugh. 'Now I can get on with the rest of my life.'

'But Kate . . .'

Kate turned to face her. 'Don't say a word, Elizabeth,' she said. She felt too fragile to listen to Elizabeth taking Alex's part in this matter. 'Please, just don't say a word. It was leading *nowhere*, don't you understand? I had to end it. And I've made the right decision, I know I have.'

Yet even as she spoke she could hear the bleak hollowness of her own voice.

## 18

'*A*re we packed?'

'Almost. Just the last few things of Henrietta's to squeeze in.'

Kate took one final look around the drawing room. She had no regrets about leaving this place. Maymyo might be pleasant enough with its hills and clement climate, but to her it would only serve to remind her of one thing: that last embittered meeting with Alex.

She went through to the shuttered bedroom and snapped shut her suitcase, fastening the leather straps tightly. The two meagre bags lying on top of the bed were all she had left now. With each step they took on the path out of Burma, her possessions grew smaller and smaller. She wondered how much she'd have left by the time they finally reached India.

A crash from the drawing room made her look up.

'You all right, Elizabeth?'

'Fine. Rather a lot of stuff, that's all. Hope it all fits in.'

Kate came out into the drawing room to find Elizabeth surrounded by a mountain of baggage, to rival Mount Everest.

'Goodness,' she remarked with a grin, 'we have been strong-minded about cutting down to bare essentials, haven't we?'

Elizabeth made a face. 'Honestly, none of it's mine,' she protested. 'It's all Henrietta's stuff. All absolutely crucial.'

'Like three teddybears?' Kate enquired ruthlessly.

'Oh, but Kate! You know how much she adores the one with the tartan ribbon, and the little brown one with the funny ears she can't sleep without . . .'

Kate laughed. 'Really, Elizabeth, you're impossible. Too sentimental by half. All I can say is, I'm jolly glad we're not thinking of leaving by plane. You're only allowed three pounds of luggage then and they positively won't let you come on board with even half an ounce more.'

'I hope Dick Ferris won't make the same stipulations,' Elizabeth said, going to her bedroom to bring through the last of her bags. 'It does look rather a lot, I admit.'

'I doubt Dick will say anything,' Kate reassured her. 'His wife's even worse than you. He was telling me yesterday that he's going to attach a trailer to his car to accommodate all Pam's luggage. They've been here for so long, that's the trouble. Collected so much.'

'I can imagine.' Elizabeth tried not to think about the precious belongings that they themselves had left behind in Rangoon.

'Anyway, I'm glad they're going to travel in convoy with us,' Kate went on. 'Makes me feel just that little bit less vulnerable. I'm pretty useless when it comes to the inside of cars. Just about manage to change a tyre, but that's about it.' She sat down on the sofa stretching out her legs. At least Dick had persuaded some army mechanic to have a good look over both vehicles, so hopefully that shortcoming would not be put to the test.

'There, that's the last of it.' Elizabeth re-arranged the trio of teddies on top of the pile and came to sit beside Kate on the sofa. 'When did Dick say we'd be leaving?'

'In about half an hour,' Kate replied. 'We should start to pack the rest of the things into the car, I suppose. You'd better tell me what you'll need for Henrietta so I can put it somewhere that's easily accessible.'

'Consider it done.' Elizabeth stood up and began hastily to sort through her bags. 'Really it's only these two that matter. Oh, and perhaps this one . . .'

In twenty minutes the old Buick was packed and loaded. Dick Ferris had already stowed the petrol and water in the boot for them and it only remained for Kate and Elizabeth to put in their personal belongings, the boxes of food and the tent and bedding.

The pale grey and pink light of early morning was hardening as Elizabeth carefully carried out the Moses basket and placed it in the back seat. She stood, looking back at the house, white-faced and silent. Kate knew she was thinking of Martin.

'Ready?' she asked gently.

Elizabeth nodded. With one last look across the hills she climbed into the front of the car beside Kate.

Next door, Dick Ferris was squeezing his short bulky frame into the driver's seat ready for the long journey. A taciturn man at the best of times he had no wish to talk now. He had loved Burma and like his wife, Pam, was leaving with only regret.

'All set?' he asked his wife.

Beside him, Pam blew her nose briskly. The worst of it all had been saying goodbye to the other VADs at the Hospital. In a short time they had all become the closest of friends, and she couldn't bear to think of Meisha and some of the others staying on without her. But, as Dick had pointed out to her, her health was not robust enough to risk staying to the bitter end and she didn't want to end up being a burden to anyone.

Kate saw Dick edge his car out of the driveway and, starting up the Buick, followed him out down the Mandalay road. Gradually the neat little houses of Maymyo, the polo ground and the club, fell behind them as they began their descent to the plains below.

'It's going to be hot,' said Elizabeth, winding down the window to let in the breeze. She'd become used to Maymyo's equable climate and every mile seemed to take her closer to the searing heat of the plains. 'I hope Henrietta will cope.'

'Of course she will,' said Kate, glancing over her shoulder to where Henrietta still lay sleeping peacefully. 'She's a third generation Burma baby. Old trooper.'

'Well, as long as she doesn't take after my mother,' returned Elizabeth with a wry smile, remembering how Joan had always complained bitterly about the heat. She hadn't seen her since before her father's death. It was strange to think that they were soon to meet up again, that India was now to be their home for a while.

They were making good time. The twisting roads were not nearly as crowded as Kate had expected them to be. Occasionally they would see a Chinese deserter or two scurrying up the hill in the hope of reaching China, but the bulk of the refugees from Rangoon were at Taungup or waiting in camps south of Mandalay.

It was as they were halfway down the hill to Mandalay that they heard the distant drone of planes. A wave of bombers appeared in the distance, flying low on their way to the city.

Dick stuck his head out of his window. 'Take cover!' he shouted frantically.

Quickly they pulled off the road into the safety of a wayside village which lay just ahead. Camouflaged by bamboos they sat there, waiting, as the planes flew down towards the city. Then the steady crump of bombs filled the air.

'Poor Mandalay,' said Kate grimly. 'Getting a pounding by the sound of it.' She couldn't bear to think of that lovely city with its beautiful old palace being systematically destroyed. Her memories of that place were of happier times.

'Do you think this is what our journey is going to be like all the way?' asked Elizabeth quietly. Instinctively she glanced over her shoulder at the Moses basket.

'I'm sure it won't,' Kate assured her. 'Our bad timing, that's all.' At least she hoped to heaven that she was right. Apart from the sheer danger of it all, it would double the time of the journey and she wasn't sure about whether they had enough supplies.

It was early afternoon by the time they eventually drove into Mandalay. The raid had long since finished but the acrid smoke of the smouldering buildings still hung across the city. The bombing had been heavy, the damage immense, especially to the business and shipping area. For Kate the saddest moment of all was driving past the old palace and seeing the moat brimming with floating dead bodies.

'Nothing will ever be the same again,' said Elizabeth sorrowfully, looking about her at the ruined city. 'It breaks my heart to see such ruthless destruction.'

They drove slowly on through the city and out towards the Ava Bridge. It wasn't just the morbid sight of the city which kept them moving, it was Dick's well-timed reminder that the refugee camps close by were rife with cholera.

'Five hundred dying a day of it, so they say,' said Pam grimly. Which, she supposed, was hardly surprising when they'd had no sanitation, no order, no burning of litter.

'So,' said Dick, ushering them firmly back into the cars after they'd taken a short, well earned break to stretch their legs, 'if we can just get to Sagaing, it should just put us clear a bit.'

Out beyond Mandalay a steady procession of people was trooping along the dust-choked road. Some were on bicycles, some in bullock-carts, some even in rickshaws, all moving relentlessly on, ignoring the cars and trucks blaring their horns as they tried to push through. The raid earlier that day had prompted a mass exodus from the camps, and now it seemed no one could persuade them to turn back.

Kate had been shocked by their numbers. As far as the eye could see there was a line of women with children on their backs and their worldly goods on their heads, children pushing handcarts, families clinging on top of laden, lumbering buffalo-carts, all clotting the road, ploughing purposefully on through the dust.

'This is ghastly,' said Elizabeth, carefully winding up her window to keep out the thick dust which rose about them like sulphur smoke. 'I suppose this is practically the only road out?'

'Yes, I'm afraid it is.' Kate didn't like to tell her that Dick Ferris had warned her that this stretch of road was one of the best they would travel on.

By late afternoon they seemed to have succeeded in pushing ahead of the main column of refugees. They managed to pick up a bit of speed, despite the potholes and bumps, though Kate found the glare of the sun blinding at times. It burnt ferociously down through the gullies and the trees, the harsh light shining back at them with sharp intensity.

At about six o'clock they decided to pull over and set up camp for the night. They were all tired and Henrietta, who'd been impeccably behaved for most of the journey, had become restless and fretful.

'Poor little thing doesn't know where she is,' soothed Elizabeth, taking her in her arms. 'Actually,' she said, looking at Kate, 'nor do I exactly.'

So on request Dick got out the linen map, while they had supper, and showed them the route which they were about to take. No one knew exactly how much of the road from India to Tamu had been built yet, but Dick insisted that there would be suitable fair weather tracks most of the way.

'We should be all right,' he said, carefully getting out his calipers to measure the distance. 'Bang on schedule if we're going to do the journey in a week . . .'

He ran his hand through his grey short-cropped hair, still looking down at the map, frowning. It was hard to tell the precise distances of these mountainous areas though, the contours made it so deceptive. What looked like only a mile or so on the map might be several in reality.

All he knew was, he was relieved beyond measure that they had managed to get going before the rains came. Then all the little gullies and streams which crisscrossed the tracks would be impassable and heaven only knew what would happen to the refugees who had fallen behind.

They settled down for the night in their tents, mosquito nets pegged into place. Kate lay tucked under her blankets, watching the shining orange pool of light from the Ferris' hurricane lamp flittering in the darkness like some huge, exotic moth.

'This reminds me of when I was younger and used to go up on camping trips with my father,' she said, watching Elizabeth position Henrietta beside her. 'After Mother died, we used to often travel to the Cameron Hills. Just the two of us.'

There was a silence. Outside in the night they could hear the distant sound of jackals crying.

'Have you heard anything from him, yet?' Elizabeth asked. She sounded a little cautious for she thought she knew the answer.

'No, not since the fall of Singapore,' said Kate. 'The trouble is the authorities will probably only let Sylvia know if he's . . . if he's alive and I doubt she'll bother to let me know.'

'Oh, surely not!'

Kate gave a light shrug. Elizabeth credited everyone with too much benevolence. 'Anyway now she won't even know where to write and I've no idea of her whereabouts either. When Daddy last wrote, all he said was she was about to return to Australia. Perth, I suppose.'

'At least it means Louisa is safe.'

Kate glanced across at Henrietta, lying on her back in the Moses basket, kicking her legs contentedly. 'I know. It wouldn't be much fun for a little one being held by the Japanese, would it?'

'No fun for anyone, full stop,' declared Elizabeth bluntly. 'In a way . . .' She paused, looking down at her hands suddenly, and cleared her throat. 'In a way, I'm glad Daddy died at Anapuri. He couldn't have borne to have left the place, you know, and he couldn't have borne to have been captured. Maybe if Mummy had managed to persuade him to come up to Rangoon . . .'

'You mustn't blame her, Elizabeth,' said Kate gently. 'No one was able to cajole your father into doing anything he didn't want to. And look, she didn't even manage to persuade you to leave, did she? Too stubborn, that's the trouble with you Staveleys.'

'I know. Alex always said that. Said it was both our strength and our weakness.' Elizabeth paused, glancing across at Kate with slight embarrassment. She'd been careful to avoid talking about her brother since that fateful evening.

Kate said nothing, rolling onto her side. The tough, practical side of her had determined to erase Alex from her consciousness since their quarrel, but it had been far from easy.

She hadn't realised how deeply enmeshed in her life he had become. Little things, snippets from songs, the sweet wafting smell of cheroots, even Henrietta whose dark eyes and wide mouth at times looked remarkably like Alex's, conspired to remind her painfully of him.

She closed her eyes, resolutely shutting out his image.

She pulled the thin blanket up under her chin, concentrating instead on the velvety blackness of the night and the low steady tramp of the refugees, which even now still echoed across to her from the moonlit road beyond.

Waking in the morning, Kate came out of her tent to discover that Dick Ferris had already gathered a bundle of dry wood and had started a fire for their breakfast.

'Did you manage to sleep at all?' he asked convivially as she joined him.

'A little.' She couldn't admit to more. She stretched. 'What about you?'

Dick crouched over the fire, adjusting the kettle on its wire sling. 'Not too bad. Pam had a rotten night, though. Beastly headache.'

'Not surprised. It was a terrible shock coming down from Maymyo into that dreadful heat.'

'She usually copes admirably with that,' he said, with a light shrug. 'Anyway, I've left her sleeping now.'

'Do her the world of good,' agreed Kate. She turned to glance back across the hard-baked paddy field to her own tent pitched under the trees. Neither Elizabeth nor Henrietta had stirred yet either.

Kate took the steaming cup of tea which Dick was holding out to her. Neither of them spoke. Dick, Kate knew, liked a peaceful start to the day. It was Pam who was the gregarious one of the pair.

Beyond them, on the road, the steady tramp of refugees continued, the faint haze of reddish dust rising like a plume. It seemed to Kate that the long column never rested and, like Hamlet's ghost, was destined to walk restlessly on for ever.

There was a snuffling cry from the tent and a few minutes later Elizabeth appeared clutching Henrietta in her arms.

'Come and have some tea,' called out Kate.

'In a minute. Just going to change Henrietta first,' said Elizabeth, adjusting her daughter onto her shoulder. 'Need some of her things from the car, though.'

Now that everyone was stirring, Kate started to prepare breakfast. She opened the foodbox and had just taken out the bread, ready to cut it into thin slices, when a cry rang out across the stubbled rice field and, looking up, she saw Elizabeth stumbling back towards them.

'My God! What is it?' She was on her feet and running towards Elizabeth in seconds.

Elizabeth fell into her arms, shivering.

'Elizabeth, what happened? Tell me.' She tightened her arms about Elizabeth, while Henrietta, held too tensely in her mother's arms, burst into tears too, arms and legs rigid with fright.

'By the car . . .'

Elizabeth's voice was hardly audible.

'What?'

For a moment Elizabeth couldn't speak, then she whispered: 'He was . . . dead, Kate. I went to the car and there he was.'

Kate tensed. 'Who? Who was dead?'

Kate felt her shudder again in her arms.

'An old man. One of the refugees,' said Elizabeth, swallowing hard. 'Just lying on the side of the road, close to the car. No one stopping. No one caring. Oh God, Kate, and the worst of it all is that he must have died during the night, not more than a few yards from where we were sleeping. And we didn't know. And we didn't even *know*.'

Behind them Dick cleared his throat. 'Too old to make the journey, poor fellow,' he said. 'Beats me how some

of them have got as far as this from Rangoon . . .'
He stood for a moment, watching them, then thrust his
hands into his pockets uneasily. 'I'll just go and see if
there's anything I can do,' he mumbled uncomfortably.
He was starting to realise that this journey would be
about the survival of the fittest.

Kate watched him walk across the cropless rice paddy
towards the cars. Against the tree under which they'd
parked she could just detect the hunched outline of the old
Indian, see the wizened, skeletal body lying on its side.

Elizabeth was right. How had they missed him so close
to their camp?

Hurriedly she turned back, concentrating on the fire.
But when Dick returned, shoulders bent and head hung
down, she knew by his face that what they had witnessed
here today was only just the beginning.

A long drawn-out tragedy was in progress. And like it
or not, they were now part of it.


By midday it was clear to Dick Ferris that his wife was
not at all well. They had been travelling for several hours
and, despite the searing heat which pressed like a dense
wall against the windows of the car, Pam was shivering.

He glanced at her. She was sitting with her thin body
twisted round so that her head could rest against the
inside of the door. Her eyes were closed and, except
for the two bright pink spots on her cheeks, her face
was deathly pale.

As the car jolted over a bump in the road, he saw her
wince slightly, tightening up her eyes against the pain.

'Look, old girl, do you want to stop for a while?' he
asked with concern.

She shook her head, grimacing with the effort. 'I'll be
all right.'

'Sure?'

This time, though, she did not answer. Beads of perspiration had gathered on her upper lip like pearls of dew and Dick felt a knot of alarm tighten his stomach.

'Actually, I think we could all do with a break,' he said, trying to keep a lightness to his voice he didn't feel. 'It's like a toaster in this wretched car. Do us no harm to make an early stop for lunch.'

He didn't consult her further. With a quick wave to Kate to show what he intended to do, he pulled off the road at the next suitable spot.

He drew up under the thick shade of the trees close to a sandy banked river. Pam's eyes opened the merest slit as the car stopped and the shadows of the trees brought sudden cool relief, but she made no attempt to move.

Dick stretched out and pushed back her thin dark hair from her forehead, putting his hand against her brow. It was hot to the touch, confirming his worst fears.

'Headache still bad?' he asked gently.

She nodded.

'Not feeling sick, though?'

'Only a bit. It's the heat, Dick.'

It wasn't that, though. He knew that now with a dreadful certainty.

'Don't look so worried.'

He turned to see her smiling wanly at him. Typical of her to try and deflect his concern, he thought. Pam had always been like that. Brisk and efficient, she was one of those no-nonsense people who coped indefatigably with whatever life hurled her way. She had been ideally suited to working as a VAD and he hadn't been in the least surprised at how much she had enjoyed being at the Military Hospital, where her organising skills had been given full rein.

'Honestly, Dick, I expect it's just the upset of leaving Maymyo,' she said.

He knew she was trying not to show him what an effort it was for her to talk.

'Perhaps. But I still think we should try and find a doctor for you all the same.'

'Such a bother.'

'Nonsense. There was a village a short way back, we could try there. And if that fails there's always Shwebo.'

'But that's miles away.'

'Not really. We'll be against the tide of refugees, remember? It'll be much quicker.'

The mere fact that she didn't argue with him told him that she was feeling far worse than she was letting on. He knew then that, whatever time was lost, he would take her straight down to Shwebo to the hospital there. Thirty years in the tropics had taught him that mild fevers had a notorious habit of developing into something more serious with frightening rapidity.

He pushed open the door of the car and got out. Kate and Elizabeth had taken the opportunity to stretch their legs and had walked down to the water.

He walked down the hill towards the little stream, watching the two girls as they stood at the water's edge cooling their feet. Further along the bank two bullocks were being watered and a group of Indians sat squatting by a fire cooking rice.

'How's Pam?' asked Kate as Dick approached them.

'Not terribly good, I'm afraid. I rather think we'll have to go back to Shwebo.'

'Shwebo?'

'Heavens!'

He could hear the surprise in their voices.

'Yes. I think it would be safer,' he explained. 'I'd rather not take any risks, you see. Pam wasn't terribly well before we left.' If it hadn't been for that he might have tried to keep moving on towards India, but since her illness

Pam had never quite recovered her full strength and he wasn't prepared to take any risks.

'Of course, we understand,' said Elizabeth.

Dick paused. He could see that neither of the girls fully understood the implications of his statement.

'The thing is,' he went on, thrusting his hands into his pockets a little awkwardly, 'the thing is, I'm not sure how advisable it is for you to come back with us. I think you ought to push on now you've got this far.'

'Without you?' That was Kate.

'Without us, yes.'

There was a short sharp silence. He could tell they were shocked but it was imperative to be honest with them. The more he thought about it the more he was convinced his decision was correct. 'I don't want to endanger any of you by making you go back on your tracks,' he said. 'Besides anything else you've got Henrietta to think about. The sooner you get her to India the better.'

He could see they knew it made sense. The dangers of going on alone were small compared to those of risking meeting the Japanese.

'The route should be pretty clear,' he went on, 'fair weather tracks straight through to the Tamu Pass. You've got to make sure you keep up your supply of water, that's all.'

He saw the girls exchange apprehensive glances, but in remembering the dead old Indian man, his resolve stiffened.

Pam was his main concern. Kate and Elizabeth would be safe enough.

'If you come back to the car, we'll sort out a few things now,' he said. 'And if you like, Kate, I'll give you a quick maintenance course for the car. Just a little matter of cleaning the plugs from time to time, checking the tyre pressures, that sort of thing.'

Kate and Elizabeth followed him back to the cars.
Overhead a huge black crow circled, calling in its harsh
tone, a scavenger on the hunt for pickings.

Dick glanced inside his car. Pam had not improved.
He was glad he had made his decision. He could be at
Shwebo by late this evening.

He began to unpack the car, taking out some of the
petrol and water and rearranging them onto the light
bamboo trailer which he had uncoupled from his own
car and attached to Elizabeth's.

'This should help a bit,' he said. 'I've given you a few
more supplies as well.'

'Won't you need them?' asked Elizabeth.

'No. We can stock up again if needs be. Besides . . .'
He gave a small shrug. It seemed unlikely that they'd
attempt this journey again. He would make sure Pam, at
least, was put on one of the planes out. She'd probably
be considered a priority case now anyway.

A short while later Dick had sorted everything out and
they were ready to go their separate ways.

'We'll see you in India,' Elizabeth called out to him
cheerfully, as he climbed into his car. 'The Great Eastern
in Calcutta for a lime juice and ice.'

'Or back in Maymyo when it's all over,' he rejoined
with a confident wave of his hand. 'A stengah at the
club.'

He waited until Kate and Elizabeth had turned back
onto the road, then slipped the car into first gear, edging
it slowly forward. As he cut across the seething mass of
refugees he was aware of his sense of isolation, the sole
car heading back along the bustling line.

He turned to look behind him. Kate and Elizabeth were
already out of sight, lost in a great plume of dust.

A Chevrolet with an Englishman at the wheel swept
past on the other side of the road.

'You're going the wrong way!' he shouted with an amused, frantic signal at Dick as he passed.

And though Dick laughed and waved back cheerfully enough, he couldn't help but feel that the fellow might just, in fact, be right.

## 19

*T*he track from Ye-U to Shwegyin had been treacherous. It was narrow, twisting and intersected by
numerous dry, sandy *chaungs* which threatened to bog
down the car.

Now, exhausted by the sheer strain of the drive, Kate
and Elizabeth were waiting to cross the River Chindwin. It
was about six hundred yards wide here and swift-flowing,
and in the absence of a bridge the only means of crossing
it was by ferry.

There'd been some sort of delay the previous day and by
the time Kate and Elizabeth arrived late in the afternoon,
crowds of refugees had already begun to congeal along the
river banks, waiting to be taken across. Some had been
waiting for days, and the stench of death and sickness
hung in the air.

'Is there nowhere else to cross?' Elizabeth asked Kate,
holding Henrietta protectively to her, appalled by what
she could see.

'There isn't, no,' Kate returned bluntly. 'Not unless
you want to abandon the car.'

'Which I don't.'

'Then there's no alternative but to wait, I'm afraid.'

'Damn.'

Henrietta began to grizzle. She was flushed and had
red pimples on her arms and neck and face, prickly heat
caused by the sweltering temperature in the car over the
past few days.

Elizabeth put her against her shoulder and patted her

back, talking to her in a soft comforting voice. The effect of calming her daughter gradually soothed her as well.

Kate stirred. 'Do you want some tea?' she asked after a moment.

'If we've time. But doesn't it look as if things are moving at last?'

Kate glanced down the steep hill to the jetty below. The traffic of refugees was forging ahead again. Several small boats and bamboo rafts had appeared from nowhere to help ease the congestion, and now the little groups of families who had been sitting with such infinite patience, resigned not to get across until the next day, started to stir hopefully. They hung over the glassy shallows in the afternoon sunlight like a multi-coloured haze, several splashing forward into the water in their eagerness to be on their way.

'You're right,' said Kate. 'Perhaps we might even have a chance of getting across tonight ourselves.'

'Be wonderful if we could,' agreed Elizabeth.

'Wouldn't it?' Kate leant on the warm bonnet of the car watching the rafts and boats being loaded. 'I'm tired of this travelling business. I just want to get to India.'

Elizabeth gave a heartfelt sigh. She hadn't quite realised how bad the roads would be. 'So do I.'

Kate stretched. 'I wonder how Dick is doing,' she remarked. She still hadn't got used to not seeing the familiar, reassuring sight of their car up ahead. 'I hope Pam's tucked up in some hospital bed by now.'

'Sure to be,' said Elizabeth. 'Though I must say, I'm glad we pushed on. I was talking to an English couple when we first arrived and they were saying that they'd heard that Yenangyaung has gone . . .'

'There are always such rumours though, aren't there?' Kate remarked. She'd heard dozens during these past few days, the most frightening being that cholera and typhoid were pursuing them up the lines far faster than any Japanese. 'One can't believe them all.'

'I suppose not.' Elizabeth bent down, concentrating on changing Henrietta on the back seat. 'Anyway, I sort of feel that once we cross the Chindwin we're more than halfway there. And the road on the other side can't be as bad as this one, can it?'

'*Nothing* can be worse than the road we've just been on, surely?' laughed Kate.

But by early the next morning they discovered they had been wrong.

The so-called 'road' to Tamu was barely more than a narrow sandy jungle track, infinitely more difficult to negotiate. It was imperative to keep a slow steady pace. It was all too easy to send the car into a skid on the soft surface or to make the wheels lose their fragile grip and to set them spinning uselessly.

'Is it going to be like this all the way?' Elizabeth asked Kate on the second day.

'Probably.' Once they reached Tamu it would get easier, but that was still fifty miles or so away. 'Dick said they were supposed to be improving the road, but I assume they didn't have time. He was right about one thing, though: if we're finding the going arduous now, heaven knows what it will be like when the monsoons start.'

Outside a flock of green parakeets burst up from the thick sunless trees which bordered the track. The countryside had changed now. They had left the friendly looking villages with their palm-thatched huts and terraced rice paddies, and were climbing ever upwards into the high, inhospitable jungle.

Up ahead Kate saw two lumbering bullock-carts blocking the road. They were loaded high with bundles, on top of which were piled numerous small children. Strung out behind them for about fifty yards trailed a straggling mass of people, presumably the rest of the party.

Kate slowed down, for the track had narrowed to such a degree it would be almost impossible to pass unless the carts pulled in closely. She gave a quick toot of the horn, afraid that unless they moved over she would be forced to a virtual standstill. At the last minute the bullock-carts edged in and Kate managed to ease the car past.

Elizabeth glanced at her without comment. Kate heard her let out her breath.

'Sorry, a bit close, wasn't it?'

'A bit. Though I can't see there's any other way. The road's simply too narrow.'

And it was becoming increasingly more so, thought Kate observing how the road ahead wound tightly on between the densely treed hills.

At the next corner, as she swerved to avoid an old woman stumbling along in the centre of the track, the car hit a submerged rock, bouncing up into the air like a jack-in-the-box. Kate felt the wheel of the car turn in her hand and the next moment they were plunging across the road with frightening speed. Kate swung the wheel sharply back again, the car skidded and then stopped, bogged down in one of the seemingly bottomless pockets of sand which dotted the road.

'Damn.' Kate put the car into reverse then pushed it into first gear again, revving the engine, hoping to edge out, but this time the car stuck fast.

They both got out and stared dismally down at the bogged wheels.

'Do you think we could push it out?' asked Elizabeth.

'We'd have to unload all our luggage, I think. And even then I'm not sure we'd be strong enough. What we really need is something to stick under the wheels to give them more grip.'

'Bamboo,' said Elizabeth suddenly. 'Once when I was with Alex on one of our treks he used poles of bamboo under the wheels when we were stuck.'

'Bamboo might work,' said Kate, a little peeved that the idea had been Alex's. 'It's worth a try, I suppose.'

An hour later, dripping with sweat, they had at last succeeded in getting the car out. They started on their journey again, dust-covered, tired and exhausted, and in no mood to discover that the two bullock-carts they had been at such pains to pass earlier on that day were now in front of them again.

At the next small village they came to they decided to stop for a wash and some much-needed tea. It was late afternoon now and the pungent smell of charcoal fires hung in the air as little groups of refugees pulled in off the track for the night. Families were busy setting up camp, tying up their weary dust-covered bullocks, and gathering wood for their fires.

Kate got out of the car. There was a touch of coolness to the air, drifting down from the higher hills. She supposed it meant that they were nearing the top of the pass and the thought gave her comfort. Perhaps India was not as far away as she had imagined.

Kate turned to Elizabeth who was busily feeding a hot and irritated Henrietta.

'Do you think we might as well set up camp now?' she asked. 'I'm not sure it's worth pushing on. It will be dark in an hour or so anyway.'

'I was going to suggest the same thing,' admitted Elizabeth, readjusting her position slightly to look at Kate. 'Henrietta's just about had enough of travelling today. Poor little mite's had her fill of being constantly jolted about in the back of the car.'

'Unanimous decision, then,' said Kate with a grin. 'I'll go and find some wood and then we can get the fire started.

I think it may get quite cold tonight.'

By the time she got back Elizabeth had finished feeding Henrietta and was holding a calm and contented daughter against her shoulder.

Kate started to build the fire and as she did so she noticed two small wide-eyed Indian children of about six and seven standing quietly in the background.

She nodded in their direction to Elizabeth. 'You've got admirers, I see,' she teased.

'They've been there since you left,' Elizabeth said.

'Have they? Probably part of the family up the road.'

'Probably.'

As the evening progressed, though, the children made no attempt to join the other family. Instead they kept glancing back down the track they had travelled, as if waiting for someone to arrive.

After an hour Kate could stand it no longer. 'Elizabeth, you speak Urdu, don't you?'

'A little . . .' She glanced across at the children, knowing very well what Kate wanted. 'But Kate, they probably won't understand . . .'

'At least try.'

A few minutes later Elizabeth came back. 'They're waiting for their mother. She told them if she ever fell behind to wait at the next village.'

'Do you know where they left her?'

'Only a little way back. She was very tired, they said. And thirsty. From what I can gather their water supply's been very low and she's been saving it for the children.'

Kate knew how hazardous the water supply had been on this part of the journey. There had been hardly any water holes between Ye-U and Shwegyin. That was why Dick had been so insistent that they take the extra cans when they had parted company.

Kate glanced across at the children. It was impossible to ignore their plight.

'We'll have to go back and see if we can find her,' she said to Elizabeth. 'We can't just leave the children here like this.'

'I agree.'

'And we'd better give them something to eat and drink, too.'

'I'll get something from the car.'

It was agreed that since it would be virtually impossible to take the car back through the seething tide of people making their way up the track, Elizabeth and Henrietta would stay with the car while Kate and the two boys returned on foot to look for their mother.

Even as they set off Kate feared what she would find. There were too many corpses by the side of the road not to be aware of what might have happened. They lay unburied where they had fallen by the track – Indians mostly – their worldly goods strewn by their side. One poor woman, Kate noticed, had carried her precious sewing machine all this way, and it now lay beside her where she had fallen, killed by sheer exhaustion.

They pushed their way on through the crowd until eventually the elder boy stopped and caught hold of Kate's arm.

'Over there,' he said in Urdu, pointing.

Kate moved forward slowly. In the fading light, the magenta-saried figure propped up against the base of the tree seemed to be merely resting. Perhaps they were not too late. But as she came closer she saw her mistake. The face was too still, too vacant. She bent over her, reaching down to take hold of one of her thin limp hands. There was no pulse and her skin was quite cold to the touch as if she had died some time before. There had never been any chance of saving her, then.

Kate covered the woman's face with the edge of the brightly coloured sari and then gathered the boys to her. They did not cry, oddly fatalistic, as if they had accepted their mother's death long ago, but stood, looking expectantly up at Kate, waiting for her to show them what they must do next.

She took one of their small hands in each of hers and began to walk slowly back to the village with them, one on either side. Without protest they went with her and their trust in her touched her heart.

She knew she could not leave the sad little pair to their fate. Their mother had given her life for them and, knowing this, Kate could not pass them by. They would have to take the boys with them to India, that was all there was to it.

It was almost dark by the time they reached the village. Henrietta was already asleep in her Moses basket, oblivious of the dramas of the world about her. Elizabeth had sorted out some blankets for the boys, which she handed to them as they arrived, and they arranged a corner for them by the fire.

'Do you know,' said Elizabeth after they had given the boys another small meal and had settled them for the night, 'they were saying that they'd walked all the way from Rangoon.'

'Unbelievable, isn't it?'

'Their father worked on the docks there,' Elizabeth went on. 'Apparently he was killed by the Japanese in that first air-raid.'

'Good God!' said Kate. 'I remember that, it was dreadful.' She recalled Alex's face when he'd returned from helping in the hospital there. How shocked he'd been by the sheer numbers of people slaughtered. How strange it was to think that one of those he'd tried to help might very well have been these little boys' father.

'Anyway,' Elizabeth continued quietly, 'after that, their mother decided to leave for India. They've had a dreadful journey, Kate. Their little party was set upon by Burmese Dacoits just outside Rangoon and their grandmother and sister were killed. I know the Burmese have little love for the Indians, but no one came to their rescue apparently, even though there was a village close by. It was only by the grace of God that these two boys and their mother managed to escape.'

Kate glanced over at the two hunched forms asleep by the fire. Impossible to believe that such tiny scraps of humanity had been through so much and were still prepared to trust others.

'Well, they're safe now,' she said, stretching out her legs and leaning back on her hands. 'We'll make sure they get safely to India.'

'Yes.'

There was a pause while they both finished their tea. Kate looked up at the scattering of stars, intensely bright in the velvety black sky. It seemed so peaceful here, so beautiful, it was hard to believe that misery and hardship was pressing hard about them. Yet beauty and tragedy often walked hand in hand.

She remembered when they had first set out along this route and she had seen clouds of brightly coloured butterflies hovering by the side of the road. She'd marvelled at their loveliness, and been horrified when Dick Ferris had told her that the butterflies were feeding on the eggs the bluebottle flies had lain in the rotting corpses which lined the roadside. It had reminded Kate of the Bible story about the lion and the honey bee. 'Out of strength comes forth sweetness.' Out of darkness comes forth light.

She turned back to Elizabeth, aware she was speaking again.

'What did you say about a Dutch couple?'

'They were here earlier, when you and the boys had gone to look for their mother,' said Elizabeth. 'They only stopped long enough to put more petrol in the tank. But the Dutchman was saying that we're lucky we left when we did. He thinks the army will be pulling out this way soon.'

'How did he hear that?'

'I don't know. He seemed pretty sure about it. Said they've been pulling back all the way through Lower Burma, and sooner or later Alexander has got to make a decision on whether to go on fighting, and risk the whole army being taken by the Japanese, or to pull them out and to try and keep them intact to fight another day.'

'How on earth can they hope to get the whole army out using this route?' asked Kate. 'It must be quite obvious to them that the road isn't suitable.'

'I know,' agreed Elizabeth. 'What alternative is there, though? I doubt they've got the facilities to airlift them. They can't leave by the Burma Road, because the Japanese are almost at Lashio, and the Hukawng Valley would be a positive suicide route.'

'Lord, and if they don't move soon they'll be caught up in the monsoon and heaven help them then.'

'Exactly. That's what the Dutchman was saying. That they'd have to make a decision soon because of the monsoon. He reckons they won't try and hold the ground north of Mandalay and that they'll pull the main bulk out as soon as is feasible.'

'Then we'd better pray the weather holds for them.'

'Precisely. And that they can keep the Japanese from taking the Chindwin until they manage to get the troops across. The Dutchman seemed to think they'd probably employ specially trained nuisance parties to harry the

Japanese to try and prevent them from closing in too rapidly . . .' She couldn't bring herself to tell Kate that the Dutchman had actually referred to them as 'suicide parties'.

There was a silence. Elizabeth seemed to be concentrating on an invisible speck on her linen skirt.

'Nuisance parties?' Kate felt a little nub of tension in the pit of her stomach.

Elizabeth gave a little shrug. 'Yes. Commandos, I suppose.' She busied herself emptying out the dregs of her tea onto the ground beside her, not quite meeting Kate's eye.

Kate said nothing, tilting her head back to stare at the moonlit sky. She knew very well what Elizabeth was trying to tell her.

That Mike Calvert and his Bush Warfare Battalion would unquestionably be part of that harrying team.

And that Alex would be among them.

It was a master plan of deception. Alex, climbing into the back of the staff car bearing Wavell's flag and 'stars' behind Mike Calvert and his driver, Williams, listened to Peter Fleming as he ran through the scheme.

'We've got to convince the Japs that we're stronger in India than we really are,' he said as they sped southwards towards the Japanese lines, past the odd remnants of battered British units on the eastern bank of the Irrawaddy. 'So, what we intend to do is to try and ditch this briefcase of Wavell's behind enemy lines so that when the Japs find it they'll be convinced it's genuine and that they've had the unbelievable luck to come across certain secret documents of the general's . . .'

It sounded unbelievably like a *Boy's Own Paper* escapade to Alex, but it was just the sort of wild ruse that very well might work.

The attaché case was packed with papers, documents and letters – including several personal ones from the general's wife, to make the whole thing more convincing. Some of the stuff was genuine but it would tell the Japs nothing they didn't know already, and some were carefully prepared documents referring to non-existent armoured units and artillery, as well as the movement of certain ships, supposed to be in the Indian Ocean, but which were in fact somewhere else. There were also 'top secret' messages referring to reinforcements due from the United Kingdom and the Far East and other such misleading information.

'And how exactly are we intending to get it into enemy hands?' asked Alex. 'Presumably the fact that we're in a staff car with all this on it,' he nodded in the direction of Wavell's flag and 'stars', 'has something to do with it.'

'Absolutely,' said Fleming with a grin. 'Williams here is going to crash the car in the Japs' path, and then we're going to make a runner for it, leaving the attaché case behind, just as if we've mislaid it in the rush.'

'Foolproof!' said Calvert from the front seat, laughing. 'All we have to do is find the bloody Japs and then we're made.'

About thirty miles or so from the Ava Bridge they stopped on a brow of a hill overlooking the surrounding countryside. Calvert and Williams got out of the car, opened the bonnet, peering beneath it to give the impression they had stopped because of engine trouble.

'Good Jap country,' said Fleming, looking about him. 'We should be spotted in no time.'

Almost before he had spoken there was a burst of gunfire and Calvert and Williams slammed down the bonnet and jumped back into the car, Calvert at the wheel this time.

As the car swung round Alex saw several Japanese

breaking cover and heading their way, shooting as they came.

The fish had taken the bait.

'Step on it, Mike,' shouted Fleming, seeing the Japanese closing in.

Up ahead there was a sharp corner with a convenient embankment, which Calvert had spotted earlier, and he drove into it purposefully going much too fast. He slammed on the brakes and with much squealing of tyres they careered off the road as planned and over the embankment. They just had time, before the car started to turn over, to bale out. Peter flung the attaché case away from the wreck, in case of fire, just far enough to look as if it had been thrown clear on impact. Then all chaos broke out.

The Japanese had seen the crash and were running towards them, firing wildly.

'Time for a quick exit,' muttered Fleming, loosing off a few rounds.

Alex dived into the thick scrubland beside the road. Cutting through the bush he could hear the Japanese starting in behind him, shouting at each other as they struggled through the thick undergrowth. With no equipment to weigh him down, and a compass to take him in a straight line when the paths didn't run true, Alex had soon pulled clear and a few minutes later he could hear the Japanese giving up the chase.

He slowed his pace slightly, catching his breath, and then suddenly he was aware of Calvert's stocky frame slipping onto the path beside him.

'Fun, wasn't it?' said Calvert, grinning widely at him. He always treated these escapades as something of a game. 'That'll get the Japs thinking. Now let's think what else we can do to annoy them a bit.'

Alex laughed. Mike was incorrigible.

As they started back through the bush the others joined them one by one. It was getting dark.

'Just one last snag,' Mike told them almost casually as they walked on, 'I was told before leaving that the British are planning to blow the Ava Bridge at midnight tonight. So, if we're going to make it before demolition deadline, we'd better step on it.'

The thought of a half-mile swim through the muddy, swift-flowing Irrawaddy if they failed to reach the Ava Bridge in time acted like magic. Tired legs were suddenly forced into speedy action again and they pressed on through the darkness with renewed vigour. Every minute counted.

They only just made it in time. The bridge was still intact when they reached the eastern bank of the Irrawaddy, but soon after they crossed the rearguard demolition boys blew their charges.

Alex stood on the far bank, listening to the deafening roar of the explosion. It seemed to him, more even than the fall of Rangoon, to mark the end of it all.

There was a resounding splintering crash as the last sections of the two huge spans of the bridge collapsed into the river.

Then an almost shocked silence filled the air.

Calvert moved across to Alex's side. 'Time to be on our way,' he said briskly, once more the efficient commander. 'We've got to rejoin the unit. I've given orders for it to pull out as soon as the trucks arrive whether we're there or not.'

Alex nodded, taking one last look across at the crippled bridge.

The British army might be retreating but Alex knew they'd be back. However long it took them, they'd be back.

Without speaking he fell in behind Calvert and Williams as they slipped away through the darkness.

## 20

*T*o Kate the relief of being in Simla was immeasurable. The final part of the journey had been horrific and even now she recalled it with a shudder. The car had given up on the treacherous road to Tamu and they had had to walk with the other refugees, pulling the bamboo trailer which had once been attached to the car, piled high with as many of their possessions as they could manage.

Even now in her sleep she could hear the echo of their voices as they had urged each other on, 'One more step. Just one more step', as they tried to stagger up those never ending hills.

Hellish though that journey had been, Kate knew they had been the lucky ones. They had come through with little more than exhaustion, sore feet and the first stages of malnutrition. They had even had the luxury, once in India, of being able to contact Joan Staveley who had promptly arranged transport for them, so saving them the long hike up to the railhead at Dimapur.

Yet, for all that, Kate knew Elizabeth and she would be marked for ever by their experience. Not so much by their own suffering, but by that of others.

The memory of that drive, of the stench of rotting corpses, of the sheer desperation and hopelessness on the faces of so many of the refugees, still haunted Kate. Even the knowledge that she had been able to reunite the two little boys with their uncle in Calcutta did not seem to compensate.

But here in Simla, where life was reassuringly peaceful

and unchanged, she gradually felt the dark ghosts of the past fade away. Here it was possible to imagine a time before the war had torn everything so cruelly asunder.

The town, which clung precariously to the side of a mountain, still oozed the quiet confidence of the old colonials of Kipling's time. Subalterns still rode with their colonels' wives to see the dawn or sunset on Jakko Hill, the *jhimpanis* still propelled the same rickshaws, monkeys leapt noisily on the tin roofs and the acrid smell of charcoal and hookah tobacco still drifted up from the bazaar.

Under its gentle charm, Kate and Elizabeth began slowly to recuperate. Life became settled again, and as news filtered through of old friends who had got safely out of Burma they felt a new confidence grow within them.

They'd heard nothing about Alex, though.

The journey out of Burma had given Kate a more tolerant acceptance of life and she bitterly regretted the acrimonious way in which she and Alex had parted. She was to blame, she knew. She had slammed the door so tightly behind him, it was impossible to re-open. The newer, more mellow Kate might not have let the anger of the moment swamp any chance of understanding between them.

Now, standing on the balcony of the house in which they were staying, Kate wished she'd held her tongue that day in Maymyo. Too late now, of course. She didn't even know where he was.

She heard the sound of voices in the narrow street below and, looking down, saw Elizabeth and Henrietta returning from their walk. Henrietta was sitting up in her large blue Victorian pram, looking around her with button bright eyes as the *ayah* pushed her up the hill.

Kate went back into the house, listening to the clatter of their feet on the wooden steps.

'Did you go to the bazaar?' she asked Elizabeth as she came in, Henrietta balanced on her hip.

'No, we stopped at the club, actually. That's why
were so long.' Elizabeth handed Henrietta to the *ayah* an
flung herself down onto the chintz-covered sofa.

She seemed distracted.

'Is anything the matter?' Kate asked her cautiously.

Elizabeth waited until the *ayah* had left the room,
taking Henrietta off for her bath. Then she said: 'It's
the Ferrises. Bad news, I'm afraid.'

Kate did not speak. The slow, grave words hung in the
space between them, heavily, like a thick dark curtain.

'Someone at the club told me,' Elizabeth went on quietly.
'Apparently they were up in Myitkyina with them just
before the Japanese overran the place.'

'I see.' Kate cleared her throat. 'I thought when they
left us they were going to try and fly out from Shwebo.'

'They were. But they couldn't get on a flight so they
decided to go up to Myitkyina. They didn't get away in
time. Pam was killed on the airfield. Her plane was just
about to take off when the Japs attacked, shot them to
pieces . . .'

Kate closed her eyes, her hands falling to her sides. 'So
nearly safe then . . .'

'Yes.' Elizabeth nodded sadly. 'Apparently they were
actually taxiing down the airfield when it happened. Five
minutes more and they'd have been away. Poor Dick saw
it all and couldn't do a thing.'

'God, how *awful*.'

'Wasn't it?' Elizabeth drew a deep breath. 'Anyway,
then Dick had to do what everyone else in Myitkyina
was trying to do. Join up with a party and get through
to India through the Hukawng Valley.'

There was a silence. They both knew about the
Hukawng. Because of the monsoons the paths there
had been a sea of mud, sometimes chest-deep. There'd
been disaffected troops of all nationalities determined to

shoot their way out, pilfering and looting the few food stocks along the way, there'd been disease, starvation, and always, every brutal step of the way, the relentless heavy rain.

'Only one of Dick's party of ten made it,' Elizabeth said, staring down at the palm of her hand. 'Dick and two others were drowned when their raft swept them away down one of the rivers they were trying to cross. It overturned and they were never seen again. The rest . . .'

Her voice trailed off and she gave a hopeless shrug. There was no need to say anything more.

'I wish they'd come out with us,' said Kate, her throat tight with emotion.

'They couldn't. Pam was ill, remember?'

'They'd have stood a better chance, all the same.'

'They weren't to know that.' Elizabeth pushed her hands together so tightly that the knuckles gleamed white. 'It's so unfair, they were the gentlest of couples.'

'I know.'

'Oh, Kate, I do wish it would all end,' Elizabeth said suddenly, her voice shaking slightly. 'I've just got this awful feeling that it will go on and on and I'll never see Martin again . . .'

'Of course you will.'

'Will I?' Elizabeth stood up and went to the window, looking out across the hills. 'Not this year, I won't.'

'No.' Kate was too honest to lie. 'Not this year.'

'Then when?' Elizabeth asked savagely. She turned and beat the top of the sofa with a clenched fist. 'When will it all be over, Kate, just tell me that?'

Kate found she couldn't answer. Very slowly she stood up and went to Elizabeth's side and put her arms around her and they clung together, motionless, in silence.

\*      \*      \*

'When will it all be over?'

Martin Downing, lying on the floor of his darkened hut, was asking himself the very same question.

When he had taken refuge in the Karenni Hills nine months before he had viewed it as a purely temporary measure. He had thought that the Japanese would be held at Moulmein and, if not there, then certainly at Rangoon, and that in a matter of weeks he would be able to return to Elizabeth.

Now the Japanese were entrenched in Burma, the British had pulled out and he could see no end to this existence where he was constantly afraid for his life.

It had changed him, that fear. He pushed his thin hands together tightly, gripped by a bleak sense of loneliness and loss. He was tired of being on the run like this. It wasn't just the Japanese he had to worry about, it was the Burmese Independence Army as well. They had already been up to the villages around him and had massacred several Karens, using the war to settle old debts. Martin knew that if they were even to suspect that he was in hiding close by, they would send out a search party to find and capture him.

From outside he heard the hollow screaming of a band of Rhesus monkeys. He sat up, drawing his knees up to his chest. He ought to venture out and find some wood for the fire before it got too dark. He tried never to let the embers die down as he was so short of matches and he hadn't quite mastered the Karens' way with a flint and stone. The tell-tale thin trail of smoke would be lost long before it reached the jungle canopy, so there was no fear of it being detected.

He stirred and slipped outside into the hissing rain. The dense forest ringed the hut like a huge multi-textured cage and he had to push his way through the tortuous creepers and closely knit trees, stopping to bend down here and there to pick up an armful of brushwood.

He hated these necessary excursions into the surrounding forest. Despite carefully tucking his long trousers into his boots each time, the leeches always seemed to find a way of crawling in. He abhorred them, obscene bloodsucking creatures lurking in the undergrowth, standing on their anal suckers and weaving about in gleeful anticipation of attaching themselves onto some unsuspecting passerby.

They could force their way through the smallest of cracks, even the eye of his boots, squirming their way up his warm body – one of their favourite places was his crotch – and gorging themselves on his blood. The Lord in His infinite wisdom must have had a reason for creating the repulsive brutes, Martin thought, but he himself couldn't fathom why.

Back in the clearing once more he peered down at his clothes, dispensing with the few that clung to his garments. Then sitting on the steps of the hut, he began to undo his boots.

Two fat, slug-like leeches had already fastened themselves onto the lower half of his right leg. He knew better than to pull them off – that way their heads remained embedded in the flesh and had to be cut out before they festered. Instead, he took his lighted cheroot and touched them with its burning end, so that they unwound and released their grip. He gave a small shudder of disgust as he watched them drop off onto the muddy ground of the clearing. Then he began to check the rest of his body.

He had just dealt with another particularly bloated specimen on his right arm when he heard the sound of someone coming through the forest. He lifted his head quickly, tensing. There was always that fear of betrayal.

A few minutes later he saw the familiar shape of the

young son of Saw Yay, the headman of the village close by, appearing through the undergrowth. He gave a relieved wave in greeting and stood up, crossing the clearing to meet the young boy and gratefully taking the eggs and vegetables he had brought.

The Karen villagers had taken it upon themselves to look after him over the past few months. He felt somewhat of a fraud because he knew they probably thought him part of the Karen resistance movement active in the area. Martin, though, had no aspirations to join such a group, despite the villagers' assumption that he would.

Even his meeting with the remarkable Hugh Seagrim and his Karen levies had not changed his mind. He had no intention of involving himself in any activity which would blatantly encourage the Japanese to come looking for him. Let others play the hero, he had no wish to do so.

They'd tried hard enough to influence him, though.

When he had first arrived here they had told him about Seagrim and had taken him on a three day trek along barely distinguishable, steep jungle tracks to see him.

Tall, very dark and ascetic-looking, Martin could see at their first meeting that Seagrim was a most remarkable man. He had been with the Burma Rifles and had remained behind to try and raise and train a great army of Karen levies, to make raids from the hills on the Japanese lines of communication. It was immediately clear that not only did he love the Karens – adopting their customs and dress – but that he had also quickly won their respect and trust.

Heartened by the thought of no longer being on his own, Martin had relished the idea of joining Seagrim in his secure jungle hideaway, but he'd begun to suspect almost at once that the only reason he'd been brought there was so that he could help Seagrim with the resistance group.

It was a fear that was soon confirmed. After only a day

Seagrim had told Martin that he needed someone to help run the levies in the south and had asked Martin if he would go. Cornered, Martin felt he had no alternative but to agree.

On the way down, however, he had fallen ill with an attack of malaria, and had had to take refuge in Saw Yay's village.

Here he had stayed.

He was ill for so long that Seagrim had had to make other plans for the southern levies. Martin wasn't sorry. This war had choked every ounce of leadership and initiative out of him. He was happy to stay in hiding and leave the daring deeds to others.

Besides, he was well aware this conflict would not be over in just a few months. Even Seagrim agreed. One of the reasons he had wanted someone to look after the southern levies was because, while he wanted to keep up the momentum of the guerrillas, he also wanted to make sure that the Karens did not rise up against the BIA and the Japanese too soon. They would need the support of the British to succeed and that would be a long while coming.

If they ever came.

That was the crux of it. Martin had lost faith in the British. He had seen how quickly they had abandoned the Tenasserim District, how completely commitments and promises had been thrust aside in the scramble to get out, and he couldn't in all honesty rally the Karens to their support.

At the end of the day, even if the British did return and manage to push out the Japanese, would they really reward the Karens' dedication and loyalty with the granting of an independent Karen state, away from the oppression of the Burmans, as the Karens wanted?

The truth of the matter was, he doubted it.

Sacrificial lambs, that was what they were. That's what he was, too. And he wanted no part of it.

He was too tired. Too disillusioned. Too afraid of the risks.

He slowly climbed up the bamboo ladder which led to the bamboo platform of his stilted hut, clutching his small basket of eggs and vegetables, and crouched down beside the fire. Outside the light was already starting to fade. Another day over. Another night beginning.

So it went on. He shivered.

He could hardly bear it.


Mark Lawrence stood under the shade of the bread-fruit tree, leaning against its trunk and watching the Australians whack a cricket ball across the parade ground of the Changi Selarang Barracks.

He didn't know how they had the energy. He was almost fit now, having spent several months in hospital after the bomb-blast, but still found he tired easily. Perhaps it was just the sheer lack of food. For months now they had survived on meagre rations – mostly rice. He'd lost over two stone since the fall of Singapore.

He glanced about at the other men around him. On the whole they were an amazingly cheerful bunch, despite the deprivations. Pretty close-knit too.

Strangely enough it had been the Japanese who had brought that about, by trying to force them all to sign the no-escape 'parole'. Until that time there had been recriminations and accusations between the POWs, the Australians blaming the British for the fall of Singapore, and the British blaming the Australians. The friction and ill-feeling had continued to simmer for months, threatening to develop into something quite nasty, and then the Japanese had insisted that everyone sign some contemptible document agreeing not to attempt an escape.

At first everyone had refused, but after the Japanese had brought all the troops to Selarang Barracks – including the walking wounded, which had meant Mark himself – they'd been so overcrowded that dysentery had broken out and then diphtheria. In the end the senior officer in charge, the Australian Colonel 'Black Jack' Galleghan had told them to sign, assuring the men that because they were signing under duress, it wasn't legally binding.

At the signing table a thinly veiled rebellious mood had prevailed. Mark remembered that the two Australians ahead of him had signed themselves 'Ned Kelly' and 'Bob Menzies', while the man on his right had written 'Judy Garland' with a flamboyant flourish. The Japanese seemed totally unaware of the joke.

From that moment, though, the mood in the camp had changed for the better. Instead of destroying the POWs' morale the Japanese had in fact unwittingly brought them closer together.

'Hallo, Mark. How's it going then?'

The nasally Australian voice coming from beside him made Mark jump. He turned to find the fresh-faced Clarrie Ross standing beside him. Clarrie had been in St Patrick's Hospital with him, and had been moved up to the hospital at Roberts Barrack when Singapore had fallen. They'd been in adjoining beds for some time, and Clarrie's outrageous humour had carried Mark through many a dark moment.

It was Clarrie who had managed to keep Mark going when he'd discovered, waking up in Roberts Barracks, that he had been transferred to the military rather than the civilian prison camp. It had been some stupid mix-up, because when Mark had been brought in he'd come to the Australian military hospital along with two other Australian soldiers, and they'd found a dog-tag lying loose on the ambulance floor and had assumed it to be his. He'd been documented as one Private A. C. Thornton when he'd been admitted, and despite numerous complaints and depositions to the powers-that-were Mark had still not been transferred out. He was now virtually resigned to staying put, along with one or two other civilians who, for various reasons, had had the same problem.

He watched Clarrie as he walked over and leant against the trunk of the tree beside Mark. He was a good-looking lad in his mid-twenties who before the war had been working on his parents' farm outside Melbourne. He'd signed up with a group of his friends, all of whom had joined the 4th Anti-Tank Regiment. They'd been on their way to the Middle East until they'd been diverted to Singapore.

Clarrie took out a small tin from his shorts pocket and started to roll himself a cigarette, using some black wisps of appalling Java weed, which Mark felt was only marginally preferable to the crushed hibiscus leaves which some were now smoking, and a sheet of super-fine paper from his Bible. Mark knew he allowed himself only two a day and despite the Java weed tasting like seaweed, savoured every nicotine-filled breath.

Mark did not talk to him while he smoked, conscious of not spoiling the sheer pleasure of the moment. Instead he turned back to watch the game. It was always worthwhile, as there were some pretty fine cricketers at Changi.

A loud shout echoed across the padang as the batsman took the ball too early and was caught out mid-field. Mark watched him walk off the pitch shaking his head in disgust and the new batsman come in from the shade.

Mark frowned. It was that wretched Johnnie Matheson. He couldn't abide the fellow. He'd managed to steer clear of him most of the time he'd been at Changi. Matheson had been on working parties outside the barracks for most of the year, but now many of the groups had returned to base and unfortunately he was seeing him more and more.

Glancing across at Johnnie now, Mark wondered how

it was that, despite his thinness, he seemed to look fitter, or at any rate trimmer, than the rest of them. No doubt while out on the working parties he'd been able to filch some of the stuff they'd been supposed to be loading onto the Japanese ships.

Even so, Mark thought, it was more than that.

Quite simply, Matheson was one of those people who thrived on the difficulties of camp life. He was the sort of man who delighted in pilfering stuff in front of the Japs' noses, relishing the challenge of not being caught.

And he had the luck of the devil. Everyone said that about him. He had that aura of bright confidence about him which seemed to protect him against disaster. Cockiness more like, thought Mark with sudden rancour.

He hadn't forgiven the man for walking out on Kate like that. Nor was that the worst of it.

After Sylvia had left for Perth he'd met Edna Carlington and she had hinted, little black beady eyes alight, that she'd seen Sylvia in the company of a young Australian on more than one occasion. By the description he'd guessed it was Matheson.

He didn't know whether Sylvia had been unfaithful to him or not, perhaps he didn't want to know the truth of that, but it still made him view the man with loathing.

It was a pity he seemed to be so well-liked around here, but then the Australians liked the amusing dare-devil type. Even Clarrie had told him once that he reckoned a sense of humour was worth a pint of rice any day.

Mark heard a great roar from the onlookers. He hadn't been concentrating. Someone had scored a six.

'You little beauty!' cried Clarrie, emerging from his nicotine-clouded world to join in the applause. 'Hooked that fast ball right off his eyebrows!'

'Who did?' Even as he asked the question, Mark knew the answer.

Matheson.

Mark gave a little sniff of irritation and turned on his heel, telling Clarrie that he was much more interested in seeing how the rehearsals for the play were coming along.

As he walked away he could still hear the bystanders clapping.


Kate threw herself back into work with feverish intensity. She was in Delhi now. Although she could have continued her deciphering job with the Government of Burma, which was still based in Simla, she'd been offered a post in Delhi with the Far Eastern Bureau and had leapt at the chance of a change.

For one thing, Elizabeth had announced in September that she was going to go down to Bangalore to stay there for a while with her mother and sister, Charlotte, and Kate had felt Simla wouldn't be the same without her. She was going to miss Elizabeth and little Henrietta immensely.

So that autumn she'd left for her job with the FEB. She'd found rooms in Old Delhi at the Cecil Hotel, from where she could bicycle quite easily to the offices in Connaught Circus in New Delhi, and had settled into her new life with enthusiasm.

Almost from the beginning Kate found the work fascinating. The FEB dealt with all kinds of propaganda. There were the Japanese broadcasts aimed at the Japanese mainland, given extra life by Alington Kennard who'd previously been the editor of the *Straits Times* in Singapore; there were other broadcasts for the Japanese troops, and there were the strategic and tactical leaflets for both the Japanese and the Burmese, as well as a weekly serial newspaper, *Lay Nat Tha*, aimed at the Burmese villagers.

There was some scepticism among the higher powers whether this sort of propaganda achieved very much, but seeing all the behind the scenes work that went on in each section to make sure that just the precise chord was struck each week, Kate felt sure that they were onto the right idea.

Besides, as the months progressed, they were becoming more and more involved with the military. Psychological warfare and military deception were being taken a little more seriously, and now the FEB with its team of experts in matters Japanese and Burmese, was seen to have its advantages.

One morning Kate came into the office to find the head of the Burma section talking to two young Burmese who had recently come out to India, and who'd been put in touch with them by the interrogating officers who'd interviewed them at the frontiers.

The slim, round-faced man in spectacles was introduced as Thein Pe. He was a communist who had escaped from the Japanese in Burma with his younger companion, Thakin Tin Shway. Since he knew the actual conditions of the Burmese villagers under the Japanese, Kate realised what enormous help he would be to the FEB.

Thein Pe told them that the Japanese had already alienated much of the populace and the Burmese were gradually realising that the promise of 'Asiatic Brotherhood' had been mere propaganda, and that the Japanese regarded them as an inferior people.

'Murmurs of disquiet. That'll help our cause,' said David Morris, one of the many Australians on FEB's team. 'I'll try and tie my sermon round that.' Morris produced a Buddhist sermon or fable for the radio each week.

'It's the first positive bit of news we've had,' said Kate. 'Up until now the Burmese seemed to have bent over backwards to welcome the Japanese.'

'Not all of the Burmese,' Morris told her, coming to

sit on the edge of her desk. 'The BIA certainly. But from what I hear the local population are suspicious of them as well now. They haven't exactly helped their cause by their excesses and cruelties. Got a bit too big for their boots and started to throw their weight around. Think the Japanese regard them like a thorn in the flesh at the moment, too. You should hear Peter Fleming on the subject . . .'

'Who?'

'Peter Fleming. Was a travel writer before the war. Wrote about China. Haven't you met him?' Morris seemed surprised. He was obviously quite a character. 'Pops in here a lot. GHQ deception expert.'

'Oh, didn't he want to drop enormous inflated balloon figures amongst the BIA?' asked Kate, remembering something she'd heard. 'Thought it might spook the lot of them?'

Morris laughed. 'That's the chap. Not one of his better ideas, that. Amusing though, you'd like him. One of those chaps who like to flirt with danger, you know the sort?'

'Yes,' Kate said, thinking of Alex. 'Yes, I do.'

'Always up to some new trick,' Morris went on. He picked up his pencil and paper, he always carried them with him to jot down any thoughts that might come to him, and eased himself off the edge of her desk. 'I should think that he and the SOE boys will latch on to Thein Pe and his friend like fury. You wait, once they hear what little prize we've got hidden here they'll be along like a shot.'

He was right, too. Later that afternoon he came back to Kate, a thin dark-haired figure in tow.

'Kate, this is Colonel Peter Fleming,' Morris said triumphantly. 'Didn't I tell you he'd be here like lightning?'

Kate smiled. 'You did indeed.'

'Didn't know he'd be quite so quick though,' Morris confessed. 'But then Peter has his ear closer to the ground than most, don't you, old man?'

Peter grinned. 'I try to.'

'Little inner network they've got going, these behind the scenes intelligence chaps,' Morris chuckled, slipping his hands into the pockets of his baggy shorts. 'And talking of behind the scenes chaps, Peter, how's that mad-cap friend of yours, Calvert? Been on any more escapades with him recently?'

'Sadly, not since we left Burma,' Peter said. 'But I saw him up in Calcutta with Wingate a short time back. Sorting out some new plans I believe.'

At Calvert's name Kate's head jerked up. 'Are you talking about Mike Calvert?' she asked.

'That's the fellow,' said Peter, tapping out his pipe and putting it in his pocket. 'Why, do you know him?'

Kate hesitated the merest fraction. 'Not exactly. But a friend of mine's brother was with him in Maymyo.'

'Bush Warfare man, was he? Who was that? Met a few of those boys,' said Peter, with a boyish grin. Calvert's Commandos had been an entertaining bunch.

'Alex Staveley.'

It was the first time Kate had spoken his name out loud for months. She was surprised at the unsettling effect it had on her.

'Good Lord, Staveley you say? Now there's a thing. He was on the very last jaunt Calvert and I did before I pulled out to India. We only just made it over the Ava Bridge before the demolition boys took it apart.'

'Heavens.' It was the first she'd heard of it. It must have been soon after they had parted ways in Maymyo.

'Good chap, Staveley,' Peter said enthusiastically. 'Cool customer, too. He was one of the few of Calvert's men to volunteer to stay behind in Burma when the rest of us pulled out.'

'Stay behind?' Kate tried, but did not quite succeed, to keep the astonishment out of her voice. 'You mean he's been behind the Japanese lines in Burma all this time?'

'Well, not all the time,' Peter corrected, a little bemused by the stir his news had caused. 'He came out fleetingly a few months ago. Calvert wanted to brief him about something face to face. Back in Burma again now, though.'

'I see.' She sat, thin, pale and shocked behind the desk.

'But you needn't worry about the fellow,' she heard Peter continue. 'Saw him briefly in Calcutta myself. Had rather a wild evening out with Calvert together, in actual fact.'

'Did you?' By the greatest of efforts she forced some lightness into her voice. For some reason she found this new piece of information more perturbing than the fact he'd been facing untold dangers in Burma.

She stared down at her hands, pushing them tightly together. Hearing Alex's name had brought memories tumbling back. A few short words, that's all it had taken, and suddenly all her carefully built defences had come crumbling down. Why did it suddenly seem to matter that Alex had come out to India and hadn't even bothered to try and get in contact with her? Why should he, after all?

She'd given him his walking papers in no uncertain terms and Alex was not the sort of man to entreat her to change her mind. Too proud. Too stubborn. Alex would not retrace his tracks.

'I say, are you all right?' She looked up to see Peter staring anxiously down at her, leaning against the desk. 'Didn't mean to worry you. I'm sure Staveley will be fine, you know. Wily sort of chap. He'll stay well clear of the Japanese . . .'

'I just didn't know he was behind the lines, that's all,' said Kate lamely. It was preferable he think that was the cause of her despondency than guess the truth.

'Well, if I find out anything more about him I'll keep

you informed, shall I?' Peter went on, straightening up. 'Calvert would know. Perhaps if he comes out again . . .'

'It's all right,' Kate broke in hastily. 'There's no need. Please don't go to any trouble.'

The last thing she wanted was for Alex to know that she'd been asking after him. She didn't want that humiliation. He'd obviously been having a high time in Calcutta and hadn't given her a thought.

Peter paused by her desk and for a moment she thought he was going to say something more. Then at the last minute he seemed to change his mind.

Instead he turned to Morris and said, brightly: 'Well, *tempus fugit*. Can't stand around here for ever. Let me know when those things I asked for are ready, won't you?'

'Of course.'

With a quick nod of farewell to Kate they left the room and she could hear their voices slowly fading as they walked back along the long, echoing passage together.

Left alone, Kate was aware of the suspended sense of pain that hung over her.

Old memories came flooding back, so acute she could almost feel Alex's presence in the room. Peter talking about him like that had brought him very intensely out of the past and into the present again, somehow undoing the catch on the box that she had thought so carefully locked and bolted.

## 21

*T*he small wooden boat crept slowly across the water. Alex Staveley sat low in its bows watching the fast-flowing eddies push and pull against its roughly made sides. The river was at its pre-monsoon level, with a swiftly flowing current, but it was nothing like the raging torrent it would become in a few months' time. Nevertheless Alex was aware of the difficulties of this crossing.

For one thing, at these times he always felt vulnerable to attack. Not just by the Japanese, but by the BIA whose appearances were much more unpredictable. There was always the chance of being spotted, too, by a random passer-by, for whom the reward of a hundred rupees for turning him in would prove too tempting.

At least, now, having spent almost a year here, he was pretty sure of the villagers in the immediate vicinity. Again and again they had proved their loyalty, hiding him, bringing him food, alerting him to Japanese patrols.

In the beginning, when he had first left Calvert to come up to the Chin Hills, every day had been wrought with strain and tension, every step a step which might lead him into danger. Then he had had no idea which villages were still loyal to the British and which had decided to throw in their lot with the Japanese. Indeed, he suspected, at the outset, some had not decided themselves which way to turn.

In a way those villages were the worst. They would make a show of friendship when he first arrived in the village, giving him somewhere to sleep and food, while at the same time sending one of their runners down to warn the Japanese that what they assumed to be a British straggler was with them. More than once Alex had escaped by the skin of his teeth, plunging off into the jungle a mere hair's breadth ahead of a patrol.

Now life was easier. He had established where each of the village's loyalties lay. He knew which one to skirt around, which one to visit, which guides knew the shortest tracks, which boys gave the most accurate information about the movement and strength of the Japanese. He had found out, too, where other Britishers were in hiding, some raising levies, some gathering information like him, and though the nearest – Anderson and his wireless operator – were a good three days' march away, it still gave him comfort to know he was not entirely alone in this inhospitable jungle.

Above all, though, he was beginning to be able to gauge the Japanese a bit more accurately. They were formidable opponents, it was true, fearless fighters who could travel for days with only a bag of rice and water from a village pond, but they were so ruthlessly disciplined that they tended to lack initiative.

In Maymyo Alex could remember Wingate telling him that the Japs would fight like madmen in the most impossible conditions, but would be led up the straightest of garden paths and taken in by the most scarlet of herrings. Common sense, or lack of it, was their Achilles' heel.

Alex did not underestimate them, though. They were tough and determined, every one of them.

To the Japanese soldier, family honour, family tradition, were so webbed into his being that he didn't need to be commanded to fight until the last man – that was ingrained in him from birth.

No wonder they had blazed through Burma like a wild fire.

For the moment, though, they had reached an impasse.

The monsoons of the previous year had prevented them from following up their victories and chasing the British army all the way into India. Now the British sat in Imphal, with the Japanese waiting on the other side of the River Chindwin.

What would happen next, Alex had no idea. There was talk of the Japanese attempting to push on into India and there was talk of the British attempting some sort of push back into Burma.

Probably both claims were correct. Certainly during these early months of 1943 Alex had noticed more specific requests from GHQ for detailed information about Japanese positions and movements, a sure sign that something was about to happen.

In many ways, of course, though his whole *raison d'être* was to pave the way for such activity, Alex knew such a thrust would affect his own position detrimentally.

Columns of men pushing into the jungle, presumably ambushing road convoys, blowing up railway bridges and attacking isolated Japanese posts, would bring hordes of Japanese reinforcements into the area.

It would make life much more dangerous for him.

It was part of the price, he supposed, of trying to get the British back into Burma.

Now, as he edged his boat into the shoreline, he brushed aside thoughts of possible British action and concentrated on the task of bringing the dugout in to land upon the sandy promontory.

Soon it would be dark. Light from the dying sun sifted through the bamboo. Alex pulled the boat ashore, dragging it through to its hiding place, making sure it was well covered. The last thing he wanted was for the Japs to find it. Not only would they probably blast it apart, hampering his river crossings, but its discovery might also provoke an all-out search for him.

He didn't want to risk that.

He walked up the hill. The late afternoon was filled with soft sounds. A bamboo leaf fluttered to the ground, the wind whispered through the jungle, a tuck-too bird called, and at each noise Alex paused for the merest second before moving on. Just in case.

He followed the jungle path on towards his isolated hideaway, pushing his way through the thorns and clammy overhanging vines. Then he stopped.

Somewhere just ahead of him a twig cracked.

He kept very still. Instinctively his hand tightened on his rifle, his finger slipping off the safety catch.

'*Thakin!*'

There was a movement from within the trees. One of the young boys from the village, Ba Lai, stood in the shadows.

'What is it?' he asked, seeing the boy's agitated face. 'Is it the Japanese? Are they coming?' From time to time they sent up spot patrols to the area.

'Yes, *thakin*. And some of the Burmese Army with them.'

Alex frowned. The BIA were almost worse than the Japanese. They were such an unpredictable lot. They could be coming to the village to pilfer some food, or to abscond with some of the women to ease their army's needs, or they might even be coming with the Japanese, on a joint patrol to investigate any rumours of an Englishman being in the area.

He lifted his head. In the distance he could hear the faintest crackle of rifle fire. A bad sign, that. This was no mere foot patrol on the scrounge for provisions then.

He turned to Ba Lai.

'Quickly, back to the village!' he whispered. He didn't want the boy being found here with him.

He waited until Ba Lai had disappeared from sight and then, clutching his pack and gun tightly to him, started to move quickly back along the path. His only chance was to try and take the boat across to the other side and wait at one of his other hideouts until it was safe to return again.

He stumbled on, his arms and face being torn by the thorns and branches which overhung the path, but he didn't slow his pace. Just before the track swung round to drop down to the water's edge, though, he checked himself.

Ahead, close to where he had hidden the boat, a slight movement caught his eye. It didn't seem possible that the Burmese soldiers could have arrived there so quickly, yet some deep-seated instinct told Alex that the figure in the shadows was not one of the villagers.

He dropped down out of sight. He knew now that they had known exactly where to find him. He must have been seen on the river by a pro-Japanese native, someone who had noted the boat's hiding place, and the Japanese had split their patrol into two, one going to the village, the other cutting across ahead to the river.

Alex hesitated the briefest second. He knew he couldn't go back. Not only would it endanger the villagers, but also the Japanese would undoubtedly start pressing down the river when they didn't find him and he would more than likely be flushed out.

He wasn't sure how many of the patrol were guarding the boat, but at first glance he could spot only the one half-hidden sentry. He could try and move up river and swim across, but there were strong eddies around the submerged rocks with powerful back currents which made the crossing lethally dangerous.

If he could find a way to secure the boat, he would take that risk. He might have a chance.

Alex began to edge his way forward through the tall grass, then froze. The Japanese soldier was moving out of the cover of the trees which topped the sandy promontory. He'd lifted his head, tensing, bringing his gun to the ready, obviously alert to some sound or danger.

Alex pushed himself closer to the ground, hugging the earth, rock still. Only his eyes moved. Had the Jap seen him? His heart began to pound in his chest like a hammer.

The Jap moved again. This time, though, it wasn't towards Alex, but out along the finger of land towards the river. Now Alex heard what it was the guard had been listening to: the soft slap of a boat's oars against the water. Straightening to a half crouching position, Alex caught sight of a fisherman pulling his way into shore on the other side of the cove.

Very slowly, very deliberately, Alex began to edge his way forward. The Jap was standing with his back to him, absorbed in watching the fisherman. That momentary lack of concentration was the chance Alex had been waiting for. It was now or never, he knew.

Alex drew out his knife from its leather sheath and began to move cautiously forward at a crouch, coming in from behind the soldier noiselessly. If he hesitated for even a second all would be lost.

He grasped the Jap from behind, jerking his neck back to stifle the cry, hearing the man's low gurgle as he fought for breath. Then, with one quick sharp movement of the knife, left to right and back again, it was over.

With a violent shudder, Alex released the limp body, fighting back the bile as the puppet-like figure fell to the ground. He knew it had been a case of kill or be killed, but even so he found his hands were trembling fiercely as he replaced the knife in its sheath.

He tried to calm his breathing, closing his eyes in an attempt to steady himself, to collect his wits.

He shot a swift glance over his shoulder. No one else had appeared yet. If he were quick, he might still have time.

He dragged the sentry back into the cover of the bushes, uncovered the boat and began to pull it down to the water's edge.

Just as he reached the water, he heard someone coming scrambling down the hill behind him. Turning, he saw a lone soldier – a Burmese army recruit this one, though no less deadly – darting across the cove after him.

He heard a shout. Then the deafening report of a gun rang out and he felt his arm explode with the pain as the bullet tore into his shoulder. Alex didn't stop to unsling his own rifle. He knew his best chance, his only chance, was to push off from that shore, to get out into the dark shadows of the fast-moving river.

What happened next always remained a mass of confusion in his mind. Suddenly he became aware of another sound and, turning, saw Ba Lai running down through the grass towards him.

Alex shouted at him to turn back, waving him frantically away, but the boy kept on coming. It was then that Alex realised what he was trying to do: distract the soldier to give Alex a chance to make his getaway. He seemed oblivious of his own danger.

Before Alex had a chance to unsling his own gun, the soldier abruptly raised his gun and fired at the slight, willowy frame of Ba Lai. Almost before he heard the resounding shot Alex saw the frail young body lift into the air, flung backwards by the force of the bullet.

Alex had no time to think. In one swift movement he unhooked his rifle, firing so speedily he barely took aim. The soldier stumbled and fell. Alex fired another rapid shot and then ran back towards Ba Lai. Useless, of course.

He knew that even before he bent over the pathetically smashed, small body. But he had to check, had to make sure. He owed Ba Lai that much.

The green-uniformed figure of the BIA soldier lay slumped on the sand a few yards away. Alex cautiously approached him, tipping him over with the toe of his boot, rifle pointing down at his face. Just in case.

Then he froze. Horror pumped through him as he stared down at the figure before him.

Dear God, he knew this man.

The shock of recognition hit him with the force of a blow, making him stagger.

It was Maung Pe, Ma Kyin's youngest son.

He felt himself shudder violently, his stomach turning. Then with a determined shake he jerked himself out of his stupor.

There was no time for self-recriminations. He'd shot Maung Pe to try and protect himself and the boy. He must put it behind him.

If he were to survive, he must force himself to think straight, to drive himself on.

Behind him he could already hear the sound of the other soldiers, their guttural shouts becoming louder as they came along the jungle path from the village, alerted by the shots.

He ran back to the river and frantically began pushing out the boat into the water. If he moved quickly he might just get away in time. He mustn't think about Maung Pe. He mustn't think about anything but his own survival. He would try and reach Anderson's camp further north.

There he would be safe.

He clambered into the boat and struck out for the opposite shore. The last of the light was fading now, darkness closing about him. He was still shaking violently but at least he knew that the Japanese would be unlikely to try and follow him across the treacherous river in the dark.

It was when he was nearing the opposite bank that he thought he heard someone screaming out his name across the water. Ridiculous of course. It must have been the sound of a night bird screeching in the jungle.

But even as he struggled to bring the boat in to land, he knew the truth. Some deep-seated instinct warned him that the voice had been that of Ko Hla, Maung Pe's brother, calling out for revenge.

And as Alex stumbled ashore he knew that Hla would neither forgive nor forget.


There was another to whom forgiveness did not come easily at that moment.

Mark Lawrence, slithering and stumbling along a jungle path, with the other thousands of POWs, knew with a deep burning anger that they'd been lied to.

They'd been told they were being taken to rest camps in the Cameron Hills, with light duties and plenty of food, but with each mile that they'd taken from Singapore, they'd realised the hollowness of those promises.

They'd had to endure being crammed into rice trucks, thirty-six of them to each stifling steel box. They'd had no room to lie down and the men with dysentery had had to be held out of the open sliding door as the train jolted along, because the Japs refused to make adequate *benjo* stops.

They'd put up with that – and more – because for the first few days, foolishly, they had believed at the end of it all there would be the promised rest camps. But once they had left the train at Ban Pong and begun this painful, rain-sodden forced march, one by one they had been forced to face the bitter truth.

'We've been conned, haven't we?' said Clarrie Ross, staggering along beside Mark. 'So where do you think we *are* going? Not some bloody Thomas Cook rest camp, that's for sure!'

'Sorry about that,' mumbled Mark.

He was very conscious that it had been his idea to try for this force. When he and Clarrie had heard about the other groups leaving Changi for the rest camps in the Cameron Hills, they had made a pact to try and get themselves as fit as they could in order to be classified healthy and hardy enough to join the next group.

Anything to get out of Changi. Anything to join the so-called 'lucky' few who'd got themselves out of the hell-hole.

Now Mark was doubting the wisdom of that decision. It was clear to him that they were being herded up towards Siam for one reason only. Slave labour. The rumour was, to work on some mad-scheme railway. If they went on pushing them like this, thought Mark, there would be no POWs left to build their bloody railway.

He glanced back along the line. They'd all been fit men – or fit by Japanese standards – when they'd left Singapore. Now they were like the walking dead. And if they didn't stop for *yasumi* and food soon, they'd all be keeling over.

'Speedo! Speedo!'

A Korean guard came up along the line, rifle-butting the slower men. Mark and Clarrie stumbled on. They no longer paused at the sight of someone falling to the ground, no longer flinched at the sound of someone being punched and kicked by one of the guards, nor even at the sound of a rifle shot. They just kept marching. Like Eurydice, they thought it would be fatal to look behind them.

Up ahead Mark could see Johnnie Matheson. He was walking very upright, managing to seem impervious to the discomforts. Mark knew he wasn't, though. He'd seen

Matheson having to dive off into the bushes along with everyone else. He'd seen the sores on his legs, seen him grow thinner and weaker by the day, seen him shiver with the fever.

He wondered what Sylvia would think of him now. Tattered, verminous and disease-ridden. Not quite the handsome hero he'd been in Singapore, was he? Mark watched him with a sort of bitter obsession.

He heard the crack and thud of a rifle butt making contact with flesh and bone. Someone else was down then. Instinctively he tried to stiffen his knees.

If only they could finish this march. Anything would be better than this.

It was then that they turned the corner and through the thick sheet of pouring rain saw the square wooden gateway and, beyond that, a filthy, stinking, sodden area with atap huts open to the sky.

'Oh, God!' The shock at the appalling state of the camp made him stumble. If it hadn't been for Clarrie he would have fallen.

'Steady, old mate,' Clarrie said, catching hold of Mark's arm. 'We're here now. Can't give the bloody Japs the satisfaction of thinking they've got the better of us, can we?'

The rain was coming down so hard that the mud spurted up against their legs. Mark watched the remainder of the POWs come through the gate. Men with pitifully bony legs, looking more and more like the sagging skeleton they'd had at school for biology lessons, all fragile and bent.

He had the feeling that they were like the lost souls of the *Inferno*. And that there was no way out. But he couldn't let Clarrie know that.

He pushed back his drooping shoulders and lifted his head. He tried to ignore the terrible cramps in his stomach, the burning, blistering pain around his groin.

'No, you're right, Clarrie,' he said, and with a truly heroic effort forced a molecule of lightness into his voice. 'We can't let the bastards think they've beaten us, can we?'

'Well, what do you think of our friend Calvert, then?' Peter Fleming settled himself on the edge of Kate's desk and lit up his pipe. It was now well into May and he'd taken to calling in to see her for a quick chat whenever he was in the building. 'Mad Mike, the Press have nicknamed him.'

Kate took the finished sheet of paper out of her typewriter and began to insert another. 'Not surprising when you hear about some of his escapades,' she commented. 'But then the whole of that Chindit force seem to have come home heroes, don't they?'

Kate had followed Wingate's operation of leading the Chindits back into Burma with the utmost of interest. Operation Longcloth, as it had been called, had aroused enormous public enthusiasm. Kate could see why. Not only was Wingate himself a colourful figure – just the sort of general the Press liked to get their hands on – but here were British and Indian troops, for so long ridiculed as being unable to meet the Japanese in the jungle, proving that they could triumph. Not only had Wingate's men carried the fight to the enemy, but they had beaten them as well.

Kate knew that the cost in terms of lives lost had been immense, but the effect it had had on the morale of the troops here in India had been so stupendous it must have been worth the price. Now they had all seen it was possible to successfully engage and conquer the enemy.

Fleming picked up one of her pencils and began to twiddle it restlessly between his long fingers. 'By the way, doing anything for lunch? A group of us thought we might go to Maidens. Marjorie's coming . . .'

'I've got all this to do actually,' Kate told him with a

pointed wave of her hand at the pile of letters on her desk. 'John needs them rather urgently.'

'John needs everything rather urgently,' Peter said dismissively with a grin. 'Do him good to wait a bit.'

Kate smiled. 'Is that what you think?' She kept on typing.

'Yes, I do. And I also think you could do with a change of scene. You've been looking a bit peaky of late.'

'Nonsense,' said Kate briskly. But she knew it was true. She'd been worried about Alex. There'd been no news. She'd even tried surreptitiously quizzing Peter Fleming to find out if he knew anything unofficial, but to no avail. The trouble was she didn't want to probe too deeply, lest he suspect.

Peter replaced the pencil in its holder. 'What about it, then?' he asked, looking across at her. 'Lunch at Maidens would do you the world of good.'

'Colonel Fleming, are you encouraging me to abandon my post?' she asked equably.

'Absolutely.' He gave her a comfortable smile and slid easily off the desk. 'I'll pick you up in about half an hour.'

She was about to protest but he'd already slipped out of the room and she could hear his jaunty step disappearing down the long corridor.

By the time he returned, though, she was more than ready for lunch, tediously bored by having to type so many letters.

'Where's Marjorie?' she asked, as they started off towards his car.

'Went on ahead with Philip. Didn't relish the thought of making a quick pit-stop on the way.'

'Are we making a pit-stop?' asked Kate.

'Only fleeting. I promised a friend I'd call in and see him in hospital. You don't mind, do you? Only I thought the sight of a pretty face might cheer him up a bit.'

'So you had ulterior motives for inviting me to Maidens, then?'

Peter grinned. 'Sort of. Anyway, I thought you'd like to do your Florence Nightingale bit.'

'I see.' As a matter of fact she hated hospitals, had done so ever since, as a small child, she'd been taken to see her mother at the Singapore General the day before she'd died.

As they pushed open the door and entered the hall, the familiar smell of disinfectant and polish brought all those fearful memories tumbling back. She faltered slightly. She might even have turned back, but at that moment an efficient-looking nurse came briskly rustling towards them.

'Can I help you?' she asked, with a bright authoritative smile.

'Oh, we know where we're going, thanks,' said Peter, steering Kate past.

'Do we?'

'Most certainly.'

He did, too. He led her through a labyrinth of corridors until they found themselves standing outside the white swing doors of a ward.

'Before we go in,' he said, thrusting his hands into his pockets, 'I suppose there's something I ought to tell you . . .'

'He's hideously disfigured . . .' ventured Kate.

Peter smiled. 'Not at all. Handsome chap, in fact. It's just that I suppose I ought to warn you whom it is we're coming to see.'

'Well?' Kate frowned. It was unlike Peter to be so hesitant. 'Who is it?'

'Alex Staveley.'

'Alex!'

Kate felt every last inch of her breath leave her body. Small sounds echoed through the silence: a clock ticking, a short, sharp cough, the rattle of a medicine trolley.

'He came in from Imphal about a week ago,' Peter said. 'I wasn't sure whether to tell you or not. But I've watched you become more and more miserable over these past few months – and I was pretty sure it was because of Alex.'

'Oh.' And she had thought she had hidden her feelings so well. Peter was not a deception officer for nothing.

'So, Kate, it's now up to you. Through that door lies Alex. You can turn tail and run if you want to. Or you can tell me to wait downstairs while you go and see him . . . Which is it to be?'

'He might not want to see me . . .'

'Isn't it worth the risk?'

She hesitated for the briefest moment, then nodded.

Even if Alex refused to see her, it was worth that humiliation. At least she would have tried. If she didn't, she knew she would regret it for the rest of her life.

Peter pushed open the door for her. He saw that her face was now glowing above the white collar of her dress with a sort of fearful anticipation.

'Third bed on the right,' he said softly, touching her shoulder briefly in encouragement. 'I'll see you downstairs when you've finished.'

Kate nodded, then went in. A young, dark-haired nurse was pushing a trolley down the centre of the ward.

Kate paused, glancing down the line of carefully neat beds.

She saw him almost immediately. He was sitting up in bed, head bent, reading a newspaper which he'd spread out on the covers before him. The sight of him, so wonderfully, painfully familiar, made her heart skip a beat.

She stood for a moment taking in every detail of him, covertly, and then slowly began to walk towards him.

Whatever happened now, it didn't matter. She was glad she had come. If only to see him one last time.

Alex smoothed out the edge of his newspaper. A dark-haired nurse with a trolley of medicines clattered past, for once not stopping by his bed. The relief was immense. He was fed up with taking all the vile concoctions they tried to pour down his throat every day. Fed up with having his pulse and temperature taken at every given moment, fed up with the cluster of doctors who gathered round his bed, morning, noon and night . . . Never an easy patient, he found himself becoming more and more exasperated that they insisted on keeping him in hospital.

A shadow fell over the corner of his newspaper. He looked up, thinking it must be Phil coming to commandeer him into being a fourth in his wretched bridge game.

But it wasn't.

'Hallo, Alex.'

She was so precisely as he had remembered her that it took him a few seconds to recover, afraid that she was merely an apparition conjured up through his own longing.

His hesitation seemed to affect her.

'I thought I'd come to see you,' she said. He could hear the uncertainty in her voice, 'I hope . . . I hope that's all right.'

'Of course it is,' he said softly. To him it seemed like a small miracle.

'Really?' Kate realised she'd been holding her breath and let it out slowly.

'Really. I can't tell you how glad I am you came.'

There was a heartbeat of silence. Alex wasn't sure if he were ready to confess to her just yet how much he'd missed her.

Every day in the jungle he'd promised himself he

wouldn't think about her. And then he'd find himself remembering the smell of her skin, the way her hair curved back from her forehead in those coppery curls, the way she moved, her smile, her touch.

Coming back to India hadn't made much difference, either.

He moved slightly over on the bed. 'Come and sit down,' he said, indicating the space he'd made.

'Won't Matron disapprove?'

He grinned. 'Probably.' But he wanted her close so that he could drink in her every detail, her uncompromising beauty.

She hesitated the briefest moment then settled herself on his bed. As she did so she said softly: 'How are you, Alex?'

'Fine.' He couldn't tell her the truth. Not just yet. 'Still a bit shaky on my legs, that's all.'

'When did you get here?'

'A few days ago. They sent me down from Imphal for some inexplicable reason.' At the time he'd been terribly peeved by their decision. Not so now. 'How did you find out I was here?'

'Peter Fleming told me.'

Alex grinned. Trust Peter. 'That old rogue. Might have guessed.'

'Alex . . .' He looked up at her hesitation. 'Before we go any further I want to tell you how sorry I was about Maymyo. We should never have parted like that.'

It had cost her a lot to hand him that olive branch, he knew. Kate did not find apologies easy.

'I was as much to blame,' he said swiftly. 'Didn't exactly help things by losing my temper like that, did I? Regretted it bitterly afterwards.'

'I was a fool.'

'We both were.'

She took a deep, unsteady breath. 'I didn't mean what I said either. I over-reacted. I think I was just frightened for you. Can you understand that?'

'Easily.' He stretched out and covered her hand with his. 'I know I said some pretty rotten things too.' There was a breath of a pause. 'Am I forgiven?'

She nodded, swallowing hard.

'I was miserable without you, Kate.'

'I was miserable too.'

He looked down at her hand for a moment, tracing the line of her thin fingers. He cleared his throat a little awkwardly.

'Then do you think,' he said quietly, 'that it might be worth us trying again?' He was almost afraid to look up and see her reaction.

When he did, he saw that she was smiling at him through her tears and he knew that it would be all right between them.

They still had a long way to go, but the first faltering step had been taken. Now, if they stumbled, it would not be of their own making.

## 22

'*I*sn't this bliss, Alex?'

'Utter perfection. I still don't quite know how you managed it at such short notice.'

'Influence.' Kate laughed. 'Not mine, Peter's.'

She stretched, looking out across the mirror-still water to where the cloud-ruffed mountains rose beyond. The quiet beauty of Lake Dal was already working its miracle on them. After only a few days here away from the furnace heat and dust of Delhi, Kate could see the difference in Alex.

He seemed to be coming back to life again.

She hadn't realised at first what a strain the past year had been for him. She'd seen the physical evidence of it, of course. She'd seen how gaunt and thin he was, had seen the festering sores and ulcers, had seen where he'd been wounded in an encounter with a Jap, she knew about the dysentery, and the fevers, but the other side, the side which in the middle of the night would suddenly bring him jerking upright into total wakefulness, that was the side closed to her.

At first Alex wouldn't talk about those nightmare days and Kate waited, careful not to press him. Then, gradually, as if the burden of keeping it secret was greater than that of releasing it, he began to tell her something of what his life had been like.

It made her admire him all the more. It was one thing to go into battle, buoyed up by one's comrades and the general exhilaration of the moment, it was another to lie low, out of glory's limelight, day after day, week after week, month after month, with only one's own company to keep the demons from the door. It showed enormous inner strength.

Alex had managed it. Extremely well, by all accounts.

She was grateful for that. Yet, in the same breath, she knew it would probably be his downfall. Because, once he had recovered, they would want to send him back again and, more than anything, she didn't want him to be forced to take those sort of risks again.

She glanced at him now, terribly aware of how precious was their time together. She wanted to cup her hands together tightly to hold on to every second of their time here in Kashmir: Alex and she on this houseboat, Alex and she gliding in *shakaras* to visit the mogul gardens which sloped down the lake, through roses and water channels flowing over shallow terraces, or diving off one of the houseboats moored in the middle of the lake, or going up to the mountains to pony-trek or to fish in the clear streams.

She would need these memories in the dark days that lay ahead.

The sound of slapping oars on water made her turn. One of the boatmen from the little flotilla who brought their wares up to the houseboats had come up to their window to sell his goods.

'What do you think?'

Alex was holding up a little intricately carved box inlaid with ivory. 'I thought I might get one for Elizabeth,' he said. 'It's rather like one my father used to have at Anapuri.'

'She'd love it.' Though they had managed to save some pieces in Rangoon, all those from Anapuri had been lost. Kate came and stood beside Alex to admire the assortment of carvings. 'What about something for your mother?'

Alex's dark face tightened slightly. 'No, at least nothing

like this. It would only remind her of Anapuri and quite frankly she never liked the place.' He leant out to pay the boatman. 'She could just about cope with Rangoon, though from what Elizabeth told me in her letter I think she much prefers it here in India.'

'Does she?'

'Never stops entertaining, according to Elizabeth.' Alex put the wooden box down on the table. 'Elizabeth is rather disapproving. Thinks she's not showing enough respect for Father, even though it's nearly been two years.'

'Actually, I can understand her sentiments. She was always so close to him.'

'Yes, she was. She loved Anapuri, you see. It was a natural bond between them.' Alex spread out his hands in an expressive gesture. 'Whereas Mother couldn't stand the place. Not even at the beginning. It didn't bode well for their marriage.'

'No, I can see that.' Kate knew how much their uneasy relationship had worried Alex.

'In the end they were almost like strangers,' Alex went on. 'Elizabeth, of course, won't see that. She only sees that Mother left Rangoon without waiting for Father. She hasn't quite forgiven her for that yet, and I think she's finding it terribly difficult being in Bangalore with her as a result. It's all rather tense, I gather.'

'It can't help either that she hasn't heard a thing from Martin,' said Kate. 'In her last letter she sounded terribly down. I can understand that. When I didn't know what had happened to you, that was bad enough.'

'Ha!' Alex grinned and caught hold of her hand. 'So you did think about me while I was away then?'

'Occasionally,' Kate allowed with a smile.

Alex drew her to him, tipping her chin so that he could look at her before he kissed her. 'Only occasionally?'

'Definitely only occasionally.'

He laughed outright, seeing her face and knowing it to be a lie. He ran a gentle finger round the line of her mouth, tracing it lightly. Then he bent to kiss her.

Kate locked her arms round his neck, pulling him to her. She had never thought she could be this content again. Being with Alex, loving him, intensified every sense in her body.

Outside the lotus flowers were bright with colour on the still waters of the lake. The soft reflections were sharpening as the pale morning light deepened.

'Happy?' Alex stretched out to touch Kate's cheek.

She nodded. 'Very. It makes me almost afraid sometimes how much. You know what they say about making the Gods jealous . . .'

Alex laughed. 'I do. But I don't believe they would begrudge us our share of happiness. Heaven knows, there's little enough joy in the world at present.'

Kate thought about Elizabeth, desperate for news of Martin, and of her father – presumably still in Changi – who had not seen little Louisa and Sylvia for nearly two years. Alex was right. One had to snatch one's happiness where one could.

She stretched out against him, pressing herself tightly into his arms, making them as one. She knew what little time they had left would pass with unbelievable speed.

And beyond it, like a great grey wall, lay separation.

Mark Lawrence knew all about the pain of separation. Not only from loved ones, but from everything he'd ever known and cared about. He lay on the bamboo slatted bench, curled up on his side on two rice sacks. He no longer noticed the hardness of his so-called bed, nor the sounds of those about him, the moans and whimpers, oaths and sighs.

Today, though, his leg was giving him hell. It was

shocking how the tiny scratches from bamboo and thorns could so quickly turn into such festering sores. Ulcers that one moment were less than half an inch in diameter would start to spread, and in little more than a week or so could cover a leg from knee to ankle, exposing bone and tissue. If the ulcer grew so large that it encircled the leg, the circulation of blood stopped, gangrene set in then the leg had to come off. Luckily Mark hadn't got to that stage yet, but he'd still had to scoop out the infected flesh with a spoon, using the sharpened edge to gouge it out, an unbelievably painful, but necessary, process.

Tonight, though, it was not his leg which was keeping him awake. It was his fears about Clarrie.

That morning he'd awoken Mark, grey-faced and gagging, complaining about fearful cramps in his stomach. At first they'd thought it was simply the return of a bad dose of dysentery, but by the time Clarrie had dragged himself out onto the parade ground for morning tenko at seven, they both knew with a fearful dread that it was something more than that. Clarrie had even been too ill to go to work.

When Mark had returned that night from working on the railway cutting he found that his worst fears had been confirmed and that Clarrie had been moved up to the isolation hut.

He told himself that Clarrie was young and tough and that if anyone could pull through the bloody disease then Clarrie could. But when he'd gone up the hill to see his friend he couldn't believe how quickly he had deteriorated, how frail he looked.

'Don't give up on me, Clarrie,' Mark had said to him, kneeling by his slatted bench. 'You can beat this. People do.'

Clarrie turned his head slightly to look at him. His eyes were too bright in their cavernous sockets. He forced a weak smile, the effect of which seemed to stretch the yellow, papery skin tighter across his skull-like face.

'Doc says I've got a good chance.'

' 'Course you have. Look at old Philipps. He's twice your age and as frail as a newborn baby and he still managed to come through.'

Clarrie tried to reply but a sudden gripping pain made him double up, jack-knifing on his bed.

'Shall I read to you, Clarrie, would that help?' asked Mark.

From the far end of the hut he could hear the soft sound of another man reading to the huddled up form of his friend. There was something very comforting about that low insistent voice.

Mark looked up as a shadow fell across the bed. It was one of the Medical Officers.

'How you doing, Ross?' he asked, bending over Clarrie encouragingly. 'If you hang in there until tomorrow you'll be through the worst, you know . . .'

It was probably what they said to all their patients but Mark was conscious of Clarrie attempting a smile. He was full of admiration for the MOs and orderlies. They worked under appalling conditions and yet never seemed to be willing to give in. The constant sickly sweet smell from the cholera victims and, worse, that of the funeral pyre which burned day and night outside, would have been too much for Mark, but the valiant group of men who worked up here endured it without complaint.

The MO went on talking to Clarrie for a few minutes in hushed, supportive tones. Mark turned to look across the ward. The man who had been reading at the far end of the hut had moved down the line to the next bed now.

Mark experienced a wave of shock as he saw who it was.

Matheson.

The MO saw his look and said: 'Comes here most nights. Just to read to the boys.'

'Who? Matheson?'

The MO nodded. 'Started when his mate Langley was brought up here.'

Joe Langley, Mark remembered him. Matheson had known him before the war in Singapore. Both of them had worked in the tin mines, Mark was sure of it. He even thought, if his memory served him correctly, that Kate had met him on a couple of occasions. He was sure his name had come up in one of their conversations at Tanglin Road.

God! How far away all that seemed now.

The MO's voice cut into his thoughts. 'After Langley died, Matheson asked if he might be allowed to read to those chaps who wanted him to. He thought it had helped Langley keep his mind off the pain. We agreed. Besides, Matheson had had more than his share of prophylactic jabs while working in Malaya, so we felt he should be pretty safe. We thought it might help the boys.'

Mark nodded. He felt strangely humbled. Matheson, of all people.

Later that evening in the line-up for their watery slop of *meshi* Mark didn't turn away when he saw Matheson coming back down the column as had been his custom. And Matheson, passing, gave him an almost imperceptible nod.

Now, as Mark watched the moonlight seep through the bamboo walls, he regretted his squalid feuding of the past. Matheson was obviously a far more complex person than he'd given him credit for.

It was almost a relief to give up his petty private vendetta.

He hadn't the energy to hate him any more.

\*      \*      \*

'My boots . . .'

Mark bent down over Clarrie's hunched form, trying not to show his emotion. The change in just two days was appalling. Clarrie had lost almost half his body weight and was little more than an ashen, dehydrated husk.

'What about your boots?' Mark asked, trying to keep his voice steady.

'Make bloody sure you get them before that old scrounger Davies nicks them, won't you?' Clarrie mumbled hoarsely, wincing with the effort of speaking.

'Clarrie, you'll need them yourself when you get out of here,' said Mark, hating himself for the lie.

There was no response.

'Clarrie?' Mark stretched out to catch hold of the frail, claw-like hand.

Clarrie opened his eyes the merest slit.

'You've got to hang on,' urged Mark. 'Fight, for God's sake. Fight. The railway's nearly finished. We'll be out of here before too long. Back to Changi.'

Changi. Never had Mark thought he would recall that place with such a surge of tender emotion.

He was aware of Clarrie's hand twitching and closing around his. The eyes sunk shut again.

Mark was frightened now, he could almost feel the very last vestige of life slipping away from Clarrie. The worst of it all was there was nothing he could do. He wanted to shout and rave, to force Clarrie to cling on, but he could feel the skeletal body gradually beginning to relax, as if the tortuous cramps and excruciating pain had already lost their power over him.

'Clarrie?'

This time the eyes did not open. Mark tightened his grip on the brittle-thin hand, but he knew it was hopeless. He had half believed he could will Clarrie to live by his own sheer dogged determination, now he knew he had failed. Clarrie was slipping beyond his reach. His face was already that of a corpse.

Mark tried to speak, tried to give some encouraging words, but his throat felt so swollen with tears he couldn't utter a syllable. It was almost more than he could bear to lose Clarrie.

He had become Mark's friend and inseparable ally over the past two years. He had been Mark's support through all these trials, they had shared dreams and hopes and confidences. He would never forget him. Never. Clarrie knew him far more intimately than any of his old friends in Singapore, knew him better than any man on earth.

On earth.

The phrase rose up to mock him.

Mark bent his head, blinking back his tears as the child-like hand in his grew heavy and cold and the shallow rapid breathing stilled.

It was over. Clarrie was dead.

Fresh-faced, uncomplicated Clarrie, whose only dream had been that of going home to his parents' farm outside Melbourne. Lost now.

Mark sucked the air into his lungs, sagging forward.

How long he sat there, Mark didn't know, but suddenly he was aware of a shadow falling across Clarrie's bed.

He looked up to see Matheson standing there.

'Is there anything I can do?' Matheson asked gently.

Mark shook his head.

He was conscious of two orderlies standing behind Matheson and with a desperate, sickening awareness knew that they had come to take away Clarrie's body.

'Not yet.' The words were little more than a whisper.

The orderlies looked at one another uncomfortably. It was bad enough having to face the corpses without having to deal with any other complications.

'Look here,' one of them said, 'Ross has got to be moved. We need the bed.'

Mark tightened his grip on Clarrie's hand. He was aware of Matheson coming to stand by his side.

'We've all been through it, you know,' he said sympathetically. 'We all understand how you feel. All of us have lost mates. I know it's tough, but you've got to let them take Ross away. You know that.'

Mark drew a deep shuddering breath. He made a conscious effort to steady himself, digging his nails into the palm of his hand. Then he straightened and with a supreme effort let go of Clarrie's hand.

'I'll take you back to the camp,' said Matheson. 'Shall I?'

Mark was about to tell Matheson that he could manage perfectly well by himself but the truth of the matter was, when he stood up, his legs felt as flimsy as thistledown.

He hesitated, about to shrug off Matheson's helping hand, but the strength of it when placed under his arm, the prop, was such a relief he could hardly hide his gratitude.

Matheson guided him out, talking to him in a low encouraging voice all the time. Mark knew he was trying to draw his mind away from the pile of bodies by the door of the hut and the funeral pyre further up the hill, which billowed smoke and flames like some voracious medieval dragon.

Impossible to ignore it, though. Impossible to forget that that was where Clarrie was heading to now.

'Come on.' As if feeling Mark hesitate, Matheson gently urged him on down the hill. 'We'll be late for our *meshi* if we're not careful.'

'Not hungry.'

'Doesn't matter. Force yourself.'

Mark didn't argue. Food, even the disgusting, weevily

*pap*, commanded demonic respect here in the camp. It was the thread, gossamer thin, which tied each and every one of them to life.

They joined the queue and filled their mess tins with the watery rice, then came and sat under the shade of the trees by the riverbank. The emotion of the afternoon had made Mark so weary he could barely eat, but every time he stopped Matheson kept urging him on, until finally he had shovelled in the last mouthful.

'Satisfied?' he asked, a little resentfully, showing him his empty mess tin.

Matheson smiled broadly back at him, totally unmoved. He stretched out his legs. Mark could see the ulcer sores, which, though large, looked remarkably clean. He suspected that Matheson had resorted to using maggots from the latrines to eat away the rotting tissue, a well-tried method which worked efficiently but was definitely not for the squeamish.

He put down his mess tin. One or two of the men were paddling in the cool, muddy shallows. It looked inviting, but Mark hadn't got the energy to join them.

He heard Matheson stir beside him. He thought for a moment that he was preparing to leave, or even going to join the others in the water, but instead he re-settled himself and made no move to depart.

It was as if he were waiting for something.

Mark felt a little nub of tension between them. Then with a sudden flash of certainty he knew why Matheson hadn't left and what it was that he wanted to speak to him about.

Sylvia.

He expected to feel angry resentment at the thought. But strangely, face to face with it at last, it was as if all his animosity had been spent, lost in the struggle to survive in this hellhole.

He stared down at his mess tin. He couldn't quite bring himself to look at Matheson. 'She *is* safe, you know,' he said a little stiffly.

'What?' Matheson looked up, his expression guarded.

'Sylvia.'

There was a silence. Mark thought for a moment that he was going to pretend no interest, and silently cursed himself for making the first tentative move, but then he heard Matheson say: 'I did wonder about that. With so many of the ships going down . . .'

'She and Louisa arrived in Fremantle before Singapore fell,' Mark confirmed.

'Did they? They'll be up at Toodyay then, I guess.'

'Yes.' Mark was quiet for a moment. He had no idea where Toodyay was. He was aware it was familiar territory to Matheson and felt a small twinge of envy that he could probably picture Sylvia and Louisa in their new surroundings more clearly than he could.

'Thank you for that.' Matheson was getting to his feet. He hesitated a moment. 'By the way,' he said, 'you keep a diary, don't you?'

His words gave Mark a start. He thought he had kept it a well guarded secret. It was highly illegal and the Japanese were particularly paranoid about such things. There'd be hell to pay if they found out.

'Why?' Mark questioned cagily.

'It's just that I was talking to Jenkins this morning . . .'

'The interpreter?'

Matheson nodded. 'Apparently there are some bigwigs due up in the camp over the next few days and the Japs are planning a thorough search of the huts. A show of power. You know the sort of thing.'

'I do, yes.'

'So I should find a new hiding place for it, if I were you,' advised Matheson. 'Forewarned is forearmed and all that. Try the latrines. The Japs don't go there much. Can't stand the blowflies and maggots. Squeamish little lot, aren't they, for all their bravado?'

Mark nodded. The Japanese couldn't stand anything remotely connected with disease. 'The latrines, right. Thanks.'

Matheson inclined his head slightly. Then, turning, he started to make his way back to the huts.

Mark sat hugging his knees to his chest, watching the men dabbling their tired limbs in the cool shallows. It was only when one of them came out and Mark saw him sit down to put on his boots that he remembered Clarrie's last words to him.

He stood up quickly and began to hobble his way back to the hut, stumbling in his haste to get there before Davies.

But he was too late. Clarrie's precious boots had already gone.

He wasn't surprised.

'Any news, Kate?'

'From Alex? No, not yet.'

Kate was walking with Elizabeth through the Mughal Gardens in Delhi. It was now October 1943 and her leave had come to an end and she was back again at the FEB.

Alex was up near Saugor. The one consolation was that he hadn't been sent back to Burma yet, though Kate knew it was just a matter of time. Word was being put about that Wingate was trying to put together an even more ambitious project than Operation Longcloth. He'd been given no less than six brigades and this time, with the exception of one column, his men were going to be flown in by the American Air Force into specially chosen sites.

Although nothing had been said, Kate knew that Alex believed he would either be dropped back into Burma just prior to this new operation, or alternatively would join up with the Chindit force to use his knowledge of the country on the ground.

Either way, because the operation was not due to start until the following year, they still had the chance of seeing each other. Alex might be busy with his training, but he continually surprised her by being able to wangle a ride down to Delhi at short notice. A snatched evening here or there was all they managed, but it was more than most, and to Kate it seemed as if she were being handed the golden chalice.

'I can't tell you what a relief it is to be away from Bangalore,' Elizabeth said, linking arms with Kate as they continued their walk. 'You are quite sure it isn't any bother for me to stay on in Delhi a while longer with you?'

'It's no trouble at all,' said Kate. From what Elizabeth had said of her relationship with her mother, a few months' break would probably benefit them both.

'And you don't mind Henrietta being with me?'

'Of course not.' Kate watched the chubby figure of Henrietta tottering a few paces ahead of them with her *ayah*. 'I'd have been terribly disappointed if you hadn't brought her.'

'Really?'

'Really.'

They passed the butterfly gardens which Lutyens had created and then walked on to the magnificent terraced Mughal water garden.

In Lutyens' day, so Kate had been told, over four hundred men had been employed to look after these gardens, with over two thousand staff working at the great viceregal palace itself.

Was it arrogance or optimism which had prompted them to build on such a grand scale? Kate wondered.

They stood for a moment watching the cascading fountains. Elizabeth squeezed Kate's arm. 'I know I've said it before, but I'm so glad about you and Alex,' she said. 'It was such nonsense you two breaking up.'

'It didn't seem so at the time.'

'No. I remember,' said Elizabeth. 'But you have resolved things now, haven't you?'

'Yes.' Now that Kate knew a little of what had happened to Alex in Burma, she could see why he had been so loath to promise anything. How could he when he lived continually on a knife edge, not knowing what was going to be happening to him from one minute to the next?

He loved her. That was assurance enough.

She watched Elizabeth bend down, opening out her arms to her daughter. Now twenty months old, dark and placid like Elizabeth, Henrietta was beginning to take her first tentative steps.

Kate glanced at the two of them. She knew how much Elizabeth regretted that Martin had missed his daughter's first years. The first smile, the first word, the first step, all lost to him, never to be recaptured.

It hurt Elizabeth, that absence, Kate knew. She rarely mentioned Martin now. An odd, superstitious streak made her reluctant to say his name out loud, as if by talking about him she might tempt Fate.

She hadn't given up believing he would come home one day, though, despite the fact she hadn't heard anything about him since that brief note sent to them in Rangoon. At least Kate had finally been able to discover her father's name on one of the Swiss Red Cross lists drawn up in Changi, which, although not up to date, had nevertheless told her that he had survived the Japanese take-over of Singapore.

Elizabeth had not been so lucky.

She had to hold fast to a fragile eggshell of hope that

somehow Martin was still safe. She had to cling to those hazy recollections of their brief time together, shaping those indistinct memories into something durable and lasting. And with each month the task became more difficult.

Yet, for the first time, Kate felt that the mood in Delhi was changing. Tempered optimism filled the air. No one doubted the difficulties of forcing the Japanese out of Burma, but for the first time it was spoken of as more than just a slim possibility. The successes of the American and Australian forces against the Japanese in the Solomons and New Guinea were beginning to send out ripples against other shores.

A faint glimmer of hope stirred within Kate. The end, though still distant, was in sight. She was sure of it.

## 23

*I*n those autumn days of 1943 Martin Downing, still in hiding in the Karenni hills, felt none of Kate's optimism.

True, there was a whisper that a British intelligence officer had been dropped in by parachute to help prepare the Karen levies for an imminent Allied offensive, but as yet it was only a rumour. At any rate, what concerned Martin more was the very real increase in activity by the Japanese commander Captain Inoue and his *Kempeitai* detachment.

He was constantly afraid of being betrayed to them. The Japanese were not above torturing even the youngest Karen to find out what they wished to know.

It was Seagrim the Japanese were really after, of course, but Martin feared that when the net closed he himself would be caught up, too. Time and again came the rumours of spies in nearby villages, trying to winkle out information about British soldiers' whereabouts.

Now, though, lying in his dank lonely forest hideout, he was beginning to wonder if being caught might be such a disastrous event. He was stricken with another bout of malaria, he had dysentery, he had a badly poisoned foot and for the past few weeks had only been able to walk with difficulty.

He couldn't survive much longer by himself.

He seldom ventured out now. More and more he stayed in his small confined hut, incapable of movement. How laughable it was to remember that, when the war had first broken out, he'd been desperately keen to be released from the BCS so that he could join up.

He knew now he was not a fighting man. He was a peacekeeper. He sought to influence with words not swords. And knowing that, he understood why other BCS members like Fielding Hall and Dugald McCallam had taken their own lives when the Japanese had overrun the country, and all they had worked for and believed in had collapsed beneath the rubble of war.

The same despair caught at Martin now. He felt the burden of his own failure pressing on his shoulders.

He couldn't go on. It wasn't just his physical condition which had deteriorated so acutely over the past year or so, it was his mental state too. Day by day he felt himself slipping deeper into the mires of madness.

He lay there, his stick-like legs pressed against the bamboo floor, knowing that the time had come for a decision. He couldn't risk jeopardising the Karens' position by asking for further help from them, but he knew that alone quite simply he would die.

He had no choice.

He must surrender to the Japanese.

The cell Martin was thrown into contained five other men – all of them Indians or Burmese. It was ten feet by eight and the only way all of them could fit into such a confined space was for three men to squat, arms folded tightly about the knees, on either side of it. They were not allowed to speak or to move, except to use the latrine bucket which stood in one corner.

Martin looked about him, appalled. He had expected to be taken to Rangoon Jail to join the other POWs after surrendering to the Japanese officer at Papun, but instead he had been given rudimentary medical care, patched up and brought down to the infamous New Law Courts.

He realised why almost at once. The Japanese officer to whom he had given himself up had mistaken him for Seagrim and it seemed nothing could shake that belief.

Martin had denied it vehemently, of course, but the officer had merely laughed when Martin had told him that he was a BCS officer left behind during the British retreat, insisting that he wasn't fooled and knew very well that he was the much sought-after leader of the Karen resistance.

The mistake would have been comical except for one thing. Martin was now in the hands of the dreaded *Kempeitai*.

What if they didn't believe his story?

It was one thing to be a straggler, a lost civilian, quite another to be thought of as a spy or a commander of the Karen levies. The Japanese *Kempeitai* were reputed to be as vicious as the *Gestapo*. Perhaps even more so.

Already this morning he'd had a foretaste of the treatment he could expect. Two guards had come to his cell and had dragged one of the other inmates out through the trapdoor. They'd hauled him along to the interrogation rooms, beating and kicking him as they went.

Martin had lain, hunched up against the wall, listening to the thuds which echoed back down the corridor over the next two hours, trying to ignore the pitiful screams which seemed to curl their way around the prison.

When the guards had finally thrown the unconscious victim back into the cell, hurling him in through the trapdoor onto the cell floor, Martin had been white-faced and shaking.

He watched the Indian lying there now, his face beaten black and blue, his nose streaming with blood and his fingers and toes crushed and swollen, and knew with sickening dread that his turn would come soon.

He did not have long to wait.

Later that afternoon they came up to the stout, wooden bars and called for him. He had to crawl out on all fours through the trapdoor, trying to avoid the kicks from the guards as they shouted and screamed at him. Then they dragged him to his feet, pushing him along ahead of them up the stark passageway.

He was taken to one of the interrogation rooms, empty except for two chairs on which sat two Japanese soldiers with canes.

Martin was made to kneel between them.

One of the Japanese, the officer, began to shout at him in rapid, almost incomprehensible English. He was Seagrim, wasn't he? Why was he trying to hide the fact?

The trouble was, Martin very quickly discovered, they really weren't interested in discovering the truth. If he didn't answer in the way they wanted him to, they would slash at him with their canes, beating him about the head and face. All that they wanted was confirmation of what they thought they knew, as if to underline their own skill and cleverness.

Suddenly, without warning, one of the Japanese got to his feet, sword in hand, and began screaming at him. What had sparked off such anger Martin had no idea, but kneeling there, head bowed before him, he was aware of his whole body beginning to shudder, as if he were standing on the edge of a smouldering volcano and was helpless to stop himself sliding into its abyss.

He could see the point of the sword level with his eyes. Then with a great whooshing arc the officer raised it high, holding it between his two hands. Martin closed his eyes tightly, mumbling a quick prayer, waiting for the second rushing curve, the one which would end his life.

The screaming, high-pitched and savage, continued for a few seconds more. Then suddenly Martin felt a rushing displacement of air as the sword began its downward sweep.

He waited, fighting the urge to scream, frozen, like a rabbit before a snake. But then, with an extraordinary display of skill, the officer brought the sharp edge of his sword to a sudden halt, a hair's breadth before it touched Martin's skin.

Martin heard the Japanese officer let out a triumphant shout of laughter. It had been merely a game to him, a chance to practise his sword-play. A chance to humiliate his prisoner.

Martin began to shake uncontrollably. He remembered being told about this little sadistic trick of theirs. Several natives had literally died of fright as the sword had swung down towards them. He wasn't surprised. He himself had almost vomited with fear. He could still taste the sharp sour taste of bile in his mouth.

The Japanese officer returned to his seat. He stretched his hand inside his tunic pocket and took out a cigarette and lit up, still smiling bemusedly at his little trick.

'So, you say you are not Major Seagrim?' He paused, his small black eyes darting across to Martin's drawn face.

'I am Martin Downing. I was with the BCS at Mergui.'

'Ah so!' This time he gave a slight nod of his head. He leant back in his chair, taking a long suck at his cigarette. 'And when gallant Japanese army make so many victories, you run . . .'

'Yes.'

'The British always are running,' he exclaimed triumphantly.

When Martin did not answer, he lifted his sword and brought the flat edge hard against him.

'Is that not so?' he asked, a faint tinge of colour coming to his face.

'Yes.' Martin had no wish to provoke his temper again.

The officer smiled. 'The British think they are clever. They are not. We Japanese are not fooled. We know everything. We know about the two soldiers from India who were dropped by parachute earlier this month.' He took another suck at his cigarette, pausing so the full significance of his words might take effect. 'We know about the resistance groups. And we know about Major Seagrim.' Again that self-satisfied smile. 'You are not Major Seagrim. We know that. But perhaps you know where he is?'

Martin was silent. He had learnt that sometimes it paid to stall for a while. Often the Japanese would accidentally betray the fact that they already knew the answers to the questions themselves.

This time they obviously did not. A second later Martin was knocked sideways by an open fisted blow. 'Where is Major Seagrim?'

'I don't know. I was not part of the resistance,' Martin told them again. 'I saw Major Seagrim once only, when I first came up to the Karen Hills nearly two years ago. I haven't seen him since.'

'You expect us to believe that?' The officer's tone was mocking.

'It is the truth.'

Another blow sent him reeling. 'We are not fools. I ask you the same question. Where is Seagrim?'

Martin could taste the blood in his mouth from the cut on his lip. 'I don't know. I haven't seen him for two years. I've told you all I know.'

'You have told us nothing,' the Japanese officer spat out. He took his lighted cigarette and held it in front of Martin. 'You see this cigarette,' he said. 'The British are like this. Outside they are white, like this cigarette. But inside they are red-hot . . . like this.' He leant forward and applied the lighted end of the cigarette to Martin's arm.

The stench of burning flesh made him gag. He screamed out in pain.

He saw the gleam of satisfaction in the officer's eyes.

'We will find out what we need to know,' he said slowly. 'You will tell us.'

He would have told them, too, over those next few nightmare days, if only he had known. They delighted in their tortures, the 'water treatment', the beatings, the clubbings. Sometimes they would put slivers of bamboo under his finger and toenails, up his nose and in his private parts, and would then set them alight. Only after he had passed out would they allow him to be dragged half-conscious back to his cell, to await the next session.

Sometimes he felt he was verging on insanity. He would find that without warning he would burst into tuneless song, harsh and unmelodic, rocking to and fro on his haunches in his cell.

Then one morning they came for him as usual, dragging him out through the trapdoor. But this time, instead of taking him to the interrogation room, they hauled him outside and put him onto the back of a lorry.

He knew what was going to happen. They had finally realised he knew nothing and were going to execute him.

He was almost glad. He could not endure the brutalities, the horror of it all, any more.

He tried not to think of Elizabeth or of his child he had never seen. He tried not to think of his parents and sister, of his home in England, the pale Sussex stone warm under the gentle summer sun, of the meadows filled with ox-eye daisies and blood red poppies, of the quiet country lanes filled with dog-roses and columbine. But oh, to think he would never see them again . . .

He fought back a sob, rocking to and fro, intoning the old tuneless chant. Beside him, his *Kempeitai* escort stared dispassionately ahead. Martin closed his eyes, leaning up beside the side of the truck. It was something to feel the fresh air on his face, the warmth of the sun. He must try and keep himself calm. These last moments, at least, he must try and pass with dignity.

Suddenly the truck came to a halt. The escort motioned with his rifle for Martin to climb down. He got out, glancing around, confused. For this was not some deserted execution spot.

He was outside Rangoon Jail.

For a moment he did not understand, then the truth dawned on him. For reasons of their own the *Kempeitai* had obviously decided not to execute him and were letting him go. He was being handed over to the POW camp instead.

He stumbled ahead of the guards through the gates, unable to stop the tears of relief spilling down his cheeks, sobbing quite openly.

He'd found safety, of sorts, at last.

'Right mate, we're on our way.'

Mark Lawrence, starting to hobble unsteadily towards the waiting train, felt his spirits rise.

They were moving out of the disease-ridden camps at last.

The railway was finished and they were on their way back south, at least as far as Kanchanaburi, perhaps even to Singapore.

And not before time, he thought bitterly. They'd been the forgotten men of the railway so far up the line near the Burma border. It was late November now and most of the other camps had been cleared of POWs weeks before.

He lay back on the floor of the open flatcar, staring up at the cloud-shredded sky. A sober atmosphere prevailed on the train as it started on its journey southwards. There was something melancholy and grotesque about travelling by this train, clattering along tracks which had cost so many of their comrades' lives.

It was a long, slow journey. The train could only average three miles an hour, delayed by its inability to manage the gradient without some of the prisoners disembarking and walking to the next station. At other times the train ran out of fuel and the men again had to dismount and roam about the jungle, gathering wood to enable the boiler to get up a fresh head of steam.

As they travelled along they could see numerous wrecks beside the tracks, particularly at the more dangerous bends. And, judging by yet more upturned trucks by the side of the tracks, caution was also needed when crossing the bridges, especially the flimsier wooden structures which had to be negotiated at dead slow speeds.

'Jesus, some of the sleepers look as if they've just been scattered onto the tracks like matchsticks!' Mark heard Johnnie Matheson exclaim as he leant over the side of the open truck. 'It all looks remarkably unstable to me.'

Mark didn't have the energy to look himself. As the train snaked its way southwards he was feeling more and more feverish. The sun was flickering through the trees but his face felt icy. He turned on his side, curling up like a child.

'How are you feeling?'

He opened his eyes the merest slit. Johnnie was bending over him.

'All right.' He tried to muster a smile.

'We'll soon be at Kanchanaburi,' said Johnnie. The base hospital was there. 'God knows why it's taking so long.'

'We're hardly priority.'

'No, I suppose not. At least not while the Japs are trying to move so many of their troops northwards.' The train was picking up speed now. The ground was flatter, the track more solidly constructed. 'My God, though, did you see some of their pitiful returning warriors?' went on Johnnie. 'Heaven knows how long they'd been in that siding for, but they looked a sorry mess, didn't they? No water, no food, crying out for help and their wounded untended since boarding, by the looks of it. If the Japanese High Command are as callous as that to their own kind then it's little wonder that they think nothing of the way they treat us, is it?'

'Strange people, the Japanese.'

'Aren't they just? Cruel as hell one minute then crying like babies over some sentimental tosh about the wind in the cherry blossom. I'll never understand them as long as I live.'

'Nor shall I.' Mark had never been able to fathom them. In business he'd always preferred dealing with the Chinese.

Johnnie shifted his position. Like all the men he was so thin that his bones jutted sharply out, and if he sat in one position for too long the bare skin rubbed and became sore.

'Fancy a game of cards?' he asked Mark, delving into his tattered kit bag. At the beginning of his days in Changi he'd swopped several packets of cigarettes for the dog-eared pack, an exchange which he thought more judicious with each passing day. In the camps boredom was almost as debilitating as disease and lack of food.

'You can try and win back some of the vast sums you owe me,' he went on, with a grin. It was only for monopoly money that they played. He'd have been a millionaire if it had been for genuine currency.

'You have the luck of the devil,' said Mark, forcing himself up to a sitting position.

'Luck? What nonsense,' Johnnie protested, laughing. 'It's all down to skill. Years of practice up at the mines.'

He started to shuffle the pack, his long thin fingers expertly rearranging and sifting the cards. Two other prisoners, erstwhile bridge partners, asked to be counted in.

Mark leant back on his elbows, watching Johnnie as he began to deal. It seemed extraordinary to think now how much he had hated the man at the beginning of his incarceration. Since Clarrie's death, though, he'd been forced to throw aside those prejudices. He'd been obliged to concede Johnnie Matheson was a man of immense resourcefulness and inner strength. He could see now why Kate had been attracted to him. Even, though it went hideously against the grain to admit it, Sylvia.

He was canny, too. When Mark had gone down with an acute attack of beri-beri it was Johnnie who had come to his rescue.

Mark had thought he'd been finished that time. He'd gone beyond the early symptoms of wet beri-beri, the puffiness, lassitude and sponginess of the bones, and had reached the stage of being so bloated that he'd known that within a few days either his heart would stop pumping under all that strain, or the skin tension would reach bursting point. It was only a question of diet, but even Johnnie, who'd built up a good entrepreneurial trading relationship with the local natives, admitted there was little possibility of finding sufficient eggs or peanuts or bananas to cure the problem.

'And there's not a procurable jar of Marmite in the camp,' he told Mark. Marmite was like gold dust on the black market. In the early days of capture, when they'd been in Singapore unloading supplies at the docks, they'd come across a shipment of the stuff and had managed to pilfer vast quantities. The Japanese had more or less turned a blind eye, not particularly bothered at its loss, because when they'd opened one of the jars to examine the contents one of the prisoners had managed to convince them that the thick black substance was a type of boot polish, and was of little use to them whatsoever. If they'd known it was food, and such a rich source at that, they might have behaved differently.

As it was, anyway, all supplies had either been consumed long ago or were as closely guarded as the Crown Jewels.

Then, one evening, as Mark had lain in bed, unable to move, Johnnie had come to him clutching a bottle of Vitamin B tablets.

'How in God's name did you manage to get hold of that?' Mark had asked incredulously.

'Killed a snake out in the forest when we were out working a few days back.'

'And you traded it with the Japs?' Mark had seen several natives bringing huge cobras into the camp to sell. The Japs apparently considered them aphrodisiacs.

'No, this was only a little fella,' said Johnnie. 'But luckily it was large enough to clear the storeroom when placed in a suitably strategic position! Once they saw it the guards emptied the place at the speed of lightning!'

'I can imagine.' Mark laughed, knowing what chaos would have followed the discovery of a snake. It would have given Johnnie more than enough time to do a spot of pilfering.

'Here, take these,' Johnnie said, handing Mark the medicine. 'I've been told half the bottle should do the trick. If it doesn't work, take the other half.'

'What about you?'

'Got my own supply.'

Mark didn't argue. He knew if he didn't take them, he'd be dead within the week. 'Thanks,' he said, woefully aware of the inadequacy of the word.

'Think nothing of it,' Johnnie said and disappeared.

Merlin could not have worked more impressive a trick. Less than twenty-four hours after taking the tablets Mark started to pee at an alarming rate, almost non-stop for two days.

The crisis had passed. By the end of the week he had assumed normal dimensions.

He knew how lucky he was. He'd encountered men whose legs had literally burst apart with the strain of wet beri-beri and he knew he'd have gone the same way without the pills. He was well aware that without Johnnie he wouldn't have pulled through.

'Ready to play?'

A voice broke into his thoughts. Mark glanced up and saw that the others had already picked up their hands.

He gathered up his, fanning out his cards.

'All set?'

Mark nodded dully. Despite the sun, he shivered. He was feeling cold and his head seemed fuzzy. The journey was taking it out of him. He was weaker than he'd thought after that attack of beri-beri.

'So, who's bidding what?'

Mark looked down at his cards. For some reason he was having difficulty focusing. The numbers on the cards were jumbled and blurred.

'Mark?'

'What?'

'Your bid.'

'Oh.' He tried to concentrate on the wavering cards in front of him but he was conscious of the sweat starting to drip down his face and body. He shook his head to clear it. 'One spade,' he said, at last.

'Steve's already bid two hearts . . .'

'Has he? Sorry.' Mark hadn't heard him. He passed a hand over his face, rubbing it hard, trying to infuse some sort of life back into it. 'Two spades, then . . .'

Somehow he managed to complete the game. By the end of it, though, he felt as if he were gasping for breath.

He was aware of Johnnie glancing at him anxiously. 'Are you all right?'

'As a matter of fact,' said Mark through shallow breaths, 'not really.'

The trouble was there was nothing they could do about it. There was no cover on the train, no water, no food. Mark knew he must hold on until they reached Kanchanaburi. It surely couldn't be so far away now.

He closed his eyes. Kanchanaburi. Then Singapore.

Just the thought of the place made his mood lift. Once he was back in Singapore he felt all his troubles would be over. It was his city, after all. Its familiarity was like a protective cloak to him. He knew the sounds and smells, he knew every curve of every hill, every street, almost every tree and stone.

There he would not be afraid of the Japanese.

He let his head sink back slowly against the shuddering floor.

When the train finally stopped, he was too weary to try and move. Everything around him was a blur. He was dimly conscious of a figure kneeling beside him, and then of Johnnie Matheson's voice shouting for someone to bring a stretcher.


'They won't let me stay for long. Officious little buggers.'

Johnnie pulled up a rickety stool and sat down beside Mark Lawrence, trying not to show his concern.

Naively he'd believed that once they'd got Mark to the POW hospital and under medical care he would quickly pick up, but his immune system had been so enfeebled by disease and lack of nutrition that what was probably only a mild fever had taken a menacing grip on him. Beads of sweat stood out on Mark's forehead, and his deathly white face was flushed with fever. He didn't seem to have improved at all, thought Johnnie uneasily, listening to the shallow stertorous breathing.

He glanced around the makeshift hospital. Threadbare and squalid though it was, it was still an improvement on the one up at the camp.

'Do you know what the boys are calling this place?' he asked Mark, forcing some lightness into his voice. 'The Kanchanaburi Ritz.'

Mark's grey eyes fluttered open and he gave a weak smile. 'Are they?'

'Too right they are.' Encouraged, Johnnie went on to describe a few of the escapades the POWs had got up to over the past few hours. The Australians were always enterprising and some healthy scrounging had gone on, the pickings proving to be far easier here than up at the miserable border villages.

Kanchanaburi with its old walled town and market centre had been the nucleus of the administration for the whole of the railway, and it was from here that supplies had been sent out in progressively diminishing amounts to the other camps. For those who still had any valuables left, there were goods aplenty to barter for.

Johnnie had been hopeful of finding some medication on the black market that would help Mark, but though food was in plentiful supply, medicine was not. It was one of the few times he'd failed and he felt his inadequacy keenly.

He glanced down at Mark now and saw him wince slightly. The pain was obviously still acute.

'I think the Japs will be moving us out, once they've checked us over,' he said, anxious to distract him. 'Back to Singapore, I guess.' He didn't mention that there was some talk of a bunch of the lads having to go on to Japan to work there. It seemed to him that the thought of getting back to Singapore was the lifeline which Mark needed. 'Never thought I'd be pleased to be seeing Changi again.'

'I know what you mean.'

There was a pause. At the far end of the ward someone was groaning.

Johnnie adjusted his position. Sitting in one place for too long was uncomfortable. 'Is there anything I can get you? I brought some bananas.' He'd managed to get a bunch of twenty for ten cents. 'And some eggs.'

'I saw that. Thank you.'

'And what about money?'

'Money?'

'Yes. You won't survive without ready cash.'

'I can't pay you back. Not at the moment.'

'We can sort it out when you get down to Changi.'

Mark closed his eyes and gave a nod of gratitude. The muscles in his face twitched as if he were in pain.

'Head still agony?' asked Johnnie, noticing the grimace. He felt so bloody powerless sitting here.

'Like a thousand little men jumping around inside.' Mark managed a smile.

'Only a thousand, eh? You're doing well then. When it gets to a million, then you'll know you've got problems.'

Out of the corner of his eye Johnnie saw the doctor advancing down the ward towards him. He knew he was about to be shooed away. He'd only managed to get in here by sheer misrepresentation and lies.

As if sensing that he was about to leave, Mark stretched out his hand and caught his arm. 'Johnnie?'

'Yes?'

'I want you to do something for me.'

'I'll try.'

Mark started to push himself up on his elbows. 'My diary. I want you to take it back to Changi with you. If something happens to me . . .'

'Jesus, Mark, stop talking like that,' said Johnnie, fiercely. 'It won't.'

'But if it does, I want you to try and get it to Kate for me when this whole damn thing is over.'

Johnnie pushed his lips grimly together. If the Japs caught him with a diary the punishment could be very severe indeed. And yet, he knew what those few grubby bits of torn paper meant to Mark. Knew, too, he couldn't refuse.

'Look, I won't make promises but I'll try . . .'

'That's all I'm asking. I know you can do it.'

There was something oddly touching about Mark's faith in his abilities to outwit the Japanese. Johnnie felt a lump catch in his throat.

'I want them to know what happened to us. I want them to understand that we did try . . . so very hard . . . to get through it all . . .'

Johnnie saw the look in Mark's eyes.

'Listen, Mark, you can pull through this,' he said. He took hold of Mark's hand, trying to will some of his own energy back into those weak, frail bones. 'Don't give up now. We're so close to getting back to Singapore. And you've seen the Allied planes going over. Every day they grow more confident. It can't be much longer. You'll see, the Americans and the British will find a way of forcing their way back. They're beginning to do so in Europe, so the latest canary reports say . . .'

'Europe, perhaps,' conceded Mark wearily. Deep etched lines of pain showed around the mouth and eyes. 'But here? Take years to clear the Japs out, Johnnie. And if things get bad they'll just shoot the lot of us . . .'

'Nonsense,' said Johnnie forcibly. 'Even the Japs wouldn't dare to defy the Geneva Convention so blatantly.' But it was a fear that all of them had. That if the Allies closed in too tight, the Japs would just murder the lot

of them. 'Jesus, Mark, I thought you had more fighting
spirit in you.'

'Not any more.'

The finality of his words frightened Johnnie. 'And what
am I supposed to tell Kate?' he asked brutally. 'That you
just gave up?'

He saw Mark turn his head away.

'And what about little Louisa?' he went on. He was
hitting below the belt but he didn't care now. Somehow
he must give Mark something to cling to, something to
fight for. 'She needs you, Mark. Listen . . .'

'It's no good, Johnnie,' Mark broke in, his voice
faltering.

He fought to catch his breath. He could hardly bear it.
Johnnie's words had served to jolt his memory. He could
see his darling Louisa so very clearly, just as she'd looked
that last day in Singapore in her flowery smocked Tana
lawn dress and neat button shoes, remember the intense
cornflower blue of her eyes, her radiant, sweet smile as
she'd waited to board the ship.

Surely he couldn't lose that. He could fight. He could
win. And then the pain exploded in his head again, so
excruciatingly sharp that he cried out with the agony of
it.

'Mark?'

Johnnie closed his hand more tightly round Mark's.
There was a silence. Then Johnnie was aware of Mark's
lips moving, working anxiously. He bent over him.

'Sylvia . . .'

'Yes?' Johnnie stiffened, drawing back slightly.

'Sylvia and you.'

Johnnie felt a coldness enter his heart. He couldn't look
into Mark's face. He had never been a man to regret the
past or to dwell on the cost of his actions, but now Sylvia's
name hung between them, the shame of it wrapping itself

around Johnnie like a too-heavy, smothering cloak.

He drew in a deep breath, about to speak, but then he heard Mark go on: 'I was a fool.'

There was something in his toneless voice which made Johnnie inwardly shudder. 'Mark . . .'

'No, let me speak,' Mark croaked. 'It's no use. I've got to say it. Too old for her . . . see that now. But I wanted her so much, you see.'

For a moment Johnnie couldn't trust himself to speak.

'Wrong of me to marry her,' Mark went on. 'She wanted a protector. Someone to take care of her. I wanted . . . more.'

The effort of speaking was taking its toll. Mark's breaths were sharp and shallow. 'Johnnie?'

He tightened his hold on Mark's hand. 'I'm here.'

'Take care of them for me, won't you?'

He cleared his throat. 'You know I will.'

'And tell little Louisa I loved her . . . very much.'

He made a great effort to keep his voice steady. 'I won't let her forget you, Mark. I promise.'

Mark managed a small smile. He closed his eyes.

'You know, Johnnie, you're a survivor,' he said quietly. 'I used to hate that about you. Now I find I'm relying on it.'

Johnnie could only nod. Words were impossible. Yet he knew with a blinding flash of certainty that what Mark said was true. Whatever lay in front of him, somehow he would survive. He would never give up.

He felt a light touch on his shoulder and, turning, saw the short, bespectacled doctor he'd seen in the ward earlier standing behind him. 'You'll have to go, I'm afraid. The Japs come up this way most afternoons about now.'

'Right.' He hesitated, glancing back at Mark. 'Is there anything I can do . . . ?' His voice trailed off slightly.

'Very little, I'm afraid.'

Johnnie fingered his gold signet ring. It was the only possession he had left of his father's and up until now he had religiously fought against bartering with it. But: 'If it's a question of medicine, I can probably raise the funds somehow. I know it's thin on the ground and pretty pricey, but maybe . . .'

The doctor gave a quick almost imperceptible shake of his head. 'If he'd got here earlier, perhaps. But . . .' He lifted his shoulders in a helpless gesture.

'I see.' It was what he had expected and yet, faced now with the truth, he found he was strangely unprepared for it. He pressed his lips together tightly, trying to keep his emotions in check.

How strange it was that when he'd been in Singapore he had wanted so desperately for Sylvia to be free of Mark.

Now the shame of his wish had been granted.

And like Salome, presented at last with the head of John the Baptist, he found there was no joy in it.

No joy at all.

He picked up Mark's diary and started slowly to walk back down the hill.

## 24

'When are you pulling out?'

'I'm not sure exactly. In a few days.'

'I see.' Kate knew how lucky they'd been having extra time together, for the Chindit expedition had been delayed several times and it was now March, but she still couldn't keep the tautness from her voice.

'Listen,' Alex said quietly, pulling away from her slightly to prop himself up on his elbow, 'the sooner we start this thing, the sooner it will be over, Kate.'

'I know.' She stretched out her hand and traced the line of his mouth with her fingers. 'I do know.' Outside the moon rose over the domes of Old Delhi, casting its pale saffron light through the fluttering curtains of the room. 'So is this the big push we've all been waiting for?' she asked. This time she managed to keep her tone determinedly neutral.

Alex smiled. 'The little push, just before the big push.'

'Oh.' There was a pause. Kate felt his lips brush against her bare shoulder. 'And this time do you think we can beat them?'

'Yes, I do.'

'Despite the fact that they fight to the last man?'

'If morale is as low as it's rumoured to be, then I believe we'll hear of one of the Japanese battalions retreating before too long. And when that happens, Kate, you'll know it's the beginning of the end.'

She pressed herself against his body, feeling his warmth infuse into her own.

'I have to go,' he said, answering the unasked question in her eyes. 'I can't just turn my back on them. The Chins fought to protect me against the Japs and the BIA. They're brave people. I told you about Ba Lai?'

She nodded. At the lakes he had told about the young Chin boy who had befriended him there.

'There are other episodes, too,' he went on. 'One in particular stays in my mind. I'd been in the Hills almost a year by then.' He adjusted his position slightly, drawing her into the crook of his arm. 'One day the son of a headman who had been of particular help came to see me. He told me that the Japs had found out that his father had been passing on information to the British. They had come to the village that morning, they had stripped the old man and laid him face down in the sun, pinning him to the ground with bayonets through his hands and feet and had then skinned him alive.'

'Alex!' Kate swallowed hard, covering her face with her hands. 'Don't!'

'You have to know why I feel so strongly about going back, Kate,' said Alex, gently. 'Have to understand. It took that headman more than six hours to die. His village was forced to watch. Of course I said to the son that I quite understood that his village wouldn't be able to help me again. I thought that was why he had come to me. I knew they must be terrified. But he told me that the Japs, instead of making them afraid, had made them more determined than ever to help the British and that he had come to offer *his* services to me. He might not be able to come so often, he said, because the Japanese were now watching the village, but he *would* come.' Alex paused, looking deep into her face. 'Now do you see why I can't turn my back on these people? Why I can't worry about my own safety when they are prepared to put themselves into such danger for my sake?'

'Yes.'

It was barely a whisper. She almost wished he hadn't told her and yet she needed to know these things. Needed to know about the world to which he was about to return.

For even though he had told her much of what had happened in the Chin Hills, she knew there was more. Events which still lay unspoken between them, haunting his dreams. One incident, its dark shape revealed to her through his earlier nightmares, bothered her in particular. Perhaps now, before he left again for Burma, was the time to try and bring it out into the open.

Kate drew a deep breath.

'Alex, I wanted to ask you something,' she said, then hesitated slightly, already unsure if she should continue. 'You don't have to tell me if you don't want to.'

'This sounds ominous,' Alex turned on his side towards her, smiling.

'It's about Ba Lai.'

'Ba Lai?' She heard him fumble on the bedside table for his cigarettes and lighter.

'Yes. What exactly happened that day?'

'I told you . . .'

'That he was killed trying to save you?'

'Yes.'

There was a silence.

'But there was more to it, wasn't there?' she said at last.

She could feel his stillness. She knew he was remembering, seeing that scene again.

'If you don't want to talk about it. I do understand,' she said quickly. 'Really I do. I don't mean to meddle.' She heard him light the cigarette, heard the sharp intake of breath. 'It's just when you were first back here, when we went to the lakes together, you used to have nightmares.'

She could see he didn't want to remember.

'They were always the same. About Ba Lai. Trying to warn him. Trying to stop him from coming to you.' She saw Alex push a hand over his face. She hesitated for the merest fraction of a second. 'You used to mention Maung Pe, too.'

'Did I?'

The silence stretched into minutes. She knew then this was the core of his unease.

'Do you want to talk about it?'

Alex gave a shrug. She felt his body tense defensively.

'Alex, what happened?' she pressed on quietly. 'Maung Pe was there the day that Ba Lai died, wasn't he? What happened between you?' She took a deep breath. A half-formed thought took seed, but she uprooted it and thrust it away quickly. 'Alex?'

He sank his head between his hands. For a moment she thought he wasn't going to answer. Then he lifted his head.

'I killed him,' he said simply.

The relief of admitting it was immense. He let out a long, shuddering breath.

'I hadn't realised it was him, of course,' he went on quietly. 'Not until it was too late.'

'Oh Alex . . .' She knew they had been friends once. Before all this.

'I have to keep telling myself that it was kill or be killed. That he was partially to blame for my father's death anyway. That he'd killed Ba Lai. But I'm not sure it helps.'

'And Ko Hla?'

Alex finished the cigarette and stubbed it out. There was a sudden stillness. 'What about Ko Hla?'

'He was in your nightmares too.'

'Was he?'

His voice was curiously devoid of emotion. As if he'd

succeeded in boxing that part of it tightly away. She noticed, though, he wouldn't meet her eyes.

There was an instant brittle tension between them.

Suddenly, unwillingly, Kate understood it all.

It was not Maung Pe who'd been the cause of Alex's dark nightmares. It was Hla.

'Alex, he's waiting for you, isn't he?' she said, the words almost locking in her throat. 'Waiting for you to come back, to take his revenge.'

She could see by his face that it was the truth. Now she understood why he had hidden so much of those past months away from her. 'Alex, if it's true, you can't go back to Burma.'

'Kate, this is war. I don't have a choice. If I'm asked to go, I must. I thought you understood that.'

'But that was before I knew about Ko Hla.'

'That doesn't change a thing.'

She wanted to shout at him that of course it did. To try and make him see that to go back to the Chins when Ko Hla was waiting to hunt him down was merely misguided loyalty.

But she held back her emotions, determined not to show how the thought of his leaving chilled her to the heart. It would help nothing.

Kate had learnt her lesson about parting in anger.

Outside the light was changing, the pale glimmer of dawn stretching across the Delhi sky. She could hear the first faint murmur of the birds.

They were here then. Those inevitable last hours. Soon Alex would be leaving.

She pressed herself tightly against him, the smooth muscled tautness of his flesh hard against her cheekbone. She felt him reach out for her and she turned to him with a kind of silent despair.

They drew together, feeling the warm comfort of each

other's bodies, and made love with a slow, lingering
tenderness.

As if they knew it might be for the very last time.

Kate had been right about Ko Hla, Alex thought.

He was aware of his shadow behind him all the time.

The main bulk of the BIA had moved on, it was true,
but Anderson had told him that Hla was still looking for him, and Alex had a feeling, whichever way
the war went, he wouldn't stop. He couldn't afford to
drop his vigilance for a moment.

Apart from his worries about Hla, though, affairs in
Burma over the next few months started to look promis-
ing.

The unredoubtable American General, 'Vinegar Joe'
Stilwell, courageously led his Chinese forces back into
Northern Burma and the much-vaunted Japanese invasion
of India – Operation U-Go – had been halted by the sheer
grit and determination of British and Indian troops, despite
constant Japanese attacks against Kohima and Imphal.

General Mutaguchi Renya's band of Japanese veterans
were at last in retreat. Alex, remembering his words to
Kate, knew it marked the beginning of the end of Japanese
domination.

No one doubted that a lot of hard fighting still remained, but as 1944 came to a close it now seemed certain
that Burma could be reclaimed. Alex was only sorry that
Wingate, who'd been tragically killed in a plane crash at
the start of Operation Thursday, hadn't lived to see the
British successes for himself. All that he had striven for,
had sacrificed so much for, was at last coming to fruition.

The British pushed relentlessly on and by the New
Year had even crossed the Chindwin in strength. Ahead
of Slim's army lay the Irrawaddy, then Mandalay and
Meiktila, the gateways to Rangoon.

For Alex, the thought that the British would soon be back in Mandalay was perhaps the most heart-lifting news of all. Not just because Mandalay was the key to control of the Upper Irrawaddy, and therefore the key to any British advance down the river on Rangoon, but because he viewed Mandalay as the spiritual centre of Burma.

Capture that and he believed one had the people in one's hand, too.

Alex could already notice the change in the attitude of the Burmese towards the British as the Japanese were pushed back further south. It made his task far more easy.

Now the villagers openly helped him, eager to be part of the resistance against the Japanese. Even the Burmese National Army – the Burmese Independence Army had changed its name the previous year – was rumoured to be about to change their allegiance and swing their weight behind the British.

Alex did not warm to this latest news, however. He found it hateful to think that he would have to welcome with open arms an army which had fought against the British on the side of the Japanese for just as long as it suited them.

He knew what they had done to the Karens, to the Chins. Knew how they had raped their women and killed their elderly. Knew of their cruelties. All of them technically guilty of treason as far as he could see.

It filled him with a deep burning anger to think that he would probably be asked to make contact with the BNA and co-ordinate their support. How on earth could he justify the British *volte face* to those Burmans who had remained loyal and stood by the British throughout all their troubles?

He knew there were political, as well as military, reasons for welcoming Aung San and the BNA, of course. But whatever the sweet-talking of people like MacKenzie, who was in charge of Force 136 to which Alex was linked, and Mountbatten, it made no difference.

Alex still felt like a Judas.

Even the knowledge that they were working towards a swift victory against the Japanese, which would inevitably result in his early return to India and Kate, gave him little comfort.

He remembered Ba Lai and the many others who had been shot or mistreated by the BNA, who had sacrificed everything for the British cause. For what? Alex had this fearful premonition that those loyal subjects were about to be sold down the line.

Whatever his private opinions, though, Alex was determined to give the military whatever support he could. Intelligence reports were vital to the advance and Alex was active gathering material to send through to Rees of the 19th who was advancing on Mandalay and Maymyo.

On a morning in March, when in the early light a heavy ground mist lay across the paddy, Alex was sent to the front to see Rees and Masters about some vital reports he'd gathered. There in front of him, as the mist cleared, he saw the lion-like bulk of Mandalay Hill climbing over the horizon.

Mandalay Hill. It was almost like a mirage. It seemed so long since Kate and he had stood on its summit, looking down into the city and into the palace of the ancient kings of Burma.

'Packed with Japanese, so they say . . .'

The sound of a voice beside him cut into his thoughts. It was one of Rees' officers.

'Mandalay you mean?'

'No,' said the young officer, with a shake of his dark head, 'the hill. There're scores of them apparently, holed up in the subterranean chambers. Just waiting for us to attempt an assault.'

Alex remembered that, under the temples which r d the spine of the hill, there were cellars and dwellings an storage rooms. The Japanese, he supposed, held the whole complex and from it their artillery observers could direct heavy gunfire onto the leading British troops.

'We can't make any further advance until we have control of the hill,' the officer went on. 'It's going to be a hell of a task. We're sitting ducks.'

It looked that way, certainly. Every movement, particularly of vehicles, drew prompt and accurate fire from the Japs.

As Alex stood there waiting for Rees, though, he suddenly recalled the little known path of approach that he and Kate had used when they had climbed the hill all those years ago. The Japanese seemed to be guarding the main path. What if it were possible to advance with a battalion, under cover of night, using those lesser known tracks? It was worth a try, surely?

He went to seek out Rees. Despite his diminutive height – he was only five feet two inches high – the general was always easy to locate. He wore a Gurkha hat and a huge red silk scarf and had a tendency to base himself as far forward as possible in any action.

He was itching to get a move on and receptive to any ideas which would achieve that end.

'Have a word with the commanding officer of the 4th Battalion of the 4th Gurkhas,' Rees told Alex, when he'd put his suggestion to him. 'He was based round here when he was seconded to the Burma Rifles before the war. Had a similar sort of idea.'

Alex met up with Hamish Mackay later that morning. After discussing a few strategies, they both expressed the same opinion. It *might* be just possible to take the Japs by surprise.

Later that night, the assault began and under cover of

rkness Alex moved slowly across the dusty plain along with Hamish's men of the 4th Gurkhas. All night they battled up the steep, long stairway and along the flanks of the ridge. By sheer tenacity they had taken the summit at dawn.

Exhausted, but exhilarated, Alex stood at the highest point of Mandalay Hill, looking down into the city itself. Three and a half years of war had stripped the town of much of its splendour, half the houses had no roofs and to the south lay remnants of factories or warehouses.

But under that pale dawn sky, it hadn't lost its magic. Alex remembered standing here with Kate on that glorious morning, watching the Irrawaddy carve its yellow path past the palace, the brilliant white pagodas scattering the ridge down to the moat and the wall of the fortress.

Mandalay was where he'd first fallen in love with Kate.

He felt very close to her suddenly, could almost sense her presence beside him. Around him came the sound of the crackle of gunfire, the ponderous roar of the guns, but he heard little of it.

He thought only of Kate.


'Where did Alex say he was?'

'Mandalay.' Kate leaned back in her cane chair and stretched out her arms. She was on a few days' leave with Elizabeth down in Bangalore and relishing every minute of it. Though she loved her work at the FEB they'd been so busy over the past few months she'd felt in dire need of a break.

'I must say,' said Elizabeth, 'I never really imagined that they would be able to drive the Japs back so quickly, did you? It looks as if they'll actually be in Rangoon by May.'

Kate heard the excitement in Elizabeth's voice and smiled. She knew the reason. Martin was in Rangoon.

They'd had word from the Swiss Red Cross last year that he'd been taken to the POW camp there.

The news had changed Elizabeth. In Martin's absence she had started to fade, like a flower without water.

Now, Kate noticed, she had grown out her dreadful frizzy perm and was wearing her thick dark hair in a shoulder-length bob, held back from her face with a pretty jade clip. She was revitalised and invigorated.

Her change in attitude had eased her relationship with her mother too. Kate was glad of that. Although Elizabeth still found it hard to accept her mother's various admirers, Kate had been struck by the transformation in Joan Staveley since she had arrived in India.

She was a different person, bursting with vigour and vim. So much so, that it made Kate acutely aware of the strain Joan had been under when she had lived in Burma. That was the undercurrent of ill-feeling between Elizabeth and her mother, of course. The fact that it was now so obvious that her parents' marriage had not been a happy one grated against Elizabeth's sense of loyalty towards her father.

But time was healing that wound. After all, it was more than three years since Henry Staveley had died.

Besides, Kate suspected, now that Martin was likely to return home at any minute, Elizabeth was too busy with her own life to be so concerned about her mother's everyday activities.

'You do realise, Kate,' Elizabeth was saying, her face full of colour, 'that May is less than four weeks away.'

'Don't pin your hopes on May, Elizabeth,' Kate felt obliged to warn her. 'You know how the Japs could suddenly swing up reinforcements or dig themselves in. Or the weather could change.'

But she knew Elizabeth was having none of it.

Kate watched her, sitting on the cane chair, outstretched

legs crossed at the ankles, looking almost as she had done when they had sailed into Rangoon all those years ago. Then she had exuded tentative excitement, aquiver with the thought of seeing Martin again.

Kate smiled. Life had a habit of turning in circles.

Outside in the garden three-and-a-half-year-old Henrietta was chasing a brilliant blue and black butterfly. Kate wondered how she would react to having a father at last. Already she was talking excitedly about seeing him, listening enraptured to Elizabeth's tales as to how they'd met, flipping through the album of photographs which until recently Elizabeth, with fierce superstition, had kept hidden at the bottom of her bedroom cupboard.

Only last night they'd been laid out across the bed, the wedding photographs, the school photos of Martin, captain of cricket, 1st XV rugby, collecting his degree at Oxford. Little pieces of his life, spread out before them like pieces of a quilt.

Kate had picked up the wedding pictures, remembering that day at University Avenue so vividly. Both she and Elizabeth had taken those peaceful, halcyon days so much for granted, accepting them as their right. Now they knew the preciousness of a few simple, quiet moments spent with someone they loved.

There was a sound of running footsteps in the hallway. Henrietta was returning from the garden.

'Look, Mummy!' She stood in the doorway, proudly holding aloft a posy of flowers, all with treacherously short stems. 'For Daddy.'

'Darling, how lovely.' Elizabeth held out her arms to her, gathering her close. 'We'd better keep them safe then for when he comes home. Shall we go and put them in water?'

'Yes. Else they'll die.' Henrietta beamed happily.

'Daddy will be so pleased. He loves flowers you know.

When he was little, not much older than you, he used to have a flower garden all of his own. A little patch where he could plant his own seeds and watch them grow.'

'One for Hetty?' asked Henrietta, with the typical acquisitiveness of a small child.

'I don't see why not. When Daddy comes home perhaps.'

Kate watched as they both disappeared into the kitchen to find a vase, the posy already visibly beginning to wilt in the heat.

So much depended on Martin's speedy return, it worried Kate a little. And yet, she could sympathise with Elizabeth only too well.

For years she had held back, frightened to hope, frightened to dream. Now all that had changed. With the British so close to Rangoon, it was impossible not to believe that the end was in sight.

Kate heard Elizabeth's burst of laughter floating from the kitchen again and frowned. She wanted her to be happy, of course she did. Yet she couldn't help feeling that Elizabeth's optimism was running too high.

Like Icarus, she seemed to be flying too close to the sun. And there would be nothing to catch her if she fell.

It had been raining heavily for most of the morning – the so-called 'mango showers'. Already the yard below was a swirling brown lake. Martin, lying on his damp bed in Rangoon Jail, shifted his position a little, but wasn't inclined to join the cluster of other POWs.

He'd had enough of rumours. First, he'd heard that Slim's 14th Army would be in Rangoon before long, then the navy, then the air force, and still they waited. No one had come.

All around them Rangoon was being razed. Every hour another trail of blue-grey cloud of smoke billowed into the sky, yet, despite suspecting that the Japanese had pulled out of Rangoon, no one had come to rescue them.

'Downing?'

Martin closed his eyes tightly and remained as still as he could. He really was in no mood for talking.

'Downing, have you seen them? The boys are busy painting a message on the roof,' the voice persisted. 'They think Slim can't realise the bloody Japs have gone.'

Martin rolled slowly over. It was clear that Meyer, the American pilot, wasn't going to take the hint and push off.

'I thought they'd already written one message,' he commented. He was sure that yesterday Hudson and Kerr and some others had been busy up on the roofs painting up in huge lettering: JAPS GONE on one section and BRITISH HERE on another. 'I'm sure I even heard that a Beaufighter had swooped down and had a dekko . . .'

'Ah, well, there seems to have been a problem there,' said Meyer. 'You heard the furore earlier this morning?'

'Some damn fool of an RAF pilot skip-bombing the gaol wall? Of course I did.'

'Hudson seems to think that the RAF boys think our first message was a trick. That's why they're up there now. Thought they'd add a few words to persuade the RAF we really are British here and to get a move on.'

Martin could see the grin on Meyer's face. The boyish mischief. He waited.

'EXTRACT DIGIT, that's what they've put on the roof of block seven,' continued Meyer, laughing. 'Good one, isn't it? No Nip could have thought that up! Slim'll have to know that the signs are genuine now.'

'Let's hope the message gets passed on soonest,' Martin returned, a little tartly. 'It wouldn't be much fun to buy it at this stage with one of our own bombs, would it?'

He closed his eyes, turning onto his side and presenting

Meyer with his back. Conversations tired him. Over the past year he'd become increasingly withdrawn and unsociable. He started to hum quietly to himself.

Meyer took no offence. Each POW had found his own way of surviving. Downing was all right. A bit of a crank, but not as bad as some.

Undeterred, he patted Martin on the shoulder. 'I'll let you know if anything else comes up, shall I?'

Tactfully he didn't wait for a reply but slipped down into the compound to join the general throng of POWs milling about there.

Martin stayed on his bed, eyes closed. Even the sound of several planes flying at a low level over the jail didn't make him stir. He didn't know why, but he couldn't feel any exhilaration about the events of the past few days. His emotions felt strangely dead.

The truth was his last link with the warm world had been severed so long ago, and so brutally, he wasn't sure how he would cope with being part of it again.

He lay on his bed, legs drawn up, rocking slightly from side to side. Dear God, he'd been frightened of capture, now he was frightened of freedom. The knowledge of his own weakness appalled him.

Later that afternoon, Meyer came up again.

'You missed all the fun,' he said, sitting uninvited on Martin's bed. 'We've had two RAF chappies here. They were on a reconnaissance flight and landed at Mingaladon. Apparently there's an amphibious operation on its way and they've gone off to try and tip them off that the Japs have gone. If they don't get word through to them in time, they'll be knocking shit out of us, so be warned.'

'Just what we need.'

'What beats me is what all these wretched BNA and INA chappies are doing. They seem to have been in Rangoon for a while and still haven't managed to let the British know that the enemy have left. Think they're too busy fighting amongst themselves as to who'll run the city. Hudson's been out and he says there are red BNA flags everywhere.'

'Not surprised.' If the British didn't arrive soon they'd never get back into Rangoon to govern.

He heard Meyer strike a match and smelt the aroma of a cheroot.

'Want one?' Meyer was holding a thick white one out to Martin. 'The Indians handed us over a whole boxful.'

Martin pushed himself up. 'Thanks.'

There was a flash of lightning outside. The rain was now coming down in sheets. No wonder Slim and the others had been held up. Impossible to move in such conditions.

Martin lit up his cheroot and took a long satisfying puff. Tobacco, of any sort, was still a luxury to him.

'Do you know,' said Meyer, leaning back a little to watch the smoke curl up to the ceiling, 'I'm not surprised that Slim can't believe that the Japanese haven't made a last stand for Rangoon. It goes so absolutely against the Japanese way of thinking not to fight to the death, doesn't it? I can't believe General Kimura was ordered to retreat, so what do you suppose made him pull out like that?'

'Fear.' Martin knew all about that.

'But his honour depended on the defence of the city,' Meyer returned, with a small shake of his head. 'And you know about honour and the Japanese. Do you know, one of our chaps in the squadron came across an Order of the Day which had been found on the body of a Japanese. Do you know what it said?'

Martin shook his head.

'"If your hands are broken, fight with your feet. If your hands and feet are broken, use your teeth. If there is no breath left in your body, fight with your ghost. We must have the determination to defend our positions to the death, and even after death . . ." Punchy stuff, eh? So why, for Pete's sake, did Kimura slink away without firing a shot?'

Martin sucked at his cheroot and lifted his shoulders dispassionately. 'Beats me.'

'Lucky for us, though. We'd have been pounded to hell, if they'd stayed.'

'Yes.'

Downstairs there was a slight commotion. The radio operators were still frantically trying to make contact with the Allied forces, to warn them to call off their assault, but no one was acknowledging their message.

Meyer stubbed out his cheroot and went off to investigate.

All through the night there were disturbances but Martin paid them little attention. He lay there, curled up tightly into a ball, listening to the rain torrenting down. The sound of its steady rhythm comforted him somehow, reminding him of when he was a child, lying in the warm security of the nursery wing at Chilgrove, listening to the rain beating against the windowpanes.

The next morning, Hudson and the few inmates considered fit enough to join him, went out to see what they could do to repair Mingaladon airfield. Martin hobbled out onto the balcony to see them off, but then returned to his bed. The sudden bustle and activity around him was exhausting. He'd really never been well since he'd been brought here by the *Kempeitai*. He wondered if he would ever be able to move more than three or four paces without collapsing with the strain of it again.

Later that afternoon a B24 came over. Martin heard the shout from the men in the compound and stumbled across to the balcony to see what the fuss was all about. For one heart-stopping moment, when the bomb-bay doors swung open above the yard, he thought that all their desperate efforts to identify themselves as Allies had failed, and they were about to be bombed. But even as he flinched, tensing himself for the inevitable, he heard an appreciative roar go up as parachutes burst open and containers of rations floated down into the compound and adjoining streets.

Martin leaned against the railing, watching the men fall upon the containers with the rapacity of Ali Baba and his forty thieves. A few minutes later, and the irrepressible Meyer appeared by his side, clutching an armful of 'K' rations, grinning from ear to ear. Martin couldn't understand why he was so pleased. As far as he could see, if the Allies were dropping as many rations as this, then they weren't about to be rescued for a few days yet. Maybe even longer.

He felt the old black depression descending on him.

'Want any?' Meyer was holding out some large oatmeally biscuits.

'No.' He was being churlish, he knew, but the threads of despondency had wrapped themselves around him, squeezing him so tightly that it made his head hurt. He wished Meyer would leave.

Meyer shrugged, unperturbed. 'Suit yourself.'

Martin pushed himself away from the railing and hobbled back to his bed. He lay there, rocking and humming, trying to shut out the world around him. He was afraid to hope too much, lest it all slipped away from him at the last minute.

After a while he heard footsteps coming across the room towards him and he determinedly closed his eyes. This time he'd make sure he kept Meyer at bay.

He began to hum just a little bit louder.

'Martin?'

He stiffened. Meyer was playing tricks now. Changing his voice.

'Martin, are you all right?'

A hand was touching his shoulder gently. He knew instinctively it was not Meyer's. For some reason, Martin did not know why exactly, he felt terribly afraid.

'It's all over . . .'

The voice was peeling back the years, a thread leading him back down the path of time. He thought he recognised it. Yet, he had so often drifted along the borders of madness, he was frightened in case he had finally crossed into that inescapable dark abyss.

'Martin, can you hear me? It's all over.'

This time, though, he was sure.

Martin swung round. The face bending close to his was so familiar it was almost painful to behold. Martin involuntarily thrust out his thin hand to touch it.

'Alex?' His voice was disbelieving. 'It *is* you. God! I was so afraid . . .'

'It's all over.' A warm, strong hand covered his.

'I just can't believe it.'

'It's true.'

'When did you get here? How?'

'Didn't you hear the fuss when the navy chaps arrived?'

Martin shook his head. He'd been vaguely aware of some sort of commotion in the yard after one of the inmates had brought him up his lunch, but he'd had no idea what it had been about.

'So you missed the Press, too?'

'Press? Good God, what were they doing here?'

'Their usual stuff. Were supposed to come with the main invasion fleet, but it wasn't making much headway so they jumped off and walked cross-country. Were the first to arrive, apparently.'

Martin managed a smile. 'The army won't be pleased about that.'

Alex laughed. 'They weren't.'

'And you? How did you manage to get into the mixing pot?'

'Came down to do a spot of reconnaissance. Rumours have been flying all week about the Japs pulling out. Slim and his lot haven't known what to believe. Thought if I could find out one way or another for myself, I could pass on a qualified report.'

'I see.'

'And of course, once it was obvious that the city was pretty much deserted, I made my way across here . . .'

Martin slumped forward. It was almost too much for his mind to encompass.

'You're safe, now. The army boys will be coming in a minute to get you out of here.'

'You mean, tonight?'

'Tomorrow probably. They've got hospital ships standing by. You should be on your way to India before too long.'

'Oh.' All the old tensions and fears started to pour back into him.

'Is it a pretty frightening prospect?' Alex asked him gently.

Martin knew Alex could sense the instability of his mood. 'A bit.' He glanced up cautiously. There seemed to be no surprise in Alex's face. He felt himself relax a little. 'Actually, if you want the truth, it's bloody terrifying. I'm not even sure if I'm ready to leave this place.' Only to Alex would he have been prepared to admit such a thing. 'Stupid, isn't it?'

'Quite understandable, actually.'

'It's as if there are two of me, here. One wants desperately to go, the other's afraid to.'

'Just give yourself time. You've got nothing to prove.' Alex's quiet voice was soothing. 'You've done your bit.'

'I didn't, though.' Martin thought about Seagrim and his Karen levies. He'd done nothing to advance their cause at all. Seagrim had been captured and brought to Rangoon Jail only a few months after Martin's arrival. Martin had studiously avoided him, so racked with guilt that he'd done nothing to help him or the Karens, silently mourning him when he'd been executed by the Japanese a few months later.

No, he'd done nothing for any cause. Perhaps that was part of the problem.

'Once you're back in India it'll be different. You've got Elizabeth there. And Henrietta.'

'Henrietta?'

Alex beamed. 'Your daughter, Martin. A real heart-stopper.'

Martin stirred, letting out a deep breath. 'A daughter?' He felt himself come back to life again. 'When was she born?'

'Just after the Japs invaded. In Maymyo. During an air-raid.'

'Of course, I knew I must have a child, but I heard nothing, you see.'

'She's a smashing youngster, Martin. You can be very proud of her. Dark-haired, very like Elizabeth as a child . . .'

He started to talk then, to tell him all the little things about his daughter. And Martin, listening, for the first time felt some glimmer of hope for the future.

By the time the INA soldiers arrived to carry him to the landing craft at Phonngyi Jetty the next morning, he was no longer afraid of leaving.

He was ready to go home.

## 25

' *K*ate, it's Elizabeth.'
    'Can you speak up? It's a fearful line.' Kate, in her office in Delhi, cradled the phone closer to her ear. Across the crackling phone line came an unmistakable sob. 'Elizabeth, what is it? What's happened?'

'I'm all right now.' There was the sound of a nose being vigorously blown.

'But whatever's the matter? Is it Martin?'

The silence that followed spoke volumes.

'Oh dear, what's wrong?'

After the first few ecstatic moments which greeted Martin's return, it had soon become perilously clear how much he had altered.

Kate knew that Elizabeth hadn't been so naïve as to imagine that he'd returned unscathed, but even she had not been prepared for the devastating change in Martin.

It wasn't so much the physical side, though in truth they were all pretty shocked by that – poor little Henrietta quite unable to equate the razor-thin scarecrow of a man before her with the handsome broad-shouldered fellow of the photographs – rather, it was the mental state which perturbed them so.

Kate, who'd come down to Bangalore to be with the family when Martin came in from Burma, could see their distress and confusion. No one quite knew how to treat his black moods, his inability to concentrate or deal with crowds, his insistence on sleeping on the floor, his sudden withdrawals and, even more difficult, his sudden loud bursts of tuneless humming.

The worst of it all, though, was that Kate could see how desperately hard he was trying to fit back into normal life.

And how impossible he was finding it.

Now it seemed his inability to do so was causing violent outbursts. Poor, gentle Martin, who would never willingly harm a fly, suddenly reduced to throwing frustrated fits of temper which caused all the household to cower in horror from his rage.

'It's not *really* him, of course I know that,' Elizabeth was saying down the telephone. 'It's just so difficult for Henrietta. She wants so much to love him. But how can she, when one moment he's bouncing her on his knee and reading quietly to her like the most perfect father in the world, and the next acting like a madman, chucking things all over the house?'

'What do the doctors say?'

'That he just needs time. And I do know that. It's just . . .' There was a long silence. 'Kate? I know this is a lot to ask, but is there the slightest chance of you getting a short leave to come down to Bangalore?'

The anguish in her voice was unmistakable. Kate knew how bad things must be between them if Elizabeth had had to swallow her pride to ask her to come.

She heard her bite back a tearful sniff and then continue: 'I wouldn't suggest you stayed here, of course. But Mother says you could stay with her . . . if you *could* come, that is.'

'Of course I'll come.' Kate didn't allow any of her doubts to show. Somehow she'd find a way.

As it happened it was easier than she'd thought. It was now August, and since the British already had retaken most of Burma the Bureau was not quite as busy as it had once been. Kate had saved up considerable leave over the past year in the hope – misplaced, as it turned out – that Alex would get back for some furlough, so she had plenty of time due to her.

As soon as she arrived in Bangalore she could see how much Martin's condition had worsened. His mood swings were more pronounced, his outbursts more violent. It was this which worried Kate the most.

'How long has he been like this?' Kate asked Elizabeth quietly on the second day, as they took advantage of a break in the rains to sit in the garden.

'It's been gradually getting worse and worse, I suppose,' said Elizabeth. 'He was all right when he first came home. After the hospital, I mean. Then, about a month ago, he got into a fearful state with me over something terribly trivial – I can't even recall what started it off – and we seem to have regressed from there.'

'Can't you remember at all what prompted such a reaction?'

'Not really, no. I *think* it was something to do with Burma,' Elizabeth said. 'Not about the war,' she added hurriedly, 'about our earlier time there. I thought it might help him to think back on the happier moments we'd had.' Overhead a bee buzzed by, heavily laden with pollen. 'He was fine to begin with, quite communicative for him in fact, but then suddenly, I can't even recollect what we were talking about, he suddenly started thumping the table and shouting at me.'

'You'd obviously touched a raw nerve.'

'He was fine one minute, impossible the next. It was quite without warning,' Elizabeth told her. It had been terribly frightening. 'Henrietta was most awfully upset.'

'Poor little thing, I can imagine,' said Kate. She remembered how much Henrietta had been looking forward to her father's return. 'You must try and explain what's happening to her.'

'How can I when I don't understand myself?' broke in Elizabeth, unhappily. 'It's painful to see her, Kate. She tries to keep out of his way when she sees him coming now. She turns tail and runs away to hide. And the worst of it all, is Martin knows. And he minds dreadfully. It doesn't help things very much.'

'You'll have to get him to see a doctor, Elizabeth,' Kate said gently. 'Persuade him to get help.'

'I've tried. So has my mother. But he says he doesn't want to see anyone. That he can manage on his own.'

'Perhaps he doesn't want anyone to delve around too deeply,' said Kate. She could understand that. Martin had put up a thin, protective layer to shield himself from all that had happened. He didn't want to risk that being removed. 'If you dig around too much it means he has to face all his fears.'

'But he must face them some day,' said Elizabeth matter of factly.

'Naturally he must. But perhaps he needs more time.'

Kate was aware of Elizabeth's face tightening. 'I wouldn't mind for myself, but I have to think about Henrietta.'

'Of course.' Kate had noticed the change in the little girl. She was no longer the gregarious bright-eyed creature of Kate's last visit. She no longer ran to bring her father flowers.

Elizabeth adjusted her position and stirred her lemon tea. 'The trouble is . . .' she hesitated.

'Yes?' prompted Kate.

'I'm not sure how much we have in common now.'

Kate eyed her for a moment. She could see how exhausted she was feeling. 'Look, Elizabeth, he's ill now,' she said. 'It'll be different when he's better. Fundamentally he hasn't changed. All the things he used to love . . .'

'That's just the point,' Elizabeth broke in, her dark eyes

bleak. 'He used to love Burma. That's what made him fall in love with me, in the first place. Now it's the very thing he hates. That's what his outbursts are all about. That's why he finds it so difficult to be with me now. He associates me with all the misery he had to endure.'

'Oh, Elizabeth, surely not.' Yet in some peculiar way Kate saw it made sense.

'I'm certain of it, Kate. He hates Burma and I'm part of that place he hates.' Tears were flowing down her cheeks now. 'It might be different in England, but I don't know. I really don't.'

'So is that where you're going? England?'

Elizabeth nodded. 'That's about the only thing we have discussed. Martin wants to go back there as soon as he's well enough to travel. He's written to his family already.'

Kate stretched out and squeezed Elizabeth's arm reassuringly. 'It might be for the best, you know. His family were a rather convivial bunch, weren't they? You might be glad of their support.'

Elizabeth took out a lace handkerchief and dabbed at her face. 'I'll have Mother as well, of course.'

'Will you?' Kate said, surprised. 'Good heavens, is she going back to England, too?'

'Yes.' Elizabeth blew her nose. She managed a small smile. 'Believe it or not, one of her chipper colonels has proposed to her.'

'Heavens!'

'Actually, I'm terribly glad for her,' said Elizabeth. 'You know she's been absolutely wonderful about this business with Martin, she really has. If nothing else it's made us bury the hatchet.' She didn't add that her own complications with Martin had made her a mite more sympathetic to any difficulties her mother might have experienced in her own marriage. 'The colonel's got a place near Chichester. Apparently that's not too far from

Chilgrove. So Mother will be sort of off stage . . .'

Kate smiled. Being able to keep Joan Staveley, in her present sparkling form, in the background by any other means than a straitjacket was highly doubtful.

The quick treble of a child's voice came to them from the verandah and they lifted their heads. Henrietta was coming out down the steps towards them, Cassie, the black and white spaniel at her heels.

'Hello Munchkin,' said Kate, holding out her arms to her. 'How was your sleep?'

Henrietta pursed her lips together and waggled her head noncommittally. 'All right.' She ran to kiss her mother and then climbed up onto Kate's knee, settling herself comfortably and snuggling up against her.

Elizabeth stood up. 'I suppose I ought to go and see if Martin's awake yet.'

Kate stretched out her hand. 'Why don't you leave him be? He'll come out when he's ready.'

'I don't want him to feel left out. The doctor said it was important to make him feel included, part of the family.'

'Aren't you crowding him a bit?' asked Kate, who personally thought that Elizabeth was not allowing Martin enough time to himself.

'If I don't go, he'll just lie there brooding.'

'Maybe you should let him. Once in a while.'

Elizabeth hesitated. 'But he'll get depressed.'

Kate lifted her shoulders. Elizabeth had to fight her own battles in her own way.

'So,' she said to Henrietta when Elizabeth had gone back into the house, 'how was Daddy today?'

'There was a snake in the garden, today,' she said, intentionally ignoring Kate's question. 'Hari killed it. It was t-h-i-s long.' She held out her hands as far as they could go. 'Cassie found it.'

'Clever old Cassie!' The black and white spaniel lifted its head up from his paws and pricked up its ears at his name. Kate broke off a piece of cake and threw it towards him and he gobbled up the tit-bit in one hurried mouthful, thumping his tail appreciatively against the ground. She was about to break him off another piece, when Henrietta stopped her.

'Mummy will get cross, Aunty Kate,' she warned, wagging her finger. 'You know what she says: No feeding at the table. That's the rule. 'Cept when he was ill. Then it was different. Like when I'm poorly . . .'

Kate laughed, brushing her hands together to get rid of the crumbs. 'Poor old Cassie. I remember that.'

'Got knocked down by a car,' Henrietta said. He'd nearly been killed. 'Mummy says the driver was going too fast.'

'He was,' Kate agreed. There was a silence. She looked down at the child, hesitated, then decided to brave it. 'Do you remember, Henrietta, what Cassie was like when we tried to go and help him?' She was trying to choose her words carefully. 'How he snapped at us when we tried to move him?'

Henrietta nodded.

'Well, in a way that's like your father. Every time we go to try and help him at the moment he snaps, doesn't he?'

'He shouts at Mummy too!' Henrietta piped up accusingly.

'He does, yes. Just like Cassie growled at us when we tried to help. Cassie was frightened, you see. Your father's the same. He had such a horrid time when he was away that he's a little bit frightened too. But it doesn't mean he doesn't love you, darling. He does. Very much. And your mummy. But he's got to mend first, like Cassie. Only it's a bit more difficult than a broken leg.'

Henrietta tilted her head slightly, considering. 'He might go away again. Back to hospital.'

Elizabeth had been preparing the ground then. 'Yes, he might,' agreed Kate. 'But it won't be for long.'

'Then he'll be better?'

'Probably. Cassie's only got a slight limp now, hasn't he?'

'He can still spot snakes,' Henrietta said with satisfaction.

'There you are, then. Almost as good as new.'

'Better actually, Aunty Kate. When he runs off with my ball, I sometimes catch him.'

Kate laughed. 'You see.'

Happier now, Henrietta slipped off her knee to follow Cassie as he set off jauntily across the lawn on some important canine exploration.

Kate saw Elizabeth returning from the house. She was alone.

'No Martin?'

Elizabeth shook her head. 'I took your advice and left him in peace.' She slumped down in the chair beside Kate. 'I think perhaps you're right, we've all been trying *too* hard. I was so afraid of his feeling excluded, you see. While he's been away Henrietta and I have become quite a close-knit pair.'

'I know.' In Martin's absence they had filled the void in each other's lives with a solid completeness.

'I wanted to wrap him up and make him feel safe, but I think all I've succeeded in doing is to smother him,' admitted Elizabeth. She cut herself a thin sliver of cake, but didn't eat it, crumbling the piece between her fingers instead. 'I've managed it all rather badly.'

'Nonsense.'

'I have. I'm sure you were better with Alex when he first came back.'

'I'm not sure I was.'

Kate thought about those moments on the lakes when he, too, had become silent and withdrawn. Then she had purposefully held back, not probing too deeply.

In the event she wasn't sure whether it was a wiser course than Elizabeth's after all. It was only in the final hours before he left that she'd found out the truth behind his nightmares. By then it was too late to peel back the surface and to examine what lay underneath.

Now Alex was back in the jungle again. Back with Ko Hla.

There was the sound of a door opening. Kate looked up. Martin had stepped out onto the verandah. She saw him hesitate slightly, then start down the steps towards them. He still walked with a stick, hobbling slightly.

'Hallo, come and join us,' Kate called out with a wave.

'I only came to tell you,' he said, pausing to catch his breath, 'there's been an announcement on the radio. They're expecting the Japanese to agree to the Potsdam Declaration. They're awaiting an announcement by Emperor Hirohito if not today, then tomorrow.'

Elizabeth was on her feet and beside Martin in one movement. 'That means they're surrendering!' she exclaimed, flinging her arms around him. 'It's all over.'

'As long as the Imperial Guard don't have some trick up their sleeves, it is, yes.' He spoke cautiously. Everyone knew how fanatical the Imperial Guards were. Even now they could storm the Imperial Palace and try and persuade the Emperor to change his mind.

'I suppose they couldn't continue after Hiroshima,' Kate remarked. The newspaper reports had shown devastating damage. 'Truman made no bones about continuing to use atomic bombs on other Japanese cities unless they did agree to submit.'

'They wouldn't have given up otherwise.' Martin stood

staring out across the garden. He knew what single-minded extremists the Japanese soldiers had been. Remembering, he found his hands had tensed in his pockets.

'No, they wouldn't,' agreed Kate. She knew that Alex had told her the powers-that-be had estimated it would take at least three or four years to recapture Malaya completely by conventional warfare.

She took a deep breath. Now it meant Alex was coming home.

She leant back in her chair, pushing up her hair from the back of her neck with a lazy, contented movement. 'It's wonderful news, Martin. Thank you for coming down to tell us.'

He gave a slow smile, almost the Martin of old. 'Thought you'd be pleased.'

He stood for a moment, head tilted back, feeling the warmth of the sun on his face.

'Would you like some tea, darling?'

Kate saw Martin's head jerk down, alert, tensing.

'What?'

'Some tea?'

He gave a quick, sharp shake of his head. 'I'll just pop back to the house I think. See if there's any more news.'

Elizabeth leant forward, about to catch hold of his arm, about to insist that he stay. But at the last moment she glanced quickly at Kate and held back.

Martin's relief was almost palpable. He was like a swimmer caught in a strong current whose feet had touched sandy ground at last. He gave a swift nod and started to hobble back up across the lawn.

Watching him go, Kate believed she understood him a little more. She'd seen his face when he'd told her about the likely surrender. He thought he'd failed to do his bit. He couldn't accept that he was basically a man of peace, not war. Because of this belief in his own deficiency, he had suffered then and was suffering now.

What was it Alex had said? Something from Shakespeare. Something about a coward dies a thousand times, a brave man only once. So it must seem to Martin. She was sure he believed he had suffered because of his own cowardice.

There was a flurry of movement at the far side of the lawn and Cassie came romping across the lawn, Henrietta hot on his trail. Martin stopped and turned towards her.

Kate could see that his love for his daughter was painfully intense, that he was aching to stretch out to her but afraid of rejection.

Henrietta stood, firm jaw jutted out, regarding him solemnly. She took a step forward and Kate thought for one glorious moment that she was about to run to him. But at the last minute, she hesitated, turning on her heel and running back the way she'd come.

Kate could see Martin's shoulders hunch forward, the weight of his dejection pulling him down. She wished she could have urged Henrietta to go to him, but to have prompted her would only have caused humiliation to both sides.

Rebuffed, Martin was starting to hobble forward again. His faltering progress was almost excruciating to watch.

Then suddenly, back down the path came Henrietta.

'Daddy!'

Martin turned towards his daughter. She was clutching a large single dahlia which she'd gone back to pluck from the garden border.

'For you.'

For a moment they stood staring at each other, grey eye meeting grey. Then Martin ducked unsteadily down to her, holding out his arms to her. This time she didn't try to dodge his embrace but with a bright, trusting smile ran to him, arms wide.

Kate saw Elizabeth's eyes fill with tears. 'At last,' she heard her whisper, almost to herself.

A beginning, however small, had been made.

And Kate, watching Martin stagger up the steps, the red flower clutched to his chest, felt the optimism of old rise and surge within her again.

Kate, still in Bangalore over a month later, found herself increasingly enjoying being out of the heat and dust of the big city. She'd intended to return to Delhi by early September, but the Japanese surrender had prompted the closure of many of the propaganda departments, as well as the offices of D Division, and there seemed little need for her urgent return now.

Besides, she felt that if there were any news of Alex it would be delivered to the Staveleys. Apart from two quick notes, one in late June from the Sittaing, the other in July from Moulmein, Kate had heard nothing. She kept telling herself that the war was over, that nothing could happen now. Nevertheless the unspoken fear kept returning to her.

Then one day, towards the end of September, she came back to the house from visiting Elizabeth to find Joan Staveley hovering in the hallway.

'Oh, Kate, I'm so glad you're back,' she said, catching hold of her arm hurriedly. 'He's been here for hours. I didn't want to send him away.'

'Send who away?' For a split second she believed it might be Alex and her heart skipped a beat. Then she realised the impossibility of that thought.

She followed Joan into the cool sitting room. For a moment Kate didn't recognise the man sitting on the chintz-covered sofa.

'Kate!' He got hastily to his feet, smiling broadly.

It was the smile that did it. Even in that pinched, cadaverous face, there was no mistaking it.

'Johnnie. Good heavens, what are you doing here in Bangalore?'

Kate found it difficult to muster up undue warmth. The sight of him made her think of that morning in Singapore years before when she'd found him with Sylvia. She realised she still minded, not for her own sake – she'd stopped loving Johnnie long ago – but for her father's.

He hesitated slightly, aware of the threads of hostility which hung between them.

'I came to see you, actually,' he said.

He sank down again on the sofa. It was quite obvious that he was not at all well. She supposed he must have been in the camp in Singapore. He looked thinner, if anything, than Martin. But there was none of the look of the hunted, cornered animal that Martin possessed, none of the tense rigidity in his stance. He looked, quite simply, undefeated by all the hardships he'd endured.

'You know about your father, of course?' he said quietly.

'Yes.' She'd only heard the news the previous week. It had been a dreadful blow, even though in truth it hadn't been entirely unexpected.

'I'm very sorry about that.'

She lifted her head slightly. 'Easier for you and Sylvia surely?' she said, with a bitter twist of her mouth.

'Jesus, Kate. That's a bit below the belt.'

'Well, presumably you *are* going to see Sylvia in Perth when you get back, aren't you?'

She saw him look away from her for a moment.

'You see,' she said, taking his silence for vindication. Her voice was vaguely triumphant.

'You're quite wrong, Kate,' he protested. 'It isn't like that at all.'

'Isn't it?'

'No.' He took out a packet of cigarettes from his shirt pocket, offered her one, and when she refused, lit one up for himself. 'As a matter of fact,' he said, inhaling deeply, 'your father asked me to go and see her.'

'Heavens, Johnnie, do you really expect me to believe that?'

He looked at her uncomfortably. 'Whether you like it or not, Kate, it's true.'

Something in his face silenced her. His distress was obvious and unfeigned.

She squeezed her hands tightly together, knowing she was taking out on him all her sorrow and frustration that her father had not survived – as he had done. Seeing Johnnie had reawakened old memories. She still could not bring herself to forgive him for past sins.

They eyed each other warily. Johnnie stretched over and tipped the ash off the end of his cigarette.

'There was a reason for my coming,' he said, after a moment's pause.

'Oh?'

'Your father . . .' He stopped to clear his throat. 'Your father asked me to bring this out for you.' He reached over to the small mahogany table beside him and picked up a collection of frayed sheets of paper.

Kate found that her hands were shaking as she stretched out to take them from Johnnie. There was a certain poignancy to their tattered shabbiness, as if they had their own tale of hardship and endurance to tell. A dark echo of their creator's, perhaps.

Johnnie watched her for a moment, then stubbed out his cigarette and stood up. 'I'll leave you then, shall I, Kate?'

He hesitated. He would have liked to have spoken to her about her father, praising his courage and fortitude a little, but it no longer seemed appropriate.

'I'm sorry we have to part like this. I'd hoped there might be some warmth between us at least. For old times' sake.'

She lifted her shoulders lightly.

'If it helps at all, I admit I behaved badly. It was not my intention to hurt anyone.' He took a deep breath. 'Least of all, your father.'

'No, I don't suppose it was.' Her fingers touched the edges of the rough paper.

He paused. She did not offer him any encouragement.

'Well then, Kate, I suppose this is goodbye.' He crossed the room to her side and held out his hand to her. It would have been churlish of her not to take it.

'Thank you for bringing the diary.'

'I did it for him, you know.'

'I do know, yes.'

Even now he could smile at her. 'And perhaps a tiny bit for you.'

Despite everything she felt the stirrings of a smile. She'd forgotten Johnnie's easy charm. He'd always known how to use it to his advantage.

She watched him as he walked out of the room, seeing him stride down the path on those painfully thin legs of his. He held himself very upright but she could guess at the effort it took.

She went back to the sofa and sat down, then, picking up her father's notes, began to read.

It was five o'clock in the morning before she had finished.

For a long time she sat, holding the diary against her chest, not moving.

How was it possible for a man to endure so much? From that very first entry, she'd seen vividly, terribly, his day-to-day struggle for survival.

To imagine her father, her darling debonair, fastidious

father, who in Singapore had changed his clothes three or four times a day, being reduced to wearing a single piece of cloth, the inglorious 'Jap Happy', was painful enough; to live with him through his sufferings and hardships, from the day of the Selarang Incident when he'd been moved from the hospital to the main compound, through Changi, the Death March up to the railway, and the camp itself, was almost more than she could bear.

The erratic inconsistency of the entries told their own story.

She knew now how much her father had risked by keeping the diary – and Johnnie by hiding it for him – she read of friendships, the intensity of which they were likely never to experience again, of tortures and humiliations, of hunger and despair.

She saw her father, a man who on his wedding day had casually spooned caviar from an ice-sculpted swan, reduced to bartering on the black market for a rat. But above all that, above the misery and despair, she read about the spirit which had prevailed in the camps, of the sheer determination of every man to try and live one more day.

When she reached the final entry, she put the diary down, feeling very, very humble.

She saw how totally she had misjudged Johnnie. Her father had spoken of him as a friend and told of his efforts to try and save his life.

She guessed the difficulties he'd overcome in order to bring the diary to her in India, instead of returning to Australia with the other POWs. She also felt mortified by her cold reception and realised she couldn't let him leave without thanking him. Or apologising.

Even as the pale light of dawn flooded the sky Kate left the house on her way to see him. As fortune would have it, Joan Staveley, in the hour she'd spent with Johnnie before Kate's arrival, had managed to establish he was staying at the Bangalore Club, and she drove across town to see him.

He was sitting on the verandah as she came up the path, morning paper spread out on the table in front of him.

'Hello, Kate, this is a surprise,' he said, with an easy smile. 'Do you want to sit down?' He stood up, inviting her to join him, without a hint of rancour about their previous meeting.

'I've come to apologise,' Kate said, never one to duck the issue. 'I behaved rather badly yesterday.'

'I probably should have let you know I was coming.'

It was generous of him to excuse her ill-temper so. She cleared her throat.

'The diary . . . I read it last night.' For a moment, she found it difficult to speak. 'I never imagined . . . I never guessed what all those years must have been like.'

'There's no earthly reason you should have.'

His voice was light and tolerant. She saw that, with a supreme effort, he was managing to put all the horrors beside him.

He had always had that capacity, Johnnie. Even in the early days in Singapore he'd never been one to dwell on the adversities of life. He'd shouldered his father's death, his missed opportunity at university and the rigours of the tin mines, with no complaint. She could see that his ability to simply get on with life had stood him in good stead under the severity of the Japanese.

'My father thought highly of you, Johnnie.'

'Not at the beginning.' He smiled. Even now he could recall Mark Lawrence's outrage at being in the same camp as him with a stab of humour. 'But at the end, yes, I think he did.'

'He entrusted you with his diary. I hadn't realised what you must have risked in hiding it for him,' she said. Her father's stories about the punishment meted out by the

Japanese for the discovery of illicit goods were wretched. Beheadings were not uncommon.

'Kept me on my toes, at any rate,' said Johnnie, with a grin. He'd regarded it as a personal challenge to outwit the guards. 'But your father was the one, Kate. He kept that diary hidden for almost three years. I had it for little more than one.'

He was gracious with his praise.

'Were . . . were you there with him when he died, Johnnie?'

He didn't flinch or look away. 'Yes.' It wasn't quite the truth but he thought Mark would have liked Kate to have believed it. 'We were on our way back to Singapore.'

'He'd survived the railway then?' All Kate had heard was that he'd died at Kanchanaburi. 'If only he could have hung on just that little bit longer.'

'He did try, Kate.'

'I'm sure he did.' There was a catch in her voice. 'Johnnie, would you mind talking to me about what happened? I know I've got the diary, but there are one or two things . . .'

'Of course. Only too happy to.'

In the end Johnnie did most of the talking. In a low, soft voice he told her as much as he could remember about those three and a half years of captivity. He even managed a touch of grim humour, especially about those early days in Singapore when they'd had a certain freedom and could still move around the city.

'So what now?' she asked when he had finished.

'Back to Australia, I guess.' He gave a light shrug. 'The farm maybe.'

'And Sylvia?' She could ask that now without enmity.

'If she'll have me, yes.'

'She'd be a fool not to.' He'd be very good for Louisa too, she could see that.

'Sylvia might not see it that way,' he said. But there was a certain optimism in his voice. 'And what about you, Kate?'

'I'm not sure yet.'

She looked down quickly at her hands. She didn't even know if Alex was safe or not.

'I'm sorry.' Seeing the anguish in her face, Johnnie leant forward and touched her hand. 'I've obviously said something I shouldn't have . . .' His voice tapered away, unsure.

'It isn't your fault, Johnnie,' she assured him. 'It's just I don't know where Alex is. Everyone else seems to be coming home except him. I'm beginning to worry.' It was the first time she had voiced her true fears. She took a deep, shuddering breath. 'What if . . .' She couldn't bring herself to talk about Ko Hla.

Johnnie's hand tightened on hers. 'He'll come home, Kate. A wily chap like that.'

'What if he doesn't, Johnnie?' There was a measure of despair in her voice.

'He will.' Johnnie smiled. 'I know all about survivors.'

She tried to absorb some of his confidence into her chilled heart but she knew that without Alex there was nothing. He was her life.

There was a silence. Kate knew she should be heading back to the Staveleys. It was already past midday.

'Will I see you again, Johnnie?' she asked, standing up.

'You're welcome any time, you know.'

'Thank you, Kate, but I've managed to scrounge a lift on a cargo plane that leaves for Singapore this evening. I daren't miss it, not all pilots are as sympathetic as this one towards a poor POW trying to get home.'

Kate smiled. Johnnie would manage.

'You will look after yourself?'

'Of course.'

'And you'll give my love to Louisa when you see her, won't you? Perhaps when everything has settled down a bit we all might be able to spend some time together . . .'

The words hung between them. It was impossible to make plans or promises at the moment.

'Goodbye then, Kate.'

She stretched up and kissed him. Even now the overwhelming thinness of his body shocked her as she held him. His spirited manner belied his frailty.

'Goodbye, Johnnie,' she said, feeling the tears prick her eyes. 'Take care.'

He raised his hand in farewell.

He was still standing there on the verandah as she drove away, not willing to give in and collapse into the chair until she was out of sight.

His courage and determination affected her. She drove on, feeling a surge of new energy within her.

Somehow she'd get news of Alex. And when she did . . .

Suddenly she knew she could no longer wait impassively in India for him to come back. The agony of uncertainty was pressing down on her, suffocating her.

She knew then what she must do.

She must go to Burma herself.

The simplicity of the solution was so obvious it almost took her breath away.

## 26

*T*he jungle seemed to close in about him.

Alex pressed on, slowly, quietly, with the infinite care of a man walking barefoot down a still-smouldering cinder path.

He was aware that Ko Hla was somewhere closeby. Ever since Alex had returned to Burma Ko Hla had shadowed him, at times even making his presence known, as if taunting him with his proximity. Now for the past week Alex had been conscious of him again, stalking him from afar like a tiger.

But Hla had still made no move to come out into the open and challenge him.

At first this had puzzled Alex. Then in Moulmein last week, when Hla had turned up once more, he realised what was happening. Hla was stage managing their confrontation, leading him to a battleground of his own choosing.

And Alex guessed where that place would be.

Anapuri.

He walked tentatively on, pushing aside the low hanging creepers. He understood how exposed he was, how vulnerable, but he sensed he was safe for the moment. All his instincts told him that Ko Hla wanted to confront him face to face. If he'd wanted merely to annihilate him, he'd had numerous opportunities to shoot him in the back over the past year.

Alex suspected a single bullet would not have satisfied Hla's need for revenge. He wanted to corner Alex and then to mock him with his own stupidity.

Perhaps that gave Alex a chance.

Up ahead of him he saw the little bamboo bridge that led over to the first of the rubber trees. Even from here he could see how hopelessly run-down the estate had become. It had run to seed, and the weeds were so thick between the lines it would be impossible to start tapping again for some considerable time. He supposed the Japanese had had better things to do than try and produce rubber.

Seeing how shabby and ill-kempt Anapuri looked, Alex was glad that his father hadn't had to witness its devastation. It would have broken his heart to have seen all his years of hard labour turn to dust so rapidly.

It was raining again. Alex stood for a moment listening to the rattle of the rain on the leaves. There were rustlings on either side of him, and all around him, and somewhere in the distance he heard the call of a bird.

He felt himself tense, his blood pumping faster. It was merely the murmuring of the jungle, he knew, but he was constantly conscious of Ko Hla. Ready, on the alert.

The ground was steaming in the heat. Alex moved forward through the rising warm mist and crossed over the rickety bridge. Beyond the thick jungle, the light filtered through a web of branches, and he could see the track widening ahead through the rubber trees.

His breathing eased slightly. This was home territory. It would take him at least another hour to reach the house at Anapuri but at least now the terrain was familiar.

There was hardly a whisper of air. Somewhere just ahead a twig cracked. Alex edged his way on, feeling the sweat running down, soaking his shirt.

He sensed that Ko Hla was growing impatient. He knew that soon, very soon, he would make his move.

Kate sat in her hotel room in Moulmein wondering whether she had come on a fool's errand. She had got this far against the odds and now, finally, had met a complete blank wall.

The war might be over, but every conceivable obstacle had been put in her way, and if it hadn't been for Peter Fleming she would still be in Delhi. It was Peter who had managed to organise her flight to Burma. Having closed down the D Division he had arranged a tour of Burma, Malaya and Indo-China to assess the results of his deception schemes, and had managed to wangle Kate's passage with him as far as Rangoon.

Kate had then succeeded in getting herself as far as Moulmein, but now wondered if there had been any point in it. No one seemed to know anything about Alex. She knew that his last objective had been to mop up the stretch between Moulmein and Tavoy, but that had been several weeks ago. Now he seemed to have disappeared.

Shivering a little, despite the heat, she stood up and went to the window. Alex *must* be safe. Wouldn't she feel it in her heart if he were not?

The truth was she wasn't sure of anything any more. She had come to Moulmein certain that once she had arrived Alex would be conjured up like the lost Genie, and all would be well.

She had a colder vision now.

She let her head fall against her chest. Outside the sweet perfume from the frangipani blossom lifted on the warm damp air. Memories enfolded her.

Wherever he was, she sensed he was caught up in a maelstrom from which there was no escape.

And she was afraid for him.

More than she had ever been before.

The afternoon heat was beginning to fade by the time Alex reached Anapuri. He came through the last of the rubber trees, edging his way forward cautiously.

He could see the house clearly now; the shutters hung lopsidedly from their broken hinges, the windows were shattered, the roof was punctured with gaping holes. Anapuri looked like an aged and discarded courtesan, with no trace of its former elegance and allure.

Somewhere in the distance a dog barked. Alex halted. Ahead of him the house looked empty and still. Almost too still. He leant back against the trunk of the tree, closing his eyes. What now? Should he stay where he was, in the protecting shelter of the rubber trees, or should he risk trying to make for the house?

His heart pounding, Alex crouched down. Had he been blindly foolish to pick up the gauntlet which Hla had thrown down to him?

The trouble was, whatever his misgivings, Alex knew there'd been no choice. Hla was like a terrier, he would never have let go, never given up the chase. He would have waited for him, even if it had taken years. He'd always been determined and unforgiving, even as a child.

At one time Alex had thought it might be possible to side-step Hla, to simply alert the authorities to Hla's past atrocities and leave them to deal with him.

He knew for certain that Hla had been responsible for several executions of pro-British Karen headmen at the start of the war. He should have been brought to trial.

But now, since it seemed unlikely that the British government were going to press charges against the BNA leader, Aung San, for similar offences (one in particular – in Thaton – had caused quite a controversy) it seemed doubtful if any indictments would be brought against his immediate followers either. They would all be allowed to walk away scot-free. Hla too.

It left Alex no alternative. He thought of Kate. By rights he should have been back in India with her now. That was where he longed to be. But he knew that they couldn't start their life together with Hla's shadow hanging over them. For Kate's sake as well, he had to finish this business once and for all.

He took a deep breath and glanced back at the house. The last of the sun glinted against the broken windows, the dancing reflections giving a notion of movement in the darkened rooms beyond.

He would have to take a look inside.

Adrenalin pumping, he ducked down and began to zig-zag his way across through the trees to the compound and up to the verandah steps. He held his breath, sweating with concentration as he came up the stairs, the splintered railings wobbling unsteadily under his touch.

He hesitated a second, then nudged the door open with his foot, hugging the outside wall of the house while it swung wide.

He waited, listening hard. Nothing.

Gently, silently, he slid his way round the doorway, stepping over the threshold. Still no sound.

He trod his way softly into the hallway and across to the staircase, putting his hand out to the banisters. They swayed precariously under the pressure of his touch, the batons rotten and worn.

It was then that he heard it, the infinitesimal whisper of a floorboard creaking. Coming from just beyond the top of the stairs.

'Ko Hla, are you there?' Alex dodged quickly to the cover of the doorway. He held his breath. 'We need to talk, Ko Hla.'

Alex heard his heart beating so loudly he thought it would burst his eardrums.

'Can you hear me?'

Alex heard a slight movement upstairs. He thought he could see Ko Hla's indistinct form in the shadows. It was too dark to be sure.

'I can hear you, *Thakin* Alex,' Hla's voice came at last. It was harsh and bitter and there was mockery and contempt in his use of the word *thakin*. 'And I can see you, too. My gun is pointing at your head . . .'

Alex's glance flicked upwards. He was pretty sure that Hla couldn't actually have him in his sights, but the claim sent a cold finger of fear down his spine all the same. In his present state of mind, Hla was capable of anything.

'You won't help things by killing me, Hla,' he called out.

'You killed my brother. When you left him to die by the river I swore that I would avenge his spirit. I have had you in my sights many times . . .' There was a taunting tone to his words.

'I know that, Hla. I saw you in Rangoon and Moulmein.'

'Then you will know also that I have been following you for some time. I have waited a long time to take my revenge for the death of Maung Pe.'

A bird had flown in through the gaping window. Alex could hear its wings beating against the rafters as it panicked, trying to find its way out again.

He adjusted his position slightly, pressing his back tightly against the wall. 'There are many tragedies in war,' he said. 'You and Maung Pe were responsible for my father's death, too, don't forget.'

'Your father deserved to die.'

Ko Hla almost spat out the words.

'My father was good to you, Hla,' Alex remarked, shocked by the venom in Hla's voice. He couldn't understand the reason for it. Henry had always treated Hla and his brother well.

'Once I thought that too,' conceded Hla. 'Then I found out what he did to my mother.' He paused. Overhead the bird flapped noisily, still seeking a resting place. 'He violated her, you know. She was fifteen when he took her to his bed. Then when he'd had his fill of her, he threw her out. Back to the village.'

At first Alex couldn't believe Hla's words, but then gradually various pieces of his own childhood began to fall into place. So many unexplained tensions between his mother and father. He saw, though, that Hla had misjudged the events totally.

'You're wrong, Hla,' he protested, seeing the truth at last. 'My father loved Ma Kyin and she loved him.' He now understood why his mother had never liked Anapuri. She had known of that love and had always felt an outsider.

'My mother never loved your father.' Hla's voice rose almost imperceptibly as he rebelled against the truth of Alex's words. 'She did not go willingly to him . . .'

'But I did, Ko Hla.'

A woman's voice, quietly insistent, came from behind them.

Alex spun round. Ma Kyin was standing in the doorway. He did not know how long she had been standing there. The commotion caused by the bird in the rafters had covered the sound of her footsteps.

'It is time you knew the truth.'

'I will never believe it.'

'Henry Staveley was a good man . . .'

Ko Hla was on his feet now. 'If he loved you, why did he go back to England to find himself a wife? He abused you, Mother, can you not see that? Like the British in Burma have misused all of its people since they arrived here.'

'That is not so,' insisted Ma Kyin. 'And as for the British they were kindlier masters than the Japanese, your so-called friends.'

'But we do not need *masters*.' Hla came up to the edge of the banisters. 'And we don't need the Staveleys.'

Alex could see Hla's face was pinched tight with anger.

He could feel dark fanatical eyes boring into him, desperate for retribution.

It was then that he realised his mistake. The conversation had lulled him into a false sense of security and Alex had left the safety of his hiding place.

Hla saw it too. He deftly swung his gun into position over the top of the banisters. The time for talking was over.

'It's your turn to die,' he shouted wildly, leaning against the wooden rail, and taking aim. 'This is for Maung Pe.'

'No!' cried Ma Kyin. 'Hla don't.'

But it was too late. He'd already begun to squeeze the trigger.

Even as she came up over the last hill which led to Anapuri, Kate heard the unmistakable crack of a rifle shot. Alex! Her heart began to pound so hard, she could hardly breathe.

She put her foot down on the accelerator, the car skidding and sliding in the wet mud in the fading light, as it careered towards the house.

She'd known this was where Alex had gone. That morning, sitting in her hotel room, when the scent of the blossom had drifted up to her window, she had thought of Anapuri and the creamy yellow frangipani flowers which edged the verandah there, and had known with unshakeable certainty where she would find Alex. She'd managed to commandeer a car and had set off, driving through the rain and mud at a breakneck speed.

Now her hands tightened on the steering wheel. Please let me be in time, she prayed silently. Please let Alex be safe.

She jammed on the brakes, skidding to a halt outside the house. Then she was running, running for all she was worth up the steps and into the house.

Inside it was dark and for a moment she faltered, trying to make out the huddle of indistinguishable shapes before her.

'Alex?'

She couldn't see him. She felt her panic rise.

'Alex?'

For a moment she thought she had arrived too late, then one of the figures stood up and broke away from the group.

She felt her heart race, her eyelids pricking with tears.

'Oh, Alex, thank God.' She ran to him, flinging her arms around his neck. He was safe. *Alive*. 'I heard the shot. I thought it was you. I thought . . .'

'Hush.' His strong arms were tight around her, drawing her against him. 'It's all right. It's all over.'

As she leaned her head against his shoulder she saw him wince slightly. She put out her hand to his arm.

'You're hurt!' she cried out, feeling the wet stickiness of the blood that now covered her hand.

'Winged, that's all.'

'Alex!'

'It's nothing, Kate. Truly.'

'We must get it seen to.'

'There are other, more important, things to do first.' He gave a small nod in the direction of the staircase and the two figures there.

Kate took in the body lying on the bare wooden floor. 'Is it Hla?' she asked slowly.

Alex nodded.

'Did you . . . did you kill him?'

He shook his head. Mercifully it had not come to that.

'He fell, Kate. He lost his footing and fell against the banisters. They gave way.'

Alex had heard the first splintering crack and had called

out a warning. But it had been too late. The struts had snapped and given way. He'd never forget the sight of Hla trying desperately to claw his way back before he fell, his mouth open, his peaked jungle cap floating down beside him as he tumbled head-first to the ground below.

He hadn't stood a chance. He had fallen heavily onto his skull, breaking his neck. Alex had actually heard the crack as it went, and even as he rushed to his side, he had known it was hopeless. He was past help.

'I'm sorry it came to this,' said Kate.

She tightened her arms around Alex, feeling the tension in him. She knew he had hoped it would be possible in some way to persuade Hla to give up his vendetta peacefully.

Behind her she heard Ma Kyin, weeping softly over Hla's body. She broke away from Alex and went to her side, kneeling down beside her.

'He is at peace, Ma Kyin,' she said quietly, recognising the inadequacy of her words. 'Nothing more can harm him now.'

'It is my fault,' Ma Kyin said, sinking her tear-stained face between her hands.

'You mustn't blame yourself,' insisted Kate.

'I should never have called out to him. Never have tried to tell him . . .' Ma Kyin's voice caught slightly.

There was a silence.

'Tell him what?' Kate urged gently.

Ma Kyin lifted her head. But it was towards Alex she directed her gaze, not Kate.

'It's all right, Ma Kyin,' said Alex aware of her torment. He came to stand beside her, putting his hand gently on her shoulder, comforting her.

Kate was aware they were holding something back from her. Neither of them spoke for a moment.

Then Alex crouched down beside Hla's body. He cleared

his throat. 'We must move him. We can't leave him like this,' he said gravely. 'We must take him out and bury him.'

'Here?' Kate couldn't hide her surprise. She'd have thought the last person Alex would have wanted to bury at Anapuri was Hla. 'Alex? Are you sure that's what you want?'

'It's where he belongs, Kate,' Alex said. He hesitated a moment, glancing quickly at Ma Kyin. 'You see,' he said quietly, 'Hla was my half-brother.'

For a moment she couldn't take it in. She stared at him in confusion. Then he said: 'Henry was his father, too. That was what Ma Kyin tried to tell him before he died.'

So much fell into place.

Listening to Alex talk through that afternoon and evening Kate began to understand the jigsaw at last.

'Hla always set himself slightly apart from the rest of us,' Alex said, allowing himself to think back to their childhood days together. 'I suppose he always felt different in some way and yet couldn't understand why. He look. Burmese you see, perhaps because my father was so dark, but no one would have ever suspected he was half English. Yet I think deep down, he sensed a conflict within himself and that was why he struggled so hard for the Burmese cause. To give himself something to cling to, some identity.'

'And he never knew?'

'That Henry was his father? No. He found out about the liaison, though. By then he was up at Rangoon and had joined the fringes of the students' revolutionary group, and he convinced himself that my father had forced Ma Kyin to submit to his attentions against her will. It suited him to believe that. Fuelled his hate. I'm not sure what he'd have done if he had learnt the truth earlier. I don't think it would have changed his beliefs, though being an Anglo-Burmese he probably would not have been welcomed into the BNA.' Alex shrugged. 'Who knows?'

'And then you killed Maung Pe. That must have inflamed his loathing of your family,' said Kate. She adjusted her position beside him on the verandah steps.

'Absolutely. The worst thing that could have happened,' agreed Alex. He could now look back at that day with a more rational perspective. Though he regretted killing Maung Pe, he knew he could not have done otherwise.

Kate glanced out across the compound. In the rays of the evening sun Anapuri looked still and serene. There was no hint of the turmoil which it had witnessed. Only the empty shell of the house and the blackened factory bore testimony to past tragedies.

'So,' she said, putting her head gently on Alex's arm. 'What now?'

'I suppose we begin again,' he said. 'Don't we?' There was a touch of sadness in his voice, but only a touch. She could see his determination rising above it.

'I suppose we do.'

He took her hand and folded it tightly against his chest. 'It'll be a colossal task rebuilding it all. And God knows what will happen here in Burma in the long-term. We may lose the lot in the end. It's a risk.'

'But one you want to take?'

'Only if you want to,' he said. 'It's your future too, Kate. If you want to go back to England after all you've been through here, I'd understand. I'd come back with you.'

She knew what that had cost him. 'You'd hate it.'

He lifted his shoulders very slightly. 'I'd survive.'

She leant over and kissed him on the lips. 'Thank you for that, Alex, but no. I'd prefer to take my chances with you here.'

She saw Alex smile. 'Probably just as well,' he said. 'I was having difficulty envisaging myself in a pin-stripe suit and bowler.'

Kate laughed. 'So was I.' It was the image of the furled umbrella which had done it.

'Besides,' Alex went on, 'there's so much to do here.' She could already sense his energy. 'I want to be part of Burma gaining its independence. I want to make sure that the Karens and the Chins and the other hill-people are given as much say in things as they deserve.'

'Surely the British wouldn't fail them?' Kate queried, appalled at such a thought. 'Not after all that they've done to help during the war?'

'Don't be too sure about that,' Alex warned her. 'As far as I can see, Aung San and his colleagues may take all the power and that will leave the hill-people with very little control over their own destinies. And you know what scant love there is between the Burmese and the Karens.'

Kate thought of all that the Karens had done to help Martin when he was hiding from the Japanese. How selflessly they had given him shelter and refuge, how courageously they'd fought against the Japanese. Were they really to be repaid so poorly for their loyalty?

She stirred, resting her head against Alex's shoulder. For every one of them, then, there were challenges ahead.

She thought about Elizabeth and Martin trying to put their marriage back together again, about Johnnie and Sylvia started anew in Perth. Of all her friends in Singapore, trying to sort out the shattered pieces of their lives. No one would find it easy. They would all need courage to meet what lay ahead.

She felt Alex reach out for her and she turned her face to him. Despite the precariousness of the future, Kate was no longer afraid. She could feel Alex's vitality and strength breathing life back into her, willing her to have faith.

Nothing could be certain. She knew that now. You had to take chances and trust in the person you loved.

And whatever else might happen in the world, she had Alex.

That was enough.

From somewhere in the distance came the soft sound of the pagoda bells fluttering in the wind. Kate smiled.

Old Burma was reasserting itself.

The time for the changing of kings had come again.